Copyright
Seco

The author has asserted their moral right under the Copyright, Designs and Patents Act 1988, to be identified as the author of this work.

All Rights are reserved. No part of this publication may be reproduced, copied, stored in a retrieval system, or transmitted, in any form or by any means, without the prior written consent of the copyright holder, nor be otherwise circulated in any form of binding or cover other than that in which it is published and without a similar condition being imposed on the subsequent purchaser.

For my son and daughter

BLOOD OF ROME: CARATACUS

John Salter

Preface

In 55 BC Rome's greatest General, Julius Caesar, landed two full legions of soldiers and a regiment of cavalry from three hundred ships onto the shores of the land known by them as Britannia. He had claimed that this was in response to an ally of Rome, King Commius of the Atrebates tribe in the southern lands, being ousted and forced to flee the enormous island by another King, Cunobelin, of the Catuvellauni.

Caesar intended to return Commius to his throne but was met with resistance from warrior Britons, a fierce and hostile people. Realising that the expedition had been badly prepared against such a dangerous foe and as bad weather hindered further progress, he and his army were forced to retreat to Gaul.

The following year he tried again, this time accompanied by a fleet of over eight hundred ships, five legions and four regiments of cavalry, an invasion force of virtually thirty thousand trained men. Although he succeeded in returning the exiled Commius to his throne, his forces were attacked by local tribes led by Cunobelin, who harassed his columns, destroyed his supply lines and eventually forced him to retreat back to Gaul once more.

Nearly a hundred years later, Roman legions returned to Britannia, this time another member of the Catuvellauni and descendant of Cunobelin, Caratacus resisted their every step.

This is his story.

BLOOD OF ROME: CARATACUS

Chapter One

It was almost the middle of summer AD 43, when a vast fleet set sail from Gesoriacum in Gaul for the distant shores of Britannia. The Emperor Claudius had spent the last two years planning for this enterprise to finally conquer the land that had not once but twice repelled the great General Julius Caesar and his own legions. Claudius's predecessor, the insane and unpredictable Caligula, had also embarked on an invasion but had been killed by his own Praetorian guard before his plans were allowed to come to fruition.

The Senate and the legions had been humiliated when instead of setting sail across the channel, Caligula had briefed his army on the shoreline of Gaul and ordered them to collect pebbles, shells and stones and to launch them as missiles into the sea. He then claimed victory over Britannia but before redeploying his forces elsewhere, instructed them to build a lighthouse from the pebbles on the beach. This was his monument to celebrate the victory over the Britons after which, his legions were dispersed around the Empire to the astonishment of the Senate.

The Praetorian Guard knew that if Rome's fortunes were to grow and her full potential was to be realised, Caligula would have to die and a more astute and clear minded leader take his place. Now a little over two years after his death, the huge fleet of nearly one thousand vessels blanketed the water as they slowly made their way across the channel to the distant island. A land where it's warriors were known to use chariots for war, make human sacrifice to their gods and fight almost naked in battle, men and women alike.

Despite the conflicts with Caesar previously, an uneasy peace had settled between the Empire and some regions of Britannia, trading eventually grew with tribes willing to exchange goods, materials and livestock. However, nearly a hundred years later after Caesar, Claudius saw that he had an ideal opportunity to gain favour with the masses of Rome, the Senate and the army and knew that a victory over Britannia would boost his popularity.

He had finally decided that it was time that the primitive barbarians known as Britons, were brought to heel under the boots of the Empire. Some tribes had already received promises of neutrality and peace; the agreement not to resist was rewarded with gold and further pledges of wealth and client Kingdoms in what would be the next Province.

Unhappy with the dominance of the most powerful tribal regions controlled by the Catuvellauni in the south and east of the country, a few lesser chieftains even pledged to fight alongside Roman forces, Briton against Briton. A few nobles also saw an opportunity to elevate themselves and swore their loyalty to the Emperor after defecting completely or after being exiled. Most notably Adminius, son of the King of the Catuvellauni, Cunobelinus and brother to Caratacus, changed his allegiance to Rome after being exiled by his own father.

Cunobelinus had ruled these lands all his life as had his father and grandfather before him. His ancestors had even fought Caesars great armies and helped send them home but as time went by treaties were drawn up and trading was established. The power hungry Adminius had broken treaties by raiding other lands and had argued that his father should ally himself fully with Rome against other Britons. His father had refused exiling him to Gaul naming Togodumnus, another son, his successor. Adminius completed his defection fully by seeking the assistance of the Emperor, with his aid he intended to return to his rightful land where he would cooperate with Rome's wishes as a client King, after the death of his brother Togodumnus and all others who stood against him.

The vessels of the fleet now moved like a giant shadow covering the sea before them. Hundreds of dots from a distance seemed to merge into one enormous entity, appearing to change the colour of the blue water, black and white, the colours of the dark wood of their hulls and white of their sails. All was not well aboard the vessels however, as rumours had spread throughout the army that the campaign ahead was cursed and likely to be the most difficult the soldiers had ever encountered. They were told that death and destruction awaited them in the lands that lay across the water.

To the common soldier, the inhabitants who were to be their enemy were barbarians, said to infest the enormous island, living in tribal conditions in little more than mud huts and fighting against each other as they had for decades and centuries before. Since Roman explorers and envoys had first set foot on the land, it had always been a target on the Empire's north western frontier. Britannia had lay waiting, unconquered and divided by warring chieftains for a ruler who would unify the tribes.

Near rebellion had spread like disease through the ranks of the men aboard the ships and a mutiny had narrowly been averted right up until the last few days before departure. The soldiers knowing that even the great Caesar had failed to capture the land were superstitious enough to believe that Britannia could not be conquered. Stories were rife in the legions that the inhabitants had used demons and magic to destroy Caesars army, many of whom were drowned at sea by serpents during vicious storms. It was after all an island at the edge of the known world, where all manner of strange creatures and magic were said to exist.

Mysticism was rife throughout the Empire and in the streets of its pagan cities where soothsayers could be found in back streets plying their trade and divining the future. Animal entrails from sacrificed animals were studied to identify a person's future fortunes as well as pledges to all manner of gods. Pagans were very superstitious and if any sign was deemed to be a bad omen, word of its existence would spread like fire and it would be avoided at all costs.

Long before the invasion, the Britons had been told of the large force gathering in Gaul and under the leadership of Togodumnus, had amassed a huge army of over one hundred thousand warriors to greet them on their shores. Chieftains and their war bands had been recruited from all over the south from all those regions willing to fight. They had waited for weeks whilst their families tended crops and cared for their livestock at home.

However, just as Spring had begun that year when the fleet was originally due to set sail, superstition took hold of the campaigning legions and despite all the efficient organisation and planning of General Aulus Plautius Silvanus, the overall commander, his men were now reluctant to take part in the war. Stories were repeated from one soldier to the next of the unimaginable horrors that awaited them and they refused to board the ships.

Plautius sent word to Rome of the delay and Claudius dispatched his own chief of staff, Narcissus to deal with the matter. He travelled to the port to resolve the problem with promises of riches for all those who took part in the campaign. Upon his arrival at the camp Plautius called an assembly where he and Narcissus stood on a raised dais, he began to address the assembled legions. However, before Narcissus could repeat the Emperor's promise of wealth, he was shouted down and ridiculed as the men knew he was a former slave and now merely a freedman and therefore not a true Roman in their eyes.

Narcissus was jeered and began to quickly leave the platform to laughter and cheers from the gathered men who shouted insults, "Hooray for the Saturnalia", referring to when slaves could actually wear the same clothes as their masters in late December every year. Narcissus reddened clearly embarrassed and humiliated by their words, turned to the General, rage building in his face. Plautius also angered by his men's behaviour, furiously shouted for order and demanded quiet from those assembled.

"Will you follow me then? A true Roman and receive rewards?" He began. "The Emperor himself has promised every single man a bonus and land, for all those who take part in the forthcoming campaign."

Those listening went quiet.

"Together we will conquer all those who stand before us," he paused, "I guarantee success and fortune." He waved his arms at the assembled equipment waiting to be loaded on the docks and at the ships in the harbour, "We will not be bested and defeated by druids and fools who live on butchered meat and milk like animals, we are Rome, we are soldiers of the Empire."

Men began to cheer, at first single odd voices in the masses.

"Are we the legions of Rome, afraid of men who live lives in little more than mud huts, who rely on their women to fight for them and paint their skin to hide their sallow weak flesh?" He surveyed the men before him and saw that some individuals were excitedly talking to others and encouraging them. The General drew his gladius from its sheath and pointed it to the heavens.

"The gods are with us and Mars God of war himself looks down on you now, with him at our side victory is assured. Join me," he looked up, "join us and your commanders and together we will conquer that barbarian place called Britannia. With four full legions, thousands of auxiliaries, cavalry and artillery we will smash all those who stand before us."

He lowered his sword and then pointed it out into the channel and quickly the attitude of the men began to alter. They exchanged looks and stopped their sarcastic calls and started to shout the name of Plautius now agreeing to go to war. Thousands of voices chanted, "Plautius, Plautius." He turned to Narcissus, who fumed and left the platform to cat calls from the men nearby, his journey not entirely wasted.

Subsequently that night the ships had begun their journey carrying their deadly cargo westward. The refusal to board the ships and the subsequent delay however, had taken many weeks all told and the usual campaigning season was already well underway. The Britons in the meantime had heard through traders of the legions refusal to take part in the invasion and had dispersed from the southern shores back to their settlements and families believing that like Caligula's invasion of a few years before, this one wouldn't happen either.

Although Britannia was to be the furthest point west these men had journeyed, their boots would be on the beaches of foreign soil the next day. Almost to a soldier they where captivated by their own thoughts wondering who amongst them would survive to see the sun rise again in the days ahead. The fleet slowly moved across the water, oars aiding sails, drums beat rhythmically like the mighty heartbeat of the gods, timing the strokes and propelling them to the land that would be the next Province of the most powerful country and Empire in the known world.

Druids were said to be all powerful, pagan religions ruled the lands where the tribes still performed human sacrifice to their gods. Warriors were known to cover their skin with a substance called woad, a plant extract, when they fought in battle, many had images tattooed onto their bodies. The hair was spiked outward in lime to make them look more ferocious, their body hair shaven except for their heads. Britannia was indeed a primitive and barbaric place where the soldiers expected to sustain heavy casualties and the loss of many of Rome's sons.

The land would be dominated, decimated if necessary and brought to book. Client Kingdoms would be established and the mineral wealth distributed throughout the Empire. Emissaries had travelled to the rich green country the year before in the knowledge that some of the inhabitants had aided Gallic allies in Gaul. They had met with two of the brothers of Adminius who ruled one of the larger tribes in the southern part of the islands, Togodumnus and Caratacus but they had refused to become just another Province and clients of Claudius. They were known to have unified some of the tribes under their banner and were now refusing to pay tributes in the form of taxes and had denied all attempts at persuading them to join the Empire. The men of the Second Augusta led by their Legate, Titus Flavius Vespasian were now determined to show them the error of their ways, along with the men of three other legions.

The soldiers were packed into the war galleys and supply ships with equipment and animals and now couldn't wait to get to dry land. The smell and noise, together with the constant rolling waves of the sea had already made many sick much to the amusement of some of the crew and marines. They had waited in Gaul for months whilst their forces gathered, their refusal to board the ships had hindered their progress further but now they now wanted nothing more than to get to what was said to be the largest island in the known world and onto firm ground.

Preparations were already underway for farmers, their families, builders and merchants to follow the first wave of vessels in order that the island could be made into the next Province. It was intended that in a short time the indigenous population would soon see the benefits of joining the other cultures and countries that now enjoyed the benefits of the eternal City. Philosophy, wealth and education would follow as it had in other lands that profited from an alliance with their Roman masters. A much different destiny awaited those that resisted and they like others before them in Gaul would be crushed under the eagle standards that now approached their lands.

Although Centurion Tiberius Albinus Varro was from Rhegium, located on the southeast coastal tip of his homeland, a large sprawling port, he didn't like the sea or anything to do with it. He didn't previously believe that the naval crews were worthy of military recognition. Not just because they were not as highly trained and less paid than he and his colleagues but because he considered that they were on a lower level, on the military scale when all was considered. They went to war at sea, whereas the men of the Second Augusta waged their battles on land, where wars were actually won and victories secured. He now however, admitted a grudging respect for these sailors and marines whose weather beaten faces creased in grimaces as they worked the sails and strained to propel them forward.

It was common knowledge that the men who manned the military vessels were ranked below their legionary counterparts and even below the auxiliaries that were drawn up from many conquered lands. The navy was considered by most to be an inferior force altogether, it was younger than the infantry and had only come into being because of Carthage and it's seaborne threat.

However, Varro had now developed some admiration for the *miles* or *manipularis* marines, as they referred to themselves and not just as sailors. They were providing an invaluable service to the Empire as this journey and its preparation were proof of. The Emperor was spreading the eagle's wings and men on foot alone could not achieve victory without the aid of their water borne comrades. His legion was at full strength and the five thousand infantry and nearly one thousand cavalry had trained and re-trained whilst waiting to board the ships for the short but uncomfortable journey across the channel. They were happy to be on the move at last and on their way after the dull routine of training and listening to superstition and rumours in their temporary garrison camp.

Varro was physically slightly shorter than most of the men in his company but only by an inch or two, but what he lacked in height, he made up for in breadth and pure physical strength. Naturally broader than most, he had built on that by training with large pots filled with water and logs cut from thick trees for years. He and his closest companions had pushed their bodies to the limit, training everyday to try and ensure that they were at their best when the time came to jump from the boats. His skin had a slight olive tint and his short wavy black hair was cut close to his head. A tight and neatly trimmed black beard made his features quite distinguished and almost uniquely Greek looking.

He and his men although mounted, were part of the Equites Legionis who were a form of cavalry attached to the legion but were actually regular legionaries taken from the ranks. Different legions had varying numbers of Equites Legionis from one hundred and twenty to one thousand troops, in addition to auxiliary cavalry. They generally worked independently as scouts or messengers and were employed in carrying out special duties on behalf of their Legate and were commanded by Centurions unlike the Decurion's of the auxiliary units. Varro commanded the scouts of the Second Augusta and therefore liked to ride horses, what he didn't like was boats.

He looked out over the side of the vessel to the white cliffs in the distance, his hands steadying his movement on the rail of the boat as it moved up and down in the swell of the water. They were only a short distance from their destination now as he felt the vessel roll slightly once more. He thought about the days ahead and of how many men, with whom he shared meals, laughed and trained, would be dead or injured during the weeks and months to come.

"Can't wait to get amongst the blue faced scum hey Varro?" His friend and second in command of their small reconnaissance group, Optio Gaius Veranius asked as he looked towards the approaching shore just as a fresh spray of salt water lashed their faces and arms. He and Veranius had lived and worked together for the last two years, since Veranius had joined the Second and they had campaigned through Gaul with the others in their company. Together they made up the section of eight their *contubernium* or tent party. They were primarily used as scouts and would travel in forward positions ahead of the marching columns on horseback and even sometimes on foot depending on the situation, reporting back to the Legate, who commanded the Legion.

It wasn't unusual for them to be literally days ahead of the main column, in fact it was routine, so each man had to be reliable, disciplined and be able to look after himself in all manner of circumstances. It was a task that most didn't envy especially when moving into unknown territory, the majority of soldiers preferred the comfortable tight knit lines of the marching columns and squares, inside main battle formations. Scouting had proven hazardous as casualties had demonstrated previously but Varro and his men wouldn't be anywhere else. They were the tip of the spear of the greatest force in the army and he wouldn't have it any other way.

"I can't wait to get off this floating stinking death trap that's all my friend." He looked at Veranius, "I don't like salt water or anything associated with it. It rots everything and you can't drink it or even bathe in it without drying your skin like ox hide." He looked down at the water. "They say that if people actually drink the stuff, it causes them to go insane, to attack and kill others, why would anyone choose to live with that when you can have dry land and fresh water?" He replied looking at the ships personnel working around the boat.

"We'll be ashore soon enough, with solid ground under our feet. I hope it's not all white like those cliffs eh," Varanius said nodding towards the land growing larger with each rowing stroke, "what do you think it is rock, chalk?"

Varro raised his eyebrows, "I don't know but it looks in keeping with the stories we've been told doesn't it? I hope those druids aren't waiting for us or the ballista will be in action before we've even landed." He nodded towards the medium sized torsion catapults located at the front and sides of the ship. Larger machines were onboard other vessels but they would be unloaded and towed by the troops with mules not like their own swifter, more agile animals.

"At least the gods have been kind and given us a calm sea and the sun." He looked up to the clear blue sky seeing small white birds circling above them. The first few ships of the fleet were approaching the beaches and the nearest boats were already rowing aground with legionaries jumping ashore. There was no resistance on the shoreline or from the cliffs above. The pebble filled coastlines below the white cliffs were empty for as far as the eye could see in both directions. The sound of the sea was soon drowned out by hob nailed boots splashing and landing in the shallow water and on the stony surface.

"I would have set up defences on the cliff top, it's a natural fortification up there just look at it." Varro said pointing to the huge cliffs whilst removing his sword and checking it again for what must have been the fifth time that day. The slightly longer cavalry sword known as a spatha had become a part of him since he had joined the legion almost ten years before. He had carried it since it had replaced the wooden training sword he had been given during his first weeks in the army and was as familiar to him now as any of his limbs, probably more so. It had saved his life and taken others on the bloody days when his unit had seen action and he couldn't now live without it.

The tough brown leather of his bracers against the skin of his wrists had now worn in but occasionally still creaked slightly as he moved his hands. Goose grease had been applied to them so they were pliable enough for comfortable movement, unlike they had been when they were first cut by the military merchant who had sold them to him. The thick leather bands were added protection not only against the elements but also provided a thick natural barrier against attack. The leather helped support the wrist especially when training or using the spatha when the strain on the wrist could become incredible. Not all soldiers wore them but to Varro they were an essential part of his kit, like a second skin.

As the first of the legionaries walked cautiously along and up the beach, fanning out in all directions, their officers red cloaks flowing in the wind, the ship containing Varro and his men crunched into the stones and onto the shore. Decimus Longinus, another of his squad leapt from the vessel and looked around.

"I claim this land and all its females on behalf of the Roman Empire." He laughed as others around him merely smirked because they were more concerned about who maybe watching from the cliffs above.

"Come on let's get up to the green areas, there." Pointing Varro indicated to a patch where the cliff swept down to the beach in a prominent valley shaped configuration, a small stream trickling water down through the ravine and spilling its contents into the sea. The plan was to secure the landing area on foot and once it was established, their mounts would be brought from the other ships that were rapidly approaching the beach.

Whilst some centuries were forming up, other legionaries were already making their way to the natural sweeping dip with sunlight glinting from the polished iron equipment they carried. To the untrained eye it would look like the soldiers were meandering around and exploring at their leisure but each had his own task within his unit and that unit in turn was attached to another. They were trying to ensure that the Britons weren't primed to ambush them on the beach and would hold their positions once they reached certain vantage points that allowed them to see the coastline and observe inland as well, the problem in the meantime was getting to them.

"We'll be up there as soon as the horses are unloaded." Varro turned to see the animals were already starting to be taken ashore from the first ship. They had received their orders the previous night on-board their vessels, the reconnaissance unit were to follow the shoreline moving east. They would rotate in two teams as they had done so successfully on previous occasions. Whilst half would return to report back to the columns of the following legions and replenish supplies, the others would continue to track ahead and scout the area looking for hostile or friendly forces.

The same system would happen in other legions as they went forward in different directions as the land became their own. In time the rear party would catch up with the forward element and resume their tracking distances, which would expand as the campaign went on. Dependant on the terrain and the situation, the reconnaissance troops would more than likely have to fend for themselves living off the land at times or if possible, the local tribe's hospitality.

Certain chieftains had already agreed to co-operate with the invading force and had received payment in gold and even weapons so the troops knew it wasn't going to be an entirely bloody campaign. Barbarians however, had a habit of reneging on treaties especially after they had already had the bargaining tool given to them. Previous meetings with spies and local intelligence, had reported that only weeks before, thousands of tribesmen had covered the cliff tops and surrounding lands but they had grown weary of waiting, had began fighting amongst themselves and had gone home once they had heard the Romans were refusing to board their vessels.

With the horses quickly unloaded, some were already mounted and Varro ordered his men to find their own as they continued to observe the cliffs. He found his own horse Staro amongst those coming ashore as he stood out amongst the mainly brown animals because he was dark black in colour.

"Slow down boy." Varro whispered, holding onto him by his saddle and reins as his horse snorted, stamping his feet as if to make sure the surface was solid after the rolling journey from Gaul.

"It's alright my friend," he stroked the horse's mane and neck as he leaned forward and spoke, "today we begin a new adventure in another land far from home. I think you will like it here on this huge rock at the edge of the earth."

Climbing onto his mount the horse reared up on his back legs and lashed out with a foreleg, whinnying as if in agreement before settling down and cantering forward a little along the beach. Men from the ship brought water for the animals to drink in large wooden buckets as others anchored vessels to the shoreline.

"Thank you," he said to a marine carrying a large bucket, "my horse and his friends will need a little water inside them before the journey ahead." He looked at Staro twitching his ears, "Only enough to wet your lips though boy, I don't want you getting ill."

The marine from the ship looked along the beach and up at the high white rocks now towering above them, turning back to the horse and rider he said. "They all had some water a while ago on-board so they'll be fine Centurion." He looked back to the cliffs that dominated the shore, "I'm glad I joined the marines but I'd like to see what this land has to offer. It's said to be so different from anything else we've seen before. I wish you and your men good fortune, may the gods watch over you."

Varro smiled, "Thank you for the good wishes." He said looking up again at the strange white cliff, "We may need them I fear." Although Varro wasn't a zealously religious man, he sometimes prayed to the gods by thought preferring his own private tribute rather than the public displays demonstrated by others.

His mount reared up again sensing that it was time to move off, neighing loudly, "You see, even Staro is ready to conquer this land." He patted the animal's neck as he landed and then he and the others raced forward and up the beach scattering pebbles in their wake. The water carrier watched them go and said a silent prayer as the sound of the waves again dominated the diminishing noise of the hooves as the horses and men on them, moved away from the relative safety of the beach and into unknown territory. Already other ships were grounding themselves ashore as the crews began to secure them to the beach, where they would wait for high tide before their return voyage to Gaul.

Some distance away, lying in the wispy long grass above the cliffs, five men watched from cover as the large vessels unloaded soldiers and horses onto the beach, more warriors waited behind the bank unseen. Togodumnus had known that the men who had invaded Gaul would soon reach out and be tempted by their lands especially after they had refused to pay the tributes demanded of them, so he had sent men to watch the shores after the others went home. The Catuvellauni were the rulers of this land, not these intruders and they would kill any man or beast that stepped foot on their soil, just like those that had already taken their tokens of corruption and cowardice.

The men had been sent to watch the sea and they now looked on intently as the Romans scurried around and slowly spread across the beach below. They saw that some but not all wore dark red cloaks and had long spears, the blades glinted in the morning sunlight. Strange helmets were worn on their heads probably for protection, or identification, large ornate colourful plumes decorated a few of the helmets, whilst others were simply plain bronze or silver. They had clearly come ready for war but they would have their teeth and bones shattered by the warriors of Britannia until they were turned and pushed back into the sea or were destroyed where they stood.

The Britons had lived by the cliff for some days after being sent by Caratacus and his brother from the north. Patiently they had waited after all the others had left weeks before, when word had arrived that the invaders had lost their appetite for battle. They had never seen so many vessels on the water and watched with interest and trepidation as their cargo was brought ashore. Some of the equipment was already packed onto mules as they left the ships, walking unsteadily down large wooden ramps; other kit was carried by men, whilst some of their goods were towed on wagons and carts. Supplies, weapons, men, horses, mules, oxen, empty wagons, carts and other equipment they didn't even recognise began to grow and spread over the stones between the water and the base of the cliff below. The Britons had never seen anything like it although stories were still told of the last time these men had come and were pushed back into the sea.

Men with armour, shields and spears were marching in columns as they were overtaken by riders on horses as they began to move away from the sea and take a hold of this part of the shoreline. Had the Britons waited in force for a few more weeks, these men would have never got ashore and would have been met by thousands of warriors but as it was, only five pairs of eyes had watched as the ships had emerged on the horizon.

"It is as Caratacus warned," One of the men said in a hushed voice, although no Roman could have heard him from this distance, "two of you ride back," he nodded at the volunteered pair, "get home as soon as you can. Tell them they are here," he paused, a look of resignation on his face, "it begins."

Two of the warriors pushed themselves back away from the edge of the cliff, getting to their feet they turned and ran to their mounts tethered some distance away. They climbed onto their horses, smaller than those of the invading Romans and galloped away, kicking soil and grass into the air. Togun the leader of the remaining men returned his gaze to the figures below. He could see the shock in his friend's faces as their eyes moved from figure to figure in the distance, like insects on the beach below, countless hundreds already staining the earth.

"They are many but a lot of them will not return to their own land, they can bring all the stars and we will bring the sun to wipe them out, we will meet them with force. Even now Caratacus and his brother are forming more alliances with other tribes. Our chariots will cut these invaders down and drive them back into the sea, have faith in them." The expressions and eyes he saw staring back at him clearly doubted his words.

"We should have waited with the other warriors and greeted them as they jumped ashore Togun. We could have repelled them and made an end of this madness before it had even begun." One of the men said.

"Crops would have spoilt and families gone hungry, they were right to go home when they did, they'd waited long enough. We are far too few at this time to do anything but we can watch and count their numbers. We were assured by our friends in Gaul that the Romans had mutinied and were not going to cross the sea but return to their own lands instead. They were wrong and the Roman curse is here to steal our food and rape our women." He looked angry, "It is at least a full day's ride at pace to get word of this back to Caratacus. By then, when they have reached our own territories more will join and will begin to move south. Togodumnus and Caratacus will find a place of their own choosing to fight these demons and force them back, you'll see. Then they will witness their men cover the ground, dead in their thousands."

He looked at the ships and men still flooding ashore and although believed his words, he wondered how exactly the sons of their former King would deal with this immense army. The enemy had equipment that they had not seen before and they carried a lot of hard metal and strange machines such as large bows attached to wooden frames and soldiers wearing full armour. Each man he thought must weigh nearly twice his own weight, weighed down as they were with weapons and tools carried on their backs. Most of the Britons were limited to a spear or maybe a sword or dagger and if they were fortunate, a small shield. Those of a higher class such as noblemen had large ornate rectangular shields but they were not available to every fighter. They were warriors however, who had lived with conflict with other tribes all their lives. Now he knew they must come together and fight a common enemy if they were to meet this threat head on and defeat them as their forefathers had before them. He and his remaining men would stay close to the Romans and try to discover how many there were and in which direction they were intending to travel. From this high position, he knew that what he saw below was certainly more dangerous than anything he had ever before encountered.

Chapter Two

Lucius another of Varro's men, caught up with him on his own horse a brown mare as they cantered above the stony beach now down below. The grass underfoot instead of pebbles meant they could talk instead of having to shout at each other over the clatter of their mounts hooves.

"How far will we travel today sir?" He asked.

Varro raised an eyebrow, "We'll keep moving while we still have good light." He said looking up at the sky. "I would say that we've only lost a few hours of the day so we should be able to follow the coast for sometime before we have to make camp."

He looked at the sun, the sky was still clear and blue and a warm breeze passed over his muscled arms and legs as he guided Staro with his hips. Roman cavalry had learned decades before to determine the direction of travel of a horse by purely using their legs and hips if required. They would use their thighs to grip onto a large four pronged wooden pommel on the saddle that was covered in leather. It enabled the riders to have free hands primarily so they could wield their swords in battle or throw javelins. Now however, it also enabled them to drink from water skins as Lucius did. His sword was stored under his leg on the saddle on the horse's right flank so that he could get to it quickly if required.

They were now a few hundred feet above sea level and slowed their animals to walking pace as they took in their surroundings, the area before them was covered in trees and rolling woodland, it was so dense they couldn't see through or beyond it. Instinctively Varro and his men viewed the obstacles with suspicion and caution as they knew enclosed areas meant that there was always a possibility of ambush. A few small tracks lay at the base of some of the trees running parallel to them which meant that either people or animals used them regularly to travel in the area.

Varro halted his men, who waited a few steps behind him, Veranius and Decimus trotted forward, the three men listened taking in their surroundings. Everything seemed natural, birds sang in the trees and bushes moved normally with the slight breeze as hares nibbled on grass a few hundred feet away, near to the safety of the undergrowth of the trees.

"I'll go in with Decimus and have a look?" Volunteered Veranius, steadying his horse and pointing to the track, his mount seemed nervous about the trees ahead. Decimus gave him a scolding look, as the horse whinnied and dragged its right hoof across the dirt under him.

"Animals sense things that we can't see my friend. You're horse doesn't seem very happy." Varro said as he looked to the tree tops. "All manner of things can lurk and conceal themselves in such places, be careful and do not go too far. Stay in sight of each other and out of javelin range of the trees, the rest of us will follow."

Veranius and Decimus acknowledged the order that seemed more like a warning with a nod as they pushed their horses forward. Veranius was a trusted friend of Varro as well as the other members of the small reconnaissance troop albeit a subordinate. They had formed friendships over years of campaigning together and were considered to be a very tight close knit unit within the legion and vital to its overall success.

As the two began to move forward, Decimus said quietly to Veranius, "Thank you so much for volunteering me my friend." He peered into the undergrowth. "Remind me to return the compliment one day."

Veranius smiled and replied, "Your horse was getting impatient and doesn't like the trees so we'll show him he's safe."

"This fool spooks at sticks and twigs," Decimus said looking down at the horses ears. "Never mind the trees but knowing our luck this time there will be something there. He threw me once on a windy day when a leaf blew across his path and swirled about in the air near his face." Decimus replied.

Veranius laughed. He was the only member of the party that was shorter in height than Varro but he too had trained continually and had developed arms that were now the size of small tree trunks and were literally wider than his head at the bicep. He had three passions, fighting, wine and food, the latter normally provided for by utilising his hunting skills.

He had grown up near Venusia on his father's farm in the south of their country. His family had a military background and it had seemed a natural step to join the army, His father had retired from the legions as a centurion in the infantry and had returned to Venusia, where he too had grown up, to start a family after twenty five years service which was the maximum permitted time. With the spoils of war and his military pension earned by his father, Veranius had a relatively comfortable upbringing.

With most of his modest military pay saved over the years and a generous wagon full of plunder, Veranius' father had bought the small farm where he grew grapes on the vine that were sold at local markets. In the second year of civilian life he had met his wife and soon-after Veranius was born, another soldier of the empire.

Decimus was the youngest member of the group of scouts and was a joker, tall and rangy, he went out of his way to find female companionship whenever he could. He had looked forward to introducing himself to the females of Britannia and had boasted, 'They will tell their children and their children's children, that they are descended from the great Decimus, ruler and Emperor of Rome.' He had often said usually followed by roars of laughter, from his friends. He was convinced that his charm alone would prevent any conflict once the women had let him entertain them. He was from the north east fishing village of Aquileia, situated on the coast of the Adriatic Sea. He had been with the legion eight years and had transferred from the infantry a year before joining the reconnaissance troop.

Varro dismounted from his horse and took off his helmet, sweat matted his short hair. He removed his water skin from Staro's side and drank, pouring water over his head when he was finished. He checked his saddle, stroking the animal's flanks as he made sure the cloth underneath the wood and leather was flat so as not to cause blistering. Hours in the saddle could cause all manner of problems for the horse where the hard wood of the saddle rubbed against the skin through the leather. It could cause a calloused area on the flesh to well up which would affect the animal, it was not something a rider wanted if they were trying to escape a horde of barbarian sword wielding madmen. Experience had shown him that if his horse was injured or wounded, then effectively so was he and he couldn't afford that in a hostile land.

"Check you horses." He ordered as the remaining soldiers jumped from their mounts. Regular cavalry units wore heavy armour a tactic that had come into being after the Roman army had come into contact with a Sarmation tribe called the Roxolina. The Roxolina had used the *cataphracti* armour, when going into battle, the legions had been so impressed with their equipment, armour and horsemanship that they had created their own. It demonstrated a respect for people and cultures outside the Empire and had proven invaluable in preserving soldiers and horses lives and of course helped in winning battles and ultimately wars.

Varro and his men had virtually the same equipment as the men in the ranks of the legions but didn't have the same heavy solid body armour because their task was to cover large areas of land in as short a space of time as possible and the armour of the heavy infantry would have slowed them and their horses down. Instead they had chainmail linked armour that covered their torsos and their horses had a hardened leather equivalent of the regular cavalry that covered vulnerable areas against sword or spear thrusts. It wouldn't stop a direct assault but many a horse's life had been saved by the thick leather armour.

He made sure the bridle constructed of an iron curb that made up the bit in the mouth wasn't causing any problems. The curbs had been designed to get an instant response for Cavalry and had a bar in the mouth and one under the animals chin. He ran his hand along the nose band over the horse's muzzle and under its chin. Staro showed no sign of it being uncomfortable, his large brown eyes watching Varro, everything seemed to be in order.

The horse's kit had been checked before departing Gaul but there had been no time to properly check the equipment immediately after they had got off the ship as more troops had piled ashore behind them and it had been tactically astute to move off the beach as soon as possible. This was their first opportunity to make sure everything was in working order in what looked to be a safe area. They were in a clearing and out of range of any weapons that could be lurking in the nearby woodland or so they hoped.

As the sound of bird song in the trees grew louder, Veranius and Decimus approached a shaded area of grass before the woodland. They could see only large tree trunks, branches and leaves before them rustling in a slight breeze. Veranius had led them to the track on the left side of the clearing. He had decided that if an ambush party were waiting for them, they didn't want to be riding towards its centre where they could be quickly encircled and trapped.

His hands moved over the chainmail covering his chest, he pulled on the links at his sides to make it more comfortable. When the linked vests were first put on, they felt very heavy but the cavalry soon got used to them, when they were in the correct position, they hardly knew they were wearing them. He looked around, his hand dropped to the hilt of his sword as the cool of the shade engulfed him.

Decimus followed at a distance behind. In the event of attack, both horses would need at least two lengths to turn and gallop to safety. It would be pointless just the two of them trying to fight if they got into trouble with another group after finding themselves outnumbered. Their task was to ensure the way was clear and report back in the event of trouble, not to take on enemy forces, in that event they would return to the clearing at speed.

Decimus adjusted his helmet so he could see up into the tree tops. The unit had been issued with standard cavalry helmets with only the eyes, nose and mouth visible. Decimus turned his head fully, watching for anything that might be a threat.

The woodland seemed vast and full of small wildlife, all of which could be heard but not seen. Along the worn paths they wound their way through the trees like small streams disappearing and re-appearing in the walls of leaves and branches. He checked the two small throwing spears tied to his horse, they were only about four feet in length so they could be carried at the side of the animal and not wound others because they were too long, especially if they were riding in formation. All the men that served under Varro were proficient throwers of the pilum and could accurately hit a target some distance away.

The air was full of differing scents from the plentiful plant life around them, it seemed almost serene. They knew that the land they were now on was split into different tribal areas just like Gaul had been. Over twenty main tribes were known to inhabit this vast island and they were now in the area known to be dominated by the tribe known as the Cantiaci, one of the tribes heavily influenced by Caratacus of the Catuvellauni and his brother who were both vehement opponents of Rome. The Catuvellauni were a large tribe, said to be the second largest in all Britannia. Varro and his men were not there to confront them if they found them but were to scout for their presence along the coastal routes as the main force came ashore.

Three other large tribes were known to inhabit the southern shores of the island and they were sure they would come into contact with all of them at some point, hopefully one tribe at a time. The Atrebates and the Durotriges were known to live in the centre of the southern shoreline and the Dumnonii dominated the south west. Numbers amongst the tribes were invariably inconsistent and depended on who you spoke to and where the intelligence had come from but it was known that each tribe could call many thousands of warriors to their banner. The majority of these people however, were not professional fighters but farmers who answered the call to arms when required from their chieftains.

After a short time Veranius and Decimus reached a clearing where they could once again feel the warmth of the sun on their skin.

"Go back and get the others, tell Varro the area is clear." Veranius instructed Decimus. He didn't reply but just nodded and turning trotted off back down the track. Veranius searched the trees around the clearing and moved forward, he didn't see or sense any movement. A little further into the ground that was clear of trees he found a small brook where clear water ran. He led his horse to it and the animal drank, ears twitching. Veranius got off and removed his helmet and scooped water up into his cupped hands. It was cool to the touch and refreshing when he splashed it over his face and rubbed his neck.

"That's nice hey boy?" He said to the horse that turned and looked at him and then returned to the water for another drink.

"This place isn't so bad is it? It's even warm and sunny, those fools back in Rome said it was freezing here and animal skins and fur had to be worn to keep out the cold." He sat on a large rock, "Maybe it was winter when they came eh?"

He took out his dagger, a weapon nearly a foot long and known as a *pugio* or *pugiones* dependant on which region of the empire the soldier came from. The bone handle was smooth and comfortable in his hand with its T-shaped pommel at the base. The blade was made of cold sharp iron and slightly stretched in a triangular shaped wedge. Almost day dreaming in the warm sunlight, he suddenly had a vivid image of the last time he had used it in combat. Under normal circumstances it would have been his sword that was used but in a battle against a Germanic tribe he had dropped his spatha as his legions flank was outnumbered and overrun, their shield wall shattered. Colliding against the side of another horseman he had found it impossible to keep a grip of his spatha's hilt and it was knocked from his hand.

The ferocity and speed of the savages had been so shocking that they had almost overwhelmed the three lines of well trained and disciplined soldiers. They immediately began to collapse with the weight of the huge fur clad tribesmen lashing and screaming at them with axes and huge swords. He remembered back to a loud drumming sound that intruded upon the madness, it came from somewhere behind them but was drowned out by the wild cries of their attackers and clashing weapons.

The next recollection Veranius had was of landing on his back with his horse falling beside him, a violent impact, the air was instantly knocked out of his lungs and he struggled to breath, gasping for air. The small cavalry detachment had been behind the thin ranks of infantry awaiting the trumpet call to outflank the barbarians on their right side when the attack had caught them by surprise. The Germanic tribe seemed to fall out of the trees and mist from nowhere and were upon them before they could react.

His horse was quickest to it's feet and fled galloping to the rear of the Roman lines vanishing into other advancing columns without it's mount. He had stood shaking his head trying to make the stars dancing before his eyes vanish as metal clashed against metal near him, ringing in his ears. Instinctively he had drawn his dagger from his right side and almost fell backwards as infantry retreated all around him taking him along with the weight and strength of their numbers.

Something had struck him against his armoured shoulder with such power he buckled at an angle, his knees bending automatically, almost taking him back to the muddy surface. He turned to see a huge hairy face grimacing next to his own. It was so close he could smell the acrid stench of the animal like being wielding the sword that had hit his chainmail. Insane, crazed eyes stared, battle madness displayed on them as the near toothless male struggled to get the large sword up again for another strike.

An overwhelming weight hit Veranius from the left from something unseen before he hit the ground again he realised it was another horse shrieking as it was impaled through the chest by one of the attackers. He was as powerless as the horse in that moment. As the animal shrieked louder and kicked its legs trying to get to its feet, its rider was dispatched by an axe blow that struck the unfortunate soldier on the neck above the folds of his armoured vest. His head was almost cut from his body, dead eyes stared out unseeing. Blood jetted from the wound and hit Veranius in the face and mouth, warm and wet, tasting foul. In that instant the fluid was down his throat and in his eyes, he choked for breath, scraping with fingers for better vision with both hands, his sword he realised had landed somewhere at his feet, unseen as he panicked to clear his eyes.

He was aware of cries of agony as iron and bronze weapons clashed all around him and those that didn't, sliced and cut into human or animal flesh. The horses made dreadful sounds, worse than the men as barbarians thrust their weapons into their bodies, seeking out arteries, bone or major organs to terrify the riders and bring them down. The soldiers on foot were furiously thrusting and stabbing their short swords into and through the fur covered attackers that were intent on killing or mortally wounding them. They peered from behind or over their shields as they put into practise their well rehearsed training and tactics of stab, thrust and withdraw. He heard feet scrambling for purchase on the muddy surface as the retreating soldiers were pushed back by the horde attacking them.

He knew if he didn't get back to his feet quickly he wouldn't leave this field alive, his remains would be ripped apart if the Germanic tribe won the day and his severed head would end up on a spear or stake. He also knew that would only happen if he was fortunate enough to die straight away. Captured troops were made the play things for the women of the Germanic tribes, who would torture them sometimes for days on end. This was usually done by women who had lost their men, brothers or sons to the invading force. Their limbs would be broken with wooden logs, their fingers cut off and fed to packs of dogs or pigs and their organs cut out while their host took its last breath in this life. It was a vile way to die and no way for a soldier to meet his end.

He leapt up frantically searching for the large barbarian whose rank breath had almost made him retch. He had blurred vision through one eye, his right smeared with blood from the axed soldier, his left eye useless entirely. Figures blurred around him, the noise of battle overwhelming, the smell of blood, the metallic aroma disgusting and repugnant. He whirled blinking unsure who or what was around or near him. Dabbing at his right eye furiously, from nowhere animal fur brushed against his face, moving violently. He thrust the blade into what he thought must be the midriff of the tribal barbarian who had to be by his side. He heard a gasp as he ripped the blade up holding the handle now with two hands. Planting his feet for purchase on the ground, he gulped in air as he pulled the blade up with all his strength slicing through skin and muscle.

As his eyes began to clear, he heard a grinding sound, as the blade so easily cutting through flesh suddenly stopped, grating as it caught against something solid maybe bone or cartilage. Warm liquid gushed out onto his hands and wrists, making them sticky and hard to manoeuvre. He felt the weight of his opponent fall against him as he pulled on the dagger trying to free the weapon from the other living bone, its metal had cut into.

As he struggled to clear the large dagger and get it free, something hit the fur clad enemy pushing him rapidly backwards. It was the booted sandal of another soldier, as he kicked him away the dagger was instantly free. In that moment, Veranius thrust it forward again, slicing the sharp blade into the right side of his enemies face near the eye. The tribesman was still fighting struggling and gurgling against his impending death. He adjusted the blade and forced it into the barbarian's eye, it popped a dull but satisfying sound to Veranius as he fought for his very existence. Pushing forward with all his weight he saw through blurred vision as his blade caused irreparable damage as it was forced fully into the eye socket.

Time had slowed as he saw the impact on the dark terrified remaining wide eye, as the tip of his weapon pierced the other organ as the being it belonged to tried to close it's eyes in a final and futile attempt to save its sight and possibly its life. It was forced back into the head and suddenly popped again, exploding blood in a sudden gush. The knife instantly sank deeper and the man fell to the floor, silent and dead that instant.

He struggled to keep a grip of the handle of his dagger with two hands that were now slippery with sticky warm blood and he moved back, the momentum helping to free the weapon as he gagged almost emptying the contents of his stomach. As quickly as time had seemed to slow, it returned to its frantic manic pace as men fought to slash, stab and hack at each other all around him.

Veranius tried to wipe the blood from his left hand whilst stabbing out at more hordes of barbarians with the dagger in his right. He knew he had to get clear of this chaos if he were to survive. There was no sense in dying for no reason in this land of primitives in a battle that would probably be forgotten tomorrow. Other soldiers were now retreating to other lines to the rear, some fell, stumbling as they tried to get to the neat rows of soldiers that were formed up some distance away, waiting to join the battle.

Through shaking vision, he saw the straight columns and lines slowly walking towards his position as he began to get clear of the combat. An eagle standard glistened with the sun reflecting off its surface as the mist began to clear and trumpets sounded the signal for the advancing troops to quicken their pace. Swords began to strike shields as they got closer and the sound grew.

He heard a trumpet echo as the troops closed in on the battle and changed their stance slightly as they walked. The front rank he saw, were preparing to throw their first pilums. These spears were much heavier weapons than those used by the Cavalry and wooden pegs secured the spear head so they would break off on impact, stopping the spear from being thrown back. The metal head would break free of the body and pierce even shields as well as flesh and bone. The killing head of the weapon could be up to twelve inches long and so would kill or cripple anything it came into contact with. Veranius had seen the damage these spears could do to the body and ducked lower as he ran thinking of the irony of being killed by his own side.

The first of the retreating soldiers met the advancing column and were allowed to melt into their straight lines as small gaps were made for their injured, retreating and stunned comrades. A quick glance to the rear showed that his reason to run was justified. Those that had survived the initial onslaught but had tried to stand their ground were now being cut down and the fortunate amongst them, hacked to death. Some were dragged screaming from the battlefield to a more uncertain and no doubt worse fate. Some screamed, the men even hardened campaigners, would take the sound to their graves in the years and decades to come. He looked to his fellow soldiers just as the front row of the advancing lines released their javelins with a great sigh of effort. They rose high, silently climbing into the misty Germanic skies above.

Large ballista bolts were launched from somewhere behind the column, the speed of them was almost supernatural as they flew only a matter of feet above his head, hissing through the air. In one instant he heard the bolts being fired and then within the blink of an eye they were over his head and within a second they were embedded into lines of the enemy, four or five men deep, impaled on the enormous spiked heads of the bolts. He ducked instinctively and stumbled falling to the ground and tumbled forward into the mud with his momentum. He briefly caught sight of a few ballista units mounted on the rear of horse drawn wagons behind the marching death machine of soldiers as their crews worked furiously to load more of their deadly accurate life taking machines.

Veranius almost immediately felt slightly stupid and foolish for ducking and falling deliberately because he knew the weapons were deadly accurate, up to three hundred yards away and these were half that distance. He didn't dare to look behind him again because every second counted now, knowing what was to come however, he almost pitied the enemy. They were going to realise that victory didn't mean brute strength and ignorance and they were about to be annihilated to a man.

Panting he reached the column as they parted to let him through their lines, he smiled briefly and was happy to see the fresh uniforms of troops not yet covered in gore and blood from battle. One of the men shouted an acknowledgement as they went to their knees as the second row launched their own pila. He struggled through to the rear line and collapsed on the muddy surface beyond, turning almost straight away to watch the carnage that was about to unfold.

A loud shrill trumpet blast sounded from a *cornicularis* trumpeter, who blew for all he was worth from somewhere in the distance ordering the centuries into a *testudo* tortoise formation. He saw the men behind the front row bring their shields up instinctively covering their heads and those in front of them, this after days, weeks and months of drilling with their left arms holding their shields up sometimes for hours at a time. The testudo was primarily used as a defensive formation but in situations like this, a legion would use it to get into fighting range comparatively safely. Those at the front turned their bodies slightly to the left with their large rectangular shields still facing the enemy, eyes peering through the gap between the scutums and helmets. The enemy were now advancing rapidly, running towards them screaming like maniacs. In the same motion the soldiers grasped the hilts of their short swords on their right sides. A loud rasp that sent a shiver even through him, indicated they had removed their *gladius* swords, the blade of which would protrude from their collective shields, to stab at the advancing, screaming hordes.

An almighty clash of men, metal, swords, axes, shields and screams ripped through the air like thunder, consuming all other noise as the opposing forces came together. The Romans dug their sandaled hobnailed boots into the earth barely pausing as they began to cut the enemy down as if they were one giant animal, its teeth wounding and killing. It was now that the angled stance of the soldiers paid off as their right boots bit into the earth behind them and they leaned forward against their shields pushing forwards with their left legs slightly angled to gain purchase against the weight of the enemy whilst all the time stabbing at them beyond the wall of shields. After a short time they rotated, the front row coming to the rear, some bloodied and injured, as the second row met the barbarians as they became the front line and so it continued, second after second, minute after minute with fresh men moving to the front rank until what was left of the enemy, who realising it was hopeless, fled the battlefield and began to retreat.

Cavalry arched galloping around the legionnaires on the flanks and pursued the running men, cutting them down with their swords. Those lying injured in the mud were killed where they lay by the infantry as they broke the testudo and despatched those who had attacked their countrymen, for them there was and could be no mercy. Horse's charged, knocking men over, whilst their riders slashed at them with their long swords. It turned into a massacre.

Months later, now in the present and in the large tranquil clearing he looked at the dagger again. It had saved his life on that occasion, the image of its blade deep inside the barbarian's skull vivid and visceral. He examined it admiring its lines turning it over and examining it's shape of ruthless efficiency. It was truly a weapon capable of causing great injury and one he was glad to have. Thinking about that day, it was a vile and disgusting experience but he reminded himself, one that would have been reversed, had he been the one killed and not the other way round, as it was it was the barbarian whose remains had surely rotted where he had died.

The memories of previous battles didn't disturb his sleep anymore as they had in his first few months of service but once in a while something would remind him of the shear barbarity of his chosen profession and the brutality that went with it. He was brought out of his contemplative state by the sound of his approaching comrades riding clear of the tall trees.

"Veranius, stop playing with that dagger," Shouted a grinning Varro as he brought Staro to a halt, "anyone would think it was your manhood the way you were gazing and fondling it." He smirked.

A chorus of laughter started from the others as they came to a halt and Lucius said, "Don't worry you'd never see that boy sized peanut from there anyway, so it couldn't have been his cock."

More laughter rippled through the group, as Veranius just grinned in response. Trying to change the subject he said, "Nice country this my friends and its nowhere near as barren and hostile as we were led to believe" he began, "I think I'll build a villa here, right here in this very wood when I retire and find a girl to keep me warm at night. It's much more pleasant than Germania don't you think?"

Varro jumped from his horse feigning a smile. He walked Staro to the small stream making sure he had a drink.

"I think that you had better wait and see how the locals greet us before you think of setting up home with one of them don't you think?" The other men dismounted and watered their animals, Lucius walked into the stream, knee deep.

"This would be an ideal spot to camp for the night but for one small detail, the enemy could surround us and we wouldn't even know they were coming, we'd be trapped with no escape."

"We'll take a few moments and then move on." Varro replied. "Lucius and Marcus, you two will go forward this time. We need to try and get free of these trees or at least find high ground somewhere within it if we can't. Have a drink and fill your water sacks before we go. We don't know when we'll find another stream like this."

Lucius had been in the army for six years, two of those had been spent with Varro. He had more than his fair share of scars, more even than the others but no-one ever seemed to know why. He came from Ravenna one of the largest military ports on the north east coast of their homeland. Unlike most of the others under the command of Centurion Varro, Lucius was tall and skinny despite days, weeks and months of physical training. His large Roman nose meant that he sometimes had the nickname Caesar, usually when others in the group had drank too much wine and became braver as the alcohol loosened their tongues. He was a good man to have around and a demon in a fight.

He actually hated the seafaring men of the empire more than his commander after his woman Rica, had run away with one of them. Rumours circulated throughout the legion that he had sought them out in a nearby port and killed them both the night before joining the army the next day. He wouldn't talk about his life prior to joining the legion except to say where he was from accompanied normally by a loud snorting, followed by him spitting huge mouthfuls of phlegm onto the floor no matter where they were. The rest of them had learned not to ask too much about his past. He was however, a joker who never missed the chance to verbally rip the bowels out of his friends and fellow soldiers and he liked to drink his share of wine.

Marcus and Lucius were close friends and were constantly bickering with each other. A daily joke was that they should make things formal and become man and wife but then the two argued about who was going to be who, bride or groom. They drank the clear cold crystal water heartily and checked their mounts before moving off.

"So what's the plan sir?" Decimus asked watching the others in their group who were all checking their equipment a few feet away. Legionary Quintus was ensuring that everything was in order. Although he was a legionary, he was one rank above the others as he commanded the other half of the men when Varro and his group were parted whilst one was scouting ahead and the other returned to the main body of the legion to report on their progress.

Quintus had been in the army for ten years and was a veteran of many campaigns, he had been offered further promotion many times but had turned it down preferring to 'keep his boots in the mud' as he could often be heard saying. He was an Optio, one rank below Centurion and had quickly risen to the rank but he knew with further promotions, came the possibility of a command post and he didn't suit managing others or writing commands on scrolls or wax tablets all day long.

Varro replied, "We are going to stay as close to the coast as we can for the time being and keep heading west until the land naturally takes us north, a few days ride from here. The map we got hold of shows that the coast is cut away with paths going north and then branching off in different directions. The General has orders for the Second to try and identify any settlements that are willing to help and engage those that aren't. Whatever the outcome of the next few days, we're to liaise with the other legions before he decides who is going in which direction but from what I could gather from the briefing, we'll continue along the southern coast."

He took out a rough map drawn on animal hide sometime before by an exiled prince. It showed the southern coastal part of the island, if this place could be called an island because of its size. There were two smaller land masses, one off the south coast and one to the west just off the land fall, beyond that was another island it was marked as 'Mona.' There was a red mark against the name.

"What's the significance of this Mona?" Decimus asked pointing as he and Veranius flattened the parchment and studied the map.

"It's thought to be crawling with druids, the spiritual leaders of these Britons. This is where Adminius tells us they have their main settlement where they train others in their spiritual beliefs. They are believed to have been the main reason some of the tribes stopped forming an alliance with Rome. It's said they worship ancient forces and commit cruel ritualistic acts and anyone that goes against them is automatically under the threat of death and eternal misery from their druidic gods. Personally I think it's a load of old bollocks just like some of our own priests. If we end up going there and there's a distinct possibility it will be us," he pointed to Mona, "the other legions will move inland to the central core of the country, one of them anyway and the other up the east coast. Fortifications will be established and those that want to join the empire will receive our help and assistance. Those Britons that do not, will be crushed and destroyed or that's the plan anyway. One other legion will stay in the south and establish forts and harbours for supplies and reinforcements." Varro paused, thinking.

"Why the hesitation?" Veranius asked, "We will destroy all those who oppose us surely?"

Varro said, "You know it's never as easy as that and there'll be a lot of fighting and dying to do first. Many of those soldiers unloading equipment on the beach right now will never see their families or homes again, it's a fact. It's not something I come to terms with as easily as some my friend."

"Come on Varro, don't be so dour, there'll be spoils a plenty here, come on lets get moving." Veranius was right he thought. There was no point in thinking about what might happen but only what they could make happen.

"Your right, okay come on." Standing he ordered, "Mount up, lets get a move on, we won't expand the empire sitting here with you fiddling with yourself." He looked at Veranius smiling, they trotted into the trees following legionaries Lucius and Marcus laughing again as Veranius muttered something about his blade and where he'd like to put it.

In time, just as the light was beginning to fade, the two leading riders emerged from the trees into a clear area but beyond it was another vast woodland or forest, which it was, they couldn't be certain of from their position.

"Trees! Who would have guessed it?" Lucius remarked, "More like a fucking forest this time though just look at that." He brushed twigs and leaves from his shoulders and legs.

"It must have been like that when you bedded that hairy fucking bitch in Gaul Marcus. Only it probably took you longer to run your sword through her, I would have thought you'd have enjoyed the ride." Decimus said, chuckling quietly.

"Gaul'ish women maybe hairy but they keep you warm on a winter's night." He retorted. "You should have tried them instead of swilling wine every night and looking for small boys."

"Ha-ha. You're funny aren't you? Wine may kill you eventually but it can't cut your throat like those harlots." Decimus replied.

The legion had eventually banned the men from 'associating' with the local women after a few didn't report for duty the next day. Their bodies, with throats cut were found floating in the local river for days afterwards. The legions Legate, Vespasian had instructed that any soldier caught breaking the rule would be flogged and for each Roman soldier killed, five local women would die. Their severed heads would be impaled on spikes as a warning to others outside the fort. It didn't stop the drunken troops however, and no legion could confine its men to barracks forever but it did stop the murders of his men.

Discipline was hard but couldn't be brought down like an iron fist and passes had still been given to the men to visit taverns after a hard days training, building, marching or riding. Ordinarily there was no time for such activities when the legion was on the march in the middle of a campaigning season. By the time they stopped, they had to construct defences every single night as they didn't know who to trust in any given area, so socialising with the locals would always come another day. Waiting for the fleet and for the legions in Gaul to gather had been different and it was unavoidable that the men would mix with the women of the local neighbourhood.

"We'll meet up by that small hill." Marcus pointed to a distant rise beyond the forest. He estimated it had to be at least two hundred feet above ground level. "It should make a good place to camp and we'll be able to see anything that moves from up there."

When Varro and the others arrived the daylight was already fading fast. A small fire was burning in a hole in the ground and Lucius was skinning a hare he had snared, three others lay dead nearby. Varro surveyed the area around the hill, he could see for miles. Each man usually carried three days rations but if they could hunt and find fresh food, it was better for them, the salted dried meat from their rations would have to wait.

"We'll rest here tonight and move forward tomorrow at first light. Quintus you can take the other men to the rear and report our progress to the Legate. We'll continue along the coast and meet up the day after tomorrow."

Quintus nodded in response as the men began preparing for the first night that would be spent under the stars in Britannia. Thick animal skins were untied from the rumps of the horses and unwrapped on the ground. Three were kept folded and placed in a triangular shape around the hole where the fire burned a foot below ground in case of prying eyes in an attempt to reduce the glow and flames of the fire.

"We'll post two guards at each edge of the rise," Varro ordered pointing, "once we've eaten as soon as the lights gone we'll put the fire out and get our heads down. It'll be a long day tomorrow for all of us, we'll take turns as usual until the sun comes up, Servius, Sextus you two are first."

He nodded to two of the men that would return to the legion with Quintus the following day. "We'll do it in pairs, two hours about so everyone will get some sleep for most of the night, tomorrow will be a more exhausting day than today, that's for sure."

He stretched his aching limbs, they had ridden more today than they had for a while and his sore backside was testament to every bumpy mile, a few more days in the saddle would cure that though. They sat around the small fire cooking the meat and ate Lucius' kills. It was tasty and succulent and just what they needed after a day in the saddle, the meat was washed down with a mouthful of water they had taken from the stream earlier that day. It was warmer now but still relatively fresh.

With the light virtually gone and the stars starting to appear, soil was kicked over the fire dousing the remaining flames. As everyone else bedded down, Servius and Sextus went out and took up their positions, both carried their javelins.

Sometime later a voice cut through the peaceful night. "Sir, come and look at this." Sextus said in a hushed whisper from a short distance away in the dark. Varro blinked himself awake and went towards him, his figure silhouetted on a starry background. He shook two others awake and instructed Veranius and Decimus to follow. The others carried on sleeping undisturbed.

Varro didn't have to ask what the problem was, he could see for himself. On the plains below fires could be seen flickering in the distance beyond the woods and forests, there were at least thirty fires burning some way off. Other fires could be seen separate from the main group but they were isolated, none could be seen in the direction they had come from.

"Looks like you were right," Decimus remarked, "tomorrow is going to be a busy day."

"That's obviously a large village or a major settlement," Veranius said pointing to the large cluster of flames. From this distance each fire was small, a dot nothing more but some were the size of a nail head, "It's probably a day's ride from here. We'll be safe enough tonight," he looked back to the area where they had eaten, "they couldn't have seen us or the fire, Lucius dug the pit deep enough to conceal the flames and if they did, they'd probably think it was more of them or groups out hunting." He pointed to the singular fires, "That's probably what they are."

It was a decision only Varro could make he knew. He looked out and thought for a while, if they went back the way they had come, they wouldn't achieve anything but it would put some space between them and whatever lay below and around those fires. He had made his decision.

"We'll stay here tonight. If you see anything and I mean anything moving towards us and getting close, wake us straight away, begin to saddle the horses and we'll withdraw and head inland and around them dependant on the situation. We're here to see what lies in the path of the column and we just achieved that to some degree." He unfurled the map.

"That large place isn't marked here, I wasn't expecting to see any inhabited settlements for a while." He marked the map and returned to the others where he instructed Quintus to note the details on his identical copy of the map that he would take back to the legion. Maybe the maps author wasn't aware of this location he thought, or it was relatively new.

"We'll scout ahead tomorrow and see exactly what's out there before you head back so you won't leave straight away. There's no reason to return to the legion when you're within a stones through of getting some real intelligence, understood?" Varro asked.

"Yes sir." He replied.

"Right let's get some sleep," he patted Quintus on the shoulder, "and hopefully we won't speak again until daylight." As Varro made one last check of the area, he went to see Servius who was unaware of their findings and explained the situation. He told both guards to make sure they positioned themselves in dead ground so they couldn't be seen from a distance, silhouetting their bodies against the night sky before settling down to get some sleep in their makeshift camp.

Being so close to potential enemy positions was not unusual for him or his men, it was one of the reasons they volunteered for such a duty but it still felt strange no matter how many times they'd done it before. In the past they had been so close to unknown groups that they had been able to hear them laughing and talking at night, in comparison, this was positively safe. The night passed without incident but it was the last good sleep they would all have for some considerable time.

That same evening just as Varro and his men were settling down, a long way to the north, two riders reached the capitol of the Catuvellauni, Camulodunum. They galloped through the open gates and found Togodumnus and told him the news of the Roman landing.

Chapter Three

When they awoke just before sunrise the next day, a damp dew covered the ground all around them and now they were wet and cold, silver thin spider's webs adorned everything from men and equipment alike and birds sang a chirpy dawn chorus all around their makeshift camp. The sun was just beginning to rise as the black of night retreated but it would be a while before it burned away the chill of the night completely. A mist covered the lowlands making it impossible to define any detail except for the tops of trees in the distance.

"Jupiter's balls it's cold." Quintus was heard exclaiming from the confines of his makeshift bed as he brushed down his damp clothing, he wasn't talking to anyone in particular, just remarking at his own displeasure and muttering to himself.

"Germania was freezing, Gaul was cold and now we find ourselves on the dampest most remote island that Rome could find, at the furthest tip of the empire. Why couldn't we have gone east where at least we could have browned our skin under the rays of the sun and baked our balls by the sea all day?" He continued to ramble on as others began to emerge from their own blankets and cloaks grinning.

"Syria would have been nice, we wouldn't have frozen our cocks off there but no, we had to come here to this giant forest and….." He looked around and saw the mist below, "Oh wonderful, just look at that." He said pointing, "There could be all manner of hairy bastards hiding down there waiting to greet us when we get down, hundreds of them, thousands even and we wouldn't have the first fucking clue they were there."

"It will soon heat up Quintus," Decimus said, "in no time at all you'll be jumping into streams with naked local women, who will help warm your blood. Now stop your whining."

Quintus shivered at the prospect of cold water and threw aside his course blanket, kneeling he began to roll it up ready to move but it didn't stop him from complaining.

"Water, streams, you have to be pulling my incredibly long foreskin my friend. If I jumped into a stream right now I'd die and you would be responsible, miserable bloody place. I can't wait to see the locals actually I bet they're covered in natural fur to keep warm, it's bound to be growing out of their skin."

Quintus' ranting at least cheered the others up as they packed away their gear and stowed it on the horses and in no time at all they were ready to move off, breakfast would have to wait, a fact that gave Quintus more to moan about. They would move from their resting place before eating, putting a few miles between them and the overnight camp. Varro informed them that he wanted to scout the area where they had seen the fires the night before. Once that was done they would split up with Quintus and his men to returning the column. The rest of the Second Augusta was probably already preparing to move but would be having a hearty breakfast before breaking camp. They made sure there was no evidence of last night's fire and gave their mounts a little food, they could go without breakfast but their means of transportation could not. Already the mist was beginning to clear as Varro slowly led the way down off the high ground. Once more they began to see that small wooded areas littered the land, with a large covering of forest to the right, the sea and rolling coastline to their left.

"We'll make for that cluster of trees over there." Varro said pointing, "Quintus take you're men and follow the line of the sea, we'll take the northern route and move along the tree line of the forest. If you make any enemy contact or suddenly come across any hairy arse Britons your unsure of and you find yourself outnumbered, you are to withdraw to here, where we'll meet you and the same applies for us. We don't know how these people will react, so be safe. Remember we're here to watch, observe and report back, not to get involved in a fight."

Quintus acknowledged the order and indicated for his men to follow his lead. Gone was the moaning man, returned was the professional soldier. Slowly they turned their horses to follow his lead and began to descend the hillock.

"Optio," Varro said to Veranius, "Lets see who's out there shall we?"

He began to move further down the hill, their party some yards behind the first, at the base of the mound, he turned left and Quintus and his men went right. The sun was slowly beginning to warm them now and Varro felt a little better than he had when he had woken just before first light. It was always an unusual feeling being so far forward, without the comfortable feeling of the quick response and safety of the rest of the legion nearby.

Initially Varro had found it hard to adapt to the duties of the unit, never quite knowing who or what lay ahead or behind. He had spent many a restless night often preferring to volunteer for guard duty rather than sleeping or trying to sleep before he got use to it. In time, he had been promoted to Optio and now he commanded his own unit and while he slept soundly, others volunteered to stay awake on guard.

He had come to realise that whatever was written in the stars or was bound to be in his destiny he couldn't change it. It was futile to fret and worry over what he could not affect or ultimately change, so he would continue to use his skill and initiative and hopefully stay alive being careful to avoid overwhelming odds. If it was his time to leave this life then that was how it was meant to be.

He was more than aware of the responsibility regarding his men and their lives, he would be loyal to the death with them and he expected the same in return, nothing more nothing less. Politics and scheming by high ranking officers was all too apparent in the army and he wouldn't abide it with his soldiers, if an individual had something to say he would listen and respect their opinions and views. It didn't of course mean he would take any notice of it however and the men respected that. He wouldn't stand for any political wrangling or men prepared to step on others to advance their own careers.

They had once had a Senators son in their ranks whose ambition was clearly more dangerous than the enemy, because of his eagerness to please the Legate and the legions tribunes. His father had insisted he join the ranks of the army as a legionary and not a thin stripe tribune, as punishment for his arrogance and bad nature. Varro had made sure he was removed from the unit within a week after he tried to volunteer them for a mission that could have killed them all, they never saw him again. He didn't always act on his men's advice or words but he did listen, he always listened. He knew he wasn't infallible and had more respect for his fellow soldiers than other officers or men wearing Senatorial robes. If they had something of value to say and it was better than his initial course of action, he was humble enough to change his mind. Too many in the army were ignorant and arrogant as they tried to advance themselves and he had seen them all too often pay the price for that with their lives. He lived for the day not some future that may never come.

The sun was now visible and the mist had all but evaporated except for a few clumps here and there. As he led his men out towards the line of trees that marked the edge of the forest, he scanned ahead expecting to see horses and men emerge quicker than they could react and pin them down, it wasn't long before his suspicions were confirmed. Somewhere in the distance, the corner of his eye caught movement to the right. He saw fleeting movement, slight and slow but movement nevertheless. At a distance of about five hundred yards he saw a human figure move back into the cover of the thick trees. As soon as his eyes were on him or her, they'd vanished but not before Varro saw the spear that they carried, confirming it was a person.

Outwardly he gave no indication that he had seen the man or woman but he adjusted the path of Staro slightly away from the trees and to at least two range lengths of a spears throw from the cover of them. He moved his right hand to his back and held it at the base of his spine clenching his fist, Veranius saw it and without a word, all the men were aware of the danger somewhere ahead on the right.

"How far? Veranius asked quietly.

"About five hundred paces, a lone man I think armed with a javelin, all I saw was a figure but he's carrying a spear for certain and as soon as I saw him he slid back into the trees." He looked to the right where an entire army could be hidden and they wouldn't know it. Quintus was out of sight now, having gone around the other side of the hill where they had spent the night. It would be sometime before they met up at the trees Varro had indicated was to be their rendezvous point.

"Well we are here to see what's here, I suppose." He turned in his saddle smiling at Veranius who had a look of mild unease etched over his face as he then checked the location of his pilums.

"Come on lets flush out this fowl." Varro said as he gently nudged Staro with his heels and the horse moved forward slowly into a canter, ears sharp and straight as if sensing something wasn't quite right, his head nodding up and down. When they were level with the point where the man had vanished, Varro brought them to a halt, to anyone watching they made it look as if they had just stopped and were getting off their horses for a stretch but inside their senses were straining.

"Marcus," Varro said, as the soldier came forward, "you're our fastest runner aren't you?" He smiled knowing that Marcus would react as expected.

"Yes sir, no-one has beaten me in the legion yet," he beamed proudly. Marcus was one of the most competitive men Varro had ever known. It didn't matter if he was growing seeds or looking after the legions dogs, he had to be better, grow more or make the dogs more obedient, run faster and be stronger. He was a good man who was as straight and honest as the flight of an arrow and could be relied upon no matter what the situation. Here he was far from Rome, the only one amongst them actually from the capitol, he had spent three years in the army and was an expert rider and knew how to treat most ailments and injuries that the animals picked up; an altogether invaluable member of the squad.

"I want you to walk casually towards those trees but don't make it obvious that you're looking to see what's there, make it look like you're going to take a piss or something." Varro turned, "Lucius," he said looking at the other soldier, "I want you to hold the reins of his horse in case he has to run back and be ready to ride."

"Understood." He acknowledged taking the reins from Marcus who began to walk forwards and started to adjust his tunic. He had taken no more than ten feet when violent loud movement disturbed the bushes at the base of a tree. The tip of a wooden spear tipped with iron appeared and was hurled towards the advancing Marcus, the throwers arm disappeared back into the bushes as quickly as it had appeared. Marcus didn't panic but quickly moved to the left avoiding the lance as it flew harmlessly past him at arm's length and landed, embedding itself into the ground its end vibrating as its deadly sharpened spike skewered the soil.

He crouched and began to move slowly backwards watching the foliage. He had left his oval shield on his horse hanging from one of the pommels, believing that to have taken it with him would have meant arousing suspicion, a decision he was now beginning to regret. He turned to check where the others were and the expression on Varro's face told him to get back quickly. As he turned to run he was aware of more movement behind him as men emerged from the trees.

In seconds he was leaping up and vaulting into his saddle, snatching the reigns from Lucius and turning his horse ready to move, he was aware the others hadn't started to gallop away, he turned the horse and saw why. Twelve men dressed in strange primitive clothing that was draped around their legs as well as their upper bodies were standing staring at the Romans. They carried small round shields and some were holding long swords as well as spears.

Some of them had limed hair that looked dirty and stiff and stood on end, a few wore it tied up at the back and most had straggly unkempt beards, blue streaks marked their faces, they were obviously tribal warriors, the first Britons they had seen. As the two opposing sides stared at each other with fascination, fear and a growing anticipation of what was to come, a silence seemed to descend over the area and the air became still.

These were the Britons, the inhabitants of this strange land, their faces looked rough and weather beaten even more so than the sailors that had brought Varro and his men here on their ships from Gaul. Some held their swords in their right hands, whilst others had them in the left, Varro presumed that this meant that they didn't form disciplined lines in battle as they themselves did but instead probably fought as individuals and not as a cohesive group. They had been told that tribes would traditionally send their best warriors to fight in single combat to decide disputes. This was something the Romans could use to their advantage because they wouldn't make such an effective force together. Some of the swords looked to be made of bronze and Varro knew they wouldn't be as strong as the iron that made their own weapons, three or more had newer iron weapons. Nevertheless, the bronze swords could still cut a man in half as some of the Gaul's swords had. They each carried two spears attached to their backs by unseen fixtures except for one, the man that had tried to kill Marcus or had tried to scare him at least.

The odds were clearly in favour of the Britons who had an advantage of more than two to one and the expressions on their faces showed that they weren't happy to find these strange looking men in their territory. They had clearly never seen men like these before, wearing shining metal armour around their heads and bodies, the Britons eyes searched their bodies and equipment taking in every detail.

The legionaries knew that when the warring tribes weren't killing, maiming, raping each other or raiding their neighbour's lands, only a delicate peace existed, normally to prevent more deaths to individual groups who had sustained large casualties already. If they killed their own neighbours when they intruded onto their lands, they wouldn't react kindly to men from a distant country stepping foot on their soil either. As Varro considered a tactical retreat and began to look around slowly, he wondered if these men were alone, a hunting party maybe or were there more of them hidden in the darkness and shadows of the trees? He couldn't tell from this distance but he knew that without Quintus and his men, he couldn't risk a direct assault even though they had horses, were better equipped and most certainly better trained.

The last thing he could afford was a wounded horse or rider, just one dead mount or worse a wounded one, could mean death for the rider or a slow dangerous ride in retreat with the horseless riders being carried by another and no doubt being picked off as they lagged behind.

Without any sign or warning, the men who had been standing still in front of them for what seemed like an age moved backwards and in an instant disappeared back into the foliage as one. The disciplined soldiers to a man risked looking at each other in bewilderment, it would have been preferable if the Briton's had charged them screaming and slashing with their weapons. An eerie silence seemed to rob the air of noise, more acute than anything Varro had experienced before. Instinctively he began to move backwards followed his by his men backing up behind him.

As they turned their horses in preparation to move away, screaming suddenly erupted from the rear, shattering the eerie silence. Varro glanced around and saw the ranks of blue faced men had at least trebled in size.

"Go!" He screamed to his men as spears were launched towards them rising into the air. "Quickly move now."

The soldiers automatically ducked down as flat as they could over their mounts and kicked at them, their horses charged forward rapidly in response, spears landed in front of them flying over their heads, at their sides and one struck Marcus' horse as it kicked out and veered violently to the left into Varro and Staro. He couldn't see where exactly it had struck but could see it waving around as the horse galloped forward as Marcus fought for control. He had no time to think about that now because they had to get free of the deadly avalanche.

As the small group moved out of range of the airborne bombardment, the attackers howled and ran forward, collecting their spears and hurling them into the air again. Varro led his men clear of their range and then turned when he felt it was safe. He saw the tribesmen, now at least forty strong, standing shaking their spears at the Romans. One of them walked clear of the group and held his sword aloft, to a man the rest stopped howling and gesturing with their weapons.

"So much for these barbarians being an undisciplined rabble then because that to me was deliberate and practised I'd say." Veranius remarked.

"Marcus, are you injured?" He asked. Marcus jumped from his own horse and went to its flank. The spear was embedded in its back, he carefully examined it and an expression of relief and then frustration flooded over his face, relief, because the long weapon was stuck in his bedding roll and frustration, because he wanted to return the compliment to the thrower of the spear.

He pulled it clear and turned the weapon in his hand, it was lighter than a pilum but just as deadly in the right hands. He ran towards the Britons taking ten paces and hurled the spear back. Marcus was a strong man and the lance arced into the air and then fell. It landed in front of the horde harmlessly sinking into the ground with a thud. Not one of the blue streaked faces had flinched or moved a muscle as the spear was thrown and landed mere feet from them. The sound of hooves suddenly came from somewhere behind, Marcus turned, "Quintus." The other joined them.

"Problems sir?" He asked Varro.

"Nothing we couldn't handle, just." He replied relief all over his face. "Come on let's get out of here." He led them away from the warriors who were now slipping back into the forest once more.

When they were clear of further attack Varro turned to Quintus, "I want you to ride back to the column and make your report. Make sure you mark this place on your map and the settlement we saw, we'll take a look at that. We'll ride along the coast until tomorrow and find somewhere to wait for you, I'll light straw flares if you don't find us, as long as the area is clear look for cover near the coastline. May the gods be with you my friend, I have a feeling we may all need them soon enough." They clasped wrists.

"And may they be with you sir, I think you may need them more than us." Quintus replied looking back to the trees.

"Come on." He ordered as he commanded his horse forward, automatically his men followed and Varro and his men were alone again. "Two days in and we've already met the locals and surprisingly they're not that pleased to see us." He said leading them further from the trees and away from danger.

"When the column gets here that rabble will pay for that." Marcus said looking back at his bed roll.

"In time my friend," Varro cautioned, "but in the meantime let's see what else we can find."

Later they had ridden back to the coast where the sea breeze was cool and refreshing in the salt air as they walked along the cliff tops. The white chalk of the landing area had been replaced by rock and sea birds were nesting and hunting in the waters below.

"Before we move on and get further away from here, I want to see what's in the village that we saw illuminated last night." Varro said and added, "I know we need to get clear of here quickly so we'll just take a brief look."

They skirted the cliff moving slowly and turned inland nearing noon. Progress was slow anyway because of the terrain but they had to be cautious in case any friends of the tribesmen were nearby. With only a few of them in their party now, they wouldn't stand a chance if they were ambushed and trapped. They avoided confined areas and places that would make good ambush points, nearing noon as they continued away from the sea, they could see tracks had been established in the grassland areas. Marcus said that he could smell smoke and soon enough small plumes were seen as they rose up into the blue sky over the trees in the distance, many plumes of smoke. Reaching the wooded area that was a natural barrier between their position and the village they dismounted.

"We'll leave the horses here." Varro said. "Marcus, you stay with them but if there are any problems get to us as soon as possible. The rest of you follow me."

He led them through the trees along a path, knowing there was a possibility of running into locals but there were no other routes, thick un-passable bushes and gorse lined the worn track on either side so they now had no other choice if they were to see what lay beyond. Before long they could hear faint voices and laughter, they slowed their pace crouching, swords were quietly drawn.

Varro looked through the thicket and saw movement and indicated for the others to stop, he peered through the thick branches. Large round brown huts with straw roofs dotted the settlement at irregular intervals, it looked like the walls were made from packed mud and straw, fires were burning drying animal skins that were hung nearby. Children ran chasing a small dog who was barking happily at its pursuers wagging its tail.

Decimus drew level with his commander, "Anything useful?" He asked.

Varro continued to watch the village, "Shhh, keep your voice down, it looks like a bunch of natives that's all, nothing worthy of a military target but good intelligence none the less."

"What's that?" Veranius asked pointing with his sword to the far left side of the roundhouses. Situated at the edge of the area he was pointing towards was a much larger hut and beyond that was a large human figure.

"It looks like they've made a large structure of a man out of wood, branches, sticks and twine, must be some pagan ritual probably." Lucius said peering through the leaves. Studying its strange formation he said, "It must be high though because that hut is twice the size of those nearer to us and they're taller than a man themselves. That straw effigy stands twice as high as the larger hut."

"It's probably a straw god or something." Varro added. "They're are known to worship the sun, stars and moon so why not something that looks over their village and provides some form of cover as well?"

Two figures cloaked in black could be seen at the base of the effigy, kneeling down. "Look they must be some of their druids, holy people, they're praying aren't they?" Decimus pointed out.

The soldiers watched as the two figures raised and lowered their arms praying and worshiping to some unseen entity.

"It's said they hold positions of great significance within their people and can even influence tribal leaders." Varro said.

"Fucking arse bandits more like, imagine that? People led by mystics and fools?" Decimus added. "We'll rule this land within the year if this is anything to go by!"

Varro counted the huts, making a mental note for later. "The village couldn't have been here that long because it's not on the map, they've probably set up here because of the fishing in the sea," he pointed out a river beyond the effigy, "fresh water and there's probably good hunting in these woodlands near where we saw our blue friends earlier."

"How many men do you see in the village?" Veranius asked. Varro counted the two men they presumed were druids and then he realised no more.

"Our blue warriors must be from this village then. They're the men of this settlement. That means they won't be back for some time unless they have horses and I doubt that." Varro said. "Anyone care for a closer look?"

"Is that wise sir? Veranius asked. "We can't see who is in those other huts if anyone and there are lots of them. If there are only three in each hut, we would be badly outnumbered we could be walking straight into a trap."

Varro thought about what he had just said and reluctantly replied, "Yes you're right." He surveyed the surrounding ground. "See that rise over there?" He pointed beyond the straw man where a grass bank beyond the river rose to a height of about a hundred feet.

"I say we get the horses and move round," he indicated with his left arm in a sweeping movement, "cross the river and hold up in the trees above. We can observe the huts from there and see if our blue friends return. If they do, our legion will be paying them a visit during the next few days."

Returning to Marcus they explained the situation in whispers and moved off cautiously crossing the river that actually turned out to be a large stream, they could still see the top of the straw man and the settlement clearly. Marcus frowned as he looked back as they led the horses on foot through the water. Decimus dragged his water sack through the stream almost filling it, reaching the other side Varro checked to make sure the druids couldn't see them and walked left further away from the settlement and then came up finally reaching the cover of the trees. The slope flattened out and they secured the horses on the far side of the plateau, where they immediately started to eat the long lush fresh grass.

"Let's get some food while we can but no fires or cooking." Varro instructed as he removed his helmet. "Veranius, make sure the horses are watered, I want them ready to move at a moment's notice."

The men settled down and ate a small meal from their rations of salted pork, the three days rations they carried always came in handy as hunting could never guarantee a successful result and so the men were always prepared. The meat was tasty and provided all the nutrients they required.

"Do you remember that banquet we attended in Ravenna with the Falernian opimian wine?" Veranius said. "They had fillet of hake, boiled mussels, milk fed snails, and the suckling pig! Oh that was gorgeous, that little bastard, I asked the cooks how they did it and got the recipe, mmm, peppers, lovage, caraway, celery seeds, asafoetida essence with wine passum, olive oil and corn flour. It was heavenly the gods couldn't have prepared it any better."

The others chuckled quietly. Veranius was a man who loved his food probably more than the soft flesh of a woman's belly. He and Decimus would compete to see who could prepare the best dish for the others while they were out in the field and Veranius usually won because he had a knack of being able to remember long lists of ingredients which he either found or if he couldn't, he would find something similar.

"Careful my friend or you'll start to drool if you carry on and the Briton's will slip on it as it drips down the slope and discover us." Varro said. "That was a marvellous feast though I remember eating until I thought my stomach would burst and then they brought out baskets of peppered sweet cake and I ate even more. I took some with me and had it the next day it was so good. I think I nearly split my arse when it all came out again."

Their Legate had organised the feast before they had begun their march to Gaul from Germania to take on the large barbarian men in the west. He had told them they needed feeding up because the enemy were a head taller than them and generally much wider. They continued to eat their dry rations quietly whilst retelling their stories of the feast as they waited for night to fall.

They finished the small meal still feeling a little hungry but knew it would pass in time and the meat would give them enough energy until night time or the next day if necessary. The two druids had returned to the base of the effigy and could be heard excitedly mumbling to each other about something.

"What do you say Veranius, I think we should pay our new hosts a visit and see what's going on here. There aren't any more men in the village at the moment that I can see and we should be okay with these two robed fools and a load of women to contend with, what do you think?" Varro had never been overly patient.

"Alright if you say so but let's not get too far away from the horses." Veranius replied looking along the river, as the two men moved along the water using the bushes as cover, they saw that the druids seemed distracted by something off in the distance behind them. Varro and Veranius maintained their positions and watched as blue painted men appeared through a tree line beyond the two waiting figures.

A struggle was going on inside the group and as the warriors approached the druids a young boy was thrown forward onto the ground at their feet. He struggled to get up but the tip of a spear from one of the Britons persuaded him not to move or to try and run. Rough, loud words clearly ordered him to remain still.

The older of the two druids said something unheard by the watching men, to the boy and then appeared to be inspecting him. Holding his jaw, he moved the boys head from side to side and then raised his arms. Satisfied, the druid said something to the barbarians guarding the youth and he was dragged towards the large wooden structure towering over them. The boy screamed now and attempted to struggle free but it was useless, he was dragged off his feet by the heavier and stronger men. Another tribesman ran forward and opened a door at the base of the wooden structure and the boy was bodily hurled inside. He shouted and screamed more but his pleas were ignored, the door was bound secure using vines.

"What in the name of all that's holy is going on here?" Veranius asked.

Varro watched as the hunters spoke to the two druids, "I don't know my friend but I think we'll find out eh?"

The sun was beginning to sink on the horizon and a red tinge marked the clouds with a sign of another warm day again in the morning. One warrior was left to guard the boy in the wooden prison as the others returned to the main village and their huts.

"Come on." Varro ordered as the two soldiers slowly left their cover, the guard was now sat with his back against the effigy facing the huts. The footsteps of the two Romans in the water, was masked by the sound of the stream as water trickled over stones as they approached the far bank. The boy continued to scream and cry but was ignored by his guard. Varro drew his dagger quietly as he came upon the Briton who was totally unaware of him, he looked up at the captured child, the boy inside the wooden prison was watching him as his eyes grew enormous taking in what was occurring before him, his sobs ceasing. Suddenly Varro reached forward and grabbed the long hair of the blue faced guard, ripping his head backwards and striking downwards with one deep and deadly blow with the other.

His blade slid unopposed into the Britons throat, his victim barely had time to raise his arms in surprise before his blood was drained from him as Varro sliced through the large vein of his neck. Veranius almost slipped on the bloody surface as he walked and untied the rope securing the boy in his prison. He had anticipated a struggle with the lad but he was clearly glad to be leaving his temporary prison and smiled beaming as he jumped clear. Whatever the locals had in store for him, it couldn't have been good especially for him to put his trust in these oddly dressed strangers. Quietly they re-crossed the river and disappeared from view, taking the boy with them.

Some miles away from the village the Romans dismounted from their horses, the boy had ridden with Varro until they were clear of the Britons. It was now almost dark and owls could be heard calling to each other in the trees as the stars began to emerge in the night sky.

"What was happening back there boy, why did they put you in that wooden man?" Varro asked. The boy frowned and when he replied it was in words that the Romans did not understand. "Of course he doesn't understand us like we don't understand him." Veranius said.

"Mm thank you Senator." Varro said sarcastically, returning his attention to the boy he said, "What were they doing to you, are you a thief?"

The boy mumbled something in reply but again it was unintelligible. He grabbed Varro by the hand and dragged him, pointing furiously in the direction of some hills in the distance. It was the opposite way from which they had come to get to the village.

"I think he's trying to tell us he's from another place and was brought here against his will." Varro said watching the boy.

Veranius wasn't too sure, "He could be lying, he's probably a thief like you said and was being punished by his tribe, that's why he wants to get away and go to the hills. These barbarians are all the same, they're dumb goat fuckers if you ask me."

Just then a shrill scream interrupted them, followed by hellish cries of pain. It came from the village and the boy's face showed complete terror.

"Lucius, I want you with me, come on, we're going to find out what that was, Veranius take charge here, don't let the boy out of your sight."

"Sir." Was all Veranius said in return as Varro and Lucius galloped away.

Moments later the two men had dismounted, tied their horses up and were now cautiously making their way through the bushes to the edge of the water, they found themselves once more on the far side of the river bank opposite the settlement. Every now and again they could hear screams and it was obvious they were actually coming from the other side of the water. As they emerged through the trees crouching by the water's edge they could see that the blue painted warriors had another boy in their clutches and appeared to be questioning him. They retreated backward a few steps to where they could see but not be seen. One of the warriors was holding him by the arm whilst shouting questions at him and pointing into the distance, the other had a long sword over a fire.

Whenever he gave them an answer they didn't seem to like he was burned with the sword, its tip heated in the flames of the fire. They had stripped his upper clothing off, the remains of which were now rags around his waist. Swollen hot welts could be seen easily from their hiding place as the Britons continued to question the boy, who in turn screamed in agony whenever the hot sword came close to his skin.

"I wish I had my bow," Lucius whispered watching, eyes glaring. "I'd pierce that blue bastards eyeballs for him, see how he likes a bit of pain."

Varro scowled as he watched, "Mm, that would be nice but I don't think it would help that youngster there unless we killed all of them and with just two of us that isn't going to happen.

"What could they want from a boy? How old would you say he is thirteen, fourteen maybe?" Lucius asked Varro.

"Something like that I should imagine." A deafening scream shattered the otherwise peaceful night as the red hot sword once again pierced the boy's skin, this time on his right shoulder. He collapsed onto the sandy surface by the river's edge, his skin glistening with sweat.

The druid said something and two of the Britons picked the boy up and dragged him to the wooden cage. One opened the door as the other dragged his unconscious body up and spilled it into the wooden form. Chanting began from the druids and the assembled painted warriors as women emerged from their roundhouses carrying flaming torches. As they approached the men, they joined in with the chanting, it seemed to stir the boy as his head moved from side to side as if drunk and an arm was raised.

Varro and Lucius watched from their hiding place in the bushes at the side of the river, their eyes glinting in the reflection of the lit torches as wafts of burning kindling reached them now. As the boy stirred from his wooden prison, the women gathered sticks and brush and began piling them under the wooden man. The boy was fully conscious again now and began screaming for mercy. His behaviour and gestures were getting more frantic but the two Romans couldn't hear him as his voice was drowned out by other chanting Britons.

"What in gods bones are they doing sir?" Lucius asked his commander, "Surely they're not going to do what I think they are?"

Varro watched almost transfixed by the horror playing out before his eyes. "I wish we could do something Lucius but we would most likely end up in the same place if we intervened. There's nothing we can do for him, all we can do in time, is ensure that it never happens again."

As the brushwood grew under the confined boy his expression changed, his cries for mercy were exchanged for cries of anger. He was cursing his captures now and reaching through the wooden bars. He stopped at one point when his injured shoulder touched the wood and he grimaced. He leant back and began pulling at the wooden bars, jerking his head backwards with effort.

When the branches, sticks and brushwood had reached the actual base of the wooden man, the women withdrew and the chanting reached a crescendo and then abruptly stopped. The boy continued to shout and hurl what Varro concluded were insults at the people who were gathered around him but finally he stopped and was quiet. As an eerie silence enveloped the area the older druid spoke out, his harsh guttural language totally unrecognisable. He spoke for some time during which he pointed up at the sky and then down at the earth, to the trees and to the water flowing by in the river. At the end of his speech the silence took over once more as the priest bowed his head.

The boy began to fidget and move around the cage once again shouting towards the druid who pointed towards the base of the wooden man. The women walked forward with expressionless faces their eyes staring at the boy. He jumped up and began to pull at the wooden struts again, screaming and shouting, wild panic now apparent in his young voice.

The druid shouted another command and the women stopped, without another word they bent down and dropped their torches onto the gathered wood. The boy stopped stock still and looked down as initially nothing happened and the woman retreated. Then a wisp of smoke grew and was followed by another, the boy went berserk, trying to climb higher into the cage that had become his death pen. The gathered Britons did nothing except watch as the horrific drama played out before them.

"For the god's sake sir, they're burning the poor lad to death." Lucius withdrew his sword.

"We can't do anything Lucius put your fucking sword away that's an order." He emphasised the point glaring at Lucius as if to say, 'one wrong move and you'll regret it soldier'. His subordinate slammed his weapon back up to the hilt.

"Come on my friend, we don't need to see this play out, the boys as good as dead already. I promise you though we'll take vengeance on those animals, I swear it."

As Varro led the way back to their tethered horses the boy's screams began to fade and finally stopped. "Hopefully the smoke knocked him out before he could burn but they will pay for what they've done."

Chapter Four

The next day the morning sun warmed Caratacus and his scouting party as they observed the invading force in the valley below. They were lying flat on the ground on their stomachs at the top of a rise hundreds of feet above the invaders.

"Either they are convinced of their invincibility or they're as dumb as the swine we keep in our fields because if we get warriors here quickly, they'll be stuck and we'll push them back into the sea."

He had come south to see for himself the army that he had been assured wouldn't land on these shores.

"How many do you think are here brother?" He asked Togodumnus.

"In this group I would say ten thousand infantry, two thousand cavalry and about the same in those auxiliary units we observed last night. If we had brought all our men we could have defeated these vermin. It looks like they have divided their force into equal groups of three. We must find out where the other two columns have marched off to, spreading their filth over our lands." Togodumnus replied.

We'll deal with them later," Caractus replied, "first we'll crush what we see before us at the great second river. We'll use her current and depth to drown these men and banish them from ours lands. Come we have plans to make." He pushed himself up and without looking back walked to his horse.

***

Varro and his men had spent a restless night trying to keep the boy they had managed to rescue quiet. They had ridden towards the hills he had pointed towards the previous day and had tried to stop and rest and let the horses feed but it was to no avail. The boy had terror in his eyes and no amount of persuasion, albeit in a foreign tongue would calm him down. The men realised that he was probably thinking he was in for an equally vile end as his fellow Britons had tried to give him.

He obviously didn't understand a word they were saying and as they rode on Varro had discussed every eventuality with his men about what to do with the boy. They had decided they would make every effort to return him to his tribe but if that in any way risked their mission he would be abandoned. Likewise if at the end of the day he was still with them and they hadn't been successful he would be left to his fate.

After the third attempt to make camp during the night, they had given up and walked the horses slowly in single file. Lucius retold the story of the night's events to the rest of the men, all of whom were equally horrified.

"Maybe he was from a different tribe and they were sacrificing the boys to appease their Gods." Marcus said looking at Lucius.

"I don't give a whores cunny Lucius. Nobody deserves to die like that especially an innocent child. These barbarians need to be taught a lesson, is it any wonder we're here to bring them civilisation?" Lucius spat out the words.

Varro leading the way listened to the conversation as they all agreed to a man that if it was humanly possible to right this terrible wrong they would. The problem was that they were only a few soldiers, lightly armed, provisioned and miles away from any real support. They would have liked nothing better than to destroy the entire village but that was out of the question.

The boy had fallen asleep eventually, strewn face down across Staro's back in front of the centurion, Varro had kept him in place with his knees, reassuringly patting his shoulder every now and again. As the first rays of light broke slowly before the dawn of another day he brought his small party to a halt raising his hand. Veranius helped carry the lad off Staro and lay his head down on a rolled blanket.

"We'll get the horses fed and watered and ourselves and try and get some rest until the suns up properly and we can get our bearings." The stars were beginning to disappear from the night sky as dark blue replaced the sparkling blackness that had enveloped everything above them.

Decimus lit a fire whilst Marcus brought water from a nearby stream to slowly boil. They may have had to live in the field but they still liked to have some comforts. They had learned from past experience that even small things like warm water were essential for moral and keeping spirits up. They had to be wary of hunting parties but a fire wasn't enough to draw too much suspicion. The boy slept on fitfully, every now and again his body pulsed as a sleeping sob wracked his small body.

"Poor little bastard eh, what are we going to do with him?" Decimus asked of his commander.

"Well we've got a couple of choices the way I see it. We can either abandon him here leaving him to his own initiative, we could end his life or, we could try and take him home." Varro replied. "I don't want to kill an innocent child. He would surely die if he was just left here so I suppose we've got one logical option left. What do you think?" He addressed the group as a whole. They liked Varro for a number of reasons, his compassion being one, another; his ability to ask the opinion of his fellow soldiers especially when their lives could depend on the outcome.

"I say we try and get the child home as we've said, at least for the duration of today." Veranius said. "If we can't find his family by nightfall, we leave him to his own abilities."

"Agreed," Varro said, "does anyone have any objections?" He surveyed the weary eyes before him and received shakes of the head in response. "Okay. Let's get some food, some sleep and we'll see what the day brings. Marcus you take first watch."

"Sir." The trooper acknowledged as he scrambled in his food bag for some dried meat to chew and began to walk away.

"I'll be on the outcrop." He indicated to a position a hundred paces or so away from the rest of the group. It would give him a good vantage point if anyone or anything approached.

"I wonder if Caesar experienced the burning of native's when he was here?" Lucius asked.

Varro a little more educated on the topic said, "Well there were two forays into the interior of this land. Although some believe both were merely reconnaissance missions, I don't see it that way. With the amount of troops, ships and materials he had, it had to be an invasion."

The others looked at him in surprise. "If you look at the facts no-one can argue that the Britons defeated him and sent him on his way, not once but twice. Some of it was down to back luck on their behalf and some of it down to fortune. Ships damaged by storms were sunk, supplies and men were lost. The Britons were prepared and lined those great white rocks we saw when we landed. This time they believed we had abandoned the invasion and so by comparison we had an easy time of it."

Decimus listening intently asked, "So that means that those Britons or their relatives that beat the greatest general we've ever had, are still out there?"

Varro smiled, "They certainly are my friend and at some point we'll surely meet them."

"So what makes you think that we'll fare any better than Caesar?" Veranius asked chewing on his salted meat.

"This time there's a difference and tactically it's enormous. We've got a foothold on their coast and our troops and equipment are pouring ashore still, even as we speak. As the ships are offloaded they're returning to Gaul for more. In no time at all we'll have over fifty thousand men on this ground." He looked at the faces reflecting the flames of the fire. "It still won't be easy but this time we're better prepared, equipped and with legions that have fought through Gaul." He smiled. "I'm sure this time Rome will give a better account of herself against these child burning primitives."

A few hours later the sun was high in the sky and was beginning to warm Varro and his small contingent. He could feel the cold evaporate from his arms and legs. It looked to be the start of another warm day and the chill of the night before had all but vanished. The boy had been awake for over an hour and was now sitting staring at the small flames in the dying fire as most of the wood had turned to ash.

With daylight came good visibility and the area where the boy had been pointing to the night before was clearly visible from their position. No structures could be seen and there weren't any smoke plumes from any villages but the rise in the land was now nearer on the horizon and was quite distinct.

Varro smiled at the boy and pointed in that direction, the boy looked towards the region indicated and raised his eyebrows. He spoke words not understood by the soldiers and slowly got to his feet. He seemed a lot more at ease now and must have realised that the strangely dressed men, were not intending to hurt but help him.

With the camp broken Varro helped the young lad climb up onto Staro lifting him with one hand and swinging him up onto the horse's rump behind him. The centurion clicked and slowly nudged his horse forward as they set off at an easy pace. He adjusted his sword under the side of the saddle flap and below his left leg, making sure it was secure as they began another day and rode on.

They continued on for about an hour and saw no-one or nothing of any significance. Varro rode slowly leading but not taking a direct route to their destination. Every so often he would change direction, so as to limit the chance of ambush by anyone who may have seen them from the high ground. Soldiers travelling straight were easily tracked, stalked and destroyed and Varro would do everything he could to avoid that.

Just before noon they picked up the smell of wood smoke and eventually a few roundhouses came into view. The boy was chattering excitedly now at the rear of Varro as he clearly recognised his surroundings.

"Stop where you are Romans." A husky female voice suddenly sounded from somewhere ahead of them in thick bushes.

"Who are you?" Varro shouted looking around trying to locate where the voice had come from.

"Come out where we can see you. We have a boy with us and we're trying to find his home," he paused, 'where he lives."

The horses came to a halt as the men strained their eyes searching the trees surrounding them but they could see nothing.

"Where did you find the boy Roman?" The voice called.

"He has been missing for a number of days along with his brother. Did you and your men take him and have your way with him?" The voice was heavily accented but clear, concise and Latin.

Varro looked at his men, anger on his face.

"We rescued him from people who wished him harm in a settlement about a half a day's ride from here. I'm afraid we could do nothing for his friend who was with him." Varro could still see nothing to give away the position of the speaker.

"Get ready for anything." He said to his men under his breath as he turned to help the boy down. The female spoke again but in a local tongue and from a different location or so it seemed, this time speaking to the boy as he stood by the side of Staro. The boy answered, speaking in a normal tone whilst pointing to the soldiers and smiling. The woman again said something and the boy broke down and began to cry moving slowly forward.

"We mean you no harm." Varro shouted. "If you wish, we will withdraw." He watched the boy as he walked towards the bushes some thirty paces in front of them and then he was out of sight within the blink of an eye. Varro turned in his saddle to gauge the feeling amongst his men, he saw suspicious, nervous glances still scouring the trees and bushes ahead.

They all knew that a number of things could happen next and at any moment and with such speed that they may not be able to do anything about it. The position they were in allowed for a safe distance from every weapon known to the Britons except the bow and that weapon was fast and not defendable if used by a good bowman. Varro clicked his tongue quietly and Staro slowly backed up, movement that was mirrored by the other horses.

Everything seemed to slow and a strange quiet descended over the group as the Romans continued to move slowly backwards. It was disturbed by whispered mumbling somewhere through the trees in front of them.

"Easy lads," Veranius almost whispered, "we don't won't to fuck this up and end up like that poor little bastard last night, easy does it, no stupid moves eh?"

Suddenly there was movement and it came from all around them. As one, their swords were drawn iron scraping against their sheaths as the soldiers prepared to defend themselves from the unseen force that was descending on them from all around them. Their spathas drawn and ready for action if required, still they backed up.

Varro glanced quickly backwards and saw that the path behind them was still open. He knew that he could give the order and within the time it took an arrow to reach them they would be literally out of the woods and free.

"Stop Roman!"

The order he knew was directed at him and not his group as a whole, it was the same female voice as before. As he again looked forward at moving branches to the front of their position, he saw a shape begin to emerge followed by another smaller figure.

"I am known as Brenna Roman. We are grateful for you returning our young man, you will not be harmed here, you are safe."

The woman standing before him was petite and dressed in colourful tribal clothing. She wore leggings that were green and yellow criss-crossed, her top a light brown. Uncovered athletic brown arms were adorned with golden torques above her elbows and above the biceps as well as one thick piece around her neck.

"You have returned Junium to us." She glanced down at the boy. "So you are regarded as friends wherever your home lies, unlike the people that took him. He has told me what happened, you saved his life at the risk of your own, please come now. We will give you food and water." She turned with the boy and began to walk away, the soldiers didn't move and looked towards Varro.

"I'm sure if they'd wanted us dead, we probably already would be. Come on let's see what a Britons hospitality is like." He said. They dismounted and followed Brenna.

A short time later they came across a large clearing where pigs and sheep were kept in pens and dogs roamed freely outside. The locals stopped their work and play as Brenna and her party approached. Some had been attending to rows of plants, some tending to their animals and some were practising with bows away to the side of the settlement, men and women alike. The expressions on the faces of the locals were a mixture of surprise, shock and disbelief. They had clearly never seen men like these before, even their horses were strange compared to the Britons who's own animals were grazing on land in a fenced off area. It wasn't a scene they had suspected to see as it was far more civilised and organised than they were led to expect in Britannia.

"Put your horses with ours Roman, they will be safe, you have my word." Brenna said. Varro thought for a moment, he could either do as she suggested or they could tie their horses up where they could get to them quickly. It was a decisive moment but he couldn't risk dying because of his misguided trust of this woman.

"We'll leave them here for now." He said tying Staro to the fencing corralling the locals horses in. Staro was interestedly watching the horses in the paddock whose curiosity got the better of them as they came over to see their new guests. Varro sheathing his sword looked about at his surroundings noting the chariots at the far side of the roundhouses. They resembled pictures he had seen and drawings of chariots used by the eastern tribes of his own country but were sleeker.

"Come, come." Brenna said as she led them to the centre of the village. Feeling a little more at ease but still alert and suspicious, the soldiers followed. The Briton had long dark brown straight hair, its sheen bright in the mid-day sun. She led them to the village centre where they were met by a large impressive brute of a man. The boy ran to him, wrapping his arms around his neck as the man bent to pick him up smiling and clearly relieved.

"This is Tevelgus my brother." Brenna announced and father to Junuim." Tevelgus spoke to Brenna who in turn translated his words. "Tevelgus says you are welcome here and will be safe as a reward for saving his son." Varro saw for the first time that Brenna's eyes were of the darkest green, the sun enhancing them and that she was quite strikingly beautiful.

"Thank you. We have come in peace to these lands in order to provide knowledge of the greater world and our empire." Varro said to Brenna.

"We have heard of your great empire Roman and of the lands that have fallen to it because they would not kneel. We have little interest of such things and merely wish to live peacefully, working our land and raising our children." She turned to her brother, "Tevelgus can speak your words but does not trust you, so I will tell you his meaning until he does."

Tevelgus spoke again with Brenna translating. "He says that some of the villages have sworn to band together with Togodumnus and Caratacus to push your army back into the sea."

Varro looked at the big man giving away nothing. Tevelgus was wearing similar clothing to Brenna, with no weapons apparent. His hair was shoulder length and covered in what Varro assumed was lime. A large moustache was also limed and extended just to the edges of Tevelgus' large head. His bare arms were ripped with muscles and easily comparable to those of Varro. He indicated for the Romans to sit on some cut down tree trunks, rudimentary seating was levelled off at the top.

Tevelgus shouted something to another Briton who quickly ran to do his bidding. Brenna explained that he had asked that ale be brought for them the soldiers looked at each other.

"What is ale?" Asked Marcus.

"Ale, you do not have ale in your great and mighty empire?"

Varro spoke, "It's their version of wine Marcus only it's made from barley and hops not grape. It has the same effect however and sometimes is a lot stronger, so be careful with the amount you drink." Marcus smiled as the other Briton re-appeared carrying large wooden pots, he gave them to the seated group, Veranius eyed the brew handed to him suspiciously.

"Here." Brenna said, offering her pot for his, "take mine."

He looked at Varro who nodded his agreement. Marcus took the drink, gave it a sniff of approval and took a swig, his eyebrows raised as he swallowed the liquid.

"Mm this ale is quite good, try it!"

They all tried the ale for themselves, to a man they smiled their agreement with Marcus and watched astonished as Brenna drained her own and asked for more.

Brenna explained to her guests that although they in their village respected the sun, the sky, the trees and the water, they did not worship it in the same way as their neighbours and they didn't sacrifice people in order to try to ensure them. They believed in spirits and a god but one, not many. She knew the Romans had lots of gods and their people prayed to whichever one they thought would provide what they required at the time of asking. Varro was coming to the conclusion that her people were quite enlightened and not the backward cave dwelling savages they were led to believe they would find.

Tevelgus was a great warrior who had become the village leader after a successful challenge to the previous chief who, the Romans were surprised to find was still alive and living amongst the group.

"We don't live like animals and fight for the right to lead, we moved on from that some time ago." Tevelgus explained through Brenna. "We are judged by our peers," he indicated the village around them, "and they decide the victor."

Varro and his men were getting a taste for the strong ale as the shadows began to draw longer along the floor around them.

"Can we stay here tonight Brenna? Me and my men are weary and could do with a good night's sleep and your brew is too hard to resist. I would like to take this opportunity also to learn more about your life here." Varro asked Brenna.

"Of course, you are welcome, soon we will be having food," she indicated to a large boar that was being led to an area away from the others, "so you can relax, eat, drink and sleep. We will forever be grateful for you for saving and returning the boy to us. It's the least we can do."

The soldiers, with the help of the ale, were properly relaxed now and Brenna explained that she had been told of the foreign language Latin from the early attempts by Caesars forces to invade the country some decades before. She had learnt it from her father who had had some involvement with the Romans at the time.

As Brenna continued to tell Varro and his men about her life there, he realised just how distinctly attracted he was to her. He watched the movement of her lips as she spoke, her eyes he was sure could see into his soul and know his every desire. He tried to shake the feelings believing it was the influence of the ale but it was to no avail, there was no doubting his desire, he wanted her.

With the pig slaughtered and prepared, its rich meat was now roasting on the spit some feet away. The smell of fresh food with the ale and the company they were in almost helped the Romans forget that they were in a hostile land. Any thought of harm coming to them was forgotten and for the first time since setting foot in Britannia, they felt safe.

"So what do your men call you Roman?" Brenna asked.

"My name is Varro. I'm from the south east of my homeland and grew up by the warm sea. I've been in the service of my country for five years and in that time have attained the rank of centurion." He indicated to the small purple stripes on his white tunic. "This is my second in command." He indicated to the Optio then introduced the others in the group. "Our function is to ride ahead of our legions and make contact with the local population."

"And to survey what's ahead of your generals and their spears I assume." Brenna asked.

"As I said," he replied smiling, "to make contact with the population." He replied guardedly. "You have many different tribes in your land and a rich history of warrior codes."

"You are referring to the repulsion of your Great Caesar I assume? That was a long time ago but the tribes came together and worked as one. It was not all war though Varro. Contacts were made and people from both sides moved to the other countries in an exchange of ideas and cultures. Sadly not everyone was glad to receive your legions and many died on both sides."

Varro thought before responding, "Rome does not seek to crush new cultures Brenna but to bring them into the empire. Client kingdoms are established, trade routes, learning, both and all grow richer from the union."

"But doesn't your emperor seek to ravage our natural wealth and resources and in some cases also put into slavery some of our people." Brenna asked already knowing the answer.

"You seem to already know much which surprises me. Don't think me wrong, I refer to your isolation here and yet you're aware of some of the things across the sea and in the greater world beyond. If Rome chose to merely enslave and rob other civilisations and put the people there into slavery, then neither I nor my men would serve her. It would be corrupt and rotten."

"Mm so you are a good man serving a good leader with many soldiers and men to persuade these other peoples. You are on a quest to change the known world for the better even if they prefer to live in wooden roundhouses like this." She said gesturing.

Varro laughed, "The subject is as vast as it is deep and that's precisely why I'm a simple soldier. I prefer my horse, my sword and the company of my men to the deceit of some but not all senators and their like are corrupt."

Brenna looked at Staro, "I see that even your horses are big and strong." Varro looked over and saw that his horse and the others men's had eaten the grass around them at their feet.

"I'd like to take up your invitation for our horses to graze with yours if it still stands?" He asked.

"Why of course, come with me." Varro following her signalled for the others to remain where they were, Brenna stroked Staro on his flanks and the animal seemed to instantly warm to her.

"Here you go big handsome boy." She said untying him and walking him to the gate. She removed his saddle and bridle, putting them onto the fence and opened the gate. She touched his neck and the animal nudged her with his nose, his dark black eyes looking into hers. Varro was standing close to Brenna and thought he saw a connection between her and Staro.

"He doesn't usually let people he doesn't know or trust, get that close to him, you've a way with animals then?" He said. She laughed, "A bit like his owner I would say Varro."

He frowned, "Well Brenna, I have, since I have been here witnessed an innocent boy being burnt alive and others try to kill me and my men."

She smiled, "I don't mean anything by it Varro." She touched his face as she had his horse her palm was warm and gentle. She turned breaking the moment.

"In you go." She said to the other horses. "Here's a friend for you all, be nice to him." She said as the local horses came over to see who had joined them. After releasing the other animals Varro and Brenna returned to the others where a roaring fire was now raging in front of them as the shadows grew long. Tevelgus handed them both pots of ale each and they sat down. Another female appeared and offered them food, roasted pork. She was joined by others who brought more food and ale.

"I want to thank you for your generous hospitality Brenna." She raised a hand cutting him off. "You owe us nothing, you returned the boy who is the son of my brother for that I owe you." She smiled warmly and Varro felt a connection between them that he hadn't experienced with another woman for a long time. He had been involved with Lucerne when he was a soldier based in Rome for nearly two years. He was part of the cities home legion after first joining the army and had met her serving wine in a tavern. Although not a whore who would prostitute herself to men, many considered her chosen trade as near as anyone could get. Lucerne had ambitions however, and the lowly grade of a soldier and his pay turned out to be little enough reward for her bed. Brenna seemed to have far more substance about her and was not blonde as Lucerne had been which he always found to be a plus. That Varro found, attractive in itself but there was more to this Briton than he would have imagined he would find or had expected to on this large and mysterious island.

As the night wore on and the sun went down, more locals joined them at the feast. They all seemed happy to see the soldiers and were even happier when it was explained that they had saved Junium from a horrible death. The men were relaxed so much so that they had even removed their armour and their swords and were happy to sit and talk wearing just their tunics albeit through Brenna. Full bellies, an alternative to wine and a warm welcome was exactly the opposite of what any of them had ever imagined would greet them in Britannia but here it was.

Later with darkness complete overhead, the only light being that of the fire, shadows danced across the faces of those sat around the flames. Varro could feel the full effects of the brew and now felt totally relaxed. Brenna was sitting as close to him as she could get and he noticed that every now and again, she would touch his arm or his thigh as they spoke, laughing and talking about how different their cultures were. He wasn't too surprised when she asked smiling, "Would you like to come for a walk? We have a beautiful lake nearby and the water would be really refreshing after such a warm day."

Briefly he looked at his men who were either engaged in broken conversations with other Britons, pointing and learning words; or they just were content to drink more ale around the fire.

"Why not?" He said taking her offered hand to help him up. They walked towards the nearby trees through the clearing, the night air cooler without the warmth of the fire near them but welcoming after the heat of the flames.

"So tell me Roman," Brenna asked still holding his hand and leading him down a worn path, "do you have a woman waiting for you in Rome?"

"No nothing like that but I'm not from Rome, I'm from a place called Rhegium in the south and no, I don't have a woman waiting there either."

"Good." Was her one word reply as they left the woods and came to a clearing, water sparkling before them in a huge expanse of the lake she had mentioned earlier. She motioned for him to stand still and walked a few paces and then turned.

He stood watching as she untied the rope belt from around her waist and grinning removed her top. Her body was tanned brown by the sun and for the first time Varro realised that she had generous and sensual breasts above a trim waist, her nipples were welcoming and erect.

She smiled at him as she grabbed the thin string that held her breeches up and she pulled gently as they fell to her ankles. She was naked underneath and had athletic legs with feminine defined muscles, developed he presumed from hunting and running, formed erotically under her skin, He felt himself began to tingle.

"Come Varro, you can't swim with your clothes on, unless of course you are too shy?" Without another word and with Brenna watching him intently, he removed his tunic. His muscles rippled as he moved and she clearly liked what she saw. Slightly embarrassed he said, "So what does your name mean Brenna? I'm told nothing is named without reason here is that correct?"

She smiled, "Most things are yes, my name means as black as a Raven." She pointed at the clothes he still wore, and the rest." She almost ordered as he removed the remainder of his clothing. She walked to him and placed a hand on his chest, gently smoothing her hand along its surface, her fingers making circles around his nipples. He could feel himself getting aroused as they looked into each other's eyes and her hand moved lower. He grew hard as her fingers sought out his erection, she smiled as he bent to kiss her but she moved away laughing.

"Are you always so impatient?" Continuing to laugh she turned and ran towards the water. He watched as she moved, 'slowly old fellow' he thought to himself wishing he was inside her. She splashed into the water and he felt the first ache of wanting as he yearned to feel her surround him. He recovered and walked to the water's edge, it was cold against the skin of his feet. An owl in a nearby tree was hooted as if shouting encouragement. The sky was clear and full of stars now and the night air was warm against his body.

"Come on, get in. Surely a big strong soldier isn't afraid of a little water?"

He walked further now nearly oblivious to the cold as it reached his thighs, a small tide lapping against him. Brenna was standing waist high motioning him forwards towards her upper body glistening with droplets of water. When he got to within touching distance she laughed again and turned, diving into the water and vanishing from sight.

She reappeared some feet away and swam further into the lake, her back visible above the dark water. Varro bent his legs and squatted allowing the water to reach his neck, he gathered some more and splashed if over his head. He shuddered slightly as he ducked underneath it and swam after her. He followed her for a while as they swam further out, the water getting colder the further they went. Eventually she turned and slowly headed back to shore.

Varro had just managed to get level with her as she began to leave the water, drips leaving her body. He saw she stopped waiting for him again smiling and he approached her. Without waiting for an invitation he held her close to him again, getting aroused as he kissed her gently on the lips. Her tongue forced his mouth open and darted in to his as her hand helped his arousal grow. He felt her slim waist and moved his right hand up her side as they kissed, gently cupping her breast. She moaned as he felt her hard nipple as they kissed more intently.

"Come." She said breaking away and once again took him by the hand. She led him to a large downed oak lying on its side. She turned drawing him closer and drew him to her. She sighed and pushed herself onto the tree and then wrapped her legs around his waist, their tongues moving against each other's. She massaged his swollen manhood carefully and slowly rubbing it against her wetness. He waited like never before wanting to thrust himself inside her. He opened his eyes and saw that hers were closed but then opened to look into his own. He was consumed by her beauty, her intelligence and passion as she reached around his hips and gently pulled him into her.

Chapter Five

    Caratacus had waited in the shadows under thick low branches of trees for the rider to come back and report on the advancing Roman column. He had met up with his younger brother Deganus that morning at their pre-arranged rallying point in case of any unusual occurrence. If either one of them hadn't arrived the other would know that there was something seriously wrong. They had spent a few hours with the war council going over tactics and possible plans dependant on what the rider reported.

    His impatience was beginning to get the better of him and he now wanted to engage the enemy as soon as possible. He had sent the scout out to determine the route and number of legionnaires heading in his direction. He knew that they had already established a working harbour and some were already preparing to move away from the shore. What he didn't know was how many would leave and where would they go, would they all go together or would they split their force and how many would stay at the shore. He knew that if the majority marched into the interior of the country, it would leave those at the harbour vulnerable and he would attack them cutting the others off from any re-supply or re-enforcements.

    One thing he was certain of was that he and the other tribes loyal to him and his brother were now gathering. Had it not been for misinformation from Gaul, the Romans would never have set foot on solid ground but there was nothing he could do about that now. He had over five thousand fighters already which at such short notice, he was happy with as it had only been two days since news of the invasion had reached him. With more of his own warriors and the rest of the tribes he would treble the amount of Britons to Romans and more. Time was against him now however and it would take days for his extra forces to reach him, whilst at the same time evading the Romans, the last thing he wanted was a relatively small war band to be taken. He knew he couldn't and wouldn't wait forever, and dependant on the report would decide how to strike an early blow against the invading army. They had to be stopped, which meant dealing them a deadly blow or one that would at least cripple them just enough to hamper their movement, once that was achieved, they would be wiped out. Amongst his five thousand warriors, he had over two hundred chariots, five hundred horsemen, the rest were made up of foot soldiers, seasoned campaigners on the whole. Once the others arrived his numbers would swell but they would be made up of farmers, men and women who were used to working the land not fighting on it. They would be fit nonetheless and most would be efficient with a bow, he would have little time to mould them into battle ready warriors.

"Sir, a rider approaches." Just then his attention was caught by the sound of cantering hooves. He got to his feet and walked to greet the man who had been sent out to spy on the Roman's progress.

"Sire," he shouted, coming to an abrupt halt, mud being thrown up by the animal's feet, Caratacus caught the horse's reins, "What did you see, what of the Romans?"

The rider jumped off the horse and landed heavily on the ground almost stumbling over in his eagerness to report.

"They have divided their force into three columns one of them is now marching west, one north and the remainder north west. It looks like they mean to cover all areas of the country. Each army is about five to six thousand strong and has cavalry, light and heavy infantry and their auxiliaries. They have wagons full of equipment to the rear containing food, more weapons, spare horses, oxen, cattle even mules for pulling the carts. At the shore, above the cliffs it looks like they are beginning to build some kind of large palisade, there are thousands of them there still. Some of the ships that delivered them to us have already begun to return to Gaul but others are still at anchor and haven't been unloaded. I would say that they have left a full legion guarding the shoreline."

Caratacus thought briefly for a few moments and then announced to his plan to the war council. "We will attack on two fronts; firstly I will take four thousand men and ambush the column heading west. If the gods are with us and I'm careful, we will then track and attack the other columns. Deganus my brother, I want you to stay in this general area and harass their supply lines." He looked at Caratacus with a bemused expression but didn't respond.

"You will attack the base on the shore but I don't want you to go head to head with them brother. You will be too few, so you are to use guile and the cunning of a wolf and only take them on when you are certain, absolutely certain of victory. These men from Rome won't last long on our soil if their supplies are destroyed, they'll starve and won't have replacement weapons or food. Remember they are the ones far from home, I want you to concentrate on those fat swollen ships at anchor. If they were lost with their goods on board, it would be a major blow for them.

I don't know when we'll see each other again but we have no choice in this, we have to destroy or at least cripple their army.' He paused thinking. 'Togodumnus will arrive soon with thousands of warriors under his banner but we can't wait until then to act. I will take all the chariots as you won't need them but you'll have enough horse."

He grabbed his brother's arm and they hugged. "May the gods protect you brother." He turned, called for his horse, mounted it and rode away.

Sometime later with the light beginning to fade, Caratacus watched from high above on a ridgeline as the wagons making up the rear of the westerly column, limped along what was left of the path, worn away by those who had gone before them. Although it was the middle of the campaigning season for the Romans and early summer, the ground had been churned and worn by the leading troops and great ruts now scarred the land. Their boots, horses and wagons had proven too much for a track that had never witnessed so much travel on its surface previously.

A small group of five wagons had become isolated by the ruined ground and now struggled to keep up with the rest of the army. They had tried and failed to use the path so had finally given up when the wheels kept getting stuck. Men were now pushing the wagons that were pulled by thickset mules along the side of the ravaged route.

"This will be a taste of what is to come." Caratacus said looking into the valley below them. "Once the other wagons have gone beyond that curve," he pointed, "these five will be all alone. No doubt the leading group will be looking for somewhere suitable to camp for the night before dark, so we have to move quickly. If we skirt the tree line and wait a few hundred feet this side of that natural bend up there, we should be safe to attack them without the others being aware of it."

His tribal chieftains nodded in agreement. "Once they have been taken care of we'll see about the rest of the column who won't have the protection of any natural defences and we'll destroy them."

It took little time for Caratacus and his war party to get into position and they didn't have long to wait before the enemy began to get close. From the safety of a thick tree line, the Britons watched eagerly for their prey to arrive. Here he had female warriors with the men, their hair limed and their skin blue. He had seen them fight before and knew what they lacked in strength they made up in ferocity, although a few he saw were well muscled and larger than the men.

"Wait, wait, wait.....NOW." Caratacus ordered as spears flew towards the struggling Romans and their animals. His plan was to try and incapacitate them before destroying each and every one of them. As warriors ran into full view of the startled soldiers, the first animal was speared through the back and screamed out in agony and began to bolt forward, its wagon bucking and twisting in its plight behind it.

One trooper was hit at the base of his throat, just above his armour, his eyes wide with shock as realisation hit him, Britons swarmed all around them. A female shrieking like a banshee swung her long sword as she grew level with him. She was rewarded with a sickening wet clunk as her weapon cut through the jaw of the man biting into the cheek guards either side of his helmet. As far as she was concerned, he had come to take her children, kill her husband and to rape her and so deserved such a death. He died almost instantly but couldn't fall flat because of the spear, so the woman now splashed with fresh blood, twisted him to one side and used her foot to pry her blade free.

Separate attacks were taking place all around as the small wagon train was assaulted and men were butchered. They were outnumbered and at a tactical disadvantage and didn't have the numbers to form up in their traditional battle lines. Caratacus now in the thick of the fight, saw one legionnaire ripping free a horn from the rear of a covered wagon, intent on warning the others of the ambush.

Caratacus ran, sprinting towards him, running past others, his large sword in his right hand as he tugged on his knife on his belt and pulled it free of its sheath. Screaming as loud as he could, he caught the attention of the soldier, who whirled around in panic, hatred in his eyes as he leapt towards him. Caratacus was so quick that the soldier only had time to jerk backwards slightly as his attacker landed his sword and knife together finding their marks as they were embedded into his chest and forced inward and upward under his armour. The eyes were dead before the knife reached its hilt as the sword had done its work and the man fell backward, silent. In a very short time, the Britons were rifling through the contents of the five wagons, the enemy slain and scattered on the ground all around them.

"Sire." One of his warriors shouted and pointed at the contents of the wagon he was searching.

"What have you found?" Caratacus asked. Looking under the sheeting he saw what looked like giant bows in pieces, pulleys and wooden frames.

"What are these?" He tried picking one of the bows up but it was attached at one side to a frame and wouldn't move. He ran over to the other wagons and found the same equipment in all but one that contained large arrows.

"I don't know what these are but they were intended to be used against us in some way I'm sure, take them north," he said to one of his men a dark smile across his face. "Once we've found out how to use them we'll turn them on their former owners."

Twenty five men, five to each cart began to prepare to take the wagons away as Caratacus gathered the rest to move forward. He had deliberately left the corpses of the enemy where they had fallen. If he had more time, he would have had them disembowelled or had their heads removed to put fear into others but that could wait, he knew they had to move quickly. As the first of the carts began to be towed away, Caratacus kicked his horse and led his warriors up into the trees. The sight of the destruction below them as they looked down onto the former column was something that none of them had ever seen before and it encouraged them and gave them heart for what was to come.

In the time that it had taken them to destroy the former custodians of the five carts, the other soldiers in the column were a few miles west and had already found somewhere to camp for the night. They had begun to set their tents up and were now busy building palisades and all round defensive positions. Soldiers were digging trenches to create six foot deep ditches, the earth they had removed was used to create walls of solid mud. In effect they would soon have a twelve foot wall around their base. They had chopped down nearby trees and were now embedding them into the earthen banks, sharpened at one end and then hammered home deep into the earth. They were then sharpened into spikes at the other once they were in place using axes.

From their position high above, the Britons watched fascinated by the energy, order and efficiency of their enemy.

"Maybe they are intending to make a permanent settlement here." One of the men offered, then added. "But why would they start building straight away? It seems odd for an army that's been on its feet marching all day." The warrior wasn't talking to any of the others specifically and no-one was answering, they were too transfixed on the scene below. As the construction continued Caratacus noted that there were sentries already posted some two hundred paces from the building going on below them. He also saw men on horses presumably scouting the area for hostile forces. He decided it was better to withdraw and make plans for the next attack.

Varro awoke the next morning with the smell of smoke in his nostrils. As he slowly became aware of his surroundings he realised he was inside a roundhouse, Brenna's to be precise. He had no recollection of how he had got there, his last memory of the night before was being with her at the lakeside.

He turned and found her lying there next to him, partially covered in a large animal fur. Her smooth tanned flesh looked very appealing and he was tempted to peel the furry warm skin back and explore her body, he felt himself getting warmer as his eyes moved over her.

"Morning." A sleepy voice said and he realised that she was waking, laying there looking at him, eyes barely open. Without hesitation she leaned up and kissed him gently on the mouth, he responded and kissed her back. Her hands sought out his body and he pushed the animal skin aside and was rewarded by the sight of her beautiful body, she smiled before her tongue moved over his as they began to meld together.

"Centurion." A voice shouted from somewhere outside. Varro recognised it as Veranius as he darted away from Brenna and struggled to his feet.

"I'll be with you shortly, Varro shouted, 'go and catch some fresh fish in the lake for breakfast." He heard something of a reply, a grumble and muttering maybe but didn't decipher what was said exactly and didn't really care as Brenna pushed him down and onto his back and mounted him, sliding him inside her.

Sometime later Varro found all his men fishing at the lake. He walked past them as they made remarks about his tardiness and made jokes about where he had been. He didn't need to answer and within seconds Brenna appeared at the side of the lake, removed her fur blanket, touched his hand and walked naked into the water. The men stared open mouthed as Varro smiled.

"You lucky fucker." Veranius said as the rest of the men laughed.

Some miles away, Caratacus and three men observed the Roman column preparing to move from their overnight position. It was clear now that they weren't building a fort at all and that last nights fortified position was just that, a fortified position for just one night. It demonstrated to the Britons just what these foreigners were prepared to do to defend themselves even after a long days march over great distances. The Britons in contrast would in all likelihood only have put lookouts around the perimeter of their own camp.

"These men will take a little more cunning to crack than our normal enemies I believe. They are most vulnerable when they are on the move and strongest when they have built their defences for the night." He said to those watching with him and the enemy. The sentries were going into their camp and he wondered how they could march all day, guard all night and then march all day again. The answer became evident as he saw the men climbing aboard carts, where they were presumably going to rest or even sleep as their comrades drove the wagons forward.

He watched as the men dismantled the temporary camp below bit by bit, piece by piece. Even the sharpened wooden stakes were hacked from the earth and stored aboard a wagon presumably for use again that night. That meant that they wouldn't need to fell more trees which also meant that their next camp would be built a lot quicker.

Caratacus had left the rest of his men some miles away, he and this small group would shadow the column watching for an opportunity to attack and their main force would be brought forward when an opportunity arose. The last thing he wanted to do now was lose a large amount of his warriors and for no good reason. He and his men shadowed the column until noon when they stopped for a rest. He saw that scouts were sent out immediately, riding on horseback to positions that gave good vantage points of the surrounding area.

"If their behaviour so far today and yesterday is anything to go by, they will have one large break again later before they stop for the night and build their walls to hide behind. We will hit them before their stakes are in position and can kill our warriors." Caratacus said to those with him.

Some hours later, once again the weary Roman soldiers came to a halt. They had been marching since sunrise and would have to make the most of this second and last break before their final push moving west. As soon as they stopped some soldiers went to carts to get food, others removed their backpacks, dropped pilums and swords and some walked away from the main body of the column to relieve themselves.

The Britons had got into position in the valley long before the noise of the marching column was within earshot. They had waited at the most likely spot twice before as Caratacus had ordered but the Romans had continued marching but not on this occasion.

As they relaxed, joked, complained and took on food or water, the Britons struck. An Optio had just hitched up his under garments and was reliving himself some twenty feet from a cart and his men. He was day dreaming and listening to the urine splash off the weeds he was watering when his gaze was broken by something that didn't make sense. A glint of iron caught his eye as he leaned down to see what it was, partially hidden by flowering thorns. He didn't even have time to move, just to see that it was a sword as it was thrust upward between his legs. The pain was instant and crippling as the sharpened blade was forced upward into his stomach from below as a fierce blue face appeared grimacing beyond it. A brief cry of pain was all that he could muster as he slumped forward, the Briton ripping the blade from him, already moving forward to find another to kill.

As spears, stone shot and arrows were fired and hurled towards the Romans, they desperately sought out their weapons and tried to form defensive perimeters. Chariots raced towards them from both directions along the valley, one occupant steering the speeding vehicles the other throwing large spears into the panicking ranks of the defenders.

Caratacus watched some hundred paces away from the battle as his warriors tore into the enemy flanks from each side of the armour clad soldiers, he had caught them by surprise and totally unaware. They had been unable to organise themselves and most were cut down where they stood. He saw one spear arching downward and a soldier waiting for one of his warriors, seconds from fighting each other for their lives. His man was screaming flailing his sword above his head the Roman stood stock still, as if frozen with his short sword out.

The comparison of the two was stark, the Briton tall, lithe and sinewy, naked from the waist up, his body painted in blue woad, hair sticking out with lime and screaming like a devil; the Roman colourful with his red cloak and shining armour, helmet glistening in the sunlight, standing waiting.

The single act of combat in the midst of the madness was ended swiftly before it could commence. The spear launched seconds before, descended from nowhere and punched a hole through the soldier's upper chest. The look of astonishment on his face was an image of battle and the reality of war, shock and horror. This invader would never see his home or family again, he would die here on Britannia's green and fertile land.

The warrior slashed out with his sword as he drew level with the soldier, the weapon slicing into the meat of the man's bare thigh, blood sprayed out. He saw the spear had pierced the armour and chest of his opponent who fell backwards. Blood spattered the shaft of the spear as the warriors hands fought to pull it free to be used again. It was a moment, a brief moment in a battle and was over virtually before it had begun.

The warriors decimated that part of the column Caratacus had chosen, towards the rear of their line. Any reinforcements were hindered by the valley and the twists and turns of the paths the Romans had used to move along but the Britons knew the terrain well and could slip in and out before becoming trapped using the maize of paths and track ways. A few of their cavalry reached the attackers but were driven back by archers and slingers high above on the valley walls.

The triumphant Britons began to withdraw, hacking and stabbing at their prone opponents who weren't fortunate to die instantly. Running up the incline towards their leader and their waiting horses, the victorious warriors raised their weapons in salute. Caratacus signalled for his men to withdraw taking one final look at the stricken column. He knew this small encounter wouldn't stop the advance but it had given the invaders a bloody and broken nose and it would sow a seed of doubt in the minds of others.

The dead and injured were spread across the valley floor below, one Briton was running from each making sure no life blood still coursed through the veins of the men littered helplessly on the ground. When he found one that he suspected still lived, he slashed his dagger across the throat and then ran to the next. Caratacus had ordered this done as he knew that if they didn't they would be healed and returned to face them another day. His grim task done, the Briton ran up the hill towards his leader.

"How many did you count?" Caratacus asked.

The man answered, "Thirty three Sire." as he ran past and mounted his horse. Caratacus looked along the ridge and saw at least ten other lone Britons racing up the slope. If they had all done as well he thought, they had slaughtered over three hundred men, it was a good start.

Legate Titus Flavius Vespasian, Commander of the Second Legion Augusta, walked amongst the dead from the third cohort. He had known they would have been vulnerable bringing up the rear but he had never expected this kind of slaughter, especially by tribal rabble. He knelt down to examine a young soldier's dead face, he couldn't have been more than twenty years of age but his life had been taken from him by a single puncture wound to the neck. The pierced entry hole blackened with arterial blood was already beginning to thicken and harden.

"I will avenge you young man, I swear by the gods I will avenge you." He stood, "Centurion," a man ran forward, "General?"

"I want these men buried before we move forward and I want scouts sent out to find the war band that did this and I want them nailed to trees in retribution for their actions today."

"Yes General." The centurion began to rattle out orders to waiting soldiers who quickly hurried off to carry out their tasks. A cavalry cohort approached summoned by the General.

"General Vespasian sir, I'm told you have quarry for us to hunt." Vespasian looked up to see an Optio on a brown horse, several riders behind the first to arrive.

"Take a good look around. I want the barbarian bastards that did this tracked down as quickly as possible. You are not to engage them but report back to me on their movement, number and position. I want this horde taken alive if possible, just so that we can make an example of them." He looked at his slaughtered men gripping the handle of his gladius at his side. "Ride out and find these scum and you will witness their deaths."

"With pleasure General." He saluted and turned his horse and then galloped away, the other riders following.

The Emperor Claudius himself had appointed Vespasian to command the Second Augusta in Britannia personally knowing his record. Vespasian knew that this would be a bloody campaign and his men would take casualties but he had hoped he would be able to determine when and where those engagements would take place.

"Macro, he shouted." The man was a Centurion of the class that could be trusted to perform any and all tasks. Vespasian had used him previously on difficult missions in Gaul and he had always been successful.

"Yes sir?" Macro slammed to attention near his superior, Cato his trusty brother in arms close behind him.

"I have a special task for you two gentlemen if you're willing?" He raised an eyebrow under his helmet. Vespasian was determined to use every means at his disposal to rid himself of these barbarian rebels and Macro and Cato were just the type of men he needed.

Some distance away, Varro and his men were preparing to say goodbye to the Britons who had welcomed them overnight. He especially was surprised that he was saddened to be leaving Brenna after their brief night together.

"Will I see you again Roman?" She asked smiling and watching him putting his spatha under his saddle and checking his equipment.

"If the gods will it lady then yes we will see each other again. I have a duty to perform for my Emperor, if it were not for that I would be willing to see your face when I awoke every morning." He smiled as she helped strap the leather to his wrists as he faced her. He kissed her gently on the lips and then mounted his horse.

"We will lay together again I'm sure of it if you are willing." He smiled and gently kicked Staro's flanks as the horse took off at a canter, the other men following.

Gaius drew level with him, "Well Centurion Varro, you certainly got more than you bargained for there didn't you?"

His commander smirked briefly, "Could you have resisted my friend?" He asked.

"Probably not, I just hope she's not full of the pox and that your old man drops off in a couple of days' time." He laughed. "I'd hate to present you to the General all scabby with your balls blistered and ruined."

Varro didn't reply but laughed and was merely content to move them in the direction of Quintus and his men for their scheduled rendezvous.

As they began to move east back towards the general area the column was heading along, Varro couldn't help but think about the image of Brenna's body and their lovemaking the previous night. She had been more than willing and assertive in their play and although he had experienced that before, there was something else, something different with this woman he couldn't quite put his finger on.

He shook his thoughts free as he concentrated on the mission to find Quintus. The day was warm and the sky bright blue with small wispy clouds overhead. They had all been warned of the inhospitable weather patterns over Britannia but so far all they had experienced was warm sunny weather which suited them and their horses. Out here free from the rest of the legion, it was different but things would change if they were called back to the ranks and ordered to form battle lines but as things were, they were happy to be away from the Second Augusta's marching columns and dust.

He imagined that Vespasian was slowly moving westward in their direction and a fast ride overnight would see them back with the column. The countryside they found themselves in was not too dissimilar from that of Gaul. Rich green rolling hills with trees seemed to cover the land almost everywhere. Shallow slow running rivers and streams cut the land in places and with little difficulty they could be crossed quite easily on horseback.

They slowed to walking pace as they approached a small group of roundhouses. They were not as well made as the others they had encountered at Brenna's settlement and there was no fencing around them. A couple of goats were tied up and a few dogs were walking around loose, it wasn't as organised or anywhere near as large as Brenna's village.

As the dogs noticed them and began to bark, a female stooped inside her roundhouse and then appeared at the door. The look on her face was of total surprise as she surveyed the five strange men on horseback. She shouted something unintelligible with a Cantiaci dialect and kept repeating it, more women appeared at their doors peering around the edges of the door frames.

"How about this lot Centurion, would you put your sword into them, as you did last night?" Asked Veranius chuckling to himself.

Varro looked at the women, "I'm no eunuch as you know my friend but I do have some standards and I think that these crones are a few levels below my last encounter." He could see rotten brown teeth in their mouths and dry cracked skin on their faces and necks.

"I reckon you'd know about it the next day if you quenched your desires on them lot eh?" Veranius made a sound of disgust as one of the women snorted up a mouth full of phlegm and spat it towards them.

"Filthy fuckin cunt." He said pulling his spatha upward out of his scabbard, the sheaving metallic sound enough to make the women scurry back inside their houses.

"Ha-ha, I think they like you Veranius," Varro said, "maybe when we come back through this way you could spend the night with that beauty eh? But for now stay alert, I don't want to lose anyone or for someone to get injured by those horrible looking witches." He moved on, "You wouldn't think they were part of the same tribal group as Brenna's would you? They look like rabble in comparison."

Varro clicked at Staro, "Come on let's get away from here." He ordered and they galloped away from the women who had been joined by others outside and were shouting abuse at the strange looking riders. They got onto a path that looked familiar and disappeared from view of the village and entered a shaded wooded area. Suspicious of possible attack they hurried through the tree covered ground and soon came out into the bright sunshine.

Ahead of them about three hundred paces in front, they saw the uniquely recognisable helmets of Roman cavalry riding in their direction. Quintus and his men smiled as they approached waving to the other part of their small detachment of reconnaissance riders.

"Greeting Centurion Varro," he said, "how has it been out here in the barbarian wasteland where they eat their children and feed the remains to the dogs?"

"Hardly my friend." Varro answered. "Although we did come across some rather unfriendly crones a few miles back, blistered sputum spewing whores by the look of them and as pox riddled as any slut of Rome by the looks of things. Although Gaius here said he'd give them a run for their money."

"With all due respect sir, fuck you Centurion." Gaius protested and laughed.

"Come lets go and water the horses at that ford over there and we can catch up." Quintus suggested. They all followed him on his brown mare as Staro nudged her as he drew level and shook his head.

"Ah, I see Staro still has a liking for Sevella eh boy?" Quintus said patting the other soldier's horse's mane.

"When this is all over, we'll give you a chance to sire your own sons eh old boy?" Varro said as they got to the water where the horses dipped their heads and drank thirstily as their riders dismounted.

"The column was attacked Varro. Some bastard barbarian war leader called Caratacus apparently. He and his brother Togodumnus have vowed to push us back into the sea or so the story goes."

"How bad was the attack, how serious?" Marcus asked.

"Bad enough, they ambushed the rear of the legion in a valley. It was well planned and orchestrated. They killed nearly four hundred men, three hundred and seventy eight to be precise. Vespasian has gone through the fucking roof and sent out riders searching for those responsible."

"Nearly four hundred!" Varro said. "Gods hell, that's a lot of the legions strength, how the fucking hell did that happen? They're bastard primitive scum with sling shot against spear, chariot against ballista!

"I'm afraid it's true my friend, we saw the records from the Tribunes clerk, it's not good." Quintus said.

"Just how many warriors do the blue nose bastards have? Does anyone have any idea? It must be quite a lot and more than we were told existed before we crossed the water if they've killed that many trained soldiers." Marcus said.

"A well planned and co-ordinated ambush could result in odds of one loss to eight dead enemy warriors by military estimates, they reckon." Varro put in. "We were told we can expect to meet as many as one hundred and seventy thousand Britons. If that many had descended on the column in a well-planned attack, there wouldn't be a man left and General Vespasian's skull would be displayed on a spear by Caratacus' roundhouse.

An attack of this nature could have been carried out by as few as five hundred of them or as many as two thousand. We know that most of the war chiefs have gone north so the whole hundred odd thousand aren't engaging us at the moment."

"Vespasian needs to draw them out into the open all of them and engage them, all at once. We could destroy the Britons resistance in one foul sweep." Quintus said as he knelt down and started to light a fire. "We'll have some food with you, before you return to the General, we brought fresh pork with us." He said gesturing for Sextus to get some out of his bag.

As the soldiers sat together around the fire and ate, they could have been anywhere, Gaul or even Italia. At that moment they could relax somewhat due to the terrain they now found themselves in. They could see to the horizon in most directions, the only blot to disturb the view was that of the wooded area but it was too far away to hide any approaching attacking force that could endanger them. So they sat in peace and took their time relishing the crispy pork Quintus had brought with him.

The first evidence that the light was about to fade was signalled by a cool breeze and a sense of lateness brought on by an owl calling out from somewhere beyond in the forest to their south as the Legion came to a halt. They were in a huge clearing, forests to their north and south but some distance away. It looked like a huge swathe had been cleared with the route west open for passing travellers.

Vespasian knew that if they didn't start their preparations to fortify their position soon, they would run out of natural light so he had decided to bring them to a halt and had given the order for the men to start the last task of the day, an all-round defensive position.

After the attack during the morning he had ordered two cohorts of cavalry to patrol along their lines on opposite sides of the column and travelling in opposite directions at all times. One century of heavy infantry now walked with and guarded the rear flank at all times to try and ensure a repeat of the mornings attack didn't occur again.

As the men released their heavy back packs and put their equipment down, the wagons containing the sharpened timber spikes were brought to them at intervals of fifty paces and unloaded. The sound of digging commenced as men bit into the previously un-dug surface with their shovels and the preparations began to complete their temporary home once more.

Some distance away, keen eyes watched the invaders digging their earth. They had seen the precautions the Romans had taken and knew they couldn't risk attacking the column with two cohorts of cavalry ready to come to the defence of any area they believed right to take advantage of and so they waited.

"A wolf can stalk their prey for days until the right moment presents itself." Caratacus said. "Patience is always rewarded in time as we will be when we destroy these men that hide themselves in metal and iron." His accomplices nodded in agreement as they backed away from the trees and bushes they had used to help conceal themselves with.

After dark had fallen and the defences were in place, fires lit up small groups of Roman soldiers sat around fires. Sentries were silhouetted as they moved along the perimeter. Lines of brown tents were visible, set up in neat rows and safely behind their fortified position. Wolf mouths lay in the dug trenches, the small spikes embedded as a horrible surprise for any wood-be attacker, they could maim or entangle anyone or anything before a pilum was hurled at the unfortunate individual or animal to put them out of their misery. Animals caught by the devices would usually find themselves being slaughtered and then cooked the next day.

Some of the soldiers relaxed in their tents talking or playing dice or betting on the outcome as old rivalries were re-ignited, others decided to get some sleep as early as possible because they knew that come the morning they would be expected to march between twenty five and thirty miles once again.

The first of the Britons reached the pit and straining his eyes in the half light, saw some of the sharpened spikes below. He turned and whispered to the man coming up behind him, giving him instructions to take back to their leader. The man wheeled quietly around on his stomach hardly making a noise and went back in the direction it had taken so long to cover.

Sometime later, much later and with the stars sparkling like diamonds in the night sky, he returned but was not alone. Other warriors struggled with thin branches and logs cut from trees far away, they had dragged them forward as other men struggled to get them across the pits. One man stood on a particularly small spike that he hadn't seen in the dim light and the iron pierced his foot. He almost screamed out in agony but stopped himself as he pulled his foot free of the sharp metal. He scrambled back up the bank and crawled towards the trees and safety, there would be no Roman heads for him this night.

The sleeping soldiers had no warning of the attack nor did the sentries except for the fizz of fire arrows as they pierced tents and set fire to others. Some landed harmlessly on the grass and burnt out straight away. In the same instant from nowhere, Britons appeared inside the perimeter moving with stealth, silently moving towards the enemy. High on aggression and incensed with fury, the warriors crashed into the tents some jumping onto them and preventing the occupants from escaping, hacking and slashing their large swords two handed into the struggling heads and limbs trying to get free of the material inside.

As a trumpet further down the line signalled the alert, it was already too late for many of the men of the Second

Augusta. Most didn't even get free of their tents, some half asleep, half dressed and some even fell half naked outside wherever they could and were hacked to death with no mercy.

"Alarm, alarm! To arms!" Shouted a sentry some hundred yards away, now running towards the burning tents, "What the fucks going on? How did those blue bastards get inside?" He cried out to no-one in particular as he ran and was joined by others as men leapt from their own tents as he passed.

The Britons were already pulling back and were now running towards the cover of the trees as some were still struggling free of the pit. The advancing Romans were too far away to reach them however and the fastest hurled their pilums at the retreating Britons, the first of which were now already entering the tree line. The furthest pilum landed feet behind the last Briton.

The Romans that got to the attacked position first, found garrotted sentries and dead and dying soldiers. Logs and branches covered the pits where they had made their escape. The Britons had somehow out thought them and had got through the defences without the alarm being sounded. Enraged a Centurion ran through the large almost vertical spikes before the pit and over the logs, waving for the following men to continue with him, they did.

Some distance away, Vespasian watched from his area of the perimeter and suddenly ordered the trumpeter to sound the retreat suspecting what was about to happen. He screamed for his men to withdraw whilst officers gathered around staring at him in disbelief as he ran forward but it was too late.

As the legionaries got to within twenty paces of the retreating Britons, the trees seemed to come to life with movement, branches swaying. The leading soldiers realised too late that they had fought their last battle as chariots raced out of the wood towards them. They carried at least three lime covered warriors at either side of the vehicles and within no time, encircled them. All but one Briton jumped off every chariot and then immediately ran at the isolated soldiers who were already weary from the chase.

Vespasian watched helplessly as at least twenty more Roman lives were lost to the blades of the frenzied madmen and women that were hacking at them. Screams disturbed the night as flaming shadows danced over the horrifying scene beyond, reflected off the trees and faces of the Britons.

Finally the screams ended but some soldiers, at least four were dragged up, put onto chariots and driven off. Vespasian looked on and realised that they must still live. He stared straining to see properly and observed one Briton standing alone, staring back at him. He was fully clothed and was wearing an enormous double plumed helmet, Caratacus! As another native approached him, Caratacus raised a large sword and pointed it at the Roman General, he stood for several moments, then turned and walked slowly into the cover of the trees and vanished from sight.

Chapter Six

With dawn came the reality of the atrocities carried out the night before. Bodies were strewn around the valley floor of the former resting place. The army in its marching line was now divided, its middle segregated where the enemy had attacked. Scorched and with some wagons still burning, it was testament to the stealth and brutality of the plan carried out by Caratacus. Vespasian had decided to isolate the ravaged land where his men had died and had reinforced the defences facing each other in the two camps running through the valley's track.

Smoke still smouldered from burnt out tents, wagons and material and even flesh, the smell was overwhelming as men moved in to clear away their fallen comrades and bury their corpses. Water was used to douse burning flames as men passed buckets from one to another from a nearby stream.

The General's anger hadn't subsided as he once again walked amongst his dead. His hands trembled with fury as he covered his mouth with one hand, the stench almost making him empty his bowels and spill its contents over the smouldering earth. Soldiers searched nearby woods where the last of the slaughter had taken place, brave men that had tried to pursue the murderers from the night before. Their corpses lay at awkward angles, limbs bent where they had fallen. Some still wore their helmets and armour but they had still died vastly outnumbered and isolated, where they had been cut to pieces.

Their only saving grace was that they had died relatively quickly and hadn't burnt to death like the poor bastards that had gone to their gods in their tents, victims of the fire arrows or hacks to the head or body by large swords and axes. The smoke from the devastating attack could be seen from some miles away as Varro and his small band approached on their horses cautiously entering the clearing from the west.

"I don't think that's smoke from the columns camp fires for some reason, it looks different, too black, it doesn't look normal." Marcus remarked.

"I think you're right." Varro replied looking at the dark plumes rising into the sky above them in the clear blue air as they drew closer.

"Maybe they caught the butchering bastards and set them on fire." Veranius remarked.

"I very much doubt it Veranius, crucified them maybe but I wouldn't have thought the General would stoop to their barbaric levels." Varro said.

They continued on, watching all around them, their imaginations producing huge men with axes in the woods waiting for the right moment to attack. Varro knew that the approach to the column was always the most dangerous. Whilst they were so close to safety and security they knew nothing of the enemy positions and so could walk directly into a trap at any moment. If the Britons had been massing for a large attack they would be close and it would be virtually impossible to get to the main force.

Eventually the fortified positions came into view and they could see soldiers moving about in camp and outside the boundaries. Dark smoke was billowing from somewhere in the centre of the position and horsemen galloped here and there no doubt carrying out different orders.

"This doesn't look good." Varro said to no-one in particular as riders came out to challenge the approaching men.

Some hours later, the dead buried and with preparations to move forward taking place, Varro made his report to Vespasian who was sat reading reports from other scouts. The tent was modest by a General's standards, a bust of the Emperor Claudius and the Legions eagle standard, the only sign of grandeur. A large map of the land was spread out on a table.

"We came across a hunting party of no-more than twelve men General. They were two days ride further west. They attempted to engage us armed with spears and swords."

Varro pointed to relevant areas on the map laid out on the table before him. "Other than that we saw no large force or organised resistance. There were a few settlements, one where druids were performing some bizarre ritual and actually burned a young boy to death in a large wooden frame." He paused. "We found another band after rescuing another lad, they were friendly and were led by a man called Tevelgus and his sister Brenna. They gave us food, shelter and rest and let us stay at their settlement."

The General rose from his seat after listening to his verbal report. "The druids have been sacrificing the lives of their people to appease their gods for decades maybe longer, we will need the location of their settlement exactly so we can make an example out of them. I wouldn't want our men blundering into any potential allies like this Tevelgus and blood being spilt. Our previous expeditionary forces have confirmed that the druids are the spiritual leaders of many of the tribal regions and although some have their differences and boundaries, the druids remain consistent throughout. Superstition and fear are used to control their people, anyone found not complying or living outside their rules are persuaded to change their attitude shall we say. If they don't abide by the druids decisions or orders they are either sacrificed and thrown into a peat bog or something else equally awful.

The druids don't exactly rule the people of this land in the usual sense but they are very influential in various ways and hold a lot of power. It's been that way for centuries, always behind a veil of secrecy and tribal elders, offering suggestions and ensuring their own way is abided by one way or another. They are said to have a large island called Mona somewhere to the north-west just off the coast where their spiritual emissaries receive their own instructions in order to control the tribes. It is one of our objectives in time and this infestation we will destroy along with any other impediment that tries to resist us." He looked up.

"Centurion Varro you have done well to find this information, it is essential we form alliances with this Tevelgus and people like him, he will also have information about the druids local to the area and other regions. We march again soon but you and your men can get some rest and re-supply. If you find any sign of this Caratacus I want to know immediately, I vow that he will pay for the lives he's taken."

The General thanked Varro again before he left the tent, his men were waiting nearby, sitting on storage sacks, their horses feeding from nose bags. He explained the situation and their orders, "I suggest we get some sleep on the sentry wagon before we ride out again." He looked up at the valley around them. "Things are going to get interesting around here."

On horseback hidden under trees, scouts sent out by Caratacus watched as the Roman war machine packed up all its equipment and began to move forward, once again moving west like some enormous metal covered snake. A golden eagle glinted near the front of the line carried by one man, reflecting the day's bright sunshine off it as did other objects; a boar was one of many carried throughout their column. One of the watching men eagerly observing their number was not a warrior but druid. He spoke to himself in whispers, almost trance like as two other men turned to look at him. They both respected and feared the man who wore no colouring to his skin or lime in his hair. He was thin with straggling hair and a long grey beard. As one, the group turned and encouraged their horses to walk away leaving the druid watching the Romans below.

After some rest aboard one of the rattling, bumpy carts, Varro led his men along the column. He never ceased to be impressed at the uniform patterns as the legions marched, Centurions with their traverse crests in front of them or to the side, shouting at any man who fell out of line even by the smallest margin. The standard bearers carried the various unit insignia just behind the Centurion so orders could be relayed quickly to the marching troops behind them. Optio's further back were keeping an eye on the men and the ground all around them. An almost rhythmic crunch, crunch reverberated along with the soldiers as their boots hit the ground. With the mornings sun shining off their armour and helmets he wondered how anyone could fail to be overawed by their presence and fear their power. One someone however, was this

Caratacus and the Britons who accompanied him. They were clearly un-impressed and weren't afraid but so far they hadn't faced them properly, army to army. Instead they had nibbled away at the legions men, tactically winning minor victories and then vanishing into the surrounding countryside, which he hoped was about to change.

As Varro and his men drew level with the leading elements of the enormous convoy of men, wagons and horses, he saluted the Generals standard, brought Staro up onto his hind legs and then galloped away, Veranius and the others following. They slowed to a canter after a while to preserve the animal's energy.

"If they find Brenna's settlement again we'll try to forge an alliance and also try to find out what they know about Caratacus and his war band." Varro said.

"Do you really think after just one night of passion, she'll be willing to turn on her own people Varro? Your cock must have extra special seed inside it if that's what you believe." Veranius commented as he trotted alongside smirking at his superior.

"You are obviously underestimating my passion my friend," he replied smiling, "I'm sure if it had been you, she'd be ready to fight alongside that barbarian right now. Fortunately it wasn't however and I'm certain she'll be willing to accommodate me again and not just inside her bed." He laughed out loud tipping his head back as he had the last laugh and had embarrassed his second in command with the others listening and laughing along with him.

The humour was brought to an abrupt halt as they rode around the next curve on the track into a vast clearing. They stopped instantly as they stared at the lines of Britons arranged in front of them…..there were thousands of them.

"Veranius take Lucius and ride back to the General as quickly as your horses will allow, he has to be warned." Varro ordered quickly,

"Sir." Was all they both said as they turned and galloped away the way they had come.

"Gods, there are thousands of them." Marcus said studying their lines. "They have horse, chariots and light infantry." He studied their formation, "There has to be an entire legions strength out there."

"But they have no heavy infantry or artillery by the look of it. They've probably got slingers hidden somewhere though I should think but I can't see any at the moment." Varro replied looking at the army arrayed before them some hundred paces distant. They must have been hoping to catch the column cold as it turned along the clearing, he thanked the gods they had gone on ahead. Following a roar of voices, arrows were launched from somewhere to the rear of the Britons. Varro watched as they gained height.

"Archers." He shouted turning Staro to the right. "Make for the woods men, now!" They all turned and were some two hundred paces from the safety of the trees when the arrows began landing harmlessly in the grass behind them. Varro saw Britons furiously waving battle axes and swords as their jeers grew at them as they entered the safe shadows of the branches.

"Those bastards have archers hidden behind their ranks. Decimus take your horse and inform the General. Marcus and I will stay here and try to keep an eye on their movements. If anything else occurs, Marcus will bring the message back, tell Veranius where we are and tell him to avoid any contact with the Britons at all costs." Decimus nodded with determination and fear imprinted across his face.

It was now noon and the sun was high in the sky but Varro and Marcus were relatively cool in the woods. They had tied their horses up some fifty paces into the woodland and had returned to the edge of the trees to observe the Britons.

"That has to be Caratacus there." Varro said pointing to the Chieftain at the front of the group, another man was standing with him. "That's probably his brother Togodunmus or whatever name he calls himself. If I had a bow I could kill one of them from here, maybe both of them." He judged the distance to be between one hundred and fifty to two hundred paces from where they were, it would have been within reach of a bow and a skilled eye.

The two soldiers watched the Britons from cover with their helmets off until the first rumbling sign of the Roman force approached. It was a cavalry cohort who had been sent forward to reconnaissance the enemies lines, four hundred of them. They had been sent ahead in force in case of ambush but they stopped in virtually the same spot as Varro and his men had as arrows were launched into the air towards them. They turned and forced their animals into a gallop as they retreated returning the same way they had come.

"Well that didn't last long." Varro said. "Those fools," he said looking at the Britons, "don't know what they've got coming their way."

Arrows fell to the ground all around them as they retreated, one hit the rump of the last horse, it shrieked and darted to the left kicking out with its hind legs so quickly it looked unnatural as the rider struggled to get it under control, the arrow lodged into its flesh waving around, blood staining its back.

"Those fuckers are going to pay for that Marcus, I fucking guarantee it." Varro said as the two of them watched the retreating cohort charge by and then saw a large testudo of a marching legionnaires slowly approaching the Britons. At least eighty soldiers made up the front wedge of the attack, their large shields covering them from a frontal assault, the second ranks shields over their heads and so it went on until the rear of the line. Soon the Britons would be faced by thousands. Soldiers at the sides left and right held their shields to the side of the formation, the whole image looking and sounding like an enormous creature. Varro wondered how the Britons would react to the sight and then the sound of the unit of troops as it engaged them.

"Those fuckers will pay for it now Marcus." He said as the testudo cleared the corner and came into full view of the enemy. An order must have been given as the giant tortoise formation came to a halt but he didn't hear it above the clump of the boots. The Britons were quiet now and stared at them in silence seemingly unmoved by the monstrosity they saw before them.

Cavalry came to a halt behind the huge square and to its sides, it was followed by heavy infantry, three huge squares filled the enormous gap between the trees of the empty ground. Behind them three centuries of auxiliary archers Syrians, made up the next line of attack. More were assembling beyond them but Varro couldn't see what tactical formation it was. An eerie silence settled over the battlefield until a single trumpet blare eventually shattered the peace.

A dip formed in the centre of the testudo at the front and a Centurion's helmet appeared along with his sword as it was thrust skyward and then forward, "Advance." He screamed out and the formation slowly marched, the soldiers beginning to bang their short swords against their shields, the noise was almost overwhelming as they advanced, boots hitting the earth.

The Britons leader instantly ordered his chariots forward as they raced to meet the Romans around the flanks of their warriors, the faint sound of trumpets could be heard somewhere behind the Roman forces but was swallowed up by the sounds reverberating around the tree trunks. The testudo continued forward slowly, swords banging on shields then the foot soldiers of the Britons ran forward wielding swords and axes screaming like demented devils. To Varro everything seemed to slow as suddenly the front ranks of the testudo dropped down onto one knee, behind them somewhere, four rows back, the soldiers in that line hurled their pilums. That was quickly followed by the next row. Arrows were launched from behind the Britons running towards the wall of shields in front of them.

As the chariots got to within twenty paces, the pilums began to land some finding their targets of flesh and bone of man, woman and horse alike. The horses made ungodly noises as the weapons embedded themselves through their flesh, into chests, necks and heads. The men guiding them towards the invaders were generally fortunate in comparison but one Varro saw was hit somewhere in the upper chest and it took him off the back off his chariot, tumbling head over heal, breaking his arms and legs at awful unnatural angles.

The arrows of the Britons landed harmlessly on the raised shields of the testudo. Just before the remaining chariots reached the shield wall, other pilum were thrust forward horizontally between the front ranks. The horses that were not wounded or killed by the first onslaught were viciously stabbed now running onto the deadly weapons, the spears ends breaking off or bending in their chests as the animals went wild trying to turn and flee the pain, some still impaled. Chariot riders were thrown to the ground their vehicles bounced and turned and some flew apart sending large wooden splitters in all directions impaling men and women alike. As those who still lived managed to turn, they were met by other screaming warriors, half naked from the waist up, men and women alike, hair limed outward and upward, blue streaks over their bare flesh and through their hair, teeth showing as they screamed and shouted toward their enemy.

Another avalanche of Roman spears rose from inside the testudo and then fell into the attacker's ranks as they became a tangled mass of arms, legs and horses struggling for freedom, to escape this madness, this certain death. The Romans continued to advance slowly their short swords now doing the cutting and stabbing. As the square came to an ordered halt at the sound of a trumpet, the front ranks turned and were replaced by fresh troops who took over the butcher's role neutralising the enemy.

The metallic stench of blood was everywhere as the grass ran red and became slippery underfoot for the barefooted warriors. They were being annihilated by the professional soldiers who were seeking to rule the land and at the same time were being taught a harsh lesson in battlefield warfare. Caratacus watched in horror as his men and women were butchered. Those not close to the Roman front line were struggling to get to it, pinning and pushing those at the front onto swords. Those who had seen the horrors it held were trying desperately to get away but were trapped by their own people and they died in masses.

"Archers, slingers, fire over our people, keep the heads of the enemy down." A shouted order was heard over the din. Within seconds the weapons launched their missiles but had little effect that Varro could see. Arrows either bounced off hardened armour or shields and the rocks flung by the slingshots had little to no effect at all and were ricocheting off targets.

The Roman wall advanced again, the iron of their swords could be seen pumping forward from behind the shields, stabbing out at the helpless attacking and trapped warriors. The rotations of the front ranks came more often now as the arms were exhausted from the thrusts and expenditure of the lives they had taken, it was hard work cutting down fellow human beings, even if they were barbarians.

A ripple went along the centre of the testudo as soldiers climbed over the bodies of their fallen enemies, once in a while the end of a spear could be seen stabbing downward as it was used to end the life of a fallen Briton somewhere in the melee.

Caratacus waved forward his next line of women and men who sprinted forward as eagerly as those who had been killed already. He believed that the Romans couldn't continue their success but was dismayed to see that his fresh forces were relieved of their lives blood as easily as the first wave.

"It's a fucking massacre sir." Marcus commented from the safety of the trees.

"It's what these dumb sub human bastards needed Marcus, a fucking good shafting and General Vespasian is just the man to fuck them good and hard."

Through the slaughter that continued on the open ground before them, the testudo suddenly stopped advancing and its men turned and quickly marched back towards the rear, still covered by their shields.

Caratacus smiled to his brother. "See Togodumnus these metal covered pigs haven't got the stomach for a real fight. We'll slaughter them as they retreat." He quickly ran to a waiting tribal chief and shouted instructions to him, he in turn ran and jumped onto a horse. The retreating metal square had now cleared all the dead bodies lying prone on the ground. Caratacus frowned as he began to realise the cost of this battle.

"Brother, we should withdraw now," Togodumnus pleaded, "we can't give them anymore of our people."

"They are cowards," he began, "and we'll smash them into the ground, look at them falling back. They haven't got an ounce of bravery compared to our men and women. We've got to take advantage of their weakness." As his words ended more warriors ran towards the enemy being overtaken by more chariots, as dust clouds swirled all around.

Togodumnus shook his head in disbelief. "I know that's what you want brother and I pray you're right but if this fails we have to withdraw, agreed?"

Caratacus looked at his older brother sweat dripping down his temples, "Agreed."

As the soldiers of the testudo got to their own lines their shields were taken down revealing the men behind them, sweating and exhausted but very few of them were missing littering the battlefield, a cheer went up celebrating their success.

Caratacus watched as another three lines of formations of soldiers advanced towards him. They were five men wide but this time they advanced their faces showing above their shields, these men were not hiding behind their shield wall as the others had, they were heavy infantry.

Caratacus held his breath as the two opposing armies came together with a horrendous crunch of weapons and bone. His warrior's battle frenzy was heightened like never before after the slaughter they had witnessed and he saw them hack and swing with their axes and swords as Roman soldiers finally began to fall. For a brief moment he dared to think that victory against these invaders was possible as his people continued their grim task. With a sudden jolting realisation he watched on as he realised what was occurring. Two Roman oblongs on the edge of their flanks began to wheel around as if one, the ends moving quicker than those towards the centre were advancing.

Within minutes the battling Britons were all but sealed in from the front and both sides and there was now no escape as the marching squares closed in. Cavalry now raced past the battle in the centre outflanking the chaos that continued on the field of battle as distant trumpet calls ordered them into the fray. Realisation dawned on Caratacus instantly that there would be no victory for him here today. He exchanged a look with his brother and turned away from the premeditated butchering of his people as a lucky few ran back escaping the enclosing wall of horses. The rest were sealed in as cavalrymen used their shortened spears and spathas to stab at the still struggling warriors hemmed in against their ranks. Togodumnus mounted his horse following his brother as they gave the order to retreat. He saw the horror in their remaining forces as they too realised there was nothing they could do for their trapped kinsmen and women.

As Caratacus began a large scale retreat, huge spears thumped into warriors around him. He turned and saw the enemy had brought forward machines on carts and they were now firing enormous arrows from a distance of some three hundred paces. The arrows ripped through horses, chariots and men and women alike, pinning them to each other as they withdrew. Some punched through individuals, sailing through flesh and embedding themselves into others through their retreating backs.

Varro and Marcus began to get up, watching as the large weapons pounded into the enemy, their crews working furiously charging the ballista again and again without mercy. The fighting battlefield grew smaller as life was snuffed out of the remaining trapped Britons. The soldiers on the periphery began to sheath their swords turning towards the retreating Britons instead who were already some distance away.

General Vespasian trotted to the rear of his heavy infantry surrounded by a cohort of cavalry and was already congratulating his men as they began to withdraw. The sound of fighting, swords clashing and screams of agony began to die away as the men in the middle finished their deadly work. The battle was won and the Britons had paid a heavy price for their bravery, but naivety had cost them many hundreds of lives as their retreating people vanished from view.

That night many miles from the blood shedding of the day, around a sombre fire, Caratacus stared into the flames still disbelieving what he had witnessed. Many hundreds of his people had lost their lives that day on the battlefield for little life in return, those missing or known to have died was nearly a thousand. He estimated that less than fifty of the enemy had died, hiding behind their large shields. He cursed the gods for allowing this defeat, where were they, why had they allowed this destruction he asked himself. Were his people so unworthy that these invaders should rout them, slaughtering them on their own ground like animals. He held his head in his hands as visions of the days hell returned again and again.

The almost drum like beat of the Roman swords clashing against their shield's as they had slowly advanced, the harsh trumpets cutting through the air, men and women screaming and horses whinnying. The smell of victim's blood, shit and dust, all these memories brought back flashes of the day, as he shook his head at the images burned deep into his mind, his soul. They would haunt him for rest of his life.

Shock was etched on the faces around him, women cried rocking where they sat, men cursed or sat clearly devastated and mute. Muttered conversations, whispers, told tales of the horrors of the day. As a few lucky but wounded warriors were treated, shrill screams broke the quiet of the night around them as their wounds were cauterised with hot iron, bandaged or poultices applied. Less than two hundred had escaped the enclosure of the Romans. They had suffered even more wounded from the huge arrows that were rapidly propelled through their ranks as they tried to escape. Gaping open wounds still bled freely where the weapons had punched through flesh. Those whose internal organs were ruptured had died virtually instantly or were disabled enough not to be able to escape, They were later put to death as the enemy swept through the field checking for those that still held breath. They would have died horribly in agony, maybe taking weeks to die in the aftermath but as the Romans checked for survivors, they were quickly expelled and sent to the afterlife.

"We can't afford another defeat like that brother." Togodumnus remarked. "These Romans have ways of defeating us that we have never encountered before." Caratacus didn't answer he looked away from his brother back to the flames.

"We have to find another way to drive them away from our lands, if we had more numbers and the ground of our choosing we could defeat such battle lines but not like today, trapped between two lines of trees and then enclosed like the jaws of a giant beast."

Caratacus sighed. "I don't want to talk of this anymore brother. My mind keeps showing me the disaster that befell us today, that's bad enough. I don't need to be told by you like an old pestering woman reminding me, pecking me to a certain death. I'm sorry brother but now isn't the time for this. Tomorrow we move north away from them, we'll stay within our territory for the day and then head back to the east and regroup our people. At the same time we'll send messengers to our neighbours telling them of this disease that's eating into our land. They have to be persuaded that alone we cannot push them from our lands but together we could number many thousands and together we can crush these Romans."

Togodumnus agreed with his brother as another cry of agony came from one of the injured where many more lay amongst far too many other wounded warriors, a lot of whom would never walk, let alone fight again.

Early the next morning soldiers from the Second Augusta checked the battlefield again. After the previous days fighting and the last Briton had been taken from the life it had so easily given, General Vespasian had ordered them back to their defensive positions. As sentries were trebled around the perimeter, quiet celebrations were allowed amongst his men although excessive wine was not permitted. There was still a possibility of a counter attack but as time went on, it was reduced with each passing moment.

As the suns warmth began to burn away the night's dew, soldiers walked slowly across the battlefield with pilums ready or swords drawn. They had only lost eighteen men with thirty six wounded, three seriously who weren't expected to recover. It was never a good thing to lose valuable, able and well trained men but at the return they had yesterday, it was hundreds to every one of their own. The Britons had suffered a crippling and humiliating defeat, they scattered the ground as the soldiers continued their grim task looking for any who may have survived the carnage and had not been found clinging to life the night before.

Once the field had been checked Vespasian ordered that large burial pits were dug. The half-naked bodies that had sustained inhuman damage were dragged and thrown into heaps on wagons and driven to the ten large holes and thrown in. Soldiers wore cloth over their faces, torn from sacks to limit the stench of death as they toiled throughout the morning to complete the task.

Chapter Seven

Varro and his small group of reconnaissance riders rode out again the next morning. They almost expected to round a corner and find thousands of Britons waiting for them but today it was not to be. The enemy were crawling away somewhere and licking their wounds after the devastating defeat the day before. Every now and again they would come across a hurriedly dug small burial mound where they had buried corpses which showed they were in a hurry as they normally burnt their warriors on funeral pyres. Some of the mounds they found were bigger than others where presumably more than one body was buried. The Romans were curious as to how the Britons had continued to move so quickly and bury their dead but eventually they stopped finding them so the subject became irrelevant.

The Britons were not difficult to track and were clearly making no attempt to disguise the route they were taking. When the sun was high in the sky overhead Varro and his small party had caught up with them, initially they stayed back out of sight and observed them from a safe distance. Stragglers walked along on foot a few hundred feet behind the rear of the main body. Carts, horses, chariots and even the walking warriors carried the wounded slowly moving along the route others walked heads bowed in the main, with little or no conversation taking place.

Some three hundred feet or so distant following at walking pace, Varro studied the Britons who had been so alive and vibrant the day before, but now looked crushed and devoid of life. He felt no sympathy however, not because he was uncaring but because if he allowed thoughts such as those to enter his head, they would eat away at him and he knew he couldn't allow that. They were after all, the enemy, an enemy that had to been destroyed or beaten so badly that they gave up fighting and never drew a sword against Rome again

He estimated that they were now half a day's walk from Brenna's settlement and wondered how her people would greet their defeated countrymen and women. Would they be welcomed with open arms, their dead mourned, their injured healed or would they be turned away to protect their own people from the wrath of the invaders. There was no doubting that the war party would overwhelm the settlement if it so desired even in its ragged state and he didn't want Brenna or her people harmed if he could avoid it. They did their best to stay hidden and out of sight as they followed and once or twice a rider would track back and they would have to retreat some distance in order not to be seen.

"We'll go round them and warn Brenna's people of their approach. Caratacus could well do anything after yesterday and I wouldn't want anyone that didn't agree with him to get in their way especially Brenna and her people." Varro said after a while.

They moved to the left angling away from the rear of the defeated enemy and began cantering up a slight rise and away around the Britons out of sight. The day was warm with a slight breeze, a good day for riding even if it was under pressure.

By late afternoon they approached familiar paths worn by years of feet, hooves and carts passing through them. The air was still as they rounded a slight bend and entered a clearing. The settlement looked quiet, no dogs or children were busy playing, no animals in the small pens and no people could be seen.

"It looks like they've already heard the news." Veranius remarked as he brought his horse to a halt. Varro looked around at the silent roundhouses, almost eerie with no souls present. Suddenly from nowhere and without any warning arrows thudded into the ground and trees behind them, to a man they turned and retreated further into cover.

"Where the fuck did they come from?" Marcus said from under the canopy of a tree.

"Anyone see how many of them there were?" Varro asked.

"Had to have been at least ten," Veranius remarked, "the good news is that they weren't close enough to throw spears."

"No-one got hit did they?" Varro said checking his horse, they were all uninjured. "We've got a choice, we can either try to find them and see how many of them there are or we can get out of here."

"Sir," Marcus cut in, "we can scout around them." He said gesturing with his arm the direction he suggested to the left. Varro nodded in acknowledgement and they began to move away up a gradual rise on the forest floor. Some moments later they began to hear horses and carts. Moving carefully through the trees above their quarry the first of the Britons came into view. They were clearly wary of their surroundings as they were looking up into the trees canopy and the foliage as they walked.

"It has to be the main body of the enemy force. We must have bumped into the stragglers back there." Varro said as they continued to watch the Britons. "Come on let's get out of here." He turned Staro quietly and moved off, the others following.

Varro opened his eyes slowly, vague memories stumbled through his thoughts. He sensed before he saw and felt that he was being restrained, arms outstretched, wrists tied as well as feet. As his eyes slowly focused, shouting became audible as if he were emerging from water, who was it, where were they? He was dizzy and his head hurt from somewhere near the left temple. He tried to shake off the dullness but it made his head thump even more, with sharp stabbing pains. More noise, voices shouting, faces, blurred faces came into view, unfocused. He closed his eyes tightly as if that would help him focus but it was to no avail. He heard screams from nearby. He turned to the left and could make out other figures standing with their backs against trees like him, he was on his feet, facing outward.

"Varro." A voice, a familiar voice called to him. Suddenly he was struck by something hard, it rocked his head back against the tree trunk he now realised he was tied to as his senses became sharp once more through a fog of pain.

"Varro!"

The voice called again. He opened his eyes to see a sea of faces before him. Faces daubed in blue streaks, swirls and stripes, limed hair sticking out, taunting and mocking. Two of his men were tied up against a tree to the left. Veranius and Decimus were as bruised as he was and were standing watching the barbarians before them, the Britons spoke in an unknown language, their voices rough and harsh, guttural.

"Thank Mars you're alive. I thought they'd killed you for sure." Veranius said, spitting blood from his mouth and wincing. A Briton, female, stepped forward and bent down looking at the blood. She stepped into it merging it with the soil with her foot. Varro looked at her muscular frame, her arms daubed with the blue war paint, bare legs and breasts, her crotch and lower legs the only areas that were covered.

Seeing he had regained consciousness she walked over to him and muttered something but he didn't understand a word she said, her breath was rank as she spat words into his face. She grabbed at his balls, squeezing them and laughing as did others gathered nearby. He realised that he was stripped naked, his clothing and armour nowhere to be seen, what the fuck had happened? She waved a sharp knife in the other hand whilst squeezing and pulling on his testicles with the other.

They had heard rumours of Britons stripping men of their flesh when they were captured, their genitals cut from them and sewn into their mouths, tongues cut out, ears and noses cut off, burned and eaten before them. It was a fate worse than death being captured by these primitive bastards but that was where they found themselves, they here and they're worst nightmare was realised. The women were said to be more terrifying than the men, taking revenge for the deaths of their families and loved ones. Women warriors whose hatred and scorn was taken out on the men who had wounded and killed their own, were now given the chance to take blood for blood.

Varro saw men watching in the background sat on a raised bank, he and his men were being used for entertainment.

They were not delirious with pleasure as the women seemed to be but sat there just watching with something akin to sympathy etched across their faces. They chewed on stripped pieces of meat and chatted with each other as the entertainment continued.

"The others, where are they?" Varro called out.

"They managed to escape when they ambushed us." Veranius said struggling against the rope binding him to the tree. The female saw him and walked over, spitting in his face. Veranius returned the gesture and was punched squarely on the nose, it crunched under the impact. Before he could register the pain another blow pounded into his face, followed by another with the flat of her palm. The female withdrew her hand, her palm already blood spattered with red snot and blood. Veranius gagged trying to breathe through his shattered nose, snorting out blood quickly to try and clear his airway.

"I hope they rode back to get help because if they didn't we're going to go to our gods here this night." Varro said watching the woman as she walked over to Decimus. She grabbed his manhood and stretched it, gathering in his balls as well she removed her knife from a belt and placed it against his organs. His head jerked back as he tried to move away from her blade, she laughed, letting go as his head dropped in relief. They would tease their prey before they mutilated them it seemed.

"Stay the fuck away from us you dirty fucking diseased cunt." Shouted Veranius. Instantly the woman turned her attention to him.

"Veranius, keep your fucking mouth shut unless you want that dirty cunt to cut your cock off and eat it raw before your dying eyes." His commander ordered.

"They're going to kill us anyway so why delay it sir?" He looked at the Briton before him almost pleading in his eyes for a quick death as she ran the sharpened blade down his chest opening a long slicing cut.

The previously vanished memories of the ambush began to return to Varro in flashes, the attack that had come without warning and that had brought them to this point. They had been guiding their horses through a twisting trail through shaded woods when the Britons had struck. Had they been

115

pushed into taking this route by the bowmen or had it been a coincidence, Varro didn't know. What he did know was that once the ambush was sprung, within seconds he and his men were captured or fleeing for their lives. They suddenly found themselves surrounded at the front and both sides. As they tried to turn quickly in the confined space, more Britons cut off the rear. Marcus and Lucius charged their horses at the linking line of barbarians and half jumped their animals through the gathering horde.

Marcus' mounts front hooves clipped the forehead of a screaming enemy, knocking him out cold instantly, even before he hit the ground. Mud flew into the air from the animals feet as the ambush tightened its grip. The horse carrying Lucius romped into the gap created by the falling native and the two galloped away. Wooden clubs were wielded by the screaming warriors as they aimed for the heads and arms of the remaining riders whilst others behind them held large spears. As Varro realised the intention was capture and not kill, a blow to the head took him from the frenzied world he had found himself in.

Veranius spat the contents of his bleeding mouth at the female as she shrieked into his face pressing the knife into his stomach, her own now covered in his blood and spittle.

"Noooooo!" Shouted Varro as his second in command braced himself. He managed a half turn to his commander as the blade pierced his flesh entering his body with ease as she leaned on the handle. Sweat glistened from the Romans head as the knife sunk deeper and he howled in agony. Varro was aware of the face of Decimus behind his wounded friend but didn't focus to look at him. Veranius could do nothing except scream. As the knife reached the hilt, the woman let go of the handle and let it stay where it had sank to and she spat at Veranius.

"Fucking cunt, you fucking whore." He shouted his voice still strong, his head dropping, eyes looking at the blade embedded in his stomach.

"Hold on Veranius, just hold on. Don't do anything else to intimidate her or she'll have your fucking balls off as well." Varro shouted almost pleading, the woman looked at him as he said it and placed her hand on the knife handle again.

"Leave him alone you fucking whore." The Roman commander shouted staring into her black eyes. She smirked and pushed down on the handle, its blade ripping up into the stomach and chest of Veranius as he let out an unearthly cry of agony. Varro thrust himself forwards and backwards furiously against the tree trying to break free, the top even shaking slightly with this effort and rage. The woman laughed and then slowly withdrew the blade. Veranius tried to scream again, his face contorted, head jerking backwards and hitting the trunk but no words came from him. Varro wasn't sure if he had lost consciousness through his head cracking the tree or the pain being inflicted upon him as his head fell forward. Whichever it was, it didn't seem to matter now as Veranius slumped forward his body limp, he was lost to the blackness.

"You fucking coward. You fucking coward! Untie me and I'll show you what pain is, you fucking vile cock sucking whore." Varro challenged.

Veranius's eyes flickered back to life as his head slowly rose back up. Varro tried to get the woman's attention but she had already seen him and had turned her focus back to his second in command. Varro was aware of a commotion from somewhere behind the ranks of watching Britons who were now screaming and almost delirious for more blood but he wasn't focusing on that, he was screaming at the woman. She turned and sneered at him baring her teeth, lowering her arms and leering at him, leaning forward.

She raised her hand holding the knife and pointed it at him, he held his breath expecting to feel the cold metal stained with his friend's blood enter his own flesh. She walked towards him, staring into his eyes, repeating words like some sort of incantation.

"Fucking whore, you fucking whore." Veranius managed weakly as she suddenly turned focusing all her attention on him again. The crowds frenzy grew wild as without warning she stabbed downwards and his eyes bulged. Varro couldn't see what she had done as she bent down near his waist, her victim suddenly white with shock. All Varro could see was a sawing motion as her arm moved forward and backwards very slowly.

Veranius slipped into unconsciousness again, his head slumping forward, blood dripped from his open mouth. The crowd went wild with delirium as the armed woman stood up straight, her blade in one hand and bloodied flesh, organs in the other. Varro strained to see what it was. Then shock hit him with a sudden realisation. She had cut off his manhood and testicles, no matter what happened next, he knew his friend was dead.

He stood there imprisoned watching as she displayed the severed organs to the baying crowd, splashing blood onto their faces and dripping it onto her own and into her laughing open mouth. When they had all had their fill she held them over a fire and then let them drop, sizzling and spitting as they landed. Varro knew there was now nothing to be gained from shouting or struggling any further not that it would have helped the situation before. He decided that whatever happened next, it was the will of the gods that was if they were even at this forsaken place.

The woman wiped her bloodied blade on the material around her waist and smiled as she approached Decimus. The horror engrained on his face was only matched by the psychopathic joy across the faces of the watching crowd. She stood directly in front of him and examined his lower body, smiling at his genitals. She shouted something that clearly amused the crowd and they laughed and balled in appreciation of her words. She leaned forward and grabbed the soldier behind his neck, pulled his head forward and then kissed him. She licked his face as he tried to push his head backwards as her other hand moved between his legs and explored.

As she withdrew from her bizarre act, Decimus suddenly whipped his head forward, his forehead crunching into the woman's face, catching her on the bridge of the nose. She staggered back, her nose shattered clutching at her face, blood flowing freely from her broken ruptured nose and she fell to the ground. The crowd went quiet.

"Fuck you whore." Decimus said as he spat at her prone body. Varro knew that they were both dead in the hands of these animals and didn't blame him for what he had done. What difference would it make if they were to die like their friend? Just then Varro heard a murmur from Veranius as blood flowed and dripped from the black hole of the wound she had created. Varro hoped his friend wouldn't awake to see what she had done to him, he knew he would prefer to die rather than see how she had disfigured him before he went to the next world.

As the barbarian female struggled to her feet holding her nose and mouth, someone pushed their way through the now quiet crowd who were watching the scene before them. Another female voice called out and the torturer turned.

Varro was struck dumb as he saw it was Brenna.

The two women exchanged angry words, the attacker pointing at Veranius. Varro allowed a brief spike of hope to enter his being as the two women argued.

However, Brenna looked over smiling at the unconscious soldier. She grabbed the other woman's knife and approached Veranius. Varro didn't know if she even knew he was there, surely she would recognise him and his men even in this awful condition. His shock was complete as she pushed the head of Veranius back and then slashed downwards across his neck, cutting open the veins within. Blood literally gushed out spraying the ground some feet from the tied Roman, splashing Brenna and the other woman, the watching crowd went wild with excitement. Brenna barked orders at those gathered and they went silent. She walked to Decimus and stood staring at him.

"Don't you fucking dare, no please don't." Varro pleaded. Brenna looked over to him, an unknowing expression sneering at him, lips curled back like a wolf about to pounce, he didn't recognise this person. This wasn't the woman he had spent time with that night, she showed no sign of acknowledging him or human emotion. She was different, remote, she was native, feral, a Briton. She turned and walked around to the rear of the tree holding Decimus in place and cut the rope freeing him, he fell forward and onto the ground. Other women ran towards him but Brenna shouted at them holding out the knife, her words harsh, they stopped before getting to the Roman who was now rubbing at his wrists where the ropes had dug into them. She walked to Varro and did the same, cutting him free. What was she doing, was she freeing them only to have the crowd, rip them apart, his exhaustion almost made him not care.

She shouted for someone unseen as Tevelgus appeared through the gathered mob, he was leading three horses. Brenna pointed at the animals and Varro recognised Staro as he stamped his front hoof as he saw his master. She indicated for the two men to get onto the animals which they did struggling after their recent experience. Their hands were tied to the pommels of the saddles. The crowd parted slowly as they moved through them, some spat as they went by.

Varro looked down at the woman with the broken and bleeding nose as she tried to shout one last insult, her attempt snuffed out as blood spattered through her mouth and nose as she began to cough and choke. He didn't try to respond as Brenna shouted something at her and kicked her horse into a canter, parting the crowd fully.

Sometime later when darkness had fallen and they were some distance from the place of torture, Brenna reminded the two soldiers not to speak, not to say a word as they had done so far. They hadn't uttered a sentence since their release so severe was the shock of the incident and Brenna didn't want anything that may be taken the wrong way, to be overheard by any listening ears. Varro now dared to believe they would live through this horror, although he felt really guilty because his friend had died so appallingly. The image of the whore cutting into him kept returning no matter what he tried to do to rid himself of the memory.

Brenna had taken his life but had she done so in pity or to reinforce the trust of the others? Were they now being led to a worse fate? He didn't know and from his current position, tied on the horses, he didn't have any other choice than to go along with whatever Brenna planned.

They were in a group of about twenty Britons, some of whom he recognised from the night at Brenna's settlement but none gave a clue as to the outcome of this journey. After a bone jarring ride and when they were far away from the other Britons, Brenna said something to the others in the group and they came to a halt.

"You were lucky we found you when we did." Tevelgus said dismounting his horse carrying his axe. "They were planning on skinning you both alive and wearing your flesh in battle."

Varro stared at the brother of Brenna in shock. "How did you find us? How did you make them release us?" He asked.

"We found you by the will of your own gods Varro," Brenna said getting off her own horse, "we very nearly didn't find you at all, at the last turn of the river, we were going to go in the opposite direction. Then we heard shouting, their joy at your torture, it brought us to you. Tevelgus is right about them skinning you but first you would have begged for death. That woman's man was killed by your army she is left to look after three children alone."

"You killed Veranius." He said looking into her eyes, the coldness he saw in her was still present.

"Would you have preferred that he died slowly of his wounds, ruined by that woman's knife?" She looked at him with eyebrows raised.

"He could not have lived with such injuries and even if your gods had let him, what would he have been? She would have cut more flesh from his body and then when there was nothing left to mutilate, it would have been your turn or your friend here." She pointed.

"Have you ever seen a person skinned when they still live Varro? It isn't something I would wish on my worst enemy."

Varro didn't answer, he couldn't. He knew she was right. Veranius was dead and had been sent to his death in a most vile and corrupt way and there was nothing he could have done to change it. He would though he vowed if given the opportunity, take revenge on those responsible.

"Why did that thing listen to you back there? She was about to kill Decimus and me as well. I can't believe she allowed you to stop it, why?" He asked.

Tevelgus who was gathering firewood nearby answered the question. "If they had not listened to their Princess, they would have been tied to the trees in your place Varro. They would have suffered an even worse fate believe me." He threw two pairs of rough material trousers at the two soldiers he had pulled from a bag on his horse.

Varro looked at Brenna, who stared back at him raising an eyebrow. "Your soldiers massacred thousands of our people, not just my own but others from different tribes fighting under the banner of the Catuvellauni. You cannot expect them to not take their revenge."

"Wait, wait I'm confused, you're a Princess?" Said Varro, his face was lined in anguish and confusion as he paced between the horses, realising he was still naked, he pulled on the rough pants quickly.

"So why have you helped us? You could have let them kill us right then and there." He paused, confused.

"You're a Princess?" He repeated, "I knew there was something about you." He almost smiled but the situation didn't allow it. "You can help put an end to this then, you can stop the killing."

"My people are warriors if they are not fighting amongst themselves they are fighting with their neighbours, if they are not fighting with their neighbours they will fight with family. Now you have come from across the great water from Gaul, they will fight you as they have united and intend to push you back into the water as they did before."

"Before, do you mean all those years ago when Caesar marched his legions across your land?" Varro asked.

"Yes when your greatest ever warrior was defeated and sent home, then as now, the tribes are uniting. Caratacus and his brother Togodumnus are intending to defeat the Romans as the Britons did before. Then your Caesar brought a great army contained in over eight hundred vessels to our shores. He had great success but was eventually stopped, made to retreat and returned empty handed to Rome through Gaul. Roman heads decorated the villages for decades, did you know that?

Weapons were displayed as battle honours. He came with many, many men, over forty thousand warriors who raped and burned our houses but for the first time here they tasted a great defeat and faced even more warriors, better warriors and warriors who were prepared to die for their land and families. Now your great Vespasian has brought even more men maybe thousands more to our shores, our spies tell us and even so success is not guaranteed." She paused letting her words sink in.

Varro sat on a fallen log. "So I ask again, if you believe that Caratacus will do the same, why did you help us when you could have let us die back there?"

She watched as her brother gathered more wood for the fire. "We have to somehow stop this spread of violence if we as a people are ever going to progress. I have heard tell of your huge settlements made of stone, teachings by Greeks, buildings with pools of warm water in them, houses with warmth in the dark of winter, water flowing from rivers and mountain streams to your cities on great stone structures and a council that rules the whole empire. It is clear you are more aware of the world in which we live and so can help my people achieve that too."

Varro looked up, "So why don't you order them to put down their weapons, return to their villages, their settlements and it will all stop if you do, you will lose many more thousands of lives if they continue to fight. This time Rome will not turn around and go home, the emperor Claudius wants a triumph, and Britannia will be the victory that gives him that triumph. He has said that he will personally set foot on your soil when that victory is complete, it will be a great honour for your people as well as my own."

Her stare hardened again, "You see Varro that's where I become confused, why would such an enlightened people want more? Why do you think that it would be an honour for us to have your Emperor here? Why do you want to enslave our people, take our gold and leave your home to achieve that? There is one thing here for your soldiers and that's death, nothing more, nothing less. The tribes will not allow you to walk in welcomed with open arms. I have to," she looked at Tevelgus pausing, "we have to do what we can to prevent bloodshed from both sides. Don't you think it's worth it Varro?"

Varro looked at Brenna and for the first time saw the woman he had been with just a few nights before as she really was, a caring loving, intelligent leader and a beautiful woman. A memory of her warm skin and touch made him flush, "I'm just a soldier, you are asking the wrong person. I just follow the orders my General gives me. I am nothing more than an extension of his words, one of his many swords."

Brenna smiled at him warming his heart, "If you were simply a tool of your magnificent General Varro, I would not have risked my life and that of my brother to save you. My people would have tied us to trees next to you if they had known of our intentions today, leaders or not."

"So what did you say to that whore who killed my friend in such a dishonourable and barbaric way?"

"I told them that you would be the highlight of the festivities tonight and that you and your friend Decimus here would pay dearly for the massacre your General created. If I had said anything less they wouldn't have hesitated in killing you both immediately I'm sure." She touched his leg reassuringly. Tevelgus had managed to light the fire and warm flames began to take away the nights chill.

"I can't get the image of what she did to Veranius out of my head." Varro said holding his head in his hands, "He didn't deserve to die like that, no-none deserves to die like that." He looked at Decimus who was clearly having the same thoughts.

"Nobody deserves to die like that not even a pig, you are right." Brenna replied. "But you have come from a different land and you don't understand our ways or customs. Our men fight with long swords and spears they do not hide behind shields or cover themselves in armour. They could but they believe it is more honourable to fight like true warriors not cowering behind shields. Only some high born cover themselves in such armour and use shields but that is because of their importance to their people."

He looked at her staring into her dark eyes, "I can assure you we do not hide behind shields because we are cowardly. We have come here to conquer and to do that we use the best tactics, weapons and equipment we have available. It would be pure stupidity to fight in the way your people do. There is no honour in that, throwing your best warriors onto spears, where is the sense?" Varro responded, seeing that he had struck a chord with her and she didn't like it. "Anyway, I'm not here to discuss tactics with you. If you're opposed to Rome, why did you save us?"

"Varro, if my people can live in peace, are not abused as slaves or taken from our land, why should I resist? Sadly I cannot stop nor will I stop those who believe you are wrong to come here, to impose your will. I know that if we are left in peace and become part of your great empire, we will flourish and grow, we would become great allies to Rome.

The Emperor has already told us that we will become client kingdoms, which means we will still rule our people but will be overseen by the Empire. This is not a bad thing because it will in time bring peace and prosperity to my people but first we have to go through all this." She emphasised her point by indicating with a wave of her arm.

Varro thought about her words, "So no matter what happens you win, I mean you with the way you think about all of this. If your tribes push us into the sea again, you retain your rule, if Rome wins, you become client kingdoms and so you will be happy?"

"What would you do in my place Varro? If you ruled this land or part of this land, would you fight or allow the invaders to have their way if they promised peace and legitimate rule?" She asked.

"I don't know but what I do know is that we are where we are and we are who we are. Our destinies are decided by others and I am merely a soldier playing my part. That is all I can do for now and all I will do until a better opportunity presents itself or I complete my service."

"Twenty five years is a long time Varro," He raised an eyebrow, clearly she knew quite a lot about a soldier's life, she continued, "by that time maybe we will know who has won the fight for my land but I doubt it. In the meantime we have to live as best as we can." She leaned forward and kissed him gently taking him by surprise. He returned the kiss briefly before the image of Veranius blood spattered body entered his mind's eye again and the horrific death he had suffered.

"I want the woman that killed Veranius," he said, "I want to take her life and make her suffer before she goes from this world."

"Shhhh." She tried to calm him. "Tevelgus will prepare food and tomorrow you can return to your army if you wish, then you can find her and take her life."

They ate their food in near silence, pork cooked over the fire. It tasted good and was washed down by some brew the

Britons had brought with them. Varro was grateful to Brenna as was Decimus especially considering the alternative. Both of them could have been dead when the first stars appeared in the night's sky or worse, cut to pieces and still breathing. Their bodies cut, torn and broken and probably either thrown to the dogs or burned.

As he tried to sleep that night, wrapped in a rough blanket near the fire, images of the day kept returning to him. He could feel the ropes cutting into his wrists and the restraints around his lower legs. That was nothing however, compared to the death that his friend had suffered. They had all known the risks they were taking before they had even set foot on the ships to come to this strange land but nothing in previous campaigns had prepared him for the torture that day.

Varro didn't know what disturbed him more, what had happened to his friend or what would have happened to he and Decimus had Brenna and Tevelgus not rescued them. He had felt that there was something special about Brenna but would never have guessed that she was a leader of her people. As he lay there staring up at the sky, he started to feel the signs of tiredness as his eyes began to feel heavy and for the first time he thought that he would sleep that night.

Lucius and Marcus had watched helplessly as their comrades were dragged through a jeering crowd. They knew they were so close to being with them when the ambush was sprung but had just escaped. They had ridden like demons, only slowing down when they realised they weren't being followed. Catching their breath and after letting horses rest, they had skirted back and round to the ambush point. Following a track up a slope, they could hear the cheers followed by screams of joy from the Britons celebrating the capture of the three men. Fifty paces from the top of an outcrop they tied their horses to branches and slowly edged forward, the noise below getting louder.

From the vantage point they saw the three soldiers kicked and punched to the ground, stripped of their armour and clothing and dragged to a small clearing. A local chieftain pushed himself through the gathered throng and shouted orders then retreated as did the other males, leaving the females with the soldiers.

"What the fuck are those whores doing? What should we do Lucius, we can't just leave them." Marcus whispered edging closer to the lip of the outcrop. Lucius looked down at the scene below and then back at Marcus, "And what should we do Marcus? What would you have us do? We barely escaped with our lives ourselves. There are two of us and there are probably hundreds of them, we wouldn't stand a chance, they'd rip us apart. The best thing we can do is get back to the Legion and report this as soon as possible, get help."

However as they continued to watch the developing scene play out, their friends were stripped naked and backed up to three trees where their hands were tied behind their backs and their feet at ground level. A woman stepped forward shrieking and shouting, motioning to the heavens with her arms outstretched. Marcus could see that she held a knife as she approached Varro. If Marcus had a bow, he could have taken her down from here. He estimated they were only two hundred paces from the men now helpless below. He didn't want to watch but he didn't want to turn his back on the three men either. He clutched his hands repeatedly sweat pouring from his forehead and almost every pore of his body.

"Come on Marcus, I can't watch this." Lucius said getting to his feet.

"I'm not leaving them. They might just tie them up for the night and that would give us a chance to get down there and release them." Marcus said unsheathing his spatha, it wasn't of any practical purpose but it made him feel a little more secure. Lucius walked back to the horses as Marcus continued watching. As the horror continued in the small clearing he saw that the men had left the three soldiers to the fate of the women totally and knew that that was probably a bad thing. Standing behind the females they stood watching, still and impassive as the women built to frenzy in front of them goading and jeering each other on, eventually some sat down as if they were about to watch a normal form of entertainment.

Marcus watched as his friends were tormented. The leading female approached Veranius and gestured at him and the others. Winding up the women around her, she built them into a crescendo and finally slowly thrust the knife into his stomach. The gathered women went wild, he saw Varro furiously struggling to free himself but to no avail. Marcus desperately wanted to close his eyes but he watched disbelievingly as the woman cut the genitals from Veranius's ravaged body and threw them into a fire.

His head jerked back automatically in response as he saw his friends own head fall forward and hang limply, gouts of blood flowing and spurting from his wounds spasmodically. Marcus finally closed his eyes and wished and prayed for them all to be somewhere else other than this barbaric land. He swore vengeance on the woman and many others and if it were physically possible, he would help make it happen.

Then the woman approached Varro, Marcus saw that there was a disturbance from somewhere towards the back of the baying mob. He could see riders talking to the men, gesturing towards the torture that was taking place. Within seconds the riders had dismounted and were pushing their way through the crowds, seemingly oblivious to their complaints and shouts.

Marcus blinked as he recognised Brenna and Tevelgus.

"Lucius," he turned to see where he was, speaking in a low voice, "Lucius get your fucking arse here now, its Brenna and Tevelgus." He got to where Marcus lay just as Varro and Decimus were cut free.

"What the fuck happened to Veranius?" He asked.

"That fucking cunny that Tevelgus is talking with cut his fucking balls off after stabbing him, he must be dead now." He replied.

Lucius gulped down almost choking on his own breath but strained his eyes watching as Brenna walked to Veranius, pushed his unconscious head back and then cut deeply into the artery of his neck.

"Oh my gods that fucking bitch." He whispered the words out. The two men watched as the surviving Romans were cut free entirely and escorted to horses, bungled up and then rode away.

"Where do you think they're taking them?" Lucius asked.

"I don't know but I know one thing," he replied staring at the torturer, "that fucker won't ever kill another Roman soldier ever again, come on."

Later a chill had fallen over the valley where the Britons had tortured their friends, camp fires still flickered below with bodies lying nearby. Nothing moved except the occasional dog wandering around scavenging scraps and leftovers from their meals. An owl hooted somewhere in the distance its call echoing across the small valley.

Slowly Marcus led Lucius down the slope, their swords sheathed their daggers in hand as they moved lower careful not to step on anything that might break or snap and alert the sleeping enemy. Marcus had a rough idea where his prey slept as he got close to the first fire its flames disturbing his vision. They moved very slowly now crouched low, stepping through and round some snoring bodies.

"There!" Marcus whispered pointing. She lay wrapped around a child, two others were close by.

"How the fuck are we going to get her? The bitch is wrapped around that little bastard." He indicated whispering with his dagger.

"Pull the child away Lucius." Marcus instructed.

"You are fucking crazy, you'll get us both killed." Lucius said kneeling down and gently grabbing the child wrists and pulling her away. Marcus got into position around the head of the sleeping barbarian woman and pressed his dagger against her throat. Her eyes opened with a start just as he hit her, knocking her out cold instantly. A few bodies stirred briefly with the sound of the impact but none woke properly. Marcus picked up the head and shoulders whilst Lucius grabbed her feet. Together they left the sleeping bodies behind as quickly as they could, the child was still sleeping, she would never see her mother alive again.

At a safe distance Marcus threw his end of the unconscious woman to the floor, her body span round as Lucius maintained a grip of her ankles, her head colliding with the ground roughly.

"Let go." He said to Lucius, whilst getting some rope.

"What are you going to do?" Marcus didn't answer as he secured her to a tree. When he was satisfied she couldn't move he said, "I vowed vengeance on this cunt and that's what I'll have." He glared at Lucius and he knew that he wouldn't argue. Secured and tied with her back to the tree, Marcus cut her clothing off as she began to stir.

"Where shall we start Lucius?" He said grabbing at her breasts, her nipples hard in the cold night air. Her eyes opened fully as she licked her lips, still bloody from the punch Marcus had delivered. Realisation dawned as she looked at her captures armour and uniforms, she tried to cry out but Marcus grabbed her mouth with his hand and squeezed tightly, his knuckles going white with the pressure. Her eyes bulged not in fear but in pain, defiance etched all over them. Her dark eyes stared out at him with a mixture of terror and hatred.

"She's a feisty fucker this cunny stinking whore eh my friend?" Marcus cut the remaining clothes from her exposing her body totally.

"Just empty the blood from her throat Marcus, we'll gain nothing from torturing her." Lucius said as he walked back to the horses.

"And where would the fun be in that Lucius? This fucking cunt killed our second in command. Not only killed him but ruined his body as well, cutting his cock and balls off in the process. Now correct me if I'm wrong but that deserves a little more than a quick death in seconds as her blood vacates her stinking carcass. No my friend this fuck stick is going to pay for her journey into the afterlife."

Lucius didn't reply but tended to the horses. "She's quite an attractive bush here Lucius." Marcus said pointing to the woman's crotch with his knife, "It's a pity there are no balls to slice off though eh? Never mind I'm sure I can think of something similar, eh my beauty." Her eyes widened as if she understood her fate.

As he said it he brought his dagger up unseen, grabbed her left ear and sliced through from the top instantly cutting down but not fully. She tried to scream as he ripped it clear of her head and threw it straight to the ground.

"Meat?" He offered Lucius. "We could start a fire and have fresh meat for breakfast." He gestured to his mouth as the woman's muffled cries died in the material he wrapped around her mouth.

Before Lucius could gather his thoughts, Marcus had reached up and cut the other ear from her, her head thrashing furiously in a vain attempt to stop him or evade the inevitable, it landed close to the first as he discarded it. Mixed with pain and terror her eyes now showed fury as well as pain.

Lucius looked away. "You see Lucius these Britons will eventually learn that they are inferior to Romans and any act to defy us will pay a heavy price, especially if they torture our men. We'll take at least five for each one they take and eventually even they will learn."

As he said it he thrust upward and cut directly into the left breast. Blood covered the knife immediately and the right hand and arm of Marcus but not as much as the female bore on her stomach and legs, they were covered by dark red running blood. She continually closed and opened her eyes, her muffled cries dying in the gagging cloth.

"Now if I were a Briton, I would probably cut her breasts from her body and pull them over her head before watching her bleed to death. It's lucky for her we are not as primitive as them though eh Lucius? Although we should have brought that child and she could have watched as we cut it to pieces as well. Shame we didn't think of that eh my friend? You," he pointed at the woman as he began to laugh, "are very lucky we are a civilised unlike you."

Unexpectedly Marcus took three quick steps back towards her, dipped his body slightly and then thrust upwards with his right arm leading with the tip of the knife. It penetrated and entered her body easily directly below and between her breasts. He stepped closer as her eyes went hazy and dull and then rolled upward into the back of her head. He thrust more upwards embedding the weapon deeper, his feet gaining purchase on the dusty surface. He worked the knife inside her rib cage, cutting through organs, tissue and sinew as he sliced and mashed the woman to death.

When he was finished Marcus picked up her torn clothing from the ground and wiped her blood from the dagger. He felt no particular satisfaction at the action he had taken but his friend had been avenged and so his conscience was clear.

"Cut the fucker down Lucius, at least you can do that I'm sure." He looked at his comrade not even attempting to hide his contempt. Marcus felt that he had allowed him alone to carry the burden of vengeance. Lucius did as he was instructed, he understood the anger in Marcus and shared it but cared for no more blood that night and wasn't prepared to violate a prisoner even though he had helped to make her one and was therefore ultimately as guilty as Marcus for the nature of her death.

Marcus crouched near a small stream and washed the blood from his hands and arms. "Let's get out of here and back to the Legion, we've got to try and free Varro from that other murdering bitch." They untied the horses, jumped onto them and rode into the night.

Quintus led his own small reconnaissance force further away from the Legion and into the open space appearing before them. The sun had been high in the sky when they had departed the fortified lines of the encampment. It was originally intended to be used for just one night as usual but instead it had now been for many and had become more solidified in its defences. Not quite permanent but not a structure that would be ripped up and abandoned like most all the same. Vespasian had decided instead that this was as good a spot as any to build a fortress of a more permanent nature and so the building had begun the day before in earnest. A century of men would be left to defend the structure which would be much smaller yet better defended using deep revetments, higher walls and watch towers than the larger temporary emplacement.

The Roman war machine knew that it was pointless to march into an area, dominate the ground and destroy the enemy just to walk away without holding the territory they had taken. They had learned to fortify specific areas especially where resistance was strong and their enemies were many. At such places they had mile forts, garrisons built on the edge of the empire, the frontier. They were manned by hardened soldiers used to remote areas and desolate places, men who knew their presence itself would bring attack.

Auxiliaries normally helped make up the numbers in such places and were usually made up of men who were not from the local vicinity. Here however, some of those men were actually Britons who were yet to be drafted into the auxiliary legions properly as most of their neighbouring tribes were yet to be conquered. Those who had agreed to join the Empire, as client Kingdoms were yet to expose themselves to the tribes still fighting Rome. This fact and reduction in numbers gave Vespasian a problem he could ill afford, leaving a full century of battle ready men behind exposed, which meant he was a large quantity of fighters down. An entire century and twenty cavalry were to be left at the new fort from where they would scout the local lands. The Britons were to provide support and knowledge of the area.

Servius had been treated by the *medicus*, doctor after receiving an arrow wound to the upper thigh during the battle a few days before. The injury had been clean and had missed any vital arteries or bone and the medic had assured him there would be no internal bleeding or permanent damage. Padded and strapped up now, every step his horse took was a jolting reminder of the injury but he was glad to be away from the Legion and in the fresh open air of the countryside.

The arrow had somehow flown further and higher than those around it landing within the confines of the well fortified and guarded position, where the reserve cavalry units were waiting to be deployed if necessary. It had sunk into his leg without warning unseen like a burning spike instantly sinking into his flesh. Fortunately its power was dwindling when it fell to the earth and Servius wasn't pinned to his horse as some had been later, nor was his bone shattered.

After reporting to General Vespasian, Quintus and his men had been ordered to link up with Varro who had left the day before. They had been instructed to track the Britons and if possible locate an area ahead of their progress that would be ideal for an ambush and killing ground, in effect, an area where Caratacus and his army would meet their demise and be destroyed. Quintus had given his second in command Servius, the opportunity of staying behind and healing properly but he wouldn't hear of it and was eager to return to active duty as soon as possible.

By noon Quintus had led his men further west, they had stayed within cover wherever possible and now stopped to let the horses feed and get some water at a stream and the men some food. They had found the water where the banks were sandy and only high in a few places so it was ideal for the horses and for the men to relax for a while. Quintus stretched removing his sword and walked into the crystal clear water still wearing his boots, it was cold on his skin.

"Ahhh!" He sighed and then continued walking further in as he said to no-one in particular, "you should try this," His men were already biting into food or drinking from their water sacks. "We'll take a few moments then keep going."

A sudden burst of movement somewhere further up the stream had the men rushing and diving for their weapons, Servius grabbed his spears and took up a stance ready to throw as horses and riders quickly came into view. They were Britons, confirmed by the appearance of chariots behind the single horses. Scrambling out of the water Quintus slid his spatha from its sheath, there was no time to get on the horses and get away. Servius ran forward, limping slightly and hurled his pilum into the air, ripping his arm forward up and over with almost unnatural speed, the weapon flew towards the enemy.

"Stop. Stop." A voice called out in his own tongue from somewhere within the group now advancing on them with terrifying speed.

"Fuck!" Shouted Quintus as he watched the spear, cut the air through the riders, it thumped into a tree behind them, buried inches deep.

"Quintus, it's me Varro, stand down." Shouted one of the riders somewhere towards the rear as the horses got closer and began to come to a halt spraying sand up at the waiting men who were standing swords ready.

"Gods teeth Varro what happened to you where's your armour, your uniform and weapons?" Quintus saw that he and Decimus were dressed like locals. "Where are the others, where's Veranius, Marcus and Lucius?"

Varro jumped from his horse splashing water and saw that Quintus was stood with his weapon pointing at Tevelgus.

"Stand down they're friends." He grabbed the spatha and lowered it. Quintus satisfied that these Britons were no threat sheathed his sword as did the others. Servius limped back to his horse and returned his second javelin.

"I'm glad you're throwing hasn't improved any." Varro said with a smile. Servius pointed to the leg wound, "You're lucky I'm wounded commander, it slowed me down and made my throw less accurate. If I hadn't been punctured by an arrow a few days ago, your blood or that of your friends would be mingling with the water in the stream."

Varro smirked and clapped Servius on the shoulder, "I for one am glad of your injury my friend. After the few days we've just been through, the last thing I need is a Roman spear through my belly." Quintus looked at the centurion his expression questioning.

"My friend, and yours Veranius, has gone to the next world." Varro felt anguish and sadness as he spoke these words, it still didn't seem real. Quintus couldn't believe the words and literally staggered back a few feet with their force

"What? How, how did it happen? It can't be true, he survived years campaigning through Gaul, survived the Germanic tribes and black forests, what happened?"

"I'm afraid it's true Quintus, we were ambushed, captured and tortured. Veranius died before Brenna and her brother Tevelgus could come to our aid. Quintus looked at the large barbarian and the female they were quite striking for locals and not the normal barbarian pig faced bastards he had been unfortunate enough to come into close contact with before. He knew these Britons like most others were descended from Celtic tribes that came from the mountains near Rome and now called themselves Britons. These however looked bigger, stronger and better looking than the usual limed faced primitives he'd seen before.

"I am Tevelgus and this is my sister Brenna we are of the Cantiaci." The large male announced with a thick accent leaping from his horse. Quintus saw he stood at least a head taller than Varro and was just as wide. Most Britons like all barbarians were taller than their Roman counterparts but thin and bug ugly but this fellow was especially large in all areas. His sister was remarkably stunning and both had darker hair and skin than most he was familiar with.

"Our tribe rule this land by the sea but many of our people have been persuaded to carry the sword and spear to your forces by Caratacus." She said to Quintus her Latin good but heavily accented. Her bare arms were well muscled and Quintus assumed she had been trained as a warrior as most females in this strange and foreboding land.

"If you rule this land why can't you control your people?" Quintus asked walking to the stream and cupping his hands to gather water to splash his onto face.

"People are led here in this land but they cannot be ruled or bent like bronze Quintus." She replied taking in his uniform.

"They saved us from a baying mob Quintus, if they could have stopped the others I'm sure they would have. If it wasn't for them Decimus and I would have been put to death as well. You can trust them my friend as I do believe me."

Quintus seemed to relax a little and took in how the Britons were dressed and their weapons. Tevelgus and Brenna must have been quite high ranking as they both carried long swords and small round shields, he knew most only used the spear as a primary weapon. Tevelgus's sword handle glistened with colourful stones and Quintus saw detailed inscriptions engraved into the handle but could not decipher the meaning.

The other Britons he noticed although large of build carried the customary spears but no swords. They eyed Quintus with suspicion as he did them. They wore no garments on their upper bodies, their muscles defined by sweat and the blue war paint they extracted from local plants called woad. The Britons believed that by dying their hair with lime it not only protected them as the hair itself became very stiff and hard and therefore negated the need for a helmet but it was also a sign of respect for Epona their horse Goddess. Their belief was that when their hair was limed they looked like they had a flowing main of a horse. The drawback from such tradition was that the chemical within the liquid of the plant eventually made their hair fall out and it never grew back.

Bald warriors were looked upon with respect and merely applied woad to their scalps as well as their arms and upper bodies. They were deemed to have served their time as warriors but most remained active and had generally risen through the ranks of local tribes.

Tevelgus and Brenna however, had full heads of hair and with the lime they appeared even larger. Quintus tried not to stare at Brenna's rounded breasts that she or someone else had covered in swirling woad curves, they accentuated her figure even more and they were already more than appealing he thought. She like her brother and the others wore long pants down to their ankles and leather sandals over their feet, almost Roman like in their appearance.

"We're ordered to scout Caratacus and find a suitable place for ambush. The General wants his army destroyed as soon as possible." Quintus reported to Varro.

"I'm certain he does," he replied, "but it won't be easy. Now that he's had his teeth smashed he won't make the same mistake again if he can help it. He hasn't ruled his own tribe with his brother for these years without being tactically aware of that I'm sure."

Quintus studied one of the Britons chariots, the workmanship was quite remarkable. Pictures of horses had been carved into the wood and intricate Celtic designs decorated the wheels, swirling in concentric interlocking patterns.

"We stopped using chariots a long time ago Tevelgus." Quintus remarked. "Why do you still use them?"

Tevelgus walked to the horses at the front of the chariots and unhooked them leading them to the water. "Some of my people worship the horse Goddess Epona, she is said to give the warriors power and speed. The people cannot show their love for the Goddess without a chariot on which to carve their pictures." He pointed out the detailed carvings. "With a chariot you have the power of two animals not just one and with a chariot you can carry more than one warrior into battle. In here," he indicated to the chariot itself, "two or more warriors can travel as well as those on the backs of the horses themselves. From these positions, spears can be thrown at the enemy before they are engaged on foot and many spears can be carried not just two." He pointed to his horse. "Men can be moved to positions around an area of conflict very quickly and sometimes can even prevent it altogether if the enemy sees that they are at a tactical disadvantage." The big Briton smiled. "We can also carry more food and water, so you see, our chariots are very useful."

"It makes you wonder why we don't use them still if they're so valuable." Quintus said still admiring the artwork on the side of the chariot.

"We don't use them because we don't need them." Varro said. "But that's only because we have the manpower to get round it. Our cavalry make up the speed in battle, our columns make up the numbers tenfold on the battlefield and our wagons and horses, mules and oxen carry the other equipment needed. It comes down to what you have I suppose and what you're used to having, I can see advantages to both. Besides I trust Staro here," he said giving his horse a pat on the nose, "if he was rigged up to another horse, I don't know how he would behave."

Tevelgus said, "Our horses are trained from an early age to pull the chariots. Children are given small versions to break them in when they are young so they are used to them at a very early age." He saw Quintus admiring the art work on the wood of the chariot. He pointed to the swirling patterns carved into the wood. "They are never-ending circles that represent life, a very important symbol for us."

As the group settled down to rest, Varro and Quintus decided on a plan of action. Varro and Decimus had to get new equipment and they could only find that with the Legion and hopefully at the same time they would find Marcus and Lucius. Quintus and his men would scout forward and try to find a good ambush point for Caratacus.

Brenna brought them food and together the two groups rested while the horses paddled in the stream and fed on the lush, rich grass at the side of the water.

"Caratacus was still heading west when we last saw him and his army. In another two or three day's he will be at the Regini land far to the west." Brenna began, "I cannot say how the Regini will react. They may try to repel Caratacus or they may join with him. He could double his strength in a matter of days and I'm sure he will have already sent riders ahead to talk to them. You could be facing far more warriors than you or your General ever expected very soon."

"That maybe the case but I'm sure he knows what he's doing. In Gaul we faced five to one enemies, sometimes six and still we were victorious. It maybe that Vespasian would actually welcome an alliance between Caratacus and other tribal leaders. They would be bolder with greater numbers and throw themselves at the shields and spears of the Legions with greater abandon. Your warriors have the bravery of any we have ever faced in battle but their bravery is also their downfall, their tactics are old and not well thought out. Hurling the bravest man at a pointed sharpened blade is foolhardy at best and stupid at worst and a tragic waste of life. I wish I had ten Legions of Britons, trained and schooled in our ways, with them I could conquer the entire world."

Brenna regarded him with an expression approaching disdain, it was the first time he had experienced such a feeling, "Why war Varro, why killing? Is there not a different way for such an enlightened people like yours to exist and co-exist with others? Can't there be another way for those who have taken so much from the Greeks?"

Varro regarded her with an expression she had never seen before and responded angrily, "The Greeks are nothing more than subservient boy fuckers Brenna. They like nothing more than to shag twelve year olds and then stare at the night sky. The only true warriors that place ever spawned were Spartans and look what Greece did to them after they had saved them from invading Saracens."

She stared at him, "Whilst I'm not sure of their sexual preferences Varro and nor do I know what their country did to them eventually, I did not mean anything detrimental to you or yours. I merely wish to exist in peace and for those around me to do so."

"Your naivety surprises me sometimes Brenna. With so many warring tribes even in your own country I'm amazed that you're still alive." He checked the war axe that Tevelgus had given him. He continued, "I'm sorry too it's hard to have a different opinion of others when all you have known is war. There are people out there that will slit your throat without even blinking and take your animals and children and use them as they choose. I would love to live in this world you see believe me, we all would but that's another reason why we do what we do. One day our children or our children's children will live in that world and all this death will have been worthwhile."

She smiled, "When that day comes, we will have all reached a level where we deserve to live in peace. I just hope your right and that the day you speak of comes soon."

The group rested and ate together before moving off in separate directions, Quintus to the west with his men scouting for Caratacus and a possible ambush site and Varro towards the safety of the second Legion and replacement weapons and armour. Varro realised that it had actually been tranquil near the stream with the relaxing trickle of the water and the sound of birds in the trees and surrounding area and wondered when he would feel like that again.

Chapter Eight

The sun was descending in the sky by the time Varro and his small party reached the outer defences and sentries of the Second Augusta. After a difficult approach made almost deadly by their local clothing an Optio had them escorted into the inner defences and past the palisades. Now the rest of the group were fed and watered as Varro briefed the senior officers and introduced Brenna and Tevelgus. They briefed them about their recent experiences and the Britons were questioned about the local lands and people. As they returned to the others he saw that Marcus and Lucius had found them.

"Marcus, Lucius," the smile on his face unable to hide his relief that they were safe. He clasped they're arms but sensed something from them, "What, what is it?"

Lucius replied, "We got the bitch that killed Veranius." He looked at Marcus, "Marcus made sure that she will never hold a knife to another soldier ever again."

Marcus made no comment, there was merely a cold look of satisfaction in his eyes that meant that he didn't have to say a word. Varro knew that she would have been made to suffer as she went to the next life and that was all he could ask. He looked at Brenna her expression also requiring no words. There wasn't any sign of sympathy for the dead woman, she turned and saw to the horses

They shared some watered wine and food, fresh bread and olives and sat watching the flames of the fire one of the men had started. Varro had known that the invasion of Britannia would prove hard but it was only now that he was beginning to realise just what price they were going to have to pay to conquer this land. They had only been on the shores a few days and already hundreds of dead heroic citizens were fertilising the soil beneath their boots. It was going to be a long campaign as the months stretched into years and maybe even decades but it was the way of things for a centurion and all the Legions who had come here, it was their life, it was how he and they lived

Brenna saw the worry and concern in his eyes but knew that words alone wouldn't help. She realised that she wanted to wrap herself around him, remove his clothing, wash his body and lose herself in their combined sensuality but now was not the time or the place. As dawn broke, the smell and crackle of the much reduced fire woke Varro. He was surprised to find Brenna lying next to him, her big brother still sleeping nearby. He sat up looking around as the Legion began to come to life all around.

Soldiers were returning from guard duty or swapping over duties laughing and joking with their counterparts. Breakfast was being cooked as the smell of cooking meat and bread wafted over to him. Horses were being fed and shod, blacksmiths hammers sounded and the more lively horses were whinnying in the distance. Weapons were being sharpened and oiled, men were briefed in small groups and patrols mounted and the sun wasn't even properly above the horizon.

An hour later wearing new armour and carrying replacement weapons Varro and his small group rode out of camp. He gently kicked at his horse whilst acknowledging a guard who saluted as he rode passed. The guard watched as they cantered away wondering where they were going in this hostile land away from the safety of the Legion and said a silent prayer to the gods in thanks that it wasn't him going into the wilderness and for their protection.

Some hours later they began to see familiar land marks.

"I suggest we go to my settlement. We can get some help and bolster our numbers and then go and find Caratacus." Brenna said. Varro nodded in agreement as they trotted forward to an area where visibility was being to beginning to fade.

Eerily through the mist and fog, very slowly, high manmade embankments began to emerge. Further up, high up there on the hill, the upper parts of trees could be made out.

The soldiers stood in their columns staring up at the emplacement some three hundred feet above them. It was the first such fortified encampment the Second Augusta had found since crossing the sea and it filled some of the less experienced with dread. The builders of this settlement had used the natural isolated hill as it dominated the land around and it made a perfect home for its inhabitants.

The Britons had obviously constructed this hill fort sometime in the past, probably to fend off neighbouring tribes. They had made the best use of natural resources and defences building it so high using height, trees and the earth itself, that had been dug out from the surrounding hillside and then built up to make high steep walls. Large trenches had been dug out of the hillside circling around the large prominence and the excess material had been used to build up the large mud packed walls slightly further up. It made the fortification easily defendable and an extremely hard emplacement to attack. That thought was now going through the minds of thousands of assembled soldiers gathered below its slopes.

Only two entrances or exits had been found at opposite sides of the hill fort with clearly defined tracks leading to both. Wagons had worn paths down the hill and in through the woods below. It would prove a difficult target where the defenders had every advantage. The Romans could choose to siege the fort and go round and continue their advance west but that wasn't their way and so the army began to dig in and make preparations to assault the site. Early reconnaissance had suggested that there were over fifty dwelling houses inside which could mean over five hundred warriors armed and prepared to fight to the death to defend their families and land.

Once in a while a horse could be heard from inside the fort along with other animals as smoke from various fires reached for the blue skies from within, so far it had been the only evidence of habitation. The mist now barley clung to the trees as it had since the area was first discovered three days before by Varro and his small group. Brenna had gone forward and had tried to persuade the inhabitants to talk to the Romans but they had refused and threatened to hang her from the nearest tree, her influence had no sway this far west. She watched now some hundreds of feet away and wondered at the hill forts fate. The Legions strength could not be denied but the natural advantage here was with her fellow country men and women.

As tactics of the attack were finalised by Vespasian and his officers, an iron fist enclosed the huge hillside. Roman forces had now encircled the area completely and the defiant Britons were alone, cut off from any help or rescue. Vespasian knew the chance of anyone coming to their aid was remote because of their tribal nature and had taken his time preparing for the inevitable attack. Neighbouring areas were at best lived with side by side at worst bitter enemies although some alliances were not to be ruled out entirely. He thought they were too primitive to organise themselves properly but hill forts like the one towering above them, proved a different threat.

All around him the instruments of war were dragged, towed and pulled into place as men and horses toiled. Varro stood nearby and saw the gathered officers talking and pointing up to the hill. He felt his stomach lurch as he contemplated the days ahead and looked around him wondering who of those he saw would still be breathing in two or three days' time. In comparison to recent battles in Gaul this would be a minor skirmish but it was like a boil and it had to be lanced.

Heavy infantry troops were briefed in their columns, as were the light, archers and artillery crews and even the equestrian, the Britons surely didn't stand a chance he concluded so why fight and die, would he if he were on the opposite side? He thought that he probably would if men from a foreign land had come and threatened his way of life. Men, women, children and livestock were about to die and be erased from the earth because their leaders had chosen to fight. The encased Britons had been given three opportunities to surrender and had turned all of them down and so now the butchers prepared their tools before the bill could be paid.

The enemy's leader a tribal chieftain called Cavaltergex had spat in the face of Brenna as she begged him to leave the fort to speak to Vespasian. He had called her a diseased whore and vessel of the invader who would pay dearly for her treachery. These Britons were stubborn but proud and now it was time to start beginning to test their determination to resist.

Brenna had still tried everything from begging and pleading to giving calm reassurance that Cavaltergex and his people would be treated well and allowed to live their lives as they had always done but it had all failed and fallen on deaf ears. He would not submit to the men below in their gleaming metal armour and so had sealed his own fate and that of all he knew. The assault would begin as soon as the sun was high in the sky the next day. Cavaltergex was breathing his last breaths and was already dead, he just didn't know it. To defy Rome was to die and be obliterated and join others who had fallen before them, these Britons would enjoy the same end.

The following morning the sky was clear, remnants of fog clung to the trees above the soldiers but it was the clearest day since they had arrived. With the defences more distinct Varro could see that the Britons had used tree trunks bound together with vines and some other material beyond the mud banks. Rows of spiked walls could be seen as the upper lengths of trees could be observed clearly now. Dark shaded bodies moved between the small gaps in between the wooden walls indistinct from this distance, the defenders waiting for the attack to begin. Several billows of smoke rose into the air from somewhere above and a dog started to bark as if sensing what was to come.

A trumpet sounded, it was followed almost immediately by the vicious sound of the gathered ballista releasing their huge bolts. Like a row of giant graceful sleek birds they rose towards the hill fort hurtling with startling speed to their target and within seconds found their mark. Most embedded themselves into the wooden fortifications, some falling short and vanishing into the mud embankments buried deep, a few hit flesh as they seared through the gaps in the wood as screams were heard from within. Frantic cries followed and shouting as the Britons experienced something even their wildest nightmares couldn't have foreseen, Roman warfare. Chunks of wood and giant splinters were thrown into the air exploding as the large arrows found targets a few of the forts walled logs were cleaved in two and gaps began to appear in their ranks.

Vespasian had ordered that the ballista continue firing until clear entry points were visible in the forts defences. After a time archers were brought forward about one hundred and fifty paces and joined in the murderous hail of fire, raining arrows up into the air to fall down on the inhabitants inside. More cries and screams of pain escaped the large compound above, the Britons were learning and learning well their mistake of defiance.

Varro watched on from the side lines as the ballista bolts took their toll. He and his party had found the hill fort a few days before and Brenna had tried her best to persuade her countrymen to yield to the advancing army. Two days from now they would ride out again after a well-deserved rest while Quintus and his men rode ahead. In the meantime he watched as the artillery teams toiled to launch their missiles, cranking tight their torsion machines, metal scraped against metal, men heaved and the large arrows loosed and whined as they sped into the air. They were making short work of the wooden walls.

Heavy infantry now took up their shields and began to move slowly forwards, a centurion signalling for his men to form a *testudo*, tortoise formation. The men lofted their big shields, those at the front hoisting them to cover their bodies at the front, those inside the column, raised them above their heads and those on the sides covered any attacks from ground level. As the shields overlapped the centurion vanished into a gap left open in the wall facing Varro and disappeared to give orders on the march, his red converse plume he saw intermittently amongst the shields and was distinct amongst the other helmets.

They didn't have to wait long for a response from inside the fort as arrows began to fall, first into the attacking archers and ballista crews, who retreated backwards out of range and then onto the advancing column. Vespasian mounted on his horse ordered another column of heavy infantry forward pointing and waving with his sword to a trumpeter who sounded the advance. The arrows of the defenders landed heavily thumping into the shields of the advancing column assisted by gravity as they swiftly returned to earth. No obvious injuries were visible yet but any screams were drowned out by the rising sound of battle. As the first heavy infantry formed into the testudo and began to pass the area where their archers had been positioned, the shower of arrows became heavier. A horn suddenly broke the sounds of battle as a length of the hill forts defensive wall fell inward. Dust was thrown up as a result from the surface masking exactly what had happened but the infantry continued slowly forward now fully on the steep slope, small steps eating the up the ground between them and the enemy.

Varro saw a large Briton appear at the side of the gap in the wall as the dust began to settle and clear. He hefted a large sword above his head and shouted something unheard at the advancing Romans. He wore scruffy looking plaid trousers and no clothing over his upper body, his skin was covered in blue woad enhancing a muscular upper frame. Long grey hair was tied at the back and swung about as he gestured down the hill. He suddenly ducked and moved to the left as a large ballista bolt flew by that was aimed directly at him, he laughed and raised his sword shaking it at his enemy. Placing the hilt at his crotch, he aimed the blade as his attackers and simulated fucking them

The second testudo was now on the base of the hillside and moving upwards as it began to take arrows to the front and above, the first already looked like a large advancing hedgehog with dozens of arrows embedded into its shields. Ballista bolts continued to fly over the advancing men as the attack was pushed forward, dust rose from the earth from their shuffling hobnail boots. As the first line of men in the original square got to within fifty paces of the now gesturing Briton, he turned and waved for something to come forward from within the settlement. Varro strained to see what was happening and stood up straighter but couldn't see clearly as the advancing troops blocked his view.

He suddenly heard shouting from above and saw Roman shields thrown into the air and men at the side of the square breaking away from the testudo and then turn and run back down the hill. He was shocked as he hadn't expected anything other than a quick assault on the relatively small hill fort. Men in the first square however, were now shouting, panicking and fully turning to retreat. Shields were thrown and abandoned as panic set in and the former square was rapidly reduced to a rabble.

As the men in the rear ranks jumped or turned to run, Varro saw what had happened. The Britons had rolled large logs into the advancing testudo knocking them over and backwards into the ranks behind sweeping the front rows of the shield wall aside. Their archers had then turned their full attention on the soldiers nearest to them and as they began to find their targets, more heavy infantry began to fall.

Injuries or loss of life was always expected in engagements of this nature but it was always a surprise when it happened especially when facing barbarians like this who were presumed to have had little tactical awareness. As the soldiers raced back down the hillside they tried to avoid the second testudo as it had now halted and had dug its shields into the ground. More Britons ran outside the hill fort and took up positions with bows and picked off the men further forward of the Roman line. Varro saw they were targeting legs in order to disable them and bring them down.

More Britons flooded out armed with spears that they hurled into the air at the retreating men. The first attack was quickly turning into disarray and more injured lay on the ground screaming in agony on the bloody hill. As the first of the rolling logs now crashed into the second testudo, it held firm but it now began to take more arrows to the front and above. The men formed up in tight ranks inside the testudo, huddled together their shields interlocked. Men from the first wave ran past them some who still had their shields tried to hold them over their backs as arrows fell.

Some of the Britons now ran forward and attacked the men who were injured, some with legs broken by the heavy rolling logs, unable to move. More screams broke the air as the Britons stabbed and slashed at the prone men already injured on the ground. Varro saw the enemy desperately searching for gaps between his comrades armour as they lay helpless on the slope, screams revealed they had found the flesh below. Where they couldn't stab deep inside the invaders flesh they ripped away the armour and found their mark or chopped at their exposed faces. The second testudo could do nothing to help or it to would start to take casualties in the same fashion, all it could was hold firm for the time being.

Shouted orders could be heard from inside the second square as it slowly began to retreat backwards. The front rank had embedded their shields into the soft earth where they left them forming a wedge between their formation and the logs as they moved away. Shields were passed forward from the rear to cover what had been the front line.

The injured troops near the top of the hill were butchered where they lay all except three who were dragged inside the fortification screaming and kicking as best they could. As soon as they disappeared from sight the wall that Varro thought had fallen down was pulled and dragged back into place and the wooden wall was whole again except for where the ballista bolts had punched holes. Where those bolts had obliterated logs and parts of the fort, the Britons worked furiously from inside to repair or replace them or cover the damage.

Vespasian shouted orders and the blast of a horn resulted in the second testudo halting and digging in where it stood, it was still within range of the missiles from above. The already retreating men reached the safety of their own lines where an Optio barked orders for the injured to get treatment from the medicus and his orderlies at the rear. Slingers ran forward and took up a position behind the remaining testudo. Vespasian's face red with rage, barked more orders, he was clearly determined to defeat the defenders above no matter what the cost.

Another horn ordered cavalry forward from somewhere in the woods, the horses cantered behind the existing testudo and slingers out of range of the falling arrows. As the ballista began to fire again, their bolts rattling forward into the air, the men already on the slope formed up in the tortoise formation began to advance once more, the slingers prepared their weapons. A direct hit from an accurate missile could kill a man as easily as an arrow or pila.

"Your general is determined to crush the settlement and isn't afraid to lose valuable men in the process it seems, surely he could just retreat?" Brenna said pulling Varro out of his concentration on the battle.

He turned to look at her, "He can't afford to do that, we can't afford to do that. Any backward step would be seen as a sign of weakness, any weakness isn't something the General does."

They watched as the formation of shield covered soldiers continued up the hill, waiting for the inevitable counter attack from those inside, they didn't have to wait long. As the testudo got to within a hundred paces the Britons appeared again and rained arrows and spears into the shields. The tempo picked up from the artillery as the ballista bolts intensified and hammered the un-armoured defenders outside the fort. Bodies stood launching arrows one second at the advancing men who were instantly propelled backwards in the blink of an eye. Some were blown and ripped backwards and vanished from sight instantly as others were pinned to the wooden walls behind them taking more with them who were unfortunate to be stood behind. The bolts even at this range, were so powerful that some passed through bodies before their victims were even aware of their injuries. Shock registered seconds later as they fell to the ground dead.

Light infantry now began the march upwards to the right as the cavalry readied themselves to join the fray from the left. More legionary archers launched their deadly volley from behind them and the skies darkened in front of the testudo as the arrows fell to their targets. Despite the barrage the Britons continued to spill out of the settlement whilst others fought in vain to repair the hill fort walls that were now succumbing to the torrent of iron hitting and shattering their timber.

Another cohort of cavalry galloped away from inside the woods, skirting around the base of the hill to support an attack elsewhere moving off to the left. The Second Legion was now throwing everything at the fort and there would be no escape for the brave natives holed up inside. As the cohort disappeared from view, astonishingly a group of Britons ran out of the front of the settlement hurling spears at the testudo now only feet from the former entrance. The first cavalry cohort galloped up in support followed by the light infantry running and struggling to keep up. Neither got to the Britons before they launched themselves onto the shields of the now dug in Roman square, who were hunched behind their overlapping shields taking cover from the onslaught. The natives were wild eyed and screaming as they tore at the shield wall trying to find its soft underbelly to stab. Sword points were thrust out at them, when they managed to force an opening wounding the attacker's hands, arms and legs. Screams of agony filled the air as furious Britons stood their ground seemingly impervious to their wounds.

In the blink of an eye the cavalry closed on the natives and unleashed their short spears throwing them at a closer range than they were used to because of the gradient of the hill. As they started to take their toll, the horses were amongst the enemy, their rider's long swords slashing and gouging at flesh and felling the enemy like wheat. A few of the defenders tried to turn and run as the men inside the testudo leapt out from their positions and joined the battle, engaging them with their short swords. The natives were trapped between them and a wall of horses as they began to meet their end.

A small group of about ten men managed to break free of the melee including Cavaltergex. They fought as they ran but didn't get far as spears and arrows cut their numbers down quickly. Cavaltergex wasn't the last to die but he fought like a lion until he was cut down by a series of blows to his head and torso from three legionaries. As the chopping and slashing began to slow and the screams began to fade, the light infantry ran past the bloody carnage straight into the ravaged fort to complete the obliteration of the enemy.

"Brenna turned to Varro once more, "Will they spare the women and children?"

He turned and walked away from her replying, "Anything that lived in there before the battle won't be alive by nightfall."

Angrily she followed him, "Is that any way to win peace, to kill women and children? What does your General hope to achieve by this?"

"It's the way of things, it's how it is. If they had surrendered when they had the chance, they would have been allowed to live but they attacked our soldiers. We have to teach these tribes that they cannot fight or defy us and get away with it, they have to be destroyed."

She grabbed his arm and he stopped and stared at her with a cold angry expression but he saw the pain in her eyes.

"I'm sorry Brenna that's the way of things." She let go and allowed him walk away.

As darkness started to fall, the former hill fort had already started to be transformed by the men of the Second. Bodies of the dead had been removed, the roundhouses burned to the ground and now a small military fort was already beginning to take shape. The three wounded men that had been taken into the settlement were found mutilated and stabbed to death. By the next night the defences would be up and the base would be better fortified than what had stood there before. The attack on the hill fort had come at a cost however, twenty three had died and twice that many were injured, at least five more weren't expected to make it through the night.

Later Varro and his small group were on their own sat round a fire eating mutton, with victory came the spoils of war and the legion would eat well tonight. Brenna had said very little since learning that that her countrymen, women and children would be cut down for daring to defy the invaders.

"Come, walk with me." She said standing and holding out her hand. Varro stood wiping his mouth with his forearm as the others watched. They walked further into the trees away from the sprawling fires of the army camped behind them.

"Where are we going?" He asked as she squeezed his hand, "I want to give you something." She said smiling.

He frowned, "I don't understand."

"You'll see soon enough" They walked until the camp fires were barley visible through the trees, a strong smell of fir in the air. She walked to a large oak tree and turned to face him, pulling him closer reaching between his legs as she kissed him.

"Oh I see." He said smiling and returning her kiss.

Sometime later they lay wrapped around each other still sweating from their exertions, their clothing was discarded all around them.

"How many days will it take the army to get to the west coast do you think?" She asked. He thought for a moment, "If today is anything to go by, I don't know. I don't think the general expected this much resistance. If we have to fight our way to the coast it could take months, maybe years. We'll know better after we ride out again and find out what lies ahead of us." His hand brushed up and down her naked back as he spoke, he felt himself getting aroused again.

"Let's not waste our time together." He pulled her up onto him grinning as they kissed again, unaware of hidden eyes watching them from some thick bushes some distance away. Eventually the watching men quietly moved off having learned how the invaders attacked the fort.

Sometime later Varro lay on his back wearing just his loin cloth, Brenna massaging his temples. "It won't always be this way, will it?" She asked.

He looked up at her, "It will for the foreseeable future, blood, death and battle, that's what the immediate future holds anyway."

"It won't be forever and it doesn't have to be that way."

He looked at her curiously and grinned, "I wish you were right but the General has his orders and after losing so many men today he'll be more cautious next time and will launch more carefully co-ordinated attacks."

She looked at the night sky where stars sparkled like jewels in the black night. Her feelings for this man were growing stronger, she felt that he wasn't just a barbaric killer as some of his comrades were, there was more to him. If only they had met under different circumstances she thought as sleep began to take her.

Chapter Nine

The next morning the sun rose casting a warm blanket of air over the earth. As Varro opened his eyes he was suddenly aware of being watched. As his adrenalin started to build and his heart race, Brenna placed a calming hand on his shoulder as he began to rise.

"Shhhhhh. It's okay, everything is fine." She smiled at him as he started to relax and lay back down.

"What were you doing?" He asked suddenly aware that his sword and dagger were not even in arms reach, as they would have been last night. They had been moved and put with his uniform, women he thought to himself 'always moving things with no idea of the consequences.'

"I was watching you sleep. Without your armour and weapons I can see you much more clearly, how you should be." She said.

He frowned obviously confused. Maybe disarming a man and leaving him open to attack enabled a better view of his unprotected skin. He looked down at his body and felt himself stirring again.

Brenna smiled, "I don't mean like that." She said as she stroked his chest and then sat back, he looked disappointed.

"I mean looking at you at your aura and who you really are, your journey and where you're going, what kind of man you really are." She tried to explain.

He looked confused. "And what kind of man am I really do you think?"

"Kind, loyal, you always try to do the right thing. Our teachings tell us how to read these things, how to translate auras and see what they mean."

He raised his eyebrows, "Do you mean like a soothsayer or druid?" He sat up on an elbow. "Is that what you mean? We have many soothsayers at home. Many people that believe they can see the future and can tell what the gods have in store for us. Nobles and common folk alike use them, it's a good living I'm told, they even sacrifice animals and read their organs, have stalls in the markets and in the shops near forums. Obviously there's no proof to what they say and by the time the things they predict either happen or don't they are long gone. Rarely do they hang around once they've been paid."

Brenna smiled, "I'm surprised that you say this. Romans accept these practices at home and yet they try to destroy them here and in Gaul. Most soothsayers as you call them move from place to place because of the suspicions they evoke. Just like you did then you don't trust in them, yet you pray to unseen gods."

The frown returned to his face but before he could respond she continued, "Lay back and relax, let me show you it's true and not made up to get money and then you can make your own mind up."

He did as he was told and Brenna moved around to his head kneeling with her knees either side and started to massage his temples, he began to relax almost straight away.

"Listen to the sounds around you, the mild breeze, the birds singing in the trees and the water of the stream nearby." Her voice softened as she spoke. They were far enough away from the Legion not to hear anything from that direction and so he let his senses become absorbed by his surroundings. Varro felt his troubles ease as Brenna's hands moved to his neck and shoulders.

"Just relax, lay back and allow all your worries to float away. I'm going push all the stress in your body out through your hands and feet." He lay still not moving enjoying the feeling of his muscles being manipulated. Brenna started to use her nails gently, lines following the curves of his flesh covering the muscle, as she brushed a nipple he smiled lightly.

"Relax." She ordered mildly, "There will be time enough for that later." He took a deep breath and exhaled leaving himself fully under her control, as her hands moved across his skin her voice lowered more.

"Feel yourself relaxing deeper as your muscles and bones relax. I'm going to push outward from your middle moving the strains and stresses to you limbs. See it in your mind like a small cloud as it moves from around your heart as I cleanse your organs and body."

Fully relaxed now, he did as she said barely clinging to consciousness seeing in his mind's eye a small cavity where the cloud was being pushed, dragged and persuaded to the sides clearing it of harmful elements. Satisfied that she had completed his trunk she moved to his limbs starting with his arms that tingled when she got to the hands. As he lay there his inner vision saw his body and now arms starting to clear as she worked her 'magic.' He didn't know what she hoped to achieve by this but no longer cared as he moved deeper into a relaxed state that he hadn't experienced before. He could see things clearly mentally but his eyes were closed and now he was aware his hearing was beginning to reduce, bird noise was no longer audible and the sound of the breeze in the trees started to disappear.

"In your mind's eye you can see a wall in front of you. In the wall is a door, a large wooden door, I want you to approach the door and stop beside it." As he 'moved' without walking he saw the door, previously unseen getting closer. It had a large round black handle.

"Reach out and take the handle and open the door." Brenna instructed and he did, seeing his arm reach out and his hand take the handle. She saw his expression change slightly as he mentally saw what she was saying.

"Turn the handle and push the door open slowly and see the steps going down beyond."

He could see numerous large sandstone steps through the door, light and sandy in colour, he moved towards them stopping at the top.

"As you take each step you will go deeper into your relaxed state. Each step will be taken very slowly, there's no rush. You can't see what's below but at the bottom you will find another door set into another wall. This wall surrounds a beautiful garden like the one you told me about from your childhood. Statues of beautiful men and women naked line the path beyond."

She was now massaging his lower ribs but he was barely aware of her touch anymore. As she asked him to move, he took a step down and could actually feel the coolness of the stone on his feet, it almost made him shiver briefly. Slowly guiding him down with her voice, he moved lower until eventually he stood below the bottom step. The ground was cooler to the touch of his feet, a worn path maybe. He stood almost floating at the door in the second wall, the air was now colder here and a little shaded. At her prompt he opened the door.

"The garden is warm and bathed in sunshine, you can feel it warming your skin." She said as if somehow making it happen. He walked forward, the grass was short and he could see various flowers of many different colours and varieties, reds, yellows, greens, purples and more than he could separate in his mind and be aware of as he tried to take everything in. As he moved forward he saw the statues lining the path in front of him, worn from feet treading the way before.

The marble slabs shone and reflected the sun brightly back into his eyes, the fact that his physical eyes weren't able to actually see what his other senses were aware of seemed irrelevant now.

"Move along the path." She instructed from somewhere distant. He barely heard the voice now and was totally unaware of the contact of her hands on his body. He was elsewhere submerged in another plain, another place. He took in the intricate details of the statues, the stone masons that worked them must have been masters of their craft. As he got to somewhere near the middle of the path he saw water beyond, a lake maybe. Tied up on the shore were small boats dug out from tree trunks, they were long and thin.

"Continue slowly forward and choose a boat to get to the other side." He heard her whisper.

Unquestioning, without thought or reason why, he reached the boats and chose which one would take him across the water.

"On the far shore amongst the trees you will see various paths, choose a path and make your way towards it and go into the woods beyond."

As he walked he reached out with his arm feeling a female statue. His hand caressed her smooth cool flat stomach, he resisted the temptation to cup her pert beautiful breast. Walking slowly past he looked down at the boats, choosing the one he had seen near the middle, he untied the rope securing it to a stump. He looked around taking in the serenity of the moment. Without further thought he pushed the boat further out into the crystal clear lake feeling the cold water surround his legs and then climbed aboard, it wobbled but didn't threaten to tip over. Taking a small oar he found in the base he rowed away from the shore slowly.

On the other side trees of different types studded the shore in dense formations, the only breaks he could see were paths leading into the woods to places unknown. He didn't feel any trepidation or fear because for some reason everything felt calm, warm and as it should be, almost as if he had come home or if as if he had been here before.

Ten paces from the bank he heard a whispered voice, "Choose a path, think carefully and take it. At the other side of the trees you will find a previous life, one you have lived before."

Had he been awake and conscious he would have dismissed the idea and laughed it off as complete bunkum but here in this place it felt normal, he didn't know why, in fact he didn't even wonder, he just did as the voice told him and rowed slowly for the shore on the other side of the water. Soon he felt the bottom of the boat crunch gently against stones as he reached the small pebbled beach.

Climbing out he headed for the path he had already decided he would take and walked into the shade of the tall trees. It only seemed like he had been on the small narrow path for seconds before he was somehow suddenly elsewhere. No longer in the place he had seen from the water.

"Go to three moments in your former life, three important times that helped mould that life and the way you are in the present." A voice instructed and instantly he was looking down on himself or someone similar, who looked different but somehow was him, a former life? Maybe, but was that possible?

He watched as the young legionnaire finished his training, dressed in the armour of Caesars Legions nearly a century before, the celebrations and wine, he and his friends enjoyed. The voice asked questions, where, when, why and then asked him to move forward. The image moved onto the next point, it showed him again but older maybe by a few years possibly as many as ten, wearing the uniform of an Optio. He was on a green hillside standing next to a Centurion whose face was familiar.

A gentle breeze brushed his face, arms and legs and he saw the horse hair of the Centurions helmet plume move slightly with the air. Behind them stood rows of Roman soldiers, quietly waiting, somewhere behind horns and trumpets blared as orders were given, it resembled the scene before a battle.

As he watched from somewhere above, apprehension gripped the faces of those on the hillside. Slowly and quietly at first another sound came to his ears but from the opposite direction down the incline of the hill, he recognised it as men moving in large numbers towards his position ascending the slope to face the gathered Roman lines. The sound of wheels or more specifically chariots joined the cacophony from somewhere unseen.

The tips of banners came into view depicting animals crudely drawn onto material fluttering in the slight breeze, on his side the eagle standard waited shining in the bright sunlight. He realised he was watching a scene from Briton but from decades before during one of Caesars forays into the country. A battle was about to be fought a pivotal battle he suspected, the final battle before Caesar ordered a retreat back to the sea and to Gaul. The Britons had been prepared on this occasion and had amassed thousands of warriors to defy the armour clad legions of Rome.

Horses whinnied from their lines, an order was given to advance towards the enemy still unseen except for their banners as the front ranks began to march slowly forward and the flats of swords began to slam into the sides of shields.

"Move forward now." The distant voice almost whispered like a memory as if inside his head and the image changed. The man he recognised as himself was lying wounded on a field surrounded by the dead and dying. He felt sharp pains in his leg and upper arm. Looking at the image he saw a deep puncture wound in his upper left thigh and a large jagged wound to his left arm just above the bicep, blood flowed from both injuries.

A medicus ran from one man to another desperately trying to staunch the blood flow sustained by men from his Legion. Some he stopped at briefly and gave aid and then ran to another where he could save a life but some he ran on from barely stopping, their lives already expired.

"Is this how you pass from this life?" The voice asked.

"Yes." He heard himself reply in a hushed tone. "The leg wound wouldn't stop bleeding, a vein was damaged inside the flesh it bled inside and stopped my heart from beating."

"And what did you learn from this life?"

"Discipline honour and duty." He whispered again accepting that what he had witnessed was somehow real or had been real and that he had lived before. Everything seemed to make sense to him now, he was a warrior that was his calling that was what he had been before, that's what he was now and that's what he would be again. Brenna calmly called him from where he had been, slowly and carefully, aware that it would be damaging to pull him too abruptly from his past. Eventually he blinked open his eyes suddenly aware of his physicality, his body and where he was, he smiled up at Brenna's beautiful face. Clenching his fists and moving his toes, he felt as if he had been asleep for days.

"That was amazing." He said attempting to rise from the ground but she held him down, "Stay still for a moment and relax."

He suddenly remembered the wounds and quickly looked at his arm and leg but there was nothing there, he frowned.

"How is this possible?" He looked at her with a frown over his face.

She smiled, "It's part of who we all are. I wanted to show you this," she gestured to the surrounding area, "everything is a part of everything else, the trees, the lakes, the animals and the people. Like all things the gods provide this and they watch. We will all live many lives and as long as we learn from each of them and grow we will live again."

"Is this how soothsayers see the future?" He asked.

"I cannot say but like some soothsayers of our people mine too sacrifice to see what the future holds but it's not always certain. Things can change the future especially where people have changed their ways or have chosen to take a different path. It's like being in a strong river, different currents can take you different ways and those currents can determine where you will finish your journey."

"I feel strangely more alive than ever before." He remarked.

"That is usual especially when someone experiences this for the first time, elation, happiness and a renewed excitement and sense of life, it rejuvenates the physical body. It comes from knowing there is more, that there is something almighty out there even though we can't always see it. Our people have always known this that is what some of our people have in common. A few tribes do not have druidic teaching but most do but even they can't agree on all manner of things such as human sacrifice. I would never take part in such barbaric practise but I wouldn't even take an animal's life for such reasons although some believe it appeases the gods.

All life is sacred and I would never take one for such a purpose only for food as the gods have provided them. The wooden cages where the young are sacrificed are vile in the extreme but some of the more desperate and power hungry druids use them to control their people with fear."

A realisation suddenly dawned on Varro and he sat up concern on his face.

"Are you a druid Brenna?"

She stared into his eyes unblinking. "I am what I am and I mean no harm to anyone or anything. Like you I'm on a journey, a journey as old as time itself. I know this word you use and if that's what you choose to call me then yes I am a druid but that is no reason for you to be concerned about me or my intentions towards you. I have nothing for you but love. You used the word soothsayer before and now you use the word druid. I call myself neither, I am just me" She smiled as her hand moved lower and he relaxed a little lying down.

As she continued talking her hand caressed his stomach and he felt himself getting aroused.

"There are some who pervert the teachings for their own purposes but there are also some who will do anything to fight against the army that you are a part of. To them its normal its natural." She smiled down at him. "It's like making love, like you and I making love."

He returned the smile as she reached down and took hold of his hard erection massaging it slowly with her hand. He moaned quietly arching his back as she manoeuvred herself to sit by his side. His hand stroked her back and slowly moved to her breast caressing a nipple. She leaned forward and licked at his shaft before taking its swollen end into her mouth. He felt her gently suck the end, warm and wet as he grew harder, tingling in anticipation. He was lost in the moment and watched as she moved and mounted him and guided herself onto him. She was beautiful, her body perfect, so sensual, he didn't want this to end. All thoughts of duty or the army and druids vanished from his mind. For now nothing else mattered except this moment and their bodies moving together as one.

Later as they lay together wrapped around each other they
kissed passionately. "Can you see a time when people don't have to fight?" She asked.

He looked into her eyes, "Maybe but not in our time, or not in this time I should say." Smiling he kissed her again.

Some miles away to the west Togodumnus and Caratacus sat in the morning sun with their tribal leaders gathered around a small fire. They ate fresh fish caught earlier and cooked on the same fire and drank strong alcoholic milk made from the herd. The mood was sombre because they had lost a lot of warriors and had seen no sign that they could stop the invader spreading through the land.

"We need to strike them hard and stop the advance." Said Tomgundum, a young warrior who had fought the enemy many times before and killed more than a dozen himself, or so he claimed.

Togodumnus looked at him, "And my young warrior just how do you propose we do this? Whilst we have the advantage of numbers and the knowledge of the ground they have their weapons, how they fight and the armour they hide behind. These men live this way, they don't work the farms and land like most of us. They fight and invade lands and no place has stopped them so far. We have to use our natural advantages or they will take this land as they have others, enslave our women and imprison us all. We did it before against their best General and we can do it again and reclaim the land that they now pollute."

There was agreement around the fire. "So what we are to do?" Asked another voice, Togodumnus looked into the eyes of those around him. Sat amongst the group was a man whose head was hooded, his body covered in a long dark grey robe, greyer even than his long straggly beard. He had sat listening to the group as they discussed the situation, he had eaten but not drank the brew. He was a druid from the far western island of Mona where many of the spiritual men and some women were trained and lived before teaching others across the lands. He like all of his kind was highly respected and revered.

"If I may," he asked his voice strange to those around him, he talked differently his accent almost rhythmic and guttural. Caratacus nodded his permission for the man to speak.

"These Romans are many and they fight in an army although not large compared to the warriors we have, you can call to your banner, they are well equipped and trained in warfare. Even as we speak now, more are coming to our shores. My scouts tell me there are at least three landing points around our east and south coasts. Those already on the beaches are fortifying their position right now while we sit here." Anxiety spread from face to face around him.

"Our lands face their greatest threat, the greatest threat they have ever faced. There are druids who tell me their Emperor sends many Legions to our people. In Gaul they say that over forty thousand trained men will soon be on our soil. Our enemy also has an advantage we haven't considered as well as those that we have." Confused faces looked at the druid as he stood and began to pace taking in their expressions.

"When these men came before a long time ago, certain peoples welcomed them and even drew up treaties, alliances, paid for peace with gold, women and children and animals so in awe were they of the invader and their power. Some even sent tribal envoys with them back to their great stone city. These Romans made friends of tribes and even gave some sanctuary across the water. Even your father Cunobelinus worked with them and we had peace. Just two years ago before this Claudius came to power, your great tribe traded with Rome and they with you. That has all gone now because certain Britons have turned their backs on their own because of their own greed and have run to Claudius and lied. We cannot trust all those who we should be able to rely on.

He looked around those sat by the fire, a new fear written over their faces. Tribal conflict had always been a way of life, it was something that they were used to and could live with, or die with as the case maybe. No one tribe now had the power to defeat another entirely after many years of war, lesser tribal lands had been swallowed up and so eventually those that survived came to agreements and fractious peace remained. None would encroach onto another's land unless under a banner of peace and then only for talks with other tribal leaders, They would respect their neighbours livestock, they would trade and even have marriages for the sake of peace and stability. It didn't always work but that was what the leaders had agreed to do.

The peace was sometimes fraught however, and every now and again an unforeseen crisis would happen and deaths would occur but conflicts were kept to a minimum. The coming of the Romans under Caesar had changed all that and certain tribes had taken advantage of it by siding with the foreign invader instead of their neighbours. For years when the wars outcome in Gaul was uncertain one tribe in particular kept a low profile but now rumours were rife that they had once again sided with the Romans and now it seemed so had others. Some who had left when the enemy were sent back into the sea were said to have returned and were able to speak the strange language of the invader. They were said to wear the clothes of the enemy and the adornments around their wrists and had promised the same for those others who had been left behind.

They spoke of the places they had seen, great settlements made of rock, shaped into blocks that towered taller than the largest tree and made into great buildings, images of the Roman leaders carved from mountains and of their gods of which there were many, buildings many levels high, plentiful water supplies from rivers and lakes many miles away carried on high man made rivers of stone, schooling of the stars and many other things the Britons hadn't even imagined.

"The invader is truly strong and powerful and they are the worse threat we have ever faced, our entire way of life is under threat, you can believe that but they will not defeat us. They will not conquer us entirely as they," he pointed eastwards, "now face an enemy they will never truly conquer. This is where they are stopped. This is where it is written that their mighty advance is halted. This is where they begin die. This is where the victorious legions of Rome will meet their end."

The gathered crowd were now on their feet cheering and roaring applause, they took heart in his words and some of the faces previously filled with anguish now had expressions of joy.

"How do you now this?" A voice asked quietly but went unheard. "I said, how do you, know this? "He shouted looking at the druid with suspicion as the crowd quietened.

He looked in the direction the voice had come from. "Our lands will face many threats over the coming years and centuries, many lives will be lost. Invaders will always come from the east. It is there the threat exists and where it will always come from but never truly succeed. Across the water is where our enemies grow and sometimes friends as well.

Long, long ago the water between our eastern coast and their shores didn't exist and we were one land until the gods separated us many, many centuries ago. This they did for a reason to protect our shores and peoples from barbarian hordes. In recent years we have enjoyed peace with our Gallic brothers across the water, for many of us came from those lands as well. Now we have trading and treaties which have helped us all live in peace. We even sent warriors to help when the call came from Gaul but the enemy crushed all who stood before them. They are now an enslaved people, their women soiled and sold around their empire along with their children but some prosper under this way of life.

Now as we begin our fight against them, they are still enslaving Gaul's and people from the great Germanic tribes but not all. Resistance will always fester for the invader like a wound that will grow and eventually kill its host. Those who take or give them gold and betray their own will be slain without hesitation. They may live like Kings and Queens for now but their time will come and they will pay dearly as those who help them will pay. Already there are some who have returned to our lands with the invader."

The lighter expressions on the faces around him were replaced by confusion. "Caratacus, it is the gods will that you and your brother lead and unite our tribes but even you have an enemy closer to home who, now walks with the Romans." Heads turned to face Caratacus and Togodumnus who both stared at the druid.

"Your brother Adminius expelled three years ago by your father has returned. He is not alone however, more lap dogs cast from our lands have returned with promises of power in exchange for their corruption."

Both Togodumnus and Caratacus stood red faced clearly offended by the druid's words, rage flowed through them as they suspected what he would say next.

Togodumnus took a step towards him, "Be careful druid. You may know many things but insulting my family is something I will not allow. My father expelled Adminius for reasons that will remain with me and my brother Caratacus. Rest assured, he was exiled for good reason and had shamed our name." He looked around at those gathered around the fire. "Know this all of you. If indeed my brother Adminius has returned and has allied himself with the enemy, he will be hunted down. It was my fathers will that he be expelled and if he has gone against those wishes he will pay for it with his life as will any others who betray us. If he is now betraying not only his father but his forefathers then this blade," he drew his long sword as it rasped out of its sheath, "shall take his life."

Cheers greeted the warrior's promise, "We cannot allow ourselves to be divided by deceit or those corrupted by the pestilence of Rome, especially those whose aim it is to flourish on the people that gave them life. All those who ally themselves with those who threaten our shores are enemies of all our people. They will be destroyed as will all those who give them shelter."

Warriors stood and began banging swords and spears as they cheered. The druid bowed to the warrior leader and turned to walk away.

"Wait druid!" Caratacus ordered, the man turned. "You spoke of others, what are their names and how do you know of these things?"

The druid faced him, "Two others are Verica of the Attrebates and Cogidubnus, the latter it is said was even taken in by Claudius the great emperor and taught their ways. It is believed he has been schooled for many years and now intends to return to Briton to make our people learn their ways. He talks their language and wears their robes, he doesn't even sound like us anymore. He is a cross breed hound who has already sealed his own fate."

He raised his eyebrows as if to emphasise his words but Caratacus felt there was no need, he knew these men, he had spared them but sent them across the water, expelling them as his father had exiled Adminius.

The druid continued, "These men will prove more lethal than swords lord, they have already betrayed their own kind and whored themselves to the Roman. Now they intend to persuade our brothers and sisters to suckle from them as well, to take their coin, dress as they do, drink their wine and prostitute our women and children.

They plan to become rulers on behalf of the invader, like a disease in our crops they intend to spread through the land. This is what the Roman does after conquering a tribe, he usurps the people and uses the weak minded to rule on their behalf. That way they think they ease themselves onto the population using a known face whilst robbing them through taxes, taking gold and silver, we have to unite to destroy them."

Togodumnus smiled and approached the druid clearly impressed by the his knowledge and defiance. "What is your name druid?" He asked.

"Mersax my lord," The hooded man replied, "Mersax of the Druidic Isle of Mona."

"Not merely a druid then but a man that teaches, you are a high priest are you not?" Togodumnus asked.

"Yes lord some call me that and in answer to your other question, I have people amongst the enemy now. They have seen the three named and recognised them, you can rest assured this is true. It is how I know where they are and their numbers, weapons and horse. Anything that you need to know will be told to you to help push them back into the sea where they belong. I knew your father Cunobelinus well. He was a wise and gracious leader, a man who would have led his people against the invader had he been alive today. He was a good man who made the Catuvellauni one of the strongest and largest, most powerful tribe in our lands." He looked away, "I'm just glad he isn't here to see their armies march across our lands."

Togodumnus studied the man's face. "I owe you a debt of gratitude Mersax, your information is invaluable and I thank you for your kind words. Our father was a great leader and I hope we can prove ourselves worthy of being his sons. I will give everything to fight no matter what it takes, where it takes me or how long. These Romans think they can come taking what they wish, killing without cost to their own but they will learn otherwise. I shall break this beasts teeth, I will blind its eyes and I shall rip out its heart and destroy its soul. I will not stop until there isn't a drop of their blood left and if I die my brother shall fight them as will our brothers and sons.

Take these words back to your priests and to the great tribes of the west, the Silures, the Demeta, the Ordovices and the Deceangli. Tell them all that Togodumnus and Caratacus of the Catuvellauni will smash these fools who come to take everything from us. Our neighbouring tribes who have been our enemies in the past and cannot be relied upon now will also die if they side with them. They envy our power and have fallen to our swords before." Mersax saw the determination in his eyes.

He continued, "I too have scouts where they are on our shores, one will return soon and I'm sure will confirm your words. I owe you a debt Mersax and my thanks." He extended his arm, Mersax took it.

"You are not indebted to me lord Togodumnus or you Caratacus, we fight the same enemy. If we don't we are all doomed. Even with some tribes united some will help and even assist those we are now at war with. We are merely at the beginning of a great and long journey and some of us will not see its end and those that do will endure great hardship and loss."

He smiled, "You are courageous and noble leaders and your own journeys are difficult. They are long and hard but you will see them through, you will live long and prosperous lives." A slight break in his expression betrayed something he knew as he spoke the words but he continued, "My people will keep you informed of anything that may be of use. I myself must return to the west, I have duties to attend to and other leaders to speak with as I travel West. I will ensure that my tendrils spread amongst our common enemies for all our sakes and I will seek out the chieftains of the tribes you named and warn them, they will know of your names as friends."

Mersax turned and walked through the gathered warriors to find his horse as did two men dressed in the same robes who had been sat around the fire previously unseen. Togodumnus turned his attention to his people and spoke of his plan to lead the Romans West for another day and then back to the North East as far as possible before engaging them. Riders would be sent to the southern tribes to warn them of the threat they faced.

By midday as the sun was high, thousands of warriors were ready to move. Chariots carried men and women, small horses pulled carts carrying families and mules and oxen dragged larger carts containing food and weapons. At the rear of the large train of humanity and animals, boys herded cattle, pigs and goats. Riders had been sent forward to Camulodunum to warn the occupants of the forthcoming battle and to prepare for war, forge weapons and re-enforce defences. Caratacus estimated that it would take three days to get back to his home land where he had grown up as a boy. He and Togodumnus already knew where they planned to take the war to the enemy.

Miles to the east Togun watched as the Romans made firm their landing area, they had only been there a matter of days but had already built a wooden fortification beyond the cliffs where they had landed. He had been a scout for Caratacus for a number of years but had never seen anything as formidable as the sight that now met his eyes. Large towers stood tall at all four corners as did two at either side in the middle walls, below which huge doors had been constructed. Sentries walked the walls and watched from the towers where ballista, were now positioned.

Palisades had been dug outside the fortification where other soldiers patrolled and scrubland had been cleared enabling the defenders a clear view of anyone or anything that approached the location. From his vantage point Togun could see Britons approaching the soldiers, he could also see Britons talking to others and passing the time of day. Anger welled up inside his chest as he watched the exchanges. He found it hard to comprehend how his own people could accept these killers of his tribal brothers and sisters. Clearly there were people who were prepared to accept them, to buy and sell and trade with them. They would share their fate. He mounted his horse and galloped off in search of Togodumnus to report his findings.

Chapter Ten

Three years earlier in AD 40, Adminius, brother to Togodumnus and Caratacus had been exiled to Gaul after exceeding his power by attacking the tribes in the far southern territories. The Catuvellauni lands were already accepted as one of the most powerful tribal regions second only in size to the Brigantes in the north. Despite this Adminius, hungry to be recognised amongst his siblings, sought his own power base and encroached across the border and began raiding the people and settlements of the Cantiaci.

Togodumnus being the eldest brother, saw this as a direct threat to his own authority as his sibling tried to expand his own influence. Action had to be taken and Adminius was stripped of all rank and power and finally exiled to Gaul with a few followers.

The remaining brothers thought they had seen the last of their ambitious sibling. However, he sought the sanctuary of the Emperor Claudius, who whilst genuinely sympathetic towards the young Briton, also recognised that there was an opportunity for him as well, whilst swearing vengeance against the grave insult to the son of a former ally.

After the initial forays into Britain by Caesar, all of those concerned had prospered. Trade routes had been set up where exchanges were made involving, gold, silver, tin, food, slaves and even technologies for items such as looms and weaving machines to manufacture cloth.

The trade allowed the Britons although not backward, to advance suddenly at a rate that they would have found difficult naturally without the influence from Rome. Trade where bartering was commonplace before using animals or weapons was now possible using coins that even began to bear the head of the Catuvellauni leadership. Coins that were originally minted in Rome were now produced in Britain, a sure sign that the times were changing.

Not all tribes were loyal to Rome however and many already saw the interlopers as people who were intent on taking anything that they could get their hands on for their own benefit after sharing some of their wealth. Disputes were an everyday part of life as some argued for what the Romans brought to their land to improve their way of life whilst some saw those chieftains who traded with them as traitors, especially by those who didn't trade or see any benefit from it. Consequently, those who were exiled for whatever reason sought assistance from Rome who at times played the part of a disciplining parent, sorting out quarrels as if from arguing children. Some of those exiled however, didn't always tell the truth and were prone to exaggerate their claims in order to try and gain favour and for Rome to come down hard on their foes. Adiminius wasn't alone in asking for help and he was joined by other influential Britons in the Roman capitol claiming barbaric behaviour by the leaders of the Catuvellauni, who it was claimed were said to be attacking other tribes loyal to Rome which of course was a lie. Adiminius also claimed that Togodumnus and Caratacus intended to defy Rome altogether and were going to cut all ties, it was all fabrication but the details or truth didn't matter as Claudius saw this as an ideal opportunity to gain favour from his people and the legions.

The Emperor had only been in power for two years and knew that a victory over the Catuvellauni would enable his empire to further its own ambitions whilst at the same time demonstrating that he was a powerful and worthy leader. Rumours were soon spreading that the situation in Britannia would have to be dealt with before it became too powerful as one tribe was unifying the others in a plot against Rome.

The stories spread like wildfire through the streets of the city from the rich to the poor alike and even without a hostile boot setting foot on the shores of the island the popularity of Claudius began to rise.

It was said that another barbaric people like the Gaul's and people of Germania had risen far away to the east. It was an uncivilised land where druids ruled and plotted against them and that they would have to be put down before they became too powerful. What had started out as a few disenchanted individuals banished because of their own greed and avarice would soon influence every life in Britannia. Momentum built to fever pitch for another war in a foreign land that was rich in resources and people, potential slaves.

Togodumnus and Caratacus knew that this had all happened before when their father had ruled and had been victorious in battle against Commius, King of the Atrebates. Vanquished and humiliated Commius had sought sanctuary in Gaul where Caesar seized the opportunity to come to the assistance of an ally. He had subsequently led an expeditionary force to Britannia intending to put the exiled King back on his throne. However the Catuvellauni led by their father had defeated Caesar's two legions who had barely managed to gain a foot hold on their shores before being forced back into the sea and then to Gaul.

Caesar had learned that the warrior race across the channel were not to be treated with contempt and so was forced to withdraw to think again. He had assumed that his professionally trained soldiers would be more than a match for the disorganised hordes who were said to live in mud huts, eat butchered raw meat and drink ale made from milk. He had in reality vastly underestimated his foe and was forced into retreating and it was recognised by some as a humiliating defeat.

However, with the aid of some intelligent propaganda the great General had turned a defeat into a victory by means of a tactical withdrawal impressing some of his superiors in Rome with the aid of clever propaganda. Subsequently, the following year, he tried again this time setting sail with five full legions and successfully returned Commius to the Atrebatic throne. Cunobelinus though was neither bowed or defeated and despite many losses to his own, continued to attack the invaders who were forced to marshal their legions and to once again return to Gaul, their original aim accomplished.

Claudius now repeated history by using Caesars excuse for war. One of the successors to the Atrebates throne after Commius was his descendant Verica, who in a mirror of the past had been defeated by Adminius. Verica now appealed for Roman assistance as an ally and Claudius was more than willing to help the client King and loyal trader and subject of Rome. Togodumnus and Caratacus knew that Claudius had lied to his people in order to create an excuse for war and had therefore gone back on his word to keep the peace. They now swore to resist the invaders just as their father had done so many years before.

Knowing the enemy were organised and had many professionally trained soldiers at their disposal, they knew the odds were against them especially after recent encounters, If they were to be successful they had to try and persuade their neighbours to join them but after years of conflict between the different regions it would be difficult. They hoped that the surrounding tribes would see that the years of peace living side by side would outweigh the far less occurring disputes they had been involved in, especially once they learned of the Emperors deceit.

The faltering of the legions to invade when the tribes were gathered and waiting for them had in fact now turned out to be the worst thing to happen as far as the Britons were concerned. Togodumnus upon hearing the news that the soldiers were refusing to board the ships and were on the verge of mutiny, had dispersed his warriors, sending them home believing that the planned invasion wouldn't now happen. Unknowingly, the few days hesitation by the superstitious men of the Roman army, who believed that Britannia couldn't be conquered after Caesars failures, had in reality bought themselves an unopposed landing.

The Catuvellauni were now at war with a devious and powerful former ally who had marched across the vast lands to the east but they were prepared to give a good account of themselves. The Gaul's had shown that the Romans could be halted as had happened at Alesia with more determination by Vercingetorex to take the sword to the Romans, better tactics and resolute allies and reinforcements, they would have been victorious.

Vastly outnumbered and surrounded, Caesars legions should have been crushed but instead turned certain defeat into victory against the odds and routed the Gaul's. More recently the Britons knew that three entire Roman legions led by another General, Publius Varus had been destroyed in the forests of Germania some thirty years before. They therefore knew these men were not invincible and could be beaten. It was just a case of finding the right ground and tactics to use against them.

      Togodumnus and Caratacus led their people further to the west for another entire day and then turned north. As the daylight began to fade they turned north east following paths they were familiar with, heading towards their capital Camulodunum. His true destination however, was not the settlement itself. The last thing he would do was give the enemy an opportunity to claim victory over him by crushing a major population and he didn't want to find himself under siege. He knew the enemy were very experienced and successful in siege warfare and were prepared to go to any lengths once they had their victims cornered. He had heard the stories of Julius Caesar building enormous towers and his men digging vast trenches around Alesia for as far as the eye could see and he didn't want to fall into the same trap with nowhere to run if all else failed. He couldn't turn back the days and prevent them from landing so he now had to find a way to take on the enemy that would give him the advantage.

      With the moon high in the clear sky they called a halt to their withdrawal. Cattle were milked and people quickly settled down for some sleep, exhausted after the days march. They intended to travel again before the sun rose hoping to stay ahead of the pursuing Romans.

      Earlier that day Varro had been given new orders, instead of continuing to scout in a westerly direction, he was now told to track Togodumnus but no contact was to be made with the Chieftain or his forces unless he wished to discuss terms for surrender. They were to be located and followed in order that they could be brought to battle as soon as possible. Varro led his small group with Brenna riding at his side, through a wooded area where the night had become cool and she now had a Roman cloak wrapped around her shoulders.

"We should rest for the night before it gets too late." She remarked.

Varro took in his surroundings, "We can't see if anything approaches us from here especially under the cover of darkness. It would be better to get clear of the trees first and find some high ground if possible."

"I know these lands and this woodland, it stretches a long way. We'll still be under its cover even if we kept riding until dawn. Whilst we can't see anyone approaching it also means that we are concealed. The Catuvellauni you seek will also have to rest and they can't go too far with the animals and children they have with them."

He turned to look at her smiling, "The women of these islands are not as weak as those from Rome and if they are all like you, they are the equal of their men so they won't slow them down but they will need sleep you're right. Let's try to find somewhere suitable to rest up for a few hours and get some sleep."

After finding little other than more trees he called a halt to their progress and they began to make a small camp for the night. Brenna's brother Tevelgus went to gather wood for a fire whilst the others took in their surroundings and unpacked cloaks and bed rolls to be used for bedding.

With arms full of dry branches for the fire, Tevelgus was about to return to the others when something caught his attention. Through the trees he could see the faint glimmer of a fire somewhere in the distance. He crouched and carefully placed the wood on the ground and moved forward quietly. After a while he could smell wood smoke and as he got closer he could now make out numerous small fires spread out below the level of land where he found himself.

Carefully moving slowly and looking at the ground to try to avoid broken branches, he got closer. Within a hundred paces he saw that he had found a large party of Britons but from this distance he couldn't see who they were. There were far too many for it to be a hunting party, could it be the Catuvellauni he wondered, the tribe who had dominated his own for many generations.

As he got closer he could see bodies lying on the ground huddled around the fires as they slept. A sharp snapping sound broke his attention and made him jump, he crouched lower swivelling round trying to see what had caused the noise. Through the trees he saw a lookout only about thirty paces from his position. He cursed himself for almost stumbling into him because he had been so focused on the fires and then realised that he was standing on a branch or twig.

Tevelgus saw that the sentry was holding a long spear and wore similar clothing to those of his own people. He was thick set and his muscular arms were apparent under the light from the moon and he was bare chested. From this distance, with this poor light it was impossible to establish if the man was Catuvellauni but there could be no other explanation. He waited for the man to move slowly off and then quietly and carefully he backtracked and reported his findings to Varro.

Long before the sun came up the centurion and his small party, weary from virtually no sleep after the discovery by Tevelgus, prepared to follow the large group he had found whilst foraging for wood. As they had found themselves so unexpectedly close to their target, they had decided not to make a fire and so had only eaten dried meat from the rations they carried. Tired and cold they packed their horses who were more than well fed at least on the long green grass of the woodland.

"Decimus." Varro called the legionary forward. "I want you to return to the General and tell him that Togodumnus and his army have changed direction. Tell him they are now heading north possibly intending to head to their capital at Camulodumun. If he goes north as well from their current position, they may even be able to cut them off and destroy them before they can get to reinforcements. Ride as quickly as your horse will carry you."

Decimus saluted and mounted his horse. Brenna turned to Varro. "Do you think the General will be able get to them before they reach their settlement? If they don't get to them first Camulodumun is well fortified and surrounded by ditches. It would be better to catch them out in the open." She said.

"That's why I've sent Decimus back to tell him as soon as he can. If we can get to them before they can reach the safety of their local lands and all that it would give them, we can end this war and save many more lives."

As the sun began to rise, clouds gathered overhead and soon after rain began to fall as Varro and his small group walked forward. Tevelgus had ridden ahead to scout the large party they were tracking. Varro at first had second thoughts as to whether he could fully trust the Britons and that doubt was all over his face. Brenna and Tevelgus had told Varro of their tribes disputes at the hands of their enemies and of the bitter history between the two large clans. Satisfied that he could allow the big Briton to track them he had let him go forward.

He had also decided that it would be better for the enemy to see another of their own or someone that at least looked like them who they may just ignore. Although the rain got harder it was still quite warm as they continued on, leading their horses and waiting for Brenna's brother to return. After a few more hours they had eventually got to clear land leaving the huge woodland and trees behind. Finding a stream they let the horses drink and took a short break.

Up ahead, Tevelgus tried to stay hidden from view as he continued to follow the group ahead. It was impossible for him to gauge the size of the army because he couldn't see the front of their lines as they moved slowly north. At walking pace he led his horse constantly alert for signs that he may be seen. He had decided to keep only the rear of Togodumnus's winding army in sight and they were some way ahead. He didn't know where his sister was but knew they wouldn't be far behind him. Every now and then he would find a dead body that carried wounds, someone injured from battles already fought. There had been no attempt to bury them now which showed the desperation of those they followed but it did confirm one thing, who they followed.

Later he found another body, that of a young man. He was lying in a ditch face up, his arms tucked in at his sides. His chest and stomach were stained in blood, a deep hole had perforated his chest, probably from a javelin he judged from the size of it. His face was pale and there was no longer any sign of life. He had been stripped of weapons and placed in the ditch.

"You could be my brother." Tevelgus spoke as he studied the young face. Just then something alerted him to activity nearby, a noise that indicated something was close, his other senses instantly came alive. Something had made him look round quickly, his heart beat faster as he stood and his horse cried out and whinnied rearing up. He grabbed the reins and tried to keep it quiet but it was too late. Five men stared down at him from a ridgeline only fifty paces away.

"Who are you?" One shouted from the middle of their group. They were all armed with spears and swords, wearing no tunics or robes. The rain made their woad covered upper bodies shine, their hair wet.

"I've found a body in this ditch." He shouted in reply pointing at the corpse, trying to gain some time to think out his next move. The men looked at each other and began to walk down the slight slope. Tevelgus felt his heart pounding through his body and he thought they would see his panic. He tried to stay calm but he knew that every moment he stood still, was a moment wasted when he could be escaping. He looked at his horse, now scraping at the damp surface with its front leg, kicking up mud. He knew that by the time he got onto him he would be as dead as the man in the ditch but if he didn't run he would surely be as dead if they recognised him as Cantiaci.

It was too late to run, with his heart beginning to calm slightly they got closer and he shouted out, "Did you kill him?"

"What? No. Romans!" Shouted the leader in the middle. "Romans killed him. They've landed in force to the east on the coast, thousands of them. They're invading the land intent on killing and stealing everything." He looked around as if seeing if he was alone. "Who are you, where are you from?" He placed a hand on the handle of his sword examining the face of the stranger.

"Romans, Romans? Why would Romans invade our land? There's been peace for years. We trade with them, why would they want to kill us?" He asked still trying to find time to think of something even just to delay them.

"Where are you from friend?" Asked the leader as the others stood around him, his tone had changed from curiosity to almost challenging. Tevelgus felt his heart begin to beat quicker once more.

"A days ride south." He turned pointing in the direction he had come from. The man examined him again, "Is this," he gestured at the dead man, "the first body you have seen? We have had to leave many behind in the past few days."

"I've been looking for elderberries not dead bodies." He looked at the dead man. "This is the first I've seen yes." He answered wary that this could go either way now. Just as he got the words out one of the men pointed shouting suddenly behind him, "Romans." They all ducked down, Tevelgus included who turned and saw Varro walking slowly towards them.

"Quickly friend, come with us or they'll cut you down." The leader said as he and his companions turned and scurried away scrambling back up the slope the way they had come. Tevelgus stood briefly watching them, "I've got to get my horse. I can't leave my horse."

The other Britons weren't listening, the quickest of them had already vanished over the rise. Tevelgus walked quickly to his animal, mounting it quicker than he ever had before he turned and raced off in the other direction.

Examining the punctured cold body in the ditch, Varro listened as Tevelgus related his encounter with the Catuvellauni looking up at the ridge.

"Your certain they were with Togodumnus?" He asked of Brenna's brother.

"There's no doubt in my mind." Tevelgus answered. "They didn't even suspect who I was but if you hadn't arrived when you had, I probably wouldn't be breathing anymore and would be dead along with our friend here. I had visions of being skinned alive and would have been if they'd realised who I was and what I was doing."

His sister patted his shoulder. "We should stay together from now on. We can't risk losing anyone and I don't intend losing you."

Varro looked in the direction indicated by Tevelgus, they were too close. "I think your right, we'll stay together. I don't think we could lose them now even if we tried. Let's withdraw and let them get further ahead. If those men were scouts staying behind the main group there's bound to be more. I don't want to let them get that close again, come on let's go."

Brenna took a final look at the young face in the ditch. He wasn't the first to die and he wouldn't be the last. She wondered how many more would also cross the river and spend time with the ferryman in the days and months to come.

Two days later Togodumnus had led his army to a position north of the river Medway. Crossing the water through shallows the day before at a position that few people knew of, he had given orders for his people to make camp. From this location they could see the open sea and a gentle warm salty breeze blew in every now and again.

"If only things were different brother?" Caratacus said.

Togodumnus looked at him, "If things were different we would be at home trying to resolve disputes of a different nature." He gazed out to sea. "I hope our scouts are right about there being no Roman ships along this stretch of the coast. I'm sure the river will delay them for a while but we don't want any of their reinforcements flanking us. I'm sure they'll try and cross the river close to us and when they do it will give us the opportunity to stop them."

Caratacus viewed the scene around them. They had positioned the chariots at the rear and those on foot nearer the water. Beyond the chariots there were wooded areas and marshland. They knew the Romans wouldn't be familiar with the area and had chosen this land because it would be hazardous to the enemy whilst giving them a place of escape if things didn't go according to plan. The brothers had now amassed an army of over eighty thousand warriors, mainly on foot. The next highest contingent being mounted of sorts with just over two thousand and the rest, fifteen hundred were war chariots.

"Do you think Adminius has any regrets about pledging his allegiance to the Romans?" Caratacus asked.

Togodumnus frowned, "He was exiled for good reason, he always tried to argue that we should submit to them, that paying them to be here on our ground was not a problem to him. He thought it was acceptable for us to be subservient to them." Anger rose as he thought back to all the conversations and arguments they had been involved in with their brother.

Their father had initially accepted that trading with the Romans was good for all concerned until they realised that it wasn't an equitable deal. The Romans didn't want a partnership, they wanted to envelop the Catuvellauni and slowly strangle them and their resources as they found out when they started asking for taxes. That could not be agreeable to an independent kingdom and one of the strongest tribes of the island and something had to be done as the men from the east asked for more and more.

Adminius had argued that it was better to be a client of the known world's strongest people rather than be dead or worse made their slaves. Their father and other brothers didn't agree, they argued it was better to have pride in life and to be able to stand on their own feet rather than suckle from Rome's breast and do its bidding. As the arguments grew more vocal their father raged at his son's weakness and had finally given him a simple choice; live his way or go across the water and become one of them.

They had a duty to their people he had told him. A way of life to protect, they were proud of what they had achieved and if Adminius was prepared to throw all of that away, then so be it. The remaining brothers had not discussed this since he had made his decision and gone into exile, a matter that was of no doubt once he had broken the treaty with the Cantiaci and raided their lands. The loss of Adminius was a double blow for their father, not only had he lost a son but he had lost him to Rome, the beast that was threatening to destroy their entire way of life.

Within days of Adminius setting sail their father's health started to fail. At first it was barely noticeable and he claimed he was just ill, suffering from one of the many illnesses that often swept through their people. Within ten days however, he had asked Togodumnus to deal with matters that he alone normally dealt with. Within weeks he took to his bed and had virtually stopped talking and took little food or water and he quickly began to look frail, old. In health he was normally a giant of a man but he began to rapidly go downhill. The brothers didn't have the luxury of a mother to nurse their father as she had died some years before so their wives nursed the ailing King.

Nothing however seemed to help and within three months of the departure of Adminius their father and King of the Catuvelleuni was dead. The remaining brothers believed it was because Adminius had gone against his wishes, had broken his heart and knew that had he died a warrior's death against an enemy instead of joining them, their father would have survived but to lose him in the way he had was not something he could come to terms with. Togodumnus and Caratacus blamed not only their brother but the reason for his defection, Rome. With their legions now moving through their woods, forests and pastures they swore to right that wrong or die trying. In their eyes Adminius was no longer a brother, he was lost to them and if the druid was right; a traitor who had to pay and the price was death, death for the betrayal of their father and his treachery to the tribe and themselves.

Mersax had confirmed their worse fear, their lost sibling and former brother had returned to the land of his birth with an army, intent on conquest and a foe that was more powerful than any other they had ever faced. They had agreed that at any cost, including even their own lives, Adminius must pay with his life. He was also understood to be giving the Romans strategic information about not only their own tribe and warriors but of land and tribes elsewhere, rivers and terrain. Including no doubt rivers that included the one where they were now camped.

He would also tell them of the people who would fight against them and that was an act that could not and would not go unpunished. The information he had to give was vital, vital to the success of the invaders and a possible death nail to them as defenders.

Adminius wasn't the only Briton to turn on his own people. Others who believed they had been badly treated by them were also known to be selling their souls to the enemy. The truth of the matter was that these people had broken laws and tribal rules and treaties that they had previously agreed to abide by but they had failed and they had been discovered and for that they had been exiled. A few had broken treaties, some had executed people under their protection for minor infractions and some had wanted to give their riches and resources to the men from the east in order that they would become clients of the Romans. Now they would begin to pay for their treachery and crimes with their lives.

The brothers had pushed their people hard in order to get breathing space and to lose the scouts who they knew were following them. Nothing more than small skirmishes had taken place since the landing and they now believed they had a day to prepare for what was to come.

Chapter Eleven

Through the swirling morning mist carried on an infrequent breeze, Varro slowly advanced with the cavalry cohort he had been attached to for the attack. Vespasian had deemed it necessary that all men and equipment available to him would be involved in what he believed would be the final and decisive battle against the Catuvellauni. His philosophy was that it was worth taking a greater risk to destroy Caratacus and Togodumnus and take casualties now rather than draw out the war and lose more men in the long term. Now all the Britons had to do was line-up and allow themselves to be slaughtered like never before.

When Varro and his small party including Brenna and her brother had originally ridden out in search of the enemy, they had originally lost contact with them despite being convinced that it wouldn't happen with such a large body moving together. The people they sought though had managed to evade them by moving faster and not stopping and it had forced the pursuers to spend time trying to locate them. The Britons had also used some of their carts, horses and people as diversions and he was shocked to find only old men and women when he had eventually tracked some of them down. They had posed no threat but had caused him to waste valuable time and he was angry at his own naivety. He had told those he found to return to their homes or risk losing their lives. In the main they agreed but some shouted abuse and one had even asked Varro questions.

"Why are you here Roman?" A man shouted sat on one of the carts. Varro looked at him, he assumed was about sixty years of age. He had long unkempt hair and was sat next to a woman of similar age who he presumed was his wife. Brenna translated his words but the man looked only at Varro.

"Togodumnus and Caratacus have seized the crown from Adminius of the Catuvellauni, rightful heir to the throne and loyal client King to the Emperor. They have also invaded other Kingdoms and plans on rebelling against Rome and cutting trade." Varro replied but even as he spoke his words were met with shaking heads.

"Adminius is the traitor and liar not Togodumnus or his brother. Your Emperor is either a fool or a liar and has been duped by Adminius and has allowed his greed to overtake his morals and mind. Tell me Roman what trade has ceased?" The old man stood on the plank seat of the cart as if to emphasise his point and make himself heard.

"Trade still flows from Britannia to Rome and from Rome to Britannia under Togodumnus. Adminius is the one who broke treaties and launched attacks on other regions. It is well known that it was he who was exiled by his father, a loyal King. It was he who called for rebellion here. Why else would the King have exiled him, his own son? It was he who was hungry for power and it is he who should be punished not an entire people."

Varro calmed Staro who jerked around underneath him, sensing tension. "My argument is not with you or your people old man. I am a soldier and go where I am ordered and I'm ordered to track Togodumnus down and you have delayed me long enough. I do not concern myself with politics but with what I can see, now where has he gone, which direction?"

The old man raised his eyebrows as if surprised by the question. "Do you expect me to betray my King Roman?" He looked around at the gathered Britons.

"I cannot help you no matter what you say or do. We live here and have lived here all our lives and we know what has happened. We have seen the greed of Adminius not Togodumnus. You may see yourself as an honest man merely doing his duty but you have been used as have all your soldiers. I am sorry but my new leader is a brave and proud man who is serving and trying to protect his people as you would and I cannot assist you against him." He sat down again as if to signify the end of the conversation.

Varro felt some respect for the old man and the others who were nodding in agreement to his words. He looked at Brenna and told her to translate once more.

"Take these people then and make your way to your homes where you will be safe." He turned Staro and galloped away with the others following. They continued to look to the west and eventually turned north east after picking up no fresh signs of the enemy. What the old man had said began to gnaw away at him. He had always believed in the noble nature of soldiering but things were beginning to cast doubts on his chosen way of life. He pushed the thoughts to the back of his mind and tried to concentrate on the task in hand.

Moving along a wide fairly fast flowing river he had finally found the army he had been searching for. They had made camp on the far side of the water a mile or so before it ran into the sea. Vast amounts of tents were pitched for as far as the eye could see and plumes of smoke billowed up from hundreds of small fires. People were wandering around talking to different groups some were eating and many were preparing weapons, warriors he assumed as he looked beyond them. From his position hidden amongst a wooded glade he could just make out war chariots behind the enemy lines, he lost count after fifty. The chariots were near a forest like area and maybe marsh land beyond where large reeds could be seen.

Working hard to stay out of sight, he and his small party watched the Britons from the safety of the far side of the river amongst uneven ground. It looked to Varro as if Togodumnus had decided to stand and make a fight and had chosen his ground well as he looked out over the huge encampment. He almost admired the chieftain for choosing this place as it was eminently defendable and hard to attack, there was no doubt that this enemy, was tactically astute. Crossing the river to attack them would prove difficult but he knew it would be imperative if they were to succeed.

Together with those in his group, the scouting party discussed the prospect of a battle occurring here. Brenna and her brother had volunteered to stay hidden and watch and wait for the slow moving Roman column to advance after Varro would report his findings to the General and his staff. Knowing that crossing the river was a major factor in what was to come, he had decided to travel further along the river and headed west to try and find a suitable place to cross. Although he estimated that the depth of the water was about shoulder height and therefore crossable, it wouldn't be so easy with enemy spears and arrows piercing soldiers flesh as they struggled with the water current as well.

    He rode on for about an hour and eventually found an old rickety foot bridge that was just wide enough for two men to cross at a time. It had been made from felled trees a long time before and bound together with vines but would be sufficient for a few cohorts to use to get to the other side of the twisting water. Varro had seen how the river had weaved its way through the countryside turning this way and that, almost turning back on itself at some points like a great snake. After finding no shallow areas suitable for a large crossing of men and equipment, he returned to the legion and reported his findings.

    Vespasian had listened to his report with interest often stopping him to ask questions or to clear up certain points as he studied the parchment map in detail. A plan of attack would be drawn up and developed with his officers and soon the Legion would march into battle.

    And so it was that he now found himself riding on its left flank advancing towards the great barbarian army on the far side of the river. The Legion had woken well before dawn and eaten breakfast consisting of dried hard biscuits and watered wine. It was still dark as he had checked his horse and had to use the flames from a torch burning nearby to make sure his saddle was secure and his javelins easily accessible.

    He now felt his heart began to pound and race in his chest in anticipation of the battle to come. He knew that the plan had involved his cohort being the tip of the spear of the attack but that was all, he knew no further specific details. The General had briefed Tribunes and senior Centurions who in turn briefed everyone through their own respective Centurions. There was no requirement for every single soldier to know specific details as they would receive their orders at the time.

    Slowly the horse's in front of his own came to a halt and an eerie silence descended. The noise of the flowing water and the occasional snort of a horse were the only things that broke it. They were to wait for the signal to advance into the water and to then cross the river as quickly as possible for a full frontal assault. He sat back in his saddle and felt the mists cool moisture on his arms and legs and thought about the fight to come as his stomach twisted and lurched in anticipation.

The plan that he was aware of was for the cavalry attack to withdraw as soon as their infantry reinforcements reached their position and engaged the army of Britons but before that a diversionary attack was to take place at the rear of the enemy lines. If that attack proved successful it would mean that the Britons would be virtually surrounded and cut off, unable to escape.

As far off cries of pain sounded from somewhere over on the other side of the river, he knew the assault had begun. Cohorts of Batavian cavalry had already set foot on the far side of the river a few hours before still under the cover of night. Some were to use the footbridge found by Varro and had made the way slowly to the other side and had gone to ground at the rear of the enemy, others had literally swam across the river with full kit three miles to the west.

The plan had been to attack and trap the Britons in the first instance by either killing, or disabling their horses at the rear and so knocking out their ability to use their chariots. The shrieks of pain from man and horse accounted for the guttural noises as the attack was pressed home but the incensed Catuvellauni were fighting like demons as they quickly realised that the Romans had already crossed the river and were now attacking from the rear.

The Batavians had quickly come to the conclusion that it was impossible to put all the horses out of action as they thrashed about kicking out at them and running wildly panicking as they saw what was happening to those around them. Soldiers tried in vain to hamstring as many of the animals as they could but were quickly attacked as they went about their grisly business.

The defending enemy counter attacked with a fury and a frenzy that even they, the veterans found hard to comprehend, as the first of the horses were wounded screaming out in agony, the Britons launched an assault. Running at the Romans the Catuvellauni threw themselves at the men killing and wounding their animals. The woad covered warriors attacked them like madmen swarming all around them in moments hurling spears and firing arrows into their ranks.

Individual fights broke out everywhere as the Romans not already engaged, attempted to hold off the attacking barbarians whilst others concentrated on the animals. The men of the Second Augusta started to fall in numbers as they were hacked and stabbed to death. Horses bolted, running wildly in the ensuing mayhem that descended all around and Roman and Briton alike were stampeded and knocked to the ground.

As Varro and his horse entered the water he exchanged nervous glances with those around him. The noise and cries from men and animals coming from the other side were chilling and almost unbearable. Their own mounts were already skittish, spooked by the ungodly sounds of battle. One trooper was thrown from his horse further down the line as his animal bucked, hurling him into the cold water.

Varro gasped as the water rose up his legs as man and horse got deeper into the river, he could now see the other side on the opposite shore through the mist. Whispering quietly to Staro he leaned forward and rubbed his neck trying to calm his mount as he strained to see more detail on the other side. He still couldn't see any of the enemy, just their roughly made tents and numerous campfires. The Centurion in charge of the cohort ordered them to advance further, they urged their animals forward wading deeper, moving faster through the deep cold water.

At the rear of the Britons line they were now taking control of the fight as more warriors enveloped the isolated Romans. Unable to wound any more horses and totally surrounded they fought for their lives, none were shown any mercy. Even those who tried to surrender, throwing their swords down and raising their arms were hacked to death by the incensed defenders who were crazed after what they had done to their animals. Fingers, hands, arms and heads were severed as blood clouds sprayed forming and spurting from veins in the continued attack as the Romans numbers were whittled down.

As they were cut to ribbons, the other cohorts appeared out of the mist galloping from their own river crossing. The bridge had collapsed under the weight of the animals so they had swam across, still steaming as the cold water met their warm bodies but they were too late to save their comrades. Instantly they turned to charge toward to a group of horses but the Britons got to them first and formed a human barrier. Spears were hurled through the air at the cavalry as faster flying arrows joined them in the air finding their targets.

The newly arrived troops and their horses were quickly hemmed together from all sides. Those who found themselves outermost struggled to fight such was the crush of bodies in front and behind and stood little chance. The men at the rear were unable to help, crammed in like eels in a barrel and could only watch in panic as those in front of them met a brutal death as they themselves could only wait their turn. Men fell from horses quickly as the long swords took their toll, the attackers able to stand off and swing wildly at such rich targets. For a rare moment the men fighting for the empire found that they didn't have the advantage. The Britons made short work of the heavily outnumbered and packed together cavalry. As the last of them was slaughtered the victorious Britons surveyed the damage done to their horses.

A pile of dead were left lying in a heap where they had died, bodies virtually piled up on top of each other. Severed arms and legs twisted at odd angles stuck out from the corpse pile, the stench of blood and shit was vile. Although the defence of the horses had been quick to respond to the attack, many now lay dead, others lay on the ground legs twitching, their cries of pain unworldly. Some tried in vain to get to their feet as the Britons approached them. Those who were deemed mortally wounded were dispatched with spears and swords. Others were still running around in pain large open wounds to their necks and flanks, still spilling blood.

As Varro and his own horse levelled out on the flat of the river side he heard sharp crisp snapping sounds and realised that they were under attack from bowmen. He looked to his left quickly after he heard a loud shriek and saw that a soldier had been hit in the throat. His hands grasped at the arrow embedded in his neck but his eyes began to glaze over almost immediately. Varro watched the legionary fall backwards over the rump of the horse, his body hit the water head first and was engulfed.

Instantly he was aware of the sounds around him, seemingly magnified as he tried to push Staro into a charge as water splashed around them. Another legionary was hit in the face by an arrow as it inverted his nose on impact. Varro heard yet another cry of pain from somewhere behind, it was bedlam. He leaned forward onto Staro's mane trying to present a smaller target as arrows whined past him from both sides and overhead. His head banged against his mounts neck and he got a face full of wet hair as Staro moved faster through the water raising his head.

After what seemed like an age, horse and rider began to emerge from the water on the other side. A brief thought inside his head told Varro that their position meant nothing because if anything the danger had now trebled as he saw woad covered Britons streaming forward screaming war cries. As they got to within about fifty paces they hefted their spears launching them into the air as they were joined by more arrows already on their own deadly flight. Varro swallowed briefly and thought that it would be a miracle if he survived this onslaught.

Riding clear of the water with the enemy bearing down on him, he pushed Staro up the slight embankment screaming encouragement to his horse. Those around him did the same but every second their flight was broken by cries of pain as arrows or spears found targets. Some horses hit by the deadly missiles were jumping in panic to the side, hitting other animals and dislodging their riders who splashed into the cold water, where men gasped for breath. The Britons were taking a heavy toll of both men and horses now as the two sides got closer. He turned to the rear quickly to make sure he wasn't alone and saw one dismounted soldier trying to wade through the water back to the other side, his horse already there but kicking wildly with a spear in its flank. Beyond the soldier he could see infantry walking into the water, their straight lines walking briskly, shields held high, they too were already starting to receive arrows.

From somewhere he was aware of trumpets sounding, giving orders to cohorts and centuries to pursue the attack as the chaos of battle grew. Staro began to gallop forward now clear of the water, he managed to gain a slight lead on the horses around him. Varro saw a clear gap to his left and steered towards it and then further to the left. He knew presenting himself and his horse's side to the enemy was a huge risk but he also knew that if he didn't do something quickly they would find themselves running straight onto swords or spears. From the corner of his eye he saw that more men and horses were getting hit by arrows. He saw one horse rearing upward with a number of arrows in its head and more landing as its undefended chest was bared. He kicked out at Staro mentally pleading for more speed.

'Come on boy we don't want to die here like this, not here, not today, come on faster.' He shouted. In a split second the thought was already gone from his head as from somewhere Staro found more speed. Varro clung on as he accelerated forward. From the side he was aware that he had made the right decision as the two opposing sides drew closer.

He saw that the enemy were now running flat out, sprinting towards their attackers, hurling spears, others held axes or swords aloft as they screamed and shook them in the air. They looked terrifying, their eyes and teeth prominent through their woad covered skin. Varro ripped a javelin free and hurled it forward and to the right. He didn't aim it at anyone in particular so dense was the crush of Britons massed and surging forward.

In seconds the two sides would clash and Varro worked like never before to push his horse further to the left. He didn't intend to end his life stupidly running into a sword or spiked on a spear. Briefly he was aware that some of the warriors were women amongst the men attacking them, for a second he saw breasts covered in blue bouncing as the women ran. He dismissed the thought concentrating on pushing Staro further.

'Faster boy come on.' He urged.

In the next moment he was aware of the two sides coming together behind him, clashing weapons and intensified screaming. Roman legionnaires who still had javelins worked them to find soft flesh, those without, stabbed out and slashed with their long swords as the Britons wielded their axes, swords and spears. The impact of the clash of both sides was almost ear splitting and Varro grimaced at the pain he felt in his ears but for now all that mattered was that he had escaped death.

He turned Staro quickly and saw that more Britons were running forward joining the fray. Weapons were brought up and down as they tried to find targets the sound of metal clashing together sharply. He reached for his second javelin whilst nudging Staro into a canter with his legs. Twenty paces from the battling sides he picked out a bare breasted women, he launched his weapon. Just before it struck home she was impaled by a Roman sword just below the right collarbone. His javelins point disappeared into the side of her head just in front of her ear and she fell lost amongst the struggling bodies.

He looked to the right and saw that the first of the infantry were struggling out of the water, dripping and struggling to form up. A trumpet sounded from somewhere ordering the cavalry cohort to hold their ground but it made no difference to the men fighting to stay alive. If they turned they would die, so they knew their only hope was to try and stay alive until reinforcements arrived. Varro saw that he wasn't the only one to have galloped to the left as he was now joined by three others their mounts snorting heavily, eyes wide.

"Let's hit them from the side." He shouted as he launched Staro towards the melee, the others followed. The Britons didn't see them coming so intent were they in their frenzy. They were struck by the charging war horses who ploughed into them knocking them sideways and backwards onto the floor. Varro quickly turned Staro and retreated from the fight. Another soldier wasn't so quick and was dragged from his mount and stabbed repeatedly never to rise again.

Varro charged out and away with the other two survivors but saw that the Britons were now clearly aware of him. A few peeled away from the large group and raced towards him. He didn't realise it at the time but this would save his life. He nodded at the two others to retreat and they followed him galloping further away from the battle as spears were launched towards them but fell short.

The pursuing Britons realising they wouldn't catch the horsemen and so turned and ran back towards the battle. Another trumpet sounded over the fighting and the cavalry engaged with the Britons turned and attempted to retreat. Some were dragged to the ground others were hit by spears but most managed to break free. Varro saw the reason why, the infantry were now formed up properly and were marching forward in tight lines.

The Britons didn't hesitate as they saw what they were now confronted with and started running at the neat columns of Roman soldiers. Helmets almost hidden behind the tops of large shields they advanced at the loosely running barbarians as another noise resounded over the screams and shouts, the sound of Roman short swords hitting their shields.

Varro and the other horseman began to canter back towards the water their horses breathing hard, breath billowing from flared nostrils as ballista bolts were launched for the first time from the other side of the river. They screamed over the legionaries helmets by the barest of margins and with astonishing speed slammed into the front, second and even third ranks of the running Britons.

Bolts literally spun some of the advancing Britons over backwards such was their speed and ferocity as they cut through the bodies and took their lives, other bolts merely passed through soft flesh their victims unaware until organs failed and they dropped to the ground dead. Varro saw three victims pinned together as the first then the second were slammed backwards into the third as they all then fell to the floor at the same time skewered together. Twenty feet from the front line of the Roman wall, javelins were launched by those soldiers holding them, who before they landed were already holding swords ready behind their guards. More of the enemy were taken from the battle as pila were embedded into bodies.

The first of the Britons began to reach the disciplined ranks, some threw themselves at the wall of shields, others tried to leap over them. Crashing into the large square as swords stabbed out to meet them, the warriors were easy targets. Those at the front were now caught between those following, where they met their end.

Varro halted short of the river as he and the two with him were joined by other mounted soldiers. He heard a trumpet sounding a cavalry flanking charge from the other side of the river, it seemed that Vespasian watching from somewhere unseen now intended to outflank the Britons and destroy them.

He turned his attention back to the battle and the square was doing what it did best, unleashing a murderous hell on their attackers. Unbeknown to the Britons who bravely threw themselves against the shields, it was only a matter of time before they died.

From behind the relative safety of their shields the men were stabbing at the enemy, short sharp thrusts were cutting the Britons down. At a Centurions shouted command, those at the front were replaced by the next row as the human death machine rotated its sword and shield cogs to maintain their deadly momentum. Soldiers could only remain on the front line for a few minutes at a time before they exhausted themselves. Slamming a shield boss into a determined enemy and then forcing them back or just holding the line was exhausting work. Stabbing through small gaps at a frenzied enemy and trying to avoid thrusts from spears and swords was equally tiring. It was something that the legions trained many hours and days to achieve and now their work was coming to fruition.

As more Britons ran to join the attack those at the front found themselves trapped by those behind them, there was nowhere to go and they died by the dozen, entire rows were cut down but still they came from the rear. Over the sound of mayhem, Varro heard splashing and saw that the ordered cavalry were making their way into the now almost boiling bloody and muddy water at the gallop. The wall of shields was now beginning to slowly advance over the dead in front of them and the Britons at the head of their battle line hesitated, those at the rear began to turn and retreat. Soldiers at the front were stepping onto their victims, steadily they moved over broken and bloody slippery mess trying to maintain their discipline and balance. The rear of spears could be seen stabbing downward as they moved.

In seconds the cavalry were across the river, what seemed to take an age previously now passed in the blink of an eye, the almost insurmountable dangerous water was nothing more than a slight obstacle to be overcome as the unsuspecting Britons were about to be surrounded. As the cavalry got level with Varro and his group they cantered forward and joined them in their attack on the right flank. As horses struck the fighting Britons another noise seemed to envelope the atmosphere. Varro struggling to control Staro and turned his head to see what was causing it. Starting as a low rumbling, the ground now shook as it got louder.

The Britons to a man and woman turned and were running, retreating the way they had come but the noise overriding the chaos sounded like an earthquake, he didn't know what it was but saw that the front line of troops had stopped and was standing still, no longer advancing. A line of dead were lying in front of them. Horses were turned towards the growing sound as riders turned their mounts.

Just as the last of the running Britons vanished into the mist covering the marsh, the first of the horses appeared galloping forward tethered to another followed by the men on the chariots they pulled. They emerged from the mist like avenging gods as a collective gasp ran through the men they faced.

"Flanking counter attack now!" Shouted an equestrian officer as he pulled his mount and galloped away shouting again, "Flanking Counter." Varro knew the order and quickly followed as horses moved away from their current position as if one to avoid the advancing chariots.

Togodumnus rode in the leading chariot whirling a long sword around his head and shouting encouragement and screaming at the men bouncing along in other chariots all around and behind him. Caratacus was one of them, the King his brother in his own chariot but he was convinced he could protect him. As the mobile Britons continued to advance building up speed, those on the sides of their great formation edged away to try and outflank the enemy infantry. The sound of the charging horses and chariots was nothing like anything that had gone before even the infantry now hitting their shields again were drowned out as the Britons bore down on them. Varro saw that the retreating Britons on foot had now turned and were following the chariots into battle.

"Charge. Forward!" Screamed the officer trying to encourage his own men leading their charge merely paces from the flanking chariots, seconds before the impact of the two sides. As the clash occurred some were lucky and ran through gaps in their opponents lines and lashed out with swords or spears. Others clashed head on with the enemy, tearing men from their horses, chariots were catapulted forward, tumbling into the dense mass of bodies and armour, weapons flew like missiles after being knocked from hands, horses ran into each other head on, the noise from the chaos was horrendous.

Varro was just behind this mass of madness and so survived unhurt as he pushed forward into the melee. Men on chariots hurled spears at the Roman horses, swords clashed and men and animals alike died, were mortally wounded or sustained injuries that would affect them for evermore. As the centre line of racing chariots including Togodumnus neared the Roman infantry of the Second Augusta the men were ordered to stand fast. The ground shook as the chariots got closer and closer. Centurion and legionary alike braced themselves for the shock of the impact about to hit them. They had already expended their own javelins but more had been passed forward from the rear and the men behind those at the front passed the weapons forward as quickly as possible. A centurion within the ranks had ordered that they hold them out towards the advancing horses like a giant porcupine. These pila now appeared, thrust through the shield wall by the men standing behind the front rank as they all waited for the crash.

Two independent battles broke out on the flanks as the Roman cavalry tried to stop the other chariots from getting to the sides and rear of their infantry, a few got through and raced off at angles speeding off elsewhere on the battlefield. Seconds from crashing the central chariots, helmets ducked behind shields. Spears were hurled from the charioteers and landed at random amongst the rows of legionaries.

Just before the crunching impact of animal and shield, horses saw the levelled spears and halted immediately digging their front hooves into the ground, their screaming occupants were hurled upwards over and into the square. Of the horses that didn't stop some ran straight onto the spears, those that somehow avoided them smashed into the Roman shields causing chaos, piling into and over men. Some of the passengers aboard the chariots jumped clear and ran to the areas where holes had been punched into the shield wall and attacked.

"Hold the line" Screamed voices as some soldiers knocked to the floor by the charging horses struggled to their feet while others were still on the ground unconscious or too injured to move. Others had lost their shields and some their swords. The rampaging Britons took advantage of those dazed by the onslaught and instantly hacked them apart. Around them other infantry tried to tighten their part of the shield wall and advanced as best as they could in the mayhem closing in on the attackers.

Chapter Twelve

Caratacus saw the danger instantly, even though his men and women were hacking down the Romans around him. He saw that the small victories would be short lived as their enemies reinforcements advanced. In the chaos all around he also saw that beyond the thrashing and clash of iron, more Romans were landing on his side of the river using rafts made of wood. There was little that he could do about it because the warriors were already struggling to cope with those already there. He looked to the side of the battleground and saw enemy horsemen rapidly outflanking those converged in the main fight, he had to do something or he and his people would be destroyed.

He looked around desperately looking for Togodumnus and briefly recognised his brother in the middle of one fight that was merely one part of many surrounded by other Britons fighting for their very lives. Large swords and axes were whipping up and down and from left to right as weapons clashed against the enemy shields and armour, men screamed and sprays of blood discoloured the air for the brief seconds they were airborne. The combined smell of blood and excrement from released bowels was vile, that mixed with the noise, made this place hell. He didn't know what was worse, the sight of the battle, the sound or the stench of blood and shit. Behind the Roman lines in the distance he saw a shining gold eagle held high like a nemesis advancing towards him.

"Retreat brother, retreat!" He shouted as loud as he was able but his voice was already hoarse and was swallowed up, drowned out by the noise all around him. He realised that in no time at all Togodumnus would be surrounded again but on this occasion by the enemy. The advancing armour and men hidden behind their shields were like huge waves now and nothing it seemed could stop them.

"Retreat, retreat." He shouted again.

The enemy wall of shields steadily advanced, spears were thrust out at his warriors and they began to take more injuries. All along the line the same thing was happening, there were small pockets where the chariots had punctured holes but they were being sealed again by the invaders like some natural vacuum. Britons who engaged the Romans at arms lengths were stabbed with short swords, those behind them were stabbed at with javelins from the men in the enemies second or third rows, as others received hurled javelins and those on the flanks were now engaged by the cavalry as they were slowly enveloped.

Caratacus ran forward still shouting trying to warn the men and women desperately fighting, only those directly in front of him heard the warning and began to back away. He realised he wasn't going to get to Togodumnus in time and for a brief moment decided to run forward, he would die here with his brother or somehow get him free. He saw a female warrior her lithe beautiful form staggering towards him, deep puncture wounds bled from her stomach and breasts, her face white with shock except for the woad colouring her features.

He grabbed hold of an arm and dragged her behind him and pushed the image from his head because he had to find his brother. As soon as the thought rushed through his mind another told him that he had to stay alive, retreat, stay alive and keep fighting if Togodumnus was killed. He paused watching as his brother and King was engulfed by stabbing blades, he staggered backwards overcome with shock and grief, his body shook. One of his men grabbed his arm and pulled him backwards away from the fight. He tried to resist planting his feet but another set of strong hands pulled him clear shouting at him not to resist and onto a stationary chariot, he stopped struggling.

"Ride, ride, get Caratacus clear." The man was bleeding from a head wound but Caratacus saw the determination in his clear eyes and stopped resisting altogether. From the height of the chariot he saw that his brother, King of the Catuvellauni was still fighting, swinging his sword at the moving shield wall now all around him he and his small band who were surrounded entirely. He could see the sword rise and come down onto the top of a shield and stop, it was stuck, he saw as his brother tried to prise it free. It was the last time he would see him as the chariot was quickly turned and the driver struggled to retreat through the still advancing men and women.

Togodumnus saw that those around him were being whittled down and knew he wouldn't survive this battle. He looked around for his brother but couldn't see him anywhere. He gripped his sword with two hands with all his strength to lose it now would mean instant death.

"No surrender." He shouted at the top of his voice as he hammered his sword down on the nearest shield. The double bladed sword sliced down into the top of the scutum a few blade widths and stopped. He immediately tried to pull his weapon free but found that it was lodged tight.

Men and women fell all around him struck down as iron cut through their bodies as other shields closed in. He saw one female warrior's blue painted flesh turned red with blood as a spear sliced through her throat. She didn't stop or hesitate but fought on impaled on the point of the weapon sticking through her flesh, hacking at the man responsible. He let go of his sword and pulled his dagger free of its scabbard and ran at her attacker. He wrenched another shield down and reached forward trying to stab at the man holding it who jerked his head back, his knife too short.

He suddenly felt an instant white hot pain from somewhere under his ribcage, in the centre of his stomach, it was crippling and instantly disabled any further movement. He dropped his weapon so paralysing was the pain. He looked down and saw a wooden shaft tipped with iron protruding from his stomach. Before another thought came to him, it was ripped free. Blood came with it and the pain was now such that he began to black out, the noise around him faded. Falling backwards he was aware of being struck by another blow somewhere to the side of his chest and then the world went black.

Caratacus was carried back to the rallying point of his chariots, he felt empty, cold and devastated. He staggered from the wooden chariot, sweating and shaking, white with shock. Men and women around him saw his expression but most were running and didn't register fully what had occurred. Warriors were still advancing towards the enemy, he watched as they ran but knew their bravery was in vain.

"Have them pull back." He said to the men who had saved him. "Get into the marshland, we can't beat them like this, they are too heavily armoured and protected."

"But lord your brother, the King what of him?" He asked.

"He was surrounded the last time I saw him." He pointed towards the battle, "Get them pulled back." He walked to his horse mounted it and then rode towards the marshes. Those who could, retreated, men and women on foot and chariots moved back to the rallying point and beyond into the marshes. The battle had gone on until midday and both sides had won some encounters but the first major blow had been struck by the enemy. They're unceasing shield wall supported by rapidly moving cavalry had forced the defenders back and into certain defeat. For hours the battle had raged on as they were out flanked, their warriors with their horsemen and so their chariots tried to outflank them but they simply did not have enough to stop the seemingly endless tide of men and armour.

Vespasian had called a halt to their advance when the Britons were seen to be finally retreating in larger numbers. Disciplined the soldiers had held their position as they were ordered. They even allowed their opponents to drag away the injured as they consolidated the position having won the strategic advantage over the river. Supplies were brought forward and artillery was set up in a defensive perimeter. The Britons had lost hundreds, maybe thousands their dead bodies littered the ground but Varro saw that his own force had lost men as well although not nearly as many as the enemy.

Word in the fast growing camp was that they were to pursue and destroy all those who had stood before them but it had to be done in a manner that reduced the cost in lives and injuries to their own. Things were moving rapidly, it could only be a matter of time before the Britons were defeated or forced to surrender.

"Lord, lord!" Caratacus was sat drinking water from a wooden cup, he turned to the shouting behind him somewhere in the trees. He had eventually retreated into the marshland with a large force intending to ambush the advancing army but they had paused for breath and much needed rest. Scouts informed him that the Legion of Vespasian were now reinforcing their position. He knew that the scene of the battle was lost to him and his people and for the time being there was nothing he could do. Their enemy although brutal, had allowed them to retrieve their injured and many were now being tended in areas nearby. Wails and cries from relatives of those struck down sounded from all around him as well as those of the injured. He had sent skirmishers and archers back through the trees to watch for when the Romans advanced again knowing they wouldn't have to wait long. They were ordered to engage them and then withdraw, engage and withdraw as fast as possible.

"What is it?" He asked of the man panting before him.

"The King he lives." The man pointed as Caratacus jumped to his feet dropping the cup. He saw his brother's body seemingly lifeless being carried on a war chariot towards him the horses were reigned in and brought to a halt. He heard a feint sigh from Togodumnus as the two horses pulling the chariot breathed heavily from their exertion. Caratacus ran over to him, he was appalled by what he saw. His brother had sustained multiple injuries to his upper chest and stomach. Almost black blood bubbled up out of two larger blood black holes in his chest. Most of the other injuries were wedge shaped and could have only come from short swords.

"Togodumnus." He said his voice almost breaking with emotion. His brother didn't respond, he was laid out on his back unmoving his eyes barely open, spittle and blood coming from his mouth. Caratacus tried to stop the blood flow from his body with his hands but it was useless.

"Bring cloth." He shouted not taking his eyes from his brother. "I thought you were dead." He said almost to himself as he surveyed the injuries again. "I knew in my heart you wouldn't fall, that they couldn't kill you." Even as he spoke, he knew his words were lies.

"We managed to get him free of the attack," said one of the men from the chariot, "if they had known he was the King they would have taken him. At first I thought he was dead there was so much blood but as I crouched I saw his eyes flicker and pulled him free of the bodies around where he lay." The chariot driver told him now staring down at his King.

"You did well my friend but I fear it may be too late to help him. He has received many injuries and whilst my brother will fight to the last, I fear the worst and think he maybe mortally wounded." He looked at his brother and watched as short shallow breaths escaped his racked and ruined body. He leant over him and whispered in his ear.

"Can you hear me brother?" He turned and looked at his face looking for any signs of consciousness there were none, no signs of life except for the breaths escaping his open mouth. He saw that even the top row of his teeth had been shattered and at least four were missing presumably knocked out as he had fought for his life. He was pained to see his brother this way, they had grown up together, laughed, cried and fought with each other.

"Brother, hear me." Tears welled up in his eyes, he didn't try to stop them. He looked up and realised that there were others gathered around him, their faces reflected his own, shock, sadness, fear and hate.

"Prepare for the enemy." He ordered looking at them. "They will pay dearly for this." The men and women around him picked up and gathered their weapons some of which had been dropped at the surprise of seeing their King so badly injured. None spoke, they didn't have to and with determined features they ran into the marshes.

Togodumnus' body shook and trembled as more blood pumped from his pierced and penetrated skin. The two wounds that had previously spewed dark black blood now emitted pinkish bubbling frothing fluid and Caratacus knew that his brother's lungs were damaged, he had seen this before. His breaths shortened, rasping with every effort, he didn't have long. Caratacus leaned over him again he knew he didn't have much time. He heard shouts from the men sent to watch for movement from the enemy.

"I swear by the gods I will avenge you brother, I will live to fight these invaders and become a thorn in their sides. I will give my all to take from them as they taken from us. I will have no other reason for being and if I am forced to give my life I will give it gladly, for my people, my land and our family. They will live to regret their greed and betrayal by invading our lands. This I swear on our fathers name, I will make it my life's work to avenge you." Tears dropped freely onto his brother's dirty blood stained face, the droplets smearing blood and dirt.

After a few quiet moments Caratacus looked up and saw that there were still five of his warriors stood solemnly watching him. He looked at them all in turn and saw the sorrow in their eyes.

"Car........" He looked back and saw that Togodumnus had opened his eyes, barely but they were open and he was trying to speak. Blood ran from the side of his mouth freely.

"I'm here brother." Caratacus said as he leant forward again trying to block everything else out.

"Admin...." His eyes rolled into the back of his head.

"Togodumnus." He reached down and took his brother's head in his hands raising it slightly.

"Adminius is that what you're saying, Adminius?" He felt the head rock slightly in his hands.

"I will ensure that bastard pays for what he has done, his treachery won't go unpunished. He is worse than the men behind those shields, at least they have not betrayed their own. At least they are brave enough to face us without cowering somewhere in the background beyond our reach. I promise you brother I swear it on our fathers soul."

Togodumnus closed his eyes as if the pain was too much and he sighed. Caratacus looked down at him tears rolling freely down his face. The King who was his brother opened his eyes once more and managed the briefest of smiles.

He gasped once more, eyes looking heavenward and then his brother felt the weight of his head grow heavy and saw his arms go limp as life left his body. Togodumnus was dead.

"Arrrrrrgggggggghhhhhhh!" Caratacus let out an almost inhuman howl, the men around him took a step back as the animalistic sound made them jump. It went on for some seconds before Caratacus fell forward over his dead brother cradling him in his arms. He let the grief and hatred combine through his veins, coursing as blood pumped from his still strong and beating heart.

After a few minutes he looked up staring ahead, "Take the King," he ordered not even lifting his head to look at the men, "I will not leave him here as a trophy for them."

They moved forward and carefully picked up the body of their former King as if he were still alive and carried him to the chariot where they placed his body.

"We will honour my brother as he deserves but not here, be sure to be careful with him." The men nodded and climbed aboard the chariot, two squatted down and held the Kings body gently and while one drove, the other two stood guard. Caratacus watched as he was slowly driven away.

"I'll see you soon my brother and we'll talk and laugh again." He said wiping his eyes. Picking up his sword he ran into the marshes.

The Roman advance was still halted as they dealt with the dead, dying or injured and brought forward more equipment, men and horses. Their own wounded, those unable to walk were taken to the rear where doctors and physicians tended to their injuries. The Legion as a whole had paused whilst readying themselves for the next step. War was a steady business Vespasian knew, it wasn't to be rushed or mistakes would be made and valuable lives lost.

Some dead Britons still littered the battlefield in dense patches where intense amounts of fighting and killing had taken place. Twisted pale limbs were bent at horrific angles and poked out from under legs and bodies, faces contorted in shock, anger and pain stared, dead eyes not seeing the world around them. Hundreds had gone to their gods that day but all bravely and without question or hesitation, the General realised he admired them for that.

It was midday before the army was formed up and ready to advance again. Scouts were sent forward to survey the tree line and beyond where the majority of Britons had been seen retreating towards. It was however, impossible for the main battle formation to enter the wooded area and even more so to enter the marshland beyond, the hazard the scouts had already found.

Vespasian had eventually decided to send a Batavian cohort forward after the scouts had reported their findings, marshland, water and bog dispersed amongst small patches of dry land. It was no place for the ranks of the Legion and so a different kind of advance was decided upon. He had learned harsh lessons from entering such places in their battle formations before, entire legions had been destroyed by Germanic tribes in the past. Vespasian didn't intend to make the same mistake of Varus who nearly forty years before had led over twenty thousand men to their deaths, wiped out in the forests of Teutoburg.

The temperature was cooler under the trees as they slowly moved forward on their horses taking in their surroundings. The ground had been solid enough under the branches when they had first entered the marshy woodland but was now it was getting damper and wetter. Squelching noises sounded as the horses pulled their hooves up from the muddy water as their riders tried to find firmer ground but it was becoming increasingly impossible.

An eerie quiet covered the woods and marshland elsewhere like a blanket, there were no birds singing or hares running wild here which the mounted men found disheartening. They knew something wasn't right. The men of the cohort knew that an attack would come but from where and when they didn't know, the pressure was like a physical force. Eventually the Decurion leading them, Arturius Valius found some more favourable footing where the ground was almost dry, it stretched out before them as far as he could see which wasn't very far under the circumstances because of the twines from the other trees but at least it was a better surface.

He didn't like this country, there were too many areas like this where an ambush could come from anywhere. The entire land it seemed was covered in trees from what he had seen of it so far and couldn't understand what use the Emperor could find for all this wood, marsh and bog. He had served in Rome's legions for twelve years and wanted nothing more than to be able to return home to his wife and family but he knew it wouldn't happen for a number of years yet so he had to concentrate on surviving.

He stopped momentarily and raised his right arm indicating that the men behind him halt while he paused and listened. Looking through the vines he scanned the terrain but there was nothing to hear or see. He strained his eyes trying to look beyond the trees and branches but could see nothing, nothing at all, no movement that may give away an ambush but he knew they were there, waiting, watching. He turned to his men but all he got in response was shrugs, they saw or sensed nothing also.

It went on like that for some time until he saw more watery marshland ahead. He waved his second in command forward, whispering he said to Aquilus, "There's more fucking water and mud ahead, pass the word, tell the men we'll take a break and get some water down us before we go further." The soldier did as he was ordered and the men dismounted quietly and took their water skins from the horses as the animals started to chew on the lush green grass around them.

After a while just as Valius felt as if he could fall asleep sat on the ground where he had stopped propped against the trunk of a tree, he decided it was time to move on. He beckoned for Aquilus and told him to tell the men. As he turned and went to carry out the order Valius was aware of something flying passed him at speed barely missing his eye in a blur, he even felt its passing. He heard a dull thump and saw that an arrow had hit his second in command and was embedded between the chain-link armour covering his back and the bronze of his helmet in the back of his neck. He stood still for a second and then just fell face forward onto the grass like a dead weight. The Decurion turned and couldn't believe what he saw.

Chapter Thirteen

Leaping out of the water was a large pack of enormous dogs with woad coloured Britons running behind them. Some were standing on the dry land launching arrows at the troops who were now scrambling to get to their feet. Where they had come from or how they had got so close, so quickly didn't matter, just doing something about it did.

"Stand to. Stand to." Shouted the Decurion as he stumbled to get to his own horse. Three feet from relative safety two arrows hit it either side of the saddle and it reared and bolted. He saw the Britons were closing on him and were now only about thirty feet away. Turning quickly he ran towards his men, some were already on their own mounts and were clearly panicking as some horses bolted and reared. One soldier he saw threw his pilum before getting on his horse.

"Run sir." Shouted one of his soldiers as he turned his horse and held out a hand for the officer as he sprinted back the way they had come. Shrill war cries screamed from behind and he could almost feel the dog's teeth sinking into his legs as the snarling got louder. A soldier loosed an arrow and it flew at pace passed the running Decurion closely missing him, seconds later he heard an animal yelp clearly it had hit one of the dogs but it wouldn't help against an entire pack.

He slipped forward on the damp surface, stumbling nearly falling over but somehow managed to stay on his feet. The horse and rider were gathering speed as they began their retreat as he reached out inches from safety. Arrows flew over and all around him as spears began to land but by some miracle they all missed.

"Come on sir for fucks sake." Shouted the soldier turning in his saddle and leaning forward leaving his arm outstretched. Valius jumped and grabbed for the arm and managed to cling on as the soldier swung him forward and up. He landed on the hard rump of the cantering horse as it sped up and bounced him up and down as he looped his arms around the cavalryman's waist almost falling off.

"Ride. Fucking ride soldier." He turned his head but before he could turn fully he saw the large dogs were already level with the horse, barking and snarling up at its legs, froth flying from their large sharp teeth. He wanted to reach for his sword but knew that to do so would be to risk falling. If that happened he would be ripped apart so he turned and clung on for dear life.

The horses eventually started to outpace the dogs when they got to a gallop but were soon caught up again when they reached another watery patch. As the soldiers urged their mounts through the waist high water as it splashed head high, the dogs leapt from the dry land.

Valius was suddenly aware of another attack from the front as his men began to turn and realised that they were cut off from the front and rear. Horses broke to the left and the right as dozens of animals panicked, eyes wide with fright. He knew that if they didn't stay together they would be easy prey and picked off one at a time but also knew that man and horse were panicking as they tried to survive the onslaught.

"Dogs? Dogs?" Shouted one soldier clearly in shock as the half crazed animals bit up at the horse's legs, growling and trying to gain purchase on their flesh.

"The bastards use them to hunt deer and bring them down." Valius shouted as he scrambled for a javelin at the horses side. He turned as loud splashes caught his attention where it looked like the water was boiling. He saw three of the dogs had latched onto the rear legs of a horse and were trying to pull it down. The soldier on board realising the odds were against him jumped clear splashing into the water face first, arms and legs spread. Instantly the dogs turned their attention to the man releasing the horse, before the Batavian even got his head clear of the water, the dogs were on him. Valius saw the soldiers arms were pinned to his side as the three then another bit into the flesh of his legs. He screamed in agony and vaguely struggled for his sword but was dragged down as yet another large dog attacked.

"This way," shouted the Decurion as his rider struggled to the right colliding into another horse. The confusion had allowed the Britons to get closer and they now launched numerous spears and arrows at the escaping men. Sharpened spikes penetrated the flesh of horse and man alike as the water began to turn red with blood.

Half naked warriors hurled themselves into the water as the majority of the panicked cavalry struggled to follow the Decurion. Those that had chosen to go to the left were quickly surrounded as other Britons appeared from the left side. Screams were literally drowned out as men were dragged from horses and plunged into the water by their attackers and pushed under and stabbed or drowned.

Helmets were ripped from heads and used as clubs to batter some of soldiers senseless before they were killed. Valius saw some surrendering holding their arms high weapon less. One of them he watched was run through by a long sword, the expression on his face of horrified shock. The Decurion urged the rider on, they had to escape this madness.

Caratacus withdrew his sword as the man collapsed. He would take no captives this day after seeing his brother die. Around him the enemy were cut down, those not surrounded by his warriors were torn to pieces by his hunting dogs. Soaking he saw that an element of soldiers were beginning to get away, he pointed in their direction and victimless warriors began to charge after them.

Sometime later disorientated and lost, the surviving auxiliaries had slowed their animals to a walk. They had trudged through the marshes for what seemed like an eternity and had eventually found dry land free of the bog. They rode on in silence, dirty, shocked and bloodied by the brutality and swiftness of the attack.

Valius had lost more than half the men that had gone into the watery marshland with him but he knew what was important now was survival, they would have time to mourn later. Horses had been cut down as well as men and no doubt some taken by the barbarians. The wrath he would face from the General would be nothing compared to facing the horror of the enemy in that watery grave. Images of the attack kept returning to his inner vision as his mind kept replaying men being brought down and attacked by the huge dogs. He wanted to stop and rest but didn't dare in case they caught up with them. His surviving men didn't complain, they all knew the risk and like him were prepared to keep going all night as long as they escaped with their lives.

Miles away to the south, the Roman Commander of the entire invasion, Aulus Plautius conferred with Vespasian. All major elements had now crossed the Medway and the vast Roman army was patiently waiting for further orders. Weapons were checked and re-supplied as were other stores, the casualty areas were reinforced and made more substantial. They planned to keep the ground they had taken.

Already trees were being felled in order to build a temporary crossing point across the river, a fortified bridge. For the time being the majority, were still having to cross some miles away from where the majority of combat troops were now gathered as only a few at a time could use the rafts. The crossing used during the battle was worn and eroded and too dangerous to use further. Inside the quickly assembled command tent the architects of the battle discussed their options. Vespasian poured a mug of wine and offered another to Plautius which he accepted.

"What would you recommend General?" asked the commander deferring to the experienced man under his command. Vespasian considered for a moment before answering, he examined the hastily drawn map in his hands. "We can either make camp here for the night or we can pursue them and cut them down sir."

Vespasian looked around him at those listening before going further, "We've still got daylight for maybe another four or five hour's sir. If we stop now it will give them chance to regroup, I think it's better if we push on for as long as we can while we've still got light. However, the Batavian cohort should have returned by now and we've seen no sign of them."

"Do you think the Britons have got the better of them?" The commander asked.

Vespasian shrugged, "Valius is a good man sir I hope not. His horses are quick and he's experienced. If he did get into any difficulties I'm sure he could get out of them. However, without knowing what's happened to him and his men, we can't afford to send anymore forward for the time being. We don't know what's beyond the trees except marsh and we don't know how far it extends.

I would suggest sending scouts ahead first. Centurion Varro and his men are available but if we send them on, I want them to be wary and return to our lines at the first sign of trouble. It will also give the rest of the men an opportunity to rest for a while and get some food." Vespasian said changing his decision as he spoke, war was one thing, unpredictable.

Plautius didn't hesitate, "Excellent, have the men take a well-earned break. If we're no further forward with the reconnaissance by the time it starts to get dark, we'll dig in properly and have the usual defences completed. I can't see them coming back after the beating they took but you never know. How many men does Valius have in his cohort by the way, is it at full strength?"

"Yes sir four hundred. I'm concerned that we've had no sign of them it's not like Valius at all, he can always be relied on, he's one of my best commanders. I've known him for years and would have expected him to send a runner back by now if all was well. I'll send the scouts forward and see what they can find."

"Good," Plautius replied, "I'll be here if you need anything further." Dismissed Vespasian and the other senior officers left the tent.

Varro had been summoned and given his orders and sometime later he found himself under the trees heading north into the marshes. He was accompanied by Decimus, Lucius and Marcus. Brenna and her brother had gone to try and drum up support for the Romans from local villages and settlements.

It wasn't long before Varro and his men found signs of trouble. A Batavian horse was calmly feeding on the long grass about four hundred paces after the marshes edge, it looked up at them as they approached, then continued chewing quite happily at the long grass. Varro dismounted and walked towards it.

"Hello boy." He said quietly, "Where's your master then?" The horse jerked his head up shaking away flies but didn't bolt as Varro stroked his head.

"Are you alright then, no cuts?" He looked at the horse's flanks but could see no sign of injury or tell-tale signs of battle but looking closer in the long mane he found blood. He looked around, it was quiet, the marsh unwelcoming lay ahead.

"We'll leave him here for now, we don't want him tied to our own mounts in case we need to move fast, come on lets go." He climbed aboard his own horse and walked slowly towards the muddy marsh.

"Okay let's not stay too close, twenty paces at least between each horse." He ordered as the others began to drop back. He guided his horse into the water and felt it wet and cold on his feet and legs, 'fucking country' he thought to himself.

It wasn't long before they found the first ambush site. Pushing further into the marsh they started to find bodies. Corpses floated in shallow red water, bits of equipment also, here and there was the body of a dead horse. Varro dismounted slowly and examined the men, crouching over bodies. Together with sword and arrow wounds and the occasional puncture from a spear, he found that some of them had flesh missing. Bite marks were clearly visible on the exposed skin.

"What in the god's names happened here?" Decimus asked standing at the side of his commander, he felt chills running through his skin

"I haven't got the first fucking idea, maybe dogs perhaps they used dogs to hunt them down. We know they are famous for them and before the invasion they traded their hunting dogs with the Empire. Some are waist high and used to hunt deer and even larger prey, they could even be used to bring a horse down." Varro replied. "They're heads are like this." he held his hands out nearly a foot wide showing Decimus who frowned."

"Jupiter's fucking cunt, well I don't want to come across any of them." Was all Decimus said jumping back on his horse as if being a few feet higher would be safer. Varro stood slowly, his nerves on edge even more now than he'd expected, he imagined seeing some of the large beasts advancing towards him.

"Come on." He said ordering his scouting party forward. He and his men preferred to be miles ahead of the main army or even days ahead but when battle had been joined this kind of reconnaissance was what they were used for and it was deadly.

Some miles ahead and to the north Valius and the remainder of his cohort ambled through the thick forest. They had eventually managed to get clear of the marshland but had yet to find the Second Augusta. He looked up at the sky again trying to get his bearings through the canopy of trees.

If he was correct he they were now heading in the right direction. He had led the survivors clear of the deadly bog and north initially. It wasn't so much of a tactical decision he thought to himself but one of survival and it had been the only route out of the ambush area. They had maintained their course until he was convinced as best as he could be that they weren't being followed.

Although the ground was dry now it was still slow going through the thick trees and exhausting. Since the attack he and his men had expected another ambush at any time and in the forest it could come from any direction. He scanned forward and to the side constantly on the alert for some movement or noise, he almost wished for it to cut the suspense.

The only sound was that from their horse's movement, there was no breeze which he was thankful for as they walked slowly forward. In open ground they could have covered miles already and probably would have been back behind friendly lines but here it was impossible, he cursed every step.

Images of the ambush were still raw in his mind, the men he had lost to the dogs especially. It was unbelievable yet it had happened, men and horses torn apart. The Britons were truly barbarians and reluctantly he admitted a worthy enemy as he acknowledged that they were using everything at their disposal to fight a superior force. Just as he realised that he had stopped sweating from his exertions earlier, but was now cold through damp, he heard a cry and the sound of breaking branches. He whipped his horse around and saw that Britons were jumping out of trees onto his men behind him, spears and swords in hand. Shouts of alarm also broke the silence as soldiers were jerked from horses and fell violently to the ground. How had he missed them in the branches of the trees?

"Advance, advance." He ordered as he turned again and kicked his horse forward. He knew that if he had tried to help those to the rear, he would have been cut down as well. He turned his head as two half naked bodies jumped onto each man and horse.

He shuddered as he urged his mount through the thick trees realising that this patrol was turning into a nightmare. Images of his family flashed through his mind and he briefly wondered if he would ever see their faces again.

'Faster,' he mentally coaxed his horse almost pleading for clear ground ahead but seeing none. Movement in front him, up in the trees almost made him pull up and his blood ran cold, he saw more warriors preparing to jump. Pulling his sword free of its scabbard he charged through the trunks of the trees, his horse veering this way and that. Another rider shot passed him to his right kicking up soil and mud in its panic to get clear, the rider didn't even turn to acknowledge his commander. Just as he got about twenty paces ahead a body dropped from above and landed on the horse's neck, the rider stabbed out with his spatha, striking the attacker somewhere on the upper body and he fell away to the ground.

Valius grinned in satisfaction as his horse raced past the stricken wounded Briton clutching at a hole in his chest. Looking forward he saw others emerge from behind trees with bows fifty paces ahead. He started to steer his horse at awkward angles through the trees trying to make them both a more difficult target as arrows were launched. Within seconds he was amongst the bow carriers and at first tried to hack out at them with his weapon but they merely jerked out of the way and moved aside. He clenched the hilt of his sword and just tried to concentrate on riding as he quickly realised it was virtually impossible to hit any of them.

Shouts and war cries reached his ears from behind but he didn't dare risk turning. He wasn't aware of how long it took or when it actually occurred but he suddenly realised it was quieter. He looked up into the branches of the advancing trees but saw no threat from above or any archers below. He slowed his horse and was joined by the rider who had raced past him.

"Where are the others sir?" asked the auxiliary. Valius frowned slightly bemused but realised that he couldn't hear anything behind him. He turned expecting to see some of his men but there were none. They were alone.

Varro slowed his horse when Decimus pointed over to the right of their position as they walked through the dense forest.

"I saw something move over there, about two hundred paces." He said still pointing. They stopped and listened, watching with the others behind them. At first there was nothing, everything was still and then Varro saw the head of a horse appear from behind a tree and then the rider.

"It's an auxiliary alright but where are the others?" Decimus asked as they sat staring at the man as another appeared behind him but no more.

"They can't be the only survivors." It wasn't a question just a statement. Varro and Decimus exchanged a look and then trotted forward. The advance alerted the two riders, the look of relief on their faces immediate.

"Thank the gods," Valius said, "We thought we were the only ones left." His expression suddenly changed as he saw the men's uniforms and equipment and realised they were regulars and not auxiliaries. He also saw that there were only a handful of them.

"Centurion Varro." Varro said introducing himself. "Where are the rest of your men Decurion?"

"We were ambushed with fucking huge dogs in the marsh sir and then the bastards jumped out of the trees, we got away there was nothing more to be done except escape or die."

Valius replied. "Where are the rest of your men?" He asked.

Varro tried to gauge the man but couldn't judge whether he was a coward or had just been very unfortunate.

"You rode out with four hundred men, are they all dead?" Deliberately he ignored the man's own question.

Valius stared at him, "Dead, lost or captured." There was a brief silence only broken by the next words from Varro, "Follow me, we've got to try and get back to our lines and it will be dark soon. I don't want to be out all night." He clicked at Staro and he moved off, Valius and his soldier falling in behind.

"They used dogs against us." The Decurion said again but Varro didn't hear him.

"And what would you do?" Decimus asked, "If a superior army invaded your lands and killed your people?" He saw the defiant expression written over the Decurion's face. "What happened, happened and we can't change it but dogs for fucks sake your right and you're lucky to be alive my friend." Valius didn't answer and they trotted on.

About an hour later they found themselves getting clear of the forest, Varro couldn't even estimate how far they were away from the Legion now. In trying to find the cohort they had changed direction many times and that had not helped their overall sense of direction. Although they had seen some local inhabitants, they weren't hostile and had just stared at the strangely dressed men as they rode by. They found a large river and paused to let the horses drink and fill their water sacks.

"Is this the Medway?" Decimus asked no-one in particular.

"I don't know." Varro answered. "Our maps showed another large river north of the Medway so it could be that one, either way if we keep heading south we should avoid the enemy and eventually find Vespasian and the army." He stretched his back stiff from riding.

"We're starting to lose light." Valius observed looking at the sky.

"Come on let's get moving." Varro said climbing back onto his horse.

They trotted on again and saw more locals, some walking in family groups with their animals, others at a distance clearly wary of the Romans. Varro believed they were scouts as they stayed away from them keeping their distance but as they didn't follow, they were ignored. Most if not all the

Britons were probably trying to get clear of the hostilities and wanted no part in the conflict. He knew that there were a lot of tribes that were loyal to Rome so not all they saw would be hostile.

He could understand any people defending their own land but the Catuvellauni were virtually alone, or so they had been assured. Even they had traded freely for many decades and only up until recently had that changed. With the death of their former King Cunobelinus, everything had changed. Togodumnus now ruled one of the largest of the indigenous tribes and wanted equal standing with Rome. As friction had built, trade had slowed and then stopped as the ambitions of the Catuvellauni grew.

Togodumnus ruled the lands north of the two great rivers and Caratacus the lands to the south. Adminius who had always wanted peace with Rome had been banished for what the two older brothers perceived as weakness and it was they who now led the resistance against Rome. With an estimated eighty thousand warriors to call upon they were a real threat and although they had a numerical superiority they lacked military knowledge, weaponry and tactics.

The tribes were used to taking part in small conflicts not large scale battles where opposing armies lined up in formations, their Generals trained in the art of war pitied their wits and knowledge against each from a military education. Like so many barbarian tribes before, irrespective of the odds, facts or past, he knew they would keep coming.

With the light failing Varro decided that they had to find somewhere to stop for the night. He knew that if they kept moving there was more chance of them walking into an ambush and in unfamiliar surroundings the chance of them surviving such an encounter was limited. He made sure that they hadn't been seen for a while and began to look for somewhere suitable for the night. He decided to try and find high ground and to observe the surroundings for a while, making sure they weren't being followed. As darkness began to fall he looked for any signs of life, movement or fires, if there were none they would settle down as best they could and try and get some rest. It was a method he had used before and had always worked well. He knew that they were probably a long way behind enemy lines now and would need every ounce of energy if they were to get to a safe area and the Legion.

From a distance on the horizon Caratacus watched the six Roman soldiers slowly walking through his land on horseback. He believed that they were the sole survivors of the enemy advance that he and his warriors had all but destroyed in the marshes and forests earlier that day. They had probably escaped in the chaos of the ambush and had got lost, but now they would be destroyed. One of his hunting parties had alerted him to their location after picking up their scent with dogs.

As he lay watching them from his concealed position on the ground he smiled thanking the gods that he had used the hounds. The big dogs were always an advantage when they were hunting boar and deer and had proved an excellent addition to his warriors against the Romans. Being ripped apart by huge animals was not a fate that he would wish on any man but times had changed and he had to use every advantage available to him.

He pushed himself backwards down the grass bank to where the rest of his war party waited. They had tracked down other small groups who had evaded the ambushes earlier and destroyed them all, he wondered if this were the last of them. The Romans had gained a foothold over the river but they had now been halted and had lost hundreds of men themselves. Caratacus was content with his days' work but was under no illusion about the days further ahead. He had never faced such a well organised and well-disciplined force before and now knew that facing them as they had, would not work again. He had lost many warriors that day and couldn't afford to let that continue. At the moment however that was irrelevant, what was important was removing the six Romans within his reach.

He quickly gave his orders and moved out as his men and women split up and went in different directions. He had fifty warriors with him and sent half that number away to skirt around the far side of the small rise that the Romans had paused on. If he could get half his force to the far side or somewhere near the enemy wouldn't escape.

Some hours later night had fallen and darkness covered the land, it was a cloudy moonless sky and there was little light to see by but the Romans were still in the same position. As

Caratacus edged slowly forward he strained his eyes and ears trying to find some evidence of the men he had observed some hours earlier. If they were still there, they were being very quiet, had no fire and had gone to ground, maybe they were sleeping.

The sound of an owl broke the silence of the night it was followed by shuffling from somewhere above. It had to be one of the six men he was hunting. Caratacus knew then that it wasn't an owl hooting but one of his men from the other party signalling that they were in position at the far side of the hillock.

He knew the ground flattened out on the top of the mound and so wasn't surprised that he hadn't seen the horses of the men they sought, they were probably tethered near them over the rise. Before he had time to do anything else, the sound of swords clashing against each other broke the still night. He and his group rose and charged forward screaming their battle cries. Reaching the top of the mound he saw that all six Romans were already surrounded by the other party and were desperately fighting for their lives. He saw one of his men struck down, cleaved through the skull by one of the long cavalry swords, another was run through and fell to the ground. The advantage of extra numbers however took its toll and the enemy began to fall and in seconds there were none left alive.

Caratacus surveyed the scene before him, six dead to his two, they were good odds. He knew that this result would have to be multiplied by many times if they were to succeed in pushing the invaders back. The Britons collected the weapons of the dead men and their horses and rode off shouting in celebration.

Chapter Fourteen

      Just before dawn Caratacus moved into position. He had managed to rest a little after returning to the main body of his army. A funeral pyre had been made for his brother and the warrior King's body had burned for hours. Set on a series of crisscross logs almost the height of a grown man, the square ceremonial block had flamed for a long time as those who were gathered around it watched on. All elements of the tribe attended family, close friends and high ranking members of the Catuvellauni as well as warriors who all watched the solemn ceremony. Tears were shed by those closest to him but others had a determined angry expression on their faces as they watched the flames reach for the sky above. Sadly it wasn't the only funeral that night but it was the largest, as many others burnt across the landscape.

      In times of peace Togodumnus would have been buried and a mound made for celebrating his life and for reflection, remembrance and respect with his sword and other possessions to enable him to carry them into the afterlife. Mead and food, jewels, torcs and perhaps a great war horse for him to ride in eternity. Today however was different, there was no time for such things and Caratacus would not risk his brother's body becoming a trophy for the enemy and so it was reduced by fire, a true warriors end. Caratacus had been nearest the pyre watching as his brother's flesh was turned slowly turned to ash. He stood remembering him and their days together growing up, playing, laughing and hunting. Tears burned his eyes as much as the pyre threatened to burn his flesh until they fell and flowed freely down his face. It was the only sign of emotion evident as he saw the pyre burn until eventually the flames got smaller.

Sleep had evaded him after the sight of his brothers mortally wounded flesh and the vision returned again and again every time he closed his eyes and tried to rest. He had finally sat with his wife and children and discussed their fate, what would happen, where would they go, how could they stop the mighty machine of Rome, was it even possible? His younger brothers hadn't hesitated about their decision, they had to fight and live or fight and die. He knew that honour demanded that as well, now he had to decide how to go about it. They were a proud people whose tribe had ruled for many decades. There had been conflicts with other regions but the Catuvellauni had never encroached into other tribal lands unless there was legitimate reason, they had never invaded other areas unless they had been provoked first. Even when such conflicts had arisen and they had crossed borders, they would always go back to their own lands afterward.

It was a major factor in deciding the fate of Adminius when he had crossed the border of others and why he had been punished so severely. They were not driven by conquering other people only ruling what they had and that most precious gift was now threatened as it had never been before. Not only was their entire way of life at stake from an enemy across the water but it was also threatened some who lived within their shores as well. Caratacus vowed to deal with them as he considered their treachery, they were worse than the invaders themselves.

His scouts had reported that the Romans had fortified their positions before dark the night before but as light brushed away the darkness he was surprised by how much. Palisades had been dug all around the encampment and trees cleared to construct a fortification that he barely thought possible given the time available, it was enormous, the landscape had been transformed completely from the day before. If he attacked now he knew it would be suicide so he would have to wait. Patience was something he had in abundance but he would have to employ it wisely. He considered withdrawing his forces completely to the capital but knew that the enemy would follow them there. He decided he would have to fight a tactical withdrawal and demonstrate that patience combined with an ability to fight, was probably as dangerous as head to head conflict.

    He lay watching from a hillside, observing the men that had come to his land and taken his brother's life and those of his people. He could see that guards watched from towers while other men patrolled the wooden walls, fires burned inside where row upon row of tents were laid out in straight symmetrical lines. Their army was so large that he could see another encampment over on the far side of the river and more fires burned for as far as he could see beyond that. He had known before that the task ahead of him was enormous but now that the Legion was laid out before him, he began to believe that it was near impossible.

    These soldiers were clearly used to living this way, it was how they existed and worse he knew that other Legion's had also landed. At that moment Caratacus was shaken to his roots and considered his position and that of his people. If he asked for a truce the lives of his people would be spared but the Romans would still want a heavy price for their nerve at resisting them. He knew that after the defeat of Alesia in Gaul, their leader Vercingetorex had surrendered and his people were enslaved, their chieftains became puppets and their lands robbed of their resources. Vercingetorex himself, who had managed before all others to unite the great Gallic tribes against Rome, had been imprisoned and then ritually strangled, it was not a fate that Caratacus wanted for himself or his people. He would willingly give himself to the Emperor if he knew his people would be free to live their lives but knew that wouldn't happen. Many would be taken to Rome, others would be scattered around the Empire and used as slaves and the men would even be made to serve in their legions as auxiliaries. He also knew that both men and women were used as sex slaves in the Empire or made to fight to the death. He wondered how such a people who believed that they were so enlightened and so advanced, could be so cruel.

    As he lay there looking out on the enemy before him, he knew he had no choice. In his mind's eye he saw his father, his brothers, his children and his people. He had a duty to protect them and their way of life and knew that he wouldn't be doing that if he walked forward and gave himself up. With the death of Togodumnus, he was King and with that came responsibility. He would fight and live as a free man or fight and die for his land and his people. His future decided, he thought through his battle plan.

The fight the day before had taught him many valuable lessons, lessons that he had paid for with the blood of his people, today would be different. If his tactics worked, they would smash the enemy but he believed that there may be a possibility that even if they didn't, they may be able to force the Romans into a truce and to leave their lands.

Varro was shaken awake by Decimus on the mound where they had tried to rest the night before. He had watched through clenched teeth as another group of his countrymen had been wiped out some distance away. He knew that it could have been him and the men around him and also knew that they could have tried to save those who were butchered but he had decided against it for good reasons. The attack had happened without warning, seemingly coming from nowhere and with speed, so even if they had tried to go to the aid of the other isolated group, they wouldn't have got there in time and would have died as well, outnumbered as they were. He had made the correct decision but that didn't give him any conciliation as he thought about the men who had found themselves in the same position as himself and his own men.

Almost whispering he instructed Decimus to wake the others and to prepare to move. He stood up stiff and cold from the nights chill and looked to where they had tethered their horses who at least had eaten well on the long grass. He surveyed their surroundings looking for any sign of the enemy but nothing moved. Before leaving the mound they ate their meagre rations sharing what they could with the two auxiliaries.

The direction they travelled in took them towards the hillock where the brief fight had taken place the night before. He knew there was very little chance that any of them had survived but he felt that he had to go and check, maybe one of them had managed to hide or had been left injured. He called

Decimus forward as they approached leaving the others where they were, telling them to keep their eyes open for any movement nearby.

It was slightly higher than where they had camped at their own resting place but narrower at the brow. As soon as they got to the top they saw the corpses of the auxiliaries, they had been decapitated their heads left on crude sticks in the ground. Varro looked at the expressions of the men who had given their lives. One head had a large slash wound either from an axe or sword that split his skull from the top of the forehead to the bridge of his nose. Another caught the moment of battle and death, his features contorted in agony his mouth still screaming but silently now.

He considered burning what was left of the men, they didn't deserve this end but knew to do so would risk attracting unwanted attention and being found. Burying them would mean losing time and while they were stationery they would be vulnerable. The Britons had stripped the bodies of their weapons, water and food and taken the horses. There was nothing he could do for them now, as hard as the decision was, they would be left, their own priority now was to get back to the Second.

They trotted down the hill and headed in a southerly direction, all the time scanning the countryside around them, expecting to see the enemy. He hoped that they would be concentrating on the main army and not looking for stragglers as the new day got under way. They passed more Britons in family groups in time all of whom stared at them but not saying a word or lifting a weapon in anger. Varro assumed they were farmers or just people from the local area, he couldn't determine that they were part of the war band and so ignored them.

By midday just as he was beginning to think they would never find the army, they ran into Quintus and his men from the other scouting party. They exchanged information and Quintus gave them the route back to the Legion through a valley, they found they were not too far away.

Varro was relieved to see the sight of the encampment as they approached the pickets on sentry duty. It was a welcome sight seeing familiar structures even if they were newly constructed and hadn't been there the day before. He kicked his horse eager to get behind the barricade and the relative safety of the new fort and its palisades. He instructed Valius to report to the Adjutant and to give him his report as he sought out the command tent in order to report his own findings.

Arriving at the large tent Varro had his identity verified by the guards and was allowed access. Senior officers and various commanders were on the verge of leaving, when Vespasian saw him he called Varro over to give his report.

"The Batavian's were routed sir, destroyed virtually to a man, we managed to bring back two survivors." Vespasian stared at him shocked but not surprised by his words. Nothing had been seen of the cohort from the day before.

"But there were four hundred men that went into the marsh. Are you telling me that we lost nearly all of them?" Another officer a Prefect asked Varro. Vespasian turned and introduced Varro to his brother Sabinus. "It was he who masterminded the idea of crossing the river yesterday, Vespasian said.

"Yes sir," Varro reported, "we found the bodies of many auxiliaries in the marshland and then in the forest beyond. We eventually caught up with Valius their commander and one soldier but by that time we were far behind their lines. They were the only men we found alive." He decided to leave out the information about the other group that were killed during the night.

A voice from the rear said, "We've had some men coming in throughout the night and still some this morning but their number is less than thirty. Over twenty of those are wounded and not fit for duty." It was the force commander Aulus Plautius, everyone stiffened coming to attention when they realised he had slipped into the briefing.

"Relax gentlemen." He said as they came to attention, he walked directly to the table where various maps were laid out.

"It seems our friendly Britons underestimated the Catuvellauni resistance and their ability to fight." He looked at the faces around him. "We were assured that Togodumnus and Caratacus were backward thugs who relied merely on brute strength to dominate other tribes, it seems we were ill informed." He turned to Sabinus, "Bring Adminius to me would you Prefect?"

Sabinus acknowledged the order, "Sir."

"Now that we have established ourselves here on this side of the river," the commander continued studying the map, "we will push forward today, even if we have to circumnavigate this marsh and the forest beyond. If necessary we'll encircle the Catuvellauni and starve them out and then destroy them. Centurion," he turned to Varro, "from the foray into their territory would you show us on the map what we're facing if you would please."

Varro stepped forward surprised that he had even remembered his name and began to explain the details and formation of the ground they would have to cover. A few moments later whilst they were discussing the details of the proposed advancement, Sabinus returned with a man wearing a toga. He looked like a civilian dignitary but Varro was surprised to hear his accent when he was introduced.

"Gentlemen," Plautius said, "I would like to introduce you to Adminius exiled brother of Togodumnus and Caratacus, the two men who are leading the fight against us." The man coloured as if embarrassed by his introduction and the fact that his brothers were fighting against Plautius and his army. He was taller than all the Romans gathered in the tent. He held himself proudly and spoke fluent Latin although heavily accented. He could have been Roman except for the large gold torc around his neck showing that he was in fact a Briton of high status.

"How can I be of service sir?" He asked, his eyes confidently fixed on Plautius. The commander looked around at his officers, "We were just discussing our options and it would seem that your brothers have wiped out an entire cohort of my Batavian auxiliaries."

Adminius looked as if he had been struck by the words, his confident manner evaporated.

"I don't know what to say general, for many years I had told them of the benefits of allying themselves with Rome. As you know I was exiled for my thoughts and beliefs that they and my father believed were treasonous. They cast me out because I had the vision to believe that living with the Empire and not fighting against it would benefit all our peoples. They would never listen and I lost everything I had but it was nothing to what I have gained." He looked at the men around him almost sneering pathetically.

"Do you think that you would be able to talk to your brothers again under a flag of truce?" Vespasian asked, the other officers gathered around the table exchanged looks of surprise.

Vespasian continued. "They may have won a small victory in the marshes but that is all. The casualty figures they sustained from yesterday must far outweigh our own and we have re-enforcements landing as we speak. We estimate that they lost over a thousand yesterday and those numbers will only rise when you take into account injuries. They cannot hope to defeat us so surely they can be made to see that?"

Adminius looked at Vespasian, "These conversations I had many times with them and my father when he was alive. They saw the advantages of living in harmony with Rome, trade and a better way of life but they rejected it and now it has come to this. If you wish me to try and talk to them again I will. I now serve the Emperor and will in any capacity he chooses. It is I and not them who should be the rightful heir to the Catuvellauni throne, they have shown they are not worthy of leading the people. The Emperor knows that I will serve him once they are defeated." He looked around at the assembled officers. "I will however attempt to persuade them once more if that is your wish. Perhaps they will see the error of their decisions now that they have lost so many souls."

Varro studied the man as he spoke and wondered how he could betray his own blood in such a manner but then he also considered his alternatives. Was it better to live as a free man and fight, or to live a life of servitude as a puppet to another man or even to another tribe? Was Adminius really a traitor to his people if his own leadership could afford them a better way of life? It was a difficult question and only one he himself could answer. He had clearly lived in conflict with his family and their way of life all of his own and had paid dearly for that by being exiled. Varro was glad he wasn't the man that stood before him. He wondered if the Emperor had actually promised him power if his brothers failed, the problem was more complicated than at first it seemed. Once thing was certain, Adminius was a man who would follow where others led whatever the cost as long as it was to his own benefit.

"My brothers are warriors and proud and they will not yield, they would rather die than live under the yoke of another. They would see it as shame to live that way but maybe after yesterday they have seen the error of their ways although I doubt it."

Plautius considered his words. "If I can save the lives of my men I will Adminius. I am not a bloodthirsty barbarian who wishes to wipe out all those who stand before me if there is a real alternative for peace and to save lives on both sides. My mandate is clear in this matter, it is to help you return to what you and others are entitled too however that occurs and by any means. If ultimately that means the destruction of some of your people then so be it."

"I want to avoid that as you do but my brothers are different individuals when it comes to politics. I will do whatever it takes and will speak to them if there's even a small chance it will help and to save the lives of my people." Varro was impressed by the reply given by Adminius but felt that he would rather see his brothers dead and out of the way.

"Very well then, we shall attempt to talk your brothers out of their foolish stance and to see if we can garner peace even at this late hour. Be clear about this though Adminius," the commander paused fixing his gaze on the Briton, "if your brothers chose to fight, we will wipe them out, all of them." Just as the General finished his sentence an alarm sounded from somewhere outside, it was quickly followed by another and then a third. Trumpeters sounded the general alarm the Britons were attacking in force.

From the safety of the forts defences beyond the palisades, Plautius surveyed the scene before him whilst inside men ran to their positions to join with their cohorts and maniples as the cavalry mounted their horses and infantry formed up. The guards on the walls had been re-enforced and the artillery teams looked alert stood at their ballista as they watched the terrain. Outside the area had been cleared for many hundreds of feet all around the position. To the north beyond the cleared ground, stood beneath the trees a wall of blue warriors, their hair white with lime. There were thousands of them. As senior officers organised their troops, forming up in pre-arranged columns Plautius gazed out at the wall of blue.

"I don't know sir. Maybe they're waiting for reinforcements from the rear, who knows with these people maybe they're just trying to goad us into reacting." A senior Tribune remarked as he stared at the silent mass before him. He turned to the inside of the fort and shouted down to the Cornicen, the man holding the large curling trumpet was waiting for orders. He was standing in front of the Legion that was forming up with a Centurion at his side who was bellowing orders. Dust was thrown up from the feet of the men as they ran and quickly got into position.

"Cornicen, as soon as the century and cavalry are formed up, sound the advance." The Centurion ordered as he ran forward waving his vine stick at men to hurry them along.

Plautius turned and shouted to the senior centurion waiting for the columns to be filled. "Centurion, I want you and the Legion formed up outside at the centre flanked by the auxiliary infantry with the cavalry on the flanks. As soon as you are in position I will join you, understood?"

"Yes sir." Shouted the centurion still urging his men to get formed up, saluting he turned to them and gave the order to his subordinate centurions to move and form up outside, his order was repeated by the Cornicen blowing into the large trumpet, his cheeks reddening from the effort. The men of the legion turned to the right and moved off whilst the centurions screamed orders.

The large doors to the fort at the front and rear were opened at the same time. The cavalry exited from the rear whilst the infantry hurriedly left through the front gate at the double in clear view of the Britons. Twenty paces behind the legionaries were the auxiliary infantry jogging to keep up, their equipment rattling as they moved as men fastened buckles and made sure equipment was secure. They had further to travel than the regulars and positioned themselves either side of them. As soon as they were in position the cavalry took up their place on the outer flanks bringing with them a cloud of dust. Plautius watched on with pride as Vespasian broke his concentration. "With your permission sir, I will join the men?"

Plautius turned and looked at his officer, "Good luck," he reached out and grasped Vespasian's arm, "you shouldn't need it because our men are more than a match for that rabble but I don't want too many casualties." He turned to survey the scene below but then turned again and added. "Just think Titus in the years to come people will still know of this day decades, maybe even centuries into the future, just like we talk of Caesar today, on the edge of the Empire defeating all those who stood before us. Remember this day of all days and take care of my Legion." He said smiling.

Vespasian smiled, "Don't worry sir I'll look after the men, you can count on it. You can also count on them." Without another word he turned and almost ran to the ladder that would take him to ground level. Adminius joined Plautius on the wall.

"It looks as if your brothers have signalled their response without your intervention young Adminius and now they will pay for their stupidity." Plautius said staring at the warriors under the trees.

Adminius looked out at the two vast armies now facing each other as the dust settled from the cavalry. From this position it was impossible to tell if his brothers were there but he knew they would be somewhere in the midst of the Catuvellauni. He said, "I pity their naivety sir and their stupidity, they could have maintained their lands and power but they chose a long time ago for this day to happen."

"Naïve and stupid they maybe Adminius but brave as well, they are fighting for what they believe in, their land, their families and their pride. Could you say such a thing?" The General gave him a look of disgust that shocked the former prince.

"I made my decision also a long time ago General and that choice was for the benefit of my people to ally them with Rome not to deny that and fight, in order to get wiped out. My brothers will see the error of their ways by paying with their lives and so will thousands of my people, my subjects." He turned and began to walk away.

"Pride comes in many guises Adminius and so does bravery." The Briton stopped and turned but Plautius continued. "If I were out there as I used to be and I was given a choice of who I was to stand beside, your brothers or you hiding behind these walls, my choice would be simple. You see Adminius some of us were born soldiers, it's not something we choose it's actually in our blood. It doesn't matter what the odds are, it doesn't matter if we wear fine uniforms or nearly nothing at all as your brothers do. We are all brothers, brothers of battle undivided, it is enough to stand and fight, it is a bond that you will never know. Now get out of my sight."

Adminius blushed hurt and embarrassed by the commander's words but he knew he was right but it didn't matter, he headed towards the ladder. His words had convinced even the Emperor of his loyalty and Claudius himself had thanked him but this underling presumed that he could talk to him as he would a peasant, a coward. Adminius swore to himself that he would make Plautius pay for his contempt.

Plautius returned his gaze to the front and saw that the Britons had begun to slowly advance. He felt his stomach knot not at the coming battle but at the contempt he felt for Adminius. Clearing his head he asked one of the centurions from his command group how many Britons they faced.

"It's hard to calculate sir because of their extended line and many of them are still hidden under the trees. They're front is far longer than our own and I can't see any of their chariots. I would estimate that we can see at least ten thousand now."

Plautius didn't answer but could see the Britons line did extend well beyond the width of his own formations and it was an unbroken line unlike the disciplined ranks of his squares. Trumpets sounded from below ordering his men forward and virtually as one the vast columns moved toward the Britons, the cavalry maintaining their position waiting for orders and to see what the enemy did.

Loud jeers rose above the noise of the marching boots from the blue and white line of the slowly advancing Britons as more emerged from the tree's thickening their line and swelling their number. The sight of them made a shiver quiver down the spine of Plautius. Most of them he could see carried spears or swords, some swung axes above their freshly limed stark white hair that stuck out from their blue painted heads and torso's. Had Plautius been a Briton he thought, he had no doubt that today he would have been among their number, not hiding below as Adminius was now.

Varro watched from the wall of the fort further along from the Generals position. Rumours were spreading through the troops that the Britons had received reinforcements during the night, chariots included. Without their own army dominating the ground to the south it was impossible to tell if these rumours were true or just wild stories. Nevertheless as he watched he now saw chariots appear on the flanks of the enemy. Although a lot of the chariots had been put out of action the day before and their horses hamstrung or butchered some had probably lived but they couldn't have accounted for the mass that emerged to face them now, these must be re-enforcements

"Over one hundred chariots on each flank and counting sir." He heard an observer shout to the General. Varro swallowed hard, the rumours were true then, they had swelled their numbers considerably.

Caratacus peeled off from the chariots and drove slowly along the front line of his warriors demonstrating that he was willing to face this threat with his people. In his right hand he held his sword and encouraged the warriors he had assembled by waving it in the air and pointing at the Roman lines facing them. He had seen that as he had predicted, they had concentrated their heavy infantry in the middle with cavalry on the flanks. The wall of helmets and shields from the regular infantry shone in the morning sunlight as they silently advanced. He had seen them first-hand the day before with a red stripe running through the middle from top to bottom and depicting two animals either side of the shield boss at the centre. A flying horse, Pegasus and a leaping Stag painted in bright white against a background of gold. Soon he would have them dripping in blood.

As he had considered his options for battle earlier that day whilst eating warm mutton, envoys from the Dobunni tribe had arrived with encouraging news. Their King had heard of the invasion and had marched his own army to fight and swell the ranks of his own bringing with them chariots. He now had now swollen his command with over thirty thousand more men and women with the help of his westerly neighbours. Although they were not as skilled in battle as the Catuvellauni, the Dobunni were a welcome addition to the force that now faced the Roman threat.

Caratacus surveyed the scene before him again and knew that if he advanced too far they would be within range of the mighty machines that hurled huge arrows and bolts across the battlefield. He could see that the enemy had placed a number of them on the walls. He would have to avoid getting too close and was intent on drawing the soldiers out and beyond their range. He could hear trumpets sounding from across the bare land where they had laid waste to everything in order to create a killing field clear of obstructions. He would use that to his own advantage now as it gave the chariots room to manoeuvre and harass the wall of shields and the men behind them.

He ordered his chariot driver to move forward of his battle line fifty paces to where he could be seen clearly, the chariot rumbled forward and stopped as instructed. He looked at the Roman shields once more and marvelled at their form but knew that he must do his best to destroy them. The ground was virtually clear of dust now as was the sky and the sun shone warming his exposed upper body, only small wispy clouds drifted across the sky above. On another day it would have been pleasant but not today. Today was a day that he knew could well determine the life, death or enslavement of him and his entire people.

The abuse the warriors shouted at their foe changed when they saw him and began to chant his name as he stood facing them. He calculated that the first of the advancing disciplined rows were now well beyond the effective range of their own machines and bolt throwers, the chances of success had just grown but only marginally. He waited for them to take another fifty paces and heard then saw that the soldiers were now banging their swords against the sides of their shields. He gave the signal for the chariots on the right to advance and they rumbled forward slowly at first building momentum.

As the chariots built up speed, the warriors cheered watching as they began to race forward arching in at an angle towards the middle of the approaching shield wall. A trumpet sounded from somewhere to their rear and the soldiers stopped as one bringing their shields up. The chariots now at full speed bounced along their drivers skilfully avoiding the tree stumps left in the ground. Each carried at least two others warriors, some three who were armed with spears. As they got to within range they hurled their weapons skyward to great cheers of approval of their kinsmen watching as the first volley of battle was launched.

The Roman front lines threw their javelins in return but most missed the fast moving chariots or were out of range as they raced past the ranks landing harmlessly. The Romans packed in their tight lines began to take casualties as the men covered up the best they could behind their large four foot shields, looking out from beneath their helmets. Caratacus had known the chariots would prove difficult targets and he was right.

As the first wave of chariots had nearly cleared the enemy front line he waved for the left side to advance sweeping his sword forward. These chariots gained speed quickly keen to show what they could achieve and by the time they were within range of the front line of shields their passengers, armed with bows unleashed their arrows, not at the front row of legionaries but at those behind. Caratacus could see from his elevated position that helmets fell backward as men died or were injured by the success of the arrows finding flesh and bone through narrow gaps as victims unexpectedly received missiles. Another trumpet sounded and all the squares moved covering themselves from above with their large shields except those at the front. The enemy were now wrapped in shields to the front, side and above and were stationary as the chariots stormed by firing arrows into them.

As the first wave of chariots returned to their own line and slowed, more spears were passed to those on board, they gratefully accepted them grinning manically, shouting in their joy at killing the men who had come to take their land. The warriors on foot cheered again knowing that the great machine that had come to kill them was at last vulnerable and bleeding.

Chapter Fifteen

Aulus Plautius watched from his vantage point on the raised platform, even from his position the roar of the enemy was like that of a huge beast as it yelled for the blood of his soldiers. He signalled to the senior centurion again and gave the order for cavalry on the wings to advance. The Cornicen sounded the charge which was repeated by other trumpeters strategically placed amongst the infantry and the cavalry bolted forward, their target the men and horses of the chariots.

He watched as the leading cavalrymen drew their large swords, dust obscured the view clearly, already thrown up by the barbarian's chariots and the fastest riders disappeared into the murk in no time. Swords colliding and shouts drowned the screams of the enemy previously heard encouraging their warriors as a trumpet cut the air sounding the infantry to advance once more.

Plautius was confident of his Legions ability especially on open ground where the enemy had chosen to meet his men. Initially frustrated that the Britons had not come to within range of his ballista, he now smiled looking down as he saw Vespasian draw his sword and start shouting to this men. Plautius felt the blood rush through his veins as he watched them advance wishing he could take to the field.

The Britons weren't the only ones to receive reinforcements overnight as the Second Augusta had now been joined by two other legions, the Fourteenth Gemina and Twentieth legions flanked either side of the Vespasian's Second Augusta as they marched forward. The General felt the hairs rise on the back on his neck and he wondered what it must be like to face this enormous wall of shields, swords and javelins.

Caratacus looked on through the dust kicked up by the chariots and signalled for them to retreat back to his lines. Rumbling made the ground tremor as the first of them returned closely followed by the pursuing Roman cavalry. He gave a signal and slingers launched their shot as rounded stones flew high into the air. Some of the missiles were naturally rounded rock, others hardened baked clay made for war.

He saw one of the mounted soldiers hit squarely in the face, blood splattered from his crushed nose and he fell off the back of his horse and hit the ground hard tumbling. He was hit by another horse and then another before he lay still unconscious and no doubt badly wounded. He lost sight of him amongst others horses as other missiles started to land. Horses reared and tried to swerve and turn panicked by the accuracy of the stones as they hit their heads and bodies as well as their riders. Pelting them like rain some animals actually began to turn, those not hit realising the danger as the noise of the speeding stones flew passed them or thudded into the ground or hit those nearby.

Arrows now joined the avalanche launched by the slingers and more of the enemy fell. One man was pierced through a gap of his chain mail armour near his shoulder and fell backward but somehow managed to stay on his horse as it veered, kicked and turned its eyes wild in panic, nostrils flaring. Britons now ran forward and attacked the cavalrymen who had been knocked from their mounts, they were butchered and their weapons taken, a few soldiers ran back towards their own lines vanishing into the clouds of dust. The cavalry turned and retreated, battered and bruised to tumultuous cheers behind them.

For a short time a quiet descended over the battlefield but it didn't last long. As the Roman infantry advanced through the dust the banging of swords on shields became the resounding noise that took over from all other sounds. The blare of trumpets somewhere in the distance was the only other thing that pierced the drumming as orders were given by the unseen ranks.

The enemy looked like something unearthly as they marched out of the settling dust. Caratacus could see Roman Eagles dispersed at regular intervals behind the rows and gave a signal for his chariots to charge again. Now he knew that they didn't face just one Roman Legion but his forces were already committed and to retreat would mean certain destruction.

This time it was the turn of the Dobunni as they rode their chariots as they had been ordered and headed straight into the enemy lines, two thirds along their front on the left. The slingers pebbles rattled off shields as arrows dug into them. Horses smashed into the shield wall and chariots ran over legionaries as more joined them. The men aboard the small two wheeled chariots lashed out with spears at the now stationary startled men trying to deflect blows with their large shields, others leapt clear and individual fights broke out all around.

Caratacus ordered his infantry forward and the men and women ran howling like banshees as they sprinted to join the battle. The entire Roman line now paused as more trumpets sounded somewhere in the distance. The Britons hit the flat line but didn't all push into it as they had done before, Caratacus had learned a bitter lesson the previous day. As they tried to hold their ground a column of charging warriors punched into the wall where the chariots had already created a large gap in the previously solid row of shields.

On the extremities of the main battle the Roman cavalry charged again trying to outflank the Britons and come at them from the rear but were hampered by the sheer numbers and the tree line which abruptly halted their advance. Unable to attack from the back, the cavalry fell onto the sides of the Britons but were hit again by the slingers who targeted them with deadly accurate fire. Man and horse were hit with the projectiles again and again as the lethal missiles took their toll.

Caratacus shouted encouragement again seeing that his plan was working and concentrated his own force at driving through the enemy wall, pushing the wedge in their column ten wide forward and through them. Barely perceptive at first the entire enemy line started to give as their cavalry retreated once more. It was working and he called for others to join the attack as his warriors forced their way through the auxiliary forces. In seconds the entire Roman line was moving slowly backward not willingly but through the sheer brutality and weight of numbers of their attackers.

With the enemy now in slow retreat and his wedge forcing through, slicing into the once unified ranks of the front line, he pushed his people hard to cut off a huge portion of the auxiliaries. All along the retreating formations the Britons continued to attack but didn't go beyond that invisible line. They held themselves not hurling their bodies onto the shields or trying to prise them free as they had before. They held off but continued striking shields with their long swords and axes at a distance that prevented the enemy's short swords from finding their mark. Others massed behind them but at intervals giving them all space.

Roman javelins were launched from the rear ranks landing unseen into the crowds of their attackers who showed no sign of relenting. More Britons joined those forcing their way into the human path as the entire battle reversed moving back towards the fort. Trumpets sounded again and the lines of the invaders increased their backward retreat.

The legions were used to advancing in their squares. Behind the large shields they had the advantage as they stabbed out at attackers as they threw themselves on their formed lines. In retreat however, they weren't so assured and some legionaries tripped walking backwards and others fell over them. It caused others to panic and turn as gaps began to appear.

Plautius had sounded the retreat as reports came in of the tactics being used by the Britons, his vision was still obscured by the dust. A look of sheer horror was etched over his face as he saw just how far they were being pushed back now. He had intended to call a halt as his men were re-enforced but with some soldiers stumbling and fright clearly spreading, he saw that his battle lines were in danger of failing altogether.

"Centurion." He shouted at the man to his left.

"Sir." The man turned saluting his General.

"Have the Ninth Hispana move out and flank right. Those bastards are trying to cut off the auxiliaries on that side. I want Geta fully aware of what he's up against and get those fucking ballista racked up and ready to fire they'll be within range in no time if this carries on."

The Centurion saluted again and ran off to convey the orders. Plautius looked back to the fight now only approximately a hundred yards away, his concern growing more every second. The Centurion hurriedly instructed the ballista crews to ready their weapons and then climbed down the ladder to Geta who was held in reserve within the fort.

Prefect Gnaeus Hosidius Geta stood with his senior officers talking about their experiences of Briton. He didn't think that his Legion would be called into action but as the trumpets sounded for him to prepare to move and he saw the Centurion running towards his position, he realised that something must have gone badly wrong outside. The Centurion puffing from his run ran straight to him saluted and told him the order from Plautius. After adding a brief description of the battle and what was happening outside, he drew his gladius and began to move forward.

Geta was a man of proven military experience who had campaigned all over the continent including the eastern lands. He was the longest serving Prefect in the army of Plautius and had completed six years more service than Vespasian had in the army. Plautius had always relied upon him when times were desperate as they now were. Marching ahead of his men, he signalled for them to form into columns to exit the fort and began to trot pulling his shield up, his men followed suit.

As he got clear of the gate all he could see was row upon row of retreating soldiers. He angled right as his trot became a run, running wide of the far right flank of the auxiliary's lines. Instantly he saw that the Britons had managed to separate a large block of soldiers from the rest of the army and were systematically cutting them down.

He ran his men at an angle to the battle still in rows of three in their columns. Shouting he ordered them to stop and ready their javelins, row upon row of pila were readied. They were then quick marched to within throwing distance. The Britons were blood raged and too eager in their havoc to see the danger, too intent on cutting down the auxiliary soldiers who were desperately fighting for their lives.

"Advance, release and rotate." Ordered Geta as the men in his front row ran forward and hurled their deadly arsenal into the air. Before the first javelins even landed, the second flight were already airborne as the front ranks were passed by the second and then the third. Hundreds of javelins rose and fell and took lives in their deadly hail instantaneously and wounded others.

As the first of the Britons fell, Geta reformed his lines and advanced his men, shields up, swords thrust forward beyond the moving shield wall. Britons not killed or injured turned as they realised the danger and attacked them. Blood lust heightened by their success and then the injuries, they fought like possessed maniacs. Gone was the control their leader had asked of them as they threw themselves at the deadly solid wall.

Heartened by the re-enforcements the retreating columns paused and held firm finding a steely determination now apparent through the men of the legions. Trumpets sounded again ordering the advance as men gripped shields tighter and swords firmer.

Caratacus couldn't believe what he was seeing. He had been so close to achieving his aim of dividing and isolating a large part of the enemy force ahead of him. He had intended to destroy some of the men and take the rest, the majority he hoped, as hostages having isolated them totally. He'd hoped to force those segregated back to his lines and then seek a treaty with the Roman General but his plan was now in ruins. The Dubonni who made up the majority of the warriors attacking and isolating the Roman auxiliaries were now either dying where they stood or surrendering altogether, throwing their weapons to the ground and their arms in the air. He looked around and then started to fall back as the once retreating Romans now advanced again encouraged by the re-enforcements from the fort. He saw more Dubonni surrendering and couldn't believe what his eyes were telling him.

He turned and shouted at those nearby. "Fall back, fall back." Then he began to scream as the warriors around him saw the danger and turned to run.

"Get back to the trees." He shouted waving his arms as his pace quickened. A chariot raced towards him and then slowed down turning in a great arc as the driver shouted for him to get aboard. Warriors ran all around as some still fought on trying to cover the retreat trying to slow down the marching men. Those that continued to battle, their number dwindling all the time must have known they were doomed as more and more turned to run leaving those fighting isolated.

Caratacus held on tightly as the two white horses pulling the chariot accelerated away from the mayhem. Turning his head he saw that it was the Dubonni who were now isolated and cut off as the Romans had managed to create a reverse of his tactic and they were swallowed, totally surrounded. He ground his teeth together in frustration and then shouted at the sky in anger.

"Keep riding," he said to the driver, "head for the Tamesa." He referred to the next great river further north, the last natural defence before his capital of Camulodunum.

He couldn't stop thinking about the stupid nature of the Dobunni, merely moments before they had been on the verge of a great victory. Even with the enemy re-enforcements coming from the fort they could still have held them off and isolated the targeted men. Now however, it was impossible and so was any hope of any early end to this war.

They rode on through the forest where their speed was hampered by the trees but they were out of range of the enemy who were now occupied with thousands of Dobunni. He took one look back but couldn't see beyond the foliage and could only imagine the end that the warriors who had covered their retreat had suffered.

The Dobunni would be rounded up and in all probability put to the sword or worse, sold as slaves. Caratacus vowed never to let such a fate happen to him again as he fingered the small dagger he always kept concealed inside his trousers. He and Togodumnus had agreed that should they be taken prisoner they wouldn't allow themselves to be trophies of the Romans to be put on display. They would take their own lives and wouldn't live under the boots of any enemy like sheep.

Eventually they got clear of the covering trees and moved along at a better rate on well-worn tracks. Warriors on foot couldn't keep pace but they all knew where the rallying point was beyond the great river. All the people knew where and when to cross the river safely at low tide, the Romans wouldn't, maybe that would help the retreat. That was of course providing no traitor had told them. The possibilities were small Caratacus thought as the territory had been their own for decades but then he remembered Adminius, another thorn in his skin.

Even the thought of his traitorous brother made him grip the hand guard of the chariot tighter as he saw his face in his mind's eye. His brother had often warned that he believed the tribes only chance against the Romans was if they were all united. There were always conflicts and he knew that the possibility of one unified force was impossible.

The Roman leader had apparently listened to his brother's tale with compassion or stupidity, a man who wanted an alliance with the greatest known Empire in the world but was cast out by his own people, his own family. Claudius had pledged that with the help of Adminius his legions would conquer his backward people and return him to his rightful place, the throne of Camulodunum. Caratacus pictured his former brother wearing the clothes of the invader, their robes and spat physically at the thought. He would pay for his treachery he swore again and decided to instruct others to kill him should his own life be taken.

Those who had survived the counter attack crossed the shallows of the Tamesa at low tide, the great river in their territory was even larger than the Medway. Reports reached Caratacus all the time that the Romans had followed and were close on their trail. He knew they wouldn't be able to cross the water however, because by the time they reached it, the tide would be high and the river too fast and deep or so he hoped. He had made that mistake on the Medway but the Tamesa was broader, deeper and faster moving, it would stop even them surely.

He considered what he would do if fortunes were reversed in the event that the Romans found themselves stuck on the other side of the river. Part of his territory was already occupied and he was now heading for the lands of his recently departed dead brother. Would the Romans be content to sit there or would they wait for more re-enforcements, would they need them or would they circumnavigate the waters and attack from the rear as they had before?

He had already sent scouts out to the other tribes both west and north to warn them of the invasion. It wasn't a fight that threatened just his territory after all but others as well and to stop them, they all had to fight together. He considered again those who had always preferred and had wanted to be a part of the Empire, they would surely side with Claudius now. He thought out his choices and knew that if he surrendered, he would no doubt die as other tribal Chieftains had done, strangled in front of cheering crowds in Rome. As he was bounced along in the chariot he thought through all the options available to him but there was only one real one, to resist. Now more than any time since his brother's death he wished that Togodumnus was still alive. He doubted his ability to carry the fight against Rome himself but at that moment he realised that he had no other choice and for the first time in a long time, he felt alone.

Varro cantered his horse forward and into the fort. The battle had been hard won and the Britons had pushed the legions back, a feat rarely seen. He respected their leader Caratacus for his tactics and knew that had he succeeded in isolating and taking thousands of troops, Plautius would have been put in an unenviable position. Had he made a treaty with the Briton and bargained for the soldiers' lives he would have won the respect of all his army. However, in bargaining with such a foe he would have been replaced, returned to Rome in disgrace and punished most severely.

As it turned out Geta had saved the day and the fortunes of Plautius who now it was rumoured, was about to decorate Geta for his bravery and that of his men. Varro had eventually been involved in the battle that day but only in the last attempt to outflank the enemy. He returned now to discover what his orders were as the fleeing Britons were pursued. It was said their capital was within a day's ride now with only one major obstacle in their way, another larger river.

Trotting through the gate after helping escort prisoners to a stockade he saw that Plautius was indeed already decorating his officers, centurions and legionaries after the battle. He turned aside and saw Varro approach.

"Ah Centurion Varro how good it is to see you young fellow. I trust you played your part in the today's victory?" He asked smiling up at the centurion.

"Sir, yes sir." Varro answered. "We attacked with the cavalry and took down many of their chariots, men and horse." He pulled up and got down off Staro.

"Splendid work my boy, splendid work. I suggest you go and find Legate Vespasian and see what he's got in store for you. We need to pursue the barbarians that didn't fall to our swords and give them a damn good beating as well. If things keep going at this rate, we'll have conquered their entire island within the year." He laughed walking off in the direction of his command tent. Varro led his horse to one of the equestrian enclosures and handed him over to a legionary.

"Make sure he's fed and watered will you? We'll be out again soon enough I'm sure." He said already walking away.

"Yes sir." The soldier acknowledged as Varro followed Plautius to the command tent. Inside, it took a few seconds for his eyes to adjust to the dimness compared to the bright sunshine outside. The temperature was hot and stuffy, not helped by the large standing burners liberally placed to allow sufficient light. He saw that Vespasian and the other senior officers including Geta were heavily engaged in their plans for the follow up campaign.

He was ushered to a side room where other centurions and a few optio's awaited their orders. Dirt covered most of the faces, arms and legs of those around him as they recounted their personal stories of the battle. He presumed that he was as filthy as them as none of them had time to wash as the General always insisted on debriefing his troops immediately.

Some laughed out loud as others were more serious as they told of narrow escapes or friends and comrades injured or killed and close escapes. The cavalry were in the minority of those waiting, the majority made up of the legions centurions who were well and truly in the middle of the fight. Auxiliaries were mocked at their near destruction but were able to give as good as they got in the well humoured banter. It was always at times like this that Varro thought the General and his staff should be present. He was certain that fewer men would die the next time and they would learn more than they did from the side lines watching as men were butchered, if only they spoke to those on the ground.

"Quiet." A Tribune shouted at the men as he appeared from around a corner. "The General is ready for you now gentlemen." He added smirking suddenly changing his demeanour at the standing officers. They entered the large briefing room where maps were laid on two tables.

"Good, good come in men." Plautius said moving to the rear of the table. Only a few senior officers, Tribunes and Prefects were still present in case their input was required, others had already left and were preparing to carry out their orders.

"Right gentlemen," he began, "come forward please, step forward so you can see." He waved them closer as Varro and the others did as they were instructed. He looked down at the table and saw what lay beyond the fort and the trees beyond. He could see the large river which it was estimated was an hours ride north on the map, it was named Tamesa the name given to it by the locals. The General turned and introduced a man dressed in a white toga. He recognised him immediately his Latin was the same as Brenna's and spoken with an unusual accent.

"This gentleman," the General said pausing and indicating with an outstretched arm, "is Prince Adminius soon to be King Adminius of the Catuvellauni. He was cruelly exiled by his own people as I'm sure some of you will already know."

The assembled officers looked at the man as he spoke, "Welcome to my country Centurions. I welcome you on behalf of those who do truly welcome you not the traitors that you have fought today." He raised an eyebrow as if waiting for some kind of response from the men standing at the other side of the table, he got none.

"A few years ago," he continued, "my father, then King of the Catuvellauni decided that it was better to distance his people from the great Empire of Rome." Varro decided quickly his first assumptions were correct about this man and that he was a sycophant and no doubt a traitor and liar to his own kind, he continued.

"Although trading continued as it had for many decades he, my father decided that he would not under any circumstances become a client King to the Emperor. At the time of course that was Emperor Caligula." The men bristled and he blushed slightly realising he had mentioned the lunatic who had ruled before Claudius but went on quickly. "My vision was to bring my land into the Empire and to work with it not against it."

A centurion standing behind Varro broke in, "Excuse me Prince." He said.

"By all means Centurion."

The soldier continued, "Do you speak on behalf of all Britannia? I thought there were many tribal regions?" Someone coughed as if indicating the point was well made.

"My tribe is one of the largest in all Britannia and the most powerful and we have the greatest influence over lesser regions. With the Catuvellauni at your side, I can assure you that Britannia will be one of your greatest allies." He smiled pausing, expecting applause maybe. He continued. "With us at your side the rest of Britannia will quickly fall in line and then we can all work together with common aims and goals.

"If what you say is correct Prince," the centurion continued, "then we have a real fight on our hands because it seems that your Catuvellauni are not exactly welcoming."

Quiet laughter broke an awkward silence as Adminius looked at the General clearly expecting him to come to his defence and offer support, he didn't.

"The warriors that met you in battle today have been misled. Since my father's death my own brothers, Togodumnus and Caratacus have ruled. Togodumnus to the north of the Tamesa," he pointed at the river on the map, "and Caratacus to south. They were always jealous of my vision that saw

Albion," he stopped, "sorry Britannia as a part of the Empire." He reddened slightly after referring to the island with the Britons name for it.

"Since I met the Emperor in Rome, they have clearly persuaded my people that their view was the right one to follow." He looked at the faces watching him. "They were wrong and those who follow them are wrong and they will pay for their insolence and betrayal." His face flushed again clearly angry at being embarrassed by the assembled soldiers.

The General expecting more of a history lesson that neither he, nor his men had time for, broke in before Adminius could say anymore. "I sincerely hope that those less powerful and less influential; share your vision Prince Adminius." He stared at the prince. "I can assure you that if the Catevallauni continue to resist, I will be forced to destroy them. Thank you for your time." The General said dismissing the Briton. He stared at the commander of the army in shock but bowed nonetheless and left the room.

"Gentlemen." The General said turning to his centurions. "Right men come closer," he said as if the Prince had not even been introduced to them as he began to outline his plans for the continuing campaign. Over the next hour Plautius told the centurions that the captured Dubonni were to be kept inside a newly constructed fort on the coast. It was to be manned by the Ninth Hispana who would also secure their landing area fully and build better harbours for their ships. Once hostilities had ended the tribesmen would be allowed to return to their lands, unarmed obviously. This brought a few raised eyebrows nevertheless but the General went onto explain that they didn't intend to enslave or kill the entire population of the enormous island.

They all knew that taking the Britons weapons would be insult enough and would no doubt create its own problems but that was an issue for another day. By that time Plautius mused, a Roman governor would be appointed and the law of the land would prevail over the law of the sword. He reiterated his desire that he intended to pursue the Catuvellauni and destroy those who continued to resist them. Any who surrendered would be treated the same as the Dubonni and would eventually be released.

The capital at Camulodunum would be taken as soon as practically possible with the Emperor Claudius leading the advance. This surprise raised more eyebrows especially when he said that the Emperor had even intended to bring with him a team of elephants and ride, 'Hannibal like' in person into the enemy stronghold, thereby ensuring the complete and utter capitulation of any who thought of carrying a sword against the men of Rome again.

After the briefing the men were given various duties and assignments, some more rigorous than others as those assigned to work in the fort complained about later. The men fortunate enough to be told they were to pursue the Britons with all haste, laughed at those to be left behind and quickly went to their duties.

Varro went to find his men and found them at one of the forts stable enclosures tending to the horses. Decimus, Lucius and Marcus were all relieved when told they were to ride in advance of the main body of cavalry and would be leaving as soon as they were prepared. None had sustained any injuries in the battle nor had the horses, not even a scratch, which he considered was a miracle considering the ferocious attack by the enemy and thanked Mithras, the god of the legions.

After a light meal they tacked up their animals, re-armed with javelins, food and water supplies and were ready to ride. Soon after they trotted towards the northern gate. Soldiers shouted their good luck and good fortune seeing that they were fully armed and leaving the safety of the fort. Some shouted good humoured abuse about having all the women and leaving some for them as well as their gold.

The four men smiled in response and waved as their horses kicked up dust flashing their tails as they increased their speed. As they got to within fifty yards of the gate, the great wooden doors were pulled and then pushed open allowing them to continue. More shouts of encouragement greeted them from above as they trotted below the guards manning the towers. Varro waved in acknowledgement and kicked Staro into a canter as they left the fort behind.

***

As the last of his people crossed the river, Caratacus saw that the tide had already swollen the quick flowing water. A handful of carts had to be helped across as the level grew higher and the speed of the water increased. Most of the Catuvellauni were already safely over and had or were still setting up their tents well away from the water's edge. He prayed that it was enough to form a big enough barrier between them and the Romans to keep them at bay. He didn't have long to wait to find out.

After the Romans had crossed the river further downstream over the Medway, he had ordered some of his men to patrol the rivers length inland in the event that they did the same again. If they did this again at least he would be prepared this time and would send re-enforcements to engage them. As he was talking to some of his senior leaders a warrior ran towards them carrying just a spear shouting a warning.

"Romans" he cried, "The Romans are here already."

Caratacus looked passed and beyond the young man and sure enough he saw four men of the legions looking at them sat on horses. He knew that the battle of the Medway and the surrounding area had to have taken a toll on their men, not as many lives as their own but surely enough to make them think again about mounting another attack so soon. He gestured for his horse to be brought forward as other men got their mounts. Together they rode towards the river's edge.

The Romans didn't move they just sat watching the group of Britons on horseback now numbering fifteen. They were too far away to be hit by a spear but an arrow could easily reach them. One of the Britons pulled his bow from over his shoulder but Caratacus signalled him to stop.

"Let's just see what our friends are doing shall we?" He said. "There's been enough blood shed for one day or so I would hope."

"Is the Tamesa big enough to hold them?" One of his warriors asked. He turned to look at him an expression of puzzlement on his face.

"I really don't know Cunilis. If you had asked me the same question of the Medway I would have answered yes but these men are good at getting around obstacles as well as fighting. They showed that and got to our war chariots and horses by crossing the river further south so I'm afraid I have little doubt they could do it again here given time." The young man looked nervous, so he tried to calm him.

"If I were their General however, I would question whether I wanted to face so many brave warriors again so quickly." He smiled trying to encourage Cunilis.

"Their great General lost a lot of men today and yesterday and if I were he, I would either try and make peace with the men on the other side of yet another river or at least have a rest and fill my belly." He looked out to the Romans again. "After all, how many men does anyone want to see die in a day?"

He wasn't sure if Cunilis felt any better or not but it made him quite certain that the enemy wouldn't try and cross the river immediately. Like his people, the Romans had to be tired and in need of rest and food. He looked at the sky and realised that they were only half way through the day. The soldiers of the legions had a river that was wider, faster and deeper to cross, he was sure he had time. He was wrong.

Varro and his men watched quietly from the safety of the far shoreline as the Britons made their camp. He couldn't believe that they were content to stop directly on the other side of the Tamesa especially after the battle at the Medway. He watched as a group of Britons rode towards them and stopped and stared, gauging them. They didn't try to re-cross the water as he thought was their original intention but stood talking animatedly to each other.

He watched the water current and realised it was much quicker than that of the Medway and it was wider and no doubt deeper. He followed its current with his eyes and decided that it was still crossable even with the high tide but only by those trained for such a task. Did the Britons think they were safe where they camped he wondered but it was a question only they could answer.

As other mounted troops reached them, Varro spoke to an Optio and told him to send a runner back to Plautius and inform him of the situation. With the countryside clear of the enemy all the way up to the Tamesa, the General had no obstacles to hinder their advance. It was merely a question of when they crossed the river, not if.

Within hours Caratacus looked out at a totally different scene across the great stretch of water. Where previously there had been grass, scrub land and the occasional tree, there was now a vast army arrayed waiting to attack. He couldn't believe the Romans were willing to enter into another conflict so quickly but they were here.

He watched as they drew up the flat small boats in a line that they had used so effectively to cross the Medway. Rows of soldiers covered their approach from the front carrying their large square shields as cover. Cavalry carrying oval shields waited behind them at a safe distance, out of arrow shot. The Romans had already set up their artillery pieces, some on carts and some standing alone but none had fired yet, he knew they must be in range at the river's edge.

From his position on a slight rise about thirty paces from the water, he considered his options and realised there were few open to him. The men across the river were readying themselves for action and there was little he could do about it.

"Bring the archers and slingers forward." He ordered. "And have the spear men advance beyond the tents. As soon as those dogs are in the river, I want the water to run red with their blood. If they reach our side I want the warriors to attack them straight away and push them back. If we let them get across there will be nothing to stop them reaching Camulodunum."

As his orders were carried out he looked up at the sky praying for divine intervention. His people were tired and exhausted and now had to somehow summon the strength to fight again. He watched as the boats were carried to the far shore hidden behind a wall of shields. Men peered out from the rectangular defences clearly expecting incoming arrows.

A trumpet sounded and very soon after things started to happen very quickly. As soon as the boats were pushed into the water, some of their occupants unshielded because of their efforts, Caratacus gave the signal for his archers to open fire. The Romans now struggled with the fast current and the arrows as the airborne dots grew larger and began to fall. Seconds later they were landing and injuring men and taking the lives of those on-board the small craft.

He saw their cavalry advance to the water's edge and the men dismount. They urged their horses forward clinging to the sides as they attempted to cross the river. Some riders bravely remained mounted and leaned back as their animals entered the water and began swimming. Caratacus was shocked as he watched the unbelievable sight before him, he had no idea that men and horses could swim together as if they were one, especially in such a dangerous current. Suddenly the large artillery pieces came to life and huge bolts were fired over the water indiscriminately punching into flesh as did their own arrows.

He waited for the horsemen and the boats to come within slinger range and then gave the signal to open fire. Men and horses were now hit by both arrows and stones as the noise of battle grew louder. Unable to buck and run the horses were easy and large fairly immobile targets for both slingers and archers and they whinnied and snorted as their flesh was bruised and pierced. As he watched he didn't know if his counter attack would be enough to stop them. He called his spearmen forward as the enemy got to within range and they now joined the fight hurling their javelins down at multiple targets. Men fell from horses and boats and the dead and injured were caught in the water current, taken away from the bedlam downstream. Screams rang out across the river of death as the water ran red with blood but the tide of men, horses and boats kept coming.

He was aware of his warriors on foot running past him as the first wave of the Romans reached their side of the river. They threw themselves at them hacking and slicing as missiles now from both sides hit where they landed indiscriminately all around. His warriors fought with ferocity and bravery as always and didn't give any ground but the enemy were getting into their stride and were beginning to methodically stab out from behind their shields as men leapt from their rafts. More men and horses entered the water from the other side and in time the sheer weight of numbers on the front line of the

Britons began to tell. His people were now being pushed back and less Roman dead were being taken by the waters flow.

Looking at the devastating scene just below him he knew something would give and it wasn't long before his warriors started to retreat as the enemy got a foothold on their side of the riverbank. He looked on helplessly almost frozen as time seemed to slow and stop. A young man's body broke away from the battle and floated downstream and Caratacus recognised Cunilis, the same man he had tried to encourage earlier was now dead.

"Retreat." He shouted and gave the signal with his arm. He didn't look back as he left the mound and walked to his horse. He briefly saw the shock on the faces of some of his warrior's men and women alike as he admitted defeat so quickly. He knew he could either watch them fight and die or retreat and survive, he chose the latter.

"To Camulodunum, retreat." He bayed once more and didn't look back.

Varro was surrounded by men cheering and banging their swords against their shields as the Britons began their retreat. He didn't feel like a celebration was in order looking at all the devastation around him. Most of the men were now stationary but a few still fought those few stragglers who had decided to stand and fight or who hadn't realised the battle was over in the midst of the mayhem. The remaining Britons were routed and finished off quickly as they were vastly outnumbered. A trumpet sounded as the men of the legions walked ashore and gathered on the far bank and then pushed further onto firmer ground. The main force of the Britons were still retreating, they had clearly had enough and weren't going to fight as they had at the Medway.

Orders were quickly sent out around the different cohorts. They were not to pursue the enemy but were to stand firm and secure the area which meant digging defences. As the river water cleared of blood, dead bodies were dragged ashore and lined up separately a line of Britons and a line of their own. It was apparent that there were far more dead Britons than

Romans, probably a ratio of four to one and their line stretched along the riverbank some way.

Riders were sent east to try and recover other dead that had been taken by the current. Despite the retreat of the Britons, heavy infantry were now formed up and began to advance behind the cover of their shields. They were ordered to move to a distant spot designated by woodland and stop approximately a hundred paces short. This would enable the rest of the army to get across the Tamesa safely without fear of a counter attack. Engineers were already putting together a bridge that would allow more troops to cross.

Defensive palisades would be dug and a base of operations established, this would ensure that they kept what they had gained. Varro saw Plautius cross the river on a small boat with Vespasian close behind on another with his senior officers their red cloaks billowing in the breeze. As some men took the opportunity to dress wounds others drank from water sacks and the more seriously injured were carried to an area where surgeons and doctors already waited.

He saw one legionary being carried by four others with a spear through the trunk of his body. The tip of the weapon had somehow found its way through his segmented armour. He was screaming in agony with each jarring step, the invasion for him was over.

Chapter Sixteen

Caratacus and his army retreated all the way back to the safety of Camulodunum. Some of them were on war chariots that hadn't even got involved in the fighting this time as the retreat had occurred so quickly, some were on horseback, others in carts but most were on foot. At first the inhabitants ran out of the enormous wooden walled settlement in celebration, great beaming smiles all over their faces, arms outstretched in greeting, until they saw the expressions and demeanour of the warriors coming towards them. Quickly their mood changed and they began to help those who had been injured in the battle and it became apparent that the river crossing by the enemy had turned into a rout.

As the new King entered the great open gates, women wailed mourning the loss of so many of their people and significantly Togodumnus as word spread of his death. Caratacus suddenly realised that he had always associated the great gates with happiness, security, feelings of well-being and safety but today was different. Today he felt empty, devastated and devoid of anything normal, how had this come to pass? A great darkness had descended over him and the place he had called home as a child as he looked into the faces of those standing watching them return.

People rushed to get the injured inside the many roundhouses and to get them treatment. Cries of agony from bleeding warriors and the wailing and screaming filled his ears from all around, his senses were bombarded with grief. He saw his wife Mott, for the first time since the battles and his eyes welled up with tears, he didn't try to stop them.

"Come with me quickly." She said. "You can't let the people see you like this." She grabbed his hand before he could say anything and led him through the low houses and woods that made up part of the great settlement and to the home of his brother. Ducking down under the low door he walked inside and for a second couldn't see anything as his eyes adjusted to the darkness.

"We have to go, leave." He said turning to Mott.

"Go? Go where husband, this is our home now. This is Camulodunum, where else are we supposed to go?" There is nowhere left. She looked into his eyes her face confused almost angry.

"They….the Romans" he began, "won't stay where they are you know that, they'll come straight here and slaughter every living thing. What are we supposed to do, what else would you suggest, wait and be massacred, is that what you're saying wife?" He paused, "I can't stop them I've tried time and time again and look what happened. They've killed hundreds of our people maybe thousands." He heard crying from somewhere outside as someone quickly walked passed with their own personal grief.

"Our people can expect more of this when they get here," he continued, "but it will be worse, they'll raise this place to the ground if we try and defend it. They have machines that are unstoppable and the men are too well protected inside their body metal." He looked at the smoke hole in the roof above and saw the blue sky above, it looked serene most unlike his reality below.

"What do you suggest we do husband flee, run away from our homes, our lives, all of us? I would rather die where I stand." Mott said rage now written over her pretty face.

"And what of the people, their families, friends, our own children, we have generations of people here. What about the old, I can't ask them to leave they wouldn't last a few days and would slow us down with the Romans pursuing us." He replied his frustration clear.

She was silent for a while. "Then we have to go with those who can survive, move quickly and fight. I will not stay here only to accept slavery or worse. I will not let that happen to our children, I'd rather take a blade to them and myself right now." Mott said.

"I would as well." He sat on the straw packed bed with his head in his hands. "If we do leave there's a chance that the Romans will leave our people alone," he looked up at his wife, "not kill them or sell them into slavery I mean. If we stay and fight one thing is certain, they'll wipe us out." He stood pacing, "I'll ask those who are able to join me," he paused adding, "us. We can't fight them as we have so I have to find another way. Even if we had the same weapons they would defeat us because they hide behind theirs shields, they fight without honour."

Mott stopped his pacing by placing her hands on his shoulders, he stared at her anger flaring in his eyes. She was considerably shorter than him with fair long brown hair tied in a ponytail at the back. They had known each other since they were children and had always been close even before their relationship blossomed as teenagers.

"Caratacus that's what they do, that's why they have swept all other opponents aside. They don't hide," his stare hardened, "they are wise in their way of war whilst we throw our people onto their shields to die even when we outnumber them they are victorious."

He broke free of her and turned away, "At the fort we didn't throw ourselves at them, we were close to achieving success but those fools of the Dobunni gave up too easily as soon as they began to take heavy injuries." He ground his teeth and clenched his fists in frustration. "I will not submit or surrender to these Romans. Their Emperor has betrayed the trust of my father and the generations before him and I will hold him personally responsible for my brother's death. I will now dedicate my life to fighting him and his legions and anyone who sides with them." He still paced. "Go and tell the chieftains and elders to gather. I will outline my plans to them and the people, all able bodied warriors who wish to come with me can, anyone who wishes to stay here and put their fate in the hands of Rome can do as they wish, I will not hold it against them." Mott smiled faintly and left leaving Caratacus to pace once more.

A short time later many chieftains and warriors were gathered to hear his words as he surveyed the crowd from the settlement wall.

"Loyal people of the Catuvellauni," he began struggling to control his emotions, "a great dark menace has come to our land and now threatens to destroy all that we have come to know. Many of you will have seen the devastation wreaked upon our warriors in battle. At this moment the enemy will be massing ready to advance again." He paused letting the words sink in, his audience silent.

"This time it's different, this time they advance on our home and if we chose to stand and fight…..we not only risk defeat but we risked total destruction. These people have no honour and they will utterly destroy our people if we stand and fight and if we chose to now, we will almost certainly lose." Those gathered below muttered and mumbled amongst themselves at his words.

"My family has always led the people of the Catuvellaunia as you know. I believe we have always had the interests of the people at heart. With that in mind I cannot risk this great place, the home of our forefathers being turned to dust and ash along with you and your families."

The audience had stopped mumbling to each other now and looks of confusion were exchanged, he continued, "I plan to leave and take as many warriors with me who want to continue to fight. The Trinovantes are a day's march away and have said they will join us but only their young, the strong, those able to join the struggle. I will take those from here, those who wish to fight and get away from this place."

"What about those you leave behind?" An old woman shouted.

"The Romans will kill every single living thing if we stay and fight here. If the warriors leave, those who are left will be at their mercy but even they will not kill just for the sake of killing. I will not abandon you I swear and I will return one day but I have to find another way to fight them. I have to gather more people for that fight and I cannot and will not witness the death of my entire people and place of birth, the place where I have so many memories."

A total silence now met his words.

"Those who are able and those who are willing to follow me must now make a choice and that choice is this….leave and fight but leave behind what you have known or stay and await their Legions." He looked around at the faces staring up at him and saw sadness, desperation and confusion.

"I go now to prepare for the journey. Any who wish to join me are welcome but I warn you it will be hard and difficult and I cannot guarantee when you will return. I can only guarantee you this……" His vice raised as he shouted, "I will not rest and I will give my last breath to fight these invaders and so must those who choose to join me." He punched his fist into the air. "I will go to the end of the land but will never give up, never, never, never."

Cheers rose up from the crowds as he turned and walked quickly away to prepare for the journey ahead.

It was a full six weeks later when the massed Roman army approached Camulodunum. The advance had surprised both sides involved in the war but not Plautius as he had decided to inform the Emperor of his progress after the battle of the Tamesa. It gave him and his troops the opportunity to secure their territorial gains and to ensure that harbours were properly established for re-enforcements and supplies. The wounded were treated and men rested, whilst the defences were made more substantial during the pause in fighting.

Claudius himself had sent word back to his headquarters that he would personally take the surrender of Camulodunum, it was something he thought would never actually happen. The intervening weeks had guaranteed that his army was at its strongest and in the best possible condition for the Emperor's arrival and in order to continue the conflict against the Britons. He made good use of his time and had negotiated the peaceful surrender of the enemy's capital. Local chieftains had assured him of their compliance after the battles they had already witnessed and so now waited to be subdued under the terms of the treaty and peace was promised.

Claudius with a taste for the dramatic had brought with him eleven elephants in order to demonstrate to the Britons, Rome's power. He now rode the largest of the great beasts at the centre of a long line of the huge animals that were ridden by members of his elite Praetorian guard with columns of heavy infantry behind, flanked by cavalry. The watching faces of Britons could be seen peering out from the settlements walls as the vast army approached.

Despite assurances that the Britons would not resist, Claudius had decided it wise not to take the chance and believe their words. If the Britons attacked the leading formations, which included him and his beloved elephants, the plan was for him to fall back and allow the battle hardened veterans to assault the vast settlement, which in turn would be reduced to smouldering ash along with every inhabitant.

With the large animals waving their long trunks around and walking slowly, the army got to within bow range and sharp eyes watched the walls but nothing changed from the people standing on them, they just watched eyes wide. As it turned out, the Britons were true to their word and Claudius, Emperor of Rome, entered the gates of Camulodunum without a drop of blood being spilt.

He had expected a hero's welcome from the people that he believed he was freeing from the tyranny of their barbaric ruler but instead of cheers and waving, the people of Camulodunum just stood and stared. A few ran at the sight of the huge animals but most simply watched as he entered their great settlement. Flanked by members of the Praetorian Guard with cavalry and heavy infantry close by he rode beyond the gates and then stopped to take in his victory, silence greeted him.

Over the coming days he took the surrender of the regional tribal Kings, eleven in total and various lower chieftains and pronounced that Britannia was now a part of the Roman Empire. He gave little thought to other regions or territories and believed that they would fall in line now that Caratacus had been defeated and Camulodunum was his. He ordered the construction of a temple in his honour and a triumphant arch. A great Roman City would grow on the grounds that had once been Camulodunum and he kept his previous promise that the people would be spared.

In preparation of the work to be completed some roundhouses were levelled and cleared with word that the Romans would build the Britons concrete houses of brick and stone. Great tents were erected in the meantime in which the Roman leaders and elite lived. Outside the settlement the vast army camped in their regulation patterns covering vast swathes of land with guards patrolling the living quarters inside. On the eighth day, after the celebrations, parades and a few days of hunting, Claudius left and started his journey home satisfied that his work was done taking his elephants with him. Almost immediately work began to transform the barbarian settlement into the islands first city.

Adminius breathed in as scented oils were rubbed onto his skin. They were blended with a mixture of spices and herbs from all over the empire; the current concoction was a spiced rose scent and mint. He was in one of the many luxury command tents now sited near the centre of what had been Camulodunum as it was transformed. After the lavish parades of Claudius' triumph over the rebels, small on a scale to those in Rome, he had been given his own tent. As the King in waiting, his scheduled coronation the next day, he suddenly found his status had been elevated by the Romans, if not by his new subjects.

He lay naked face down on a raised bed enjoying the touch of Asiria, a sign of things to come he thought, as she massaged his shoulders and upper back. Tomorrow he would be crowned King and rightfully take up his place as the leader of the Catuvellauni. Claudius had also taken the surrender of other Kings and leaders, lesser Kings obviously than he would become and the people would see that it was he who now ruled the province of Britannia on behalf of the great Roman Empire. He knew he would face hostility from a minority but didn't care, he had achieved his aim his ambition and that was all that mattered, they would grow to respect him one way or another.

Client King in waiting he maybe but he reasoned it was better to be a client than a vagabond on the run, with no shelter, food or military force to defend him as he imagined his brother to be. Asiria motioned for him to turn over and he moved onto his back. He looked up at her features and dark skin. She spoke with heavy accented Latin and had come from a land called Parthia far to the east many weeks ride away. She was beautiful and he drank in her body with his eyes enjoying her hands as they caressed his skin. She wore her native clothes that showed her virtually flat stomach and it stirred something primeval inside him.

When he had first been introduced to her by one of the Praetorian Centurions he couldn't believe his good fortune. She was to be his body slave from that point on, her life his to do with as he wished. She would ensure his bath was ready at the end of a hard day dealing with disputes and land issues concerning his people, she would massage, oil and scent his body and she would provide anything further he required. He had heard of body slaves when he was in Rome but had never expected to have one himself. It was no doubt a benefit of him now being a part of the upper class, a true nobleman. The nearest he had come to experiencing someone like her before was when visiting the many brothels of Rome.

It had always been his ambition above his brothers to rule but not as they had in their limited way. Whilst they were content to hunt and share their time with locals, he had studied. When he had learned all he could about his tribe and their customs and of those around them, he had sought new subjects and places and where better than Rome. His father had allowed him to travel to the great Capital aged just eight where he had seen things he would never have dreamed of before.

From an early age he had studied in their great libraries and read their scrolls and learned Latin unlike either Togodumnus or Caratacus giving him an advantage. So safe and comfortable was the young man in his new surroundings that he had stayed for five years, returning home aged thirteen to a land that had not grown or progressed since his departure. He had made friends in the world's largest capital and he was now reaping the rewards of his earliest ambitions. He groaned as his new acquisition rubbed his lower stomach and Asiria giggled quietly.

"I'm sorry master," she began, "I didn't mean to arouse you."

She looked down and saw that he was growing hard with pleasure as her hands moved lower still, she smiled. He had experienced many massages in Rome while in exile and knew that the slaves who performed them would do all they could to help their clients to relax. None however shared the beauty of this young woman taken by her homelands victor and chosen to be a body slave.

She turned and picked up the small oil bottle and poured a few drops onto his stiffening shaft. Rubbing it gently he groaned feeling her hands and the heat they generated together with the oils. You fool Adminius he thought to himself smiling more as Asiria parted his legs slightly and gently massaged his aching balls. Just when he thought it couldn't feel any better she took his taught manhood in her hand and carefully gripped the shaft. He looked into her dark eyes and saw they were intrigued by his swollen member. Slowly at first she let her hand move up and down his shaft hearing him groan with pleasure. He arched his back closing his eyes as the tingling sensation within him grew and her hand moved faster, the oils reacting and warming, her other hand gently rubbing his balls.

"Taste it." He instructed and she bent over him without hesitating and took his hardness into her mouth, her lips warm and soft. She moved along the length of his aching penis expertly, she clearly knew what she was doing. He knew he wouldn't last long as her hands and mouth worked their magic. All the stress of the last few days and weeks were forgotten, nothing else mattered except this moment in time. He was right about his longevity and with a loud sigh he let go and almost as quickly fell back onto the bed sighing and smiling.

She smiled back down at him and asked, "Was that correct master?"

He lay back laughing, his shoulders shaking, "Yes Asiria you did very well, very well indeed. I think we will make great friends you and I."

She asked, "Is there anything else I can do for you my lord?"

He smiled back totally relaxed. "Asiria you could do anything you wanted to do to me but for now I think I should get some sleep. I've got a very busy day ahead of me tomorrow but during the night we can have some more time together and I will help you relax." He touched her between the legs and she giggled.

Turning she gave him a towel as he sat up and then walked to the door of the tent of his sleeping apartment. It may be a temporary structure but it was walled and covered with dyed animal skins it was far more luxurious than anything the locals had seen before. Coloured fresco's even covered the walls interior here and there just as he had seen in the great buildings of their city. Lighted with candles on iron stands, warmed with a wood burner and guarded from the outside, he smiled hardly able to believe his good luck.

He considered what his own capital should look like. It would have to be something as imposing as the buildings he had lived in whilst in Rome but bigger. Great columns would greet visitors at the front, whilst huge corridors would welcome them inside. He would commission the best fresco artists to decorate the walls and would invite Senators from all over the Empire to witness the magnificence of the new province.

He had no regrets, well maybe one he mused, that he hadn't gone to Rome and begged Claudius to help him take the crown earlier. Whilst his backward family would have lived in mud huts for an eternity, he had realised his vision and now he could begin work on bringing civilisation to the country of his birth. He could barely wait for the day to dawn in the morning and to see the faces of the people, his people. He would win them over he was sure and if he couldn't they would rue the day they opposed him.

He tested the bed for firmness with his hand and found it sturdy but pliable. He drank from a goblet tasting the fresh wine he had enjoyed and finished it in one go. He dropped the towel and lay on the bed pulling the covers over him and within no time at all he was asleep. He dreamt of his future, of being a successful member of the Empire. He would recruit soldiers for Rome and make legions of British warriors turning them into auxiliaries. He would introduce farming methods and build villas, temples and worship the gods of Rome and one day he hoped, he would be accepted into the Senate itself. Anything was possible now that he had helped brush aside his backward brothers, the task now was to drag the people into the new world with him.

He didn't know where he was when he opened his eyes sometime later and sat up suddenly with a start, something had disturbed his sleep. Had something fallen or had Asiria come to help him relax even more? The candles still burned and he realised quickly that he was still inside the massive tent and nothing was untoward, he relaxed and lay back down quickly drifting back to his dreams. Then in his sleepy state he remembered that something had woken him, something deliberate, he remembered what it was, a voice.

Immediately he sat up again blinking his eyes open and there stood at the end of the bed was his brother, Caratacus. He stared in disbelief blinking again, as if he was dreaming, was he dreaming he wondered, he must be surely? He had to be asleep still he thought, his wayward brother was running for his life or so he had been told.

"It's me brother I'm here, you are not dreaming." The voice was undeniable and the reality so vivid, it hit him like an axe. Adminius saw him clearly but how was this possible? Caratacus stood before him wearing a Roman toga which just added to his confusion. He spoke, "Don't let these clothes fool you. I had to wear them in case someone saw me." He smirked now, a disturbing smile his gaze fixed.

"I wouldn't have been able to get to see you if I'd worn my own clothes would I?" He turned his head indicating something unseen, " Your friends outside, the large guards would have had my entrails cut out before I took a step further. You and your friends would have seen to that wouldn't you? No real local is allowed to within a hundred paces of your grand tents." He looked around. "So this is what it was all for was it?"

"How did you get in here? If they find you, you'll be crucified." He spat back in shock.

Caratacus said, "It's still just leather and leather cuts quite easily or have you already forgotten?" He produced a dagger from under the toga. Adminius recognised it as their fathers.

"This can all be yours as well brother." Adminius said trying desperately to change the subject to delay whatever

Caratacus had planned. Maybe someone would hear them talking and come to investigate. "We can rule together like one. I've many plans and we can rebuild this place for the better. I told you it would happen but you wouldn't listen. It's alright though I forgive you, I always did."

Caratacus could barely hide his hatred for his younger brother and ignored his words. "Do you know how Togodumnus died?" He said abruptly, he raised his eyebrows and walked to the side of the high bed.

"His body was punctured by their swords and spears whilst trying to defend his land, his people and he died in my arms, these arms you see before you." He held his arms out but Adminius didn't look at them, he stared at his eyes trying to determine what he intended. He held them out still as if to emphasise the point.

"I was covered in his blood, our father's blood, blood he gave for his people." He stared at Adminius his eyes looking right through him as if into his soul.

"I haven't seen you for year's brother but surely we can mend our differences now? I told you we couldn't fight the strength of Rome and I was right see." He waved his arm at the tented walls.

"Please now at least concede that and let us rejoice together and lead our people. With you at my side they too will see the error of their ways and stop resisting. It can be done, all you have to do is allow it for once in your life have the vision to see what is best." The terror was evident in his eyes as he saw the cold expression on the face of Caratacus and he began to use his words to try and save himself. He was under no illusion, he barely recognised the barbarian stood over him but he had to play for time. One of the guards was bound to hear their conversation through the thin walls.

"I have no intention of being at your side Adminius. You betrayed our father, our brother and our people and you chose them over us." He looked to the side of the tent to the unseen Romans elsewhere. "You have aided them and now you return to take a crown that wasn't yours to take, in a land that is no longer yours to own. Our people know of your betrayal, how long do you think you will live? You killed my father as you killed my brother and there has to be a price to pay for your betrayal and indulgence. You even dress like them and even whore yourself as they do for instant gratification."

Adminius looked shocked and blushed, "What do you mean by that?"

"I saw you with the Parthian whore." He paused. "Is that how far you've fallen brother, you didn't even know her did you?"

Adminius said, "Didn't know her, what have you done, have you hurt her?"

"You shouldn't concern yourself with such whores but think of your own people, the people you betrayed, the people who lay dead on the battlefields rotting even now as you lay here in a bed of betrayal. The people who tried to protect the capital from you and your kind now litter the plains, woods and forests. It's too late to worry about her now anyway, her blood is exhausted and her throat open to the world, my world."

Horror stricken at his brothers words Adminius tried to rise but Caratacus instantly thrust his knife forward in one quick movement before he could react, stabbing his brother in the middle of his chest where his heart lay, he froze, eyes wide as blood bled quickly from the wound.

"You fool, what have you done?" He gasped grabbing at the blade and looking down as the dagger was ripped wide and upwards into his chest cutting bone and internal organs alike. Blood gushed now, out and around the edges of the blade and onto his hands.

Caratacus stared at the man he had grown up with, he didn't recognise him. He realised he felt nothing for what had just happened. He pulled the dagger free and wiped it and his red hands on the bed sheet and then put it away. He walked quickly and quietly from the room into the next and into the one beyond where the body of the Parthian female lay. He didn't even look at her as he walked calmly by his movement reflected in her dead dark eyes. He found another toga and replaced the blood stained one he wore.

He went to the rear of the huge multi-roomed structure and found the cut in the leather panel where he had gained entry. He left as easily as he had entered and disappeared into the darkness of familiar pathways between the still standing roundhouses beyond.

Off duty Roman soldiers nodded acknowledging him as he walked calmly from the scene of the murder, he nodded and smiled in response. Finding his horse where he had left it he climbed aboard and looked around one last time. His capital was no longer his own and in no time he wouldn't recognise it unless he could find enough warriors to follow him again and retake it one day. That however, would have to wait especially with the invaders leader still here on the island somewhere surrounded by his guards, it would be impossible for the time being.

As he took one last final look around he decided to return when Claudius had got back to Rome. For a second he contemplated sacrificing himself in what would be a suicidal attack on the Emperor who was probably asleep after whoring himself as Adminius had somewhere to the south. He thought about finding his column, waiting until the early hours when all but a few guards were asleep. He reasoned that he may even succeed with the help of the gods but would he survive to fight afterwards? In that moment he no longer cared for his own life but then he remembered his family and knew he could not abandon them.

In that instant he decided to leave quietly and vanish into the night westward. The Romans would no doubt blame the death of his brother on the people but they wouldn't really care and probably wouldn't even want retribution, they were bound to find another puppet to control as King. Caratacus knew the Romans cared nothing for his countrymen except those who they could sell, enslave and use. He clicked at his horse and walked forward looking around at the place he and his people had called home.

He felt tears well up in his eyes as visions in his head saw his father, mother and family when they were young and happy as the horse carried him along the tracks and towards freedom. Through blurred vision he passed three people and heard his name whispered, it brought him out of his memories. He wiped at his eyes and recognised them their faces not unknown but their names, two men and a woman, the woman amongst them spoke quietly.

"Go safely Caratacus son of Cunobelinus and never stop fighting. Gather our people and fight this disease that stains our land." She smiled at him and he nodded in response not saying a word and kicked gently at his horse as it sped up into a trot. He would do as her words had said, not because she had recognised him as her rightful King but because that's what his life was now, a fight against Rome. He rode out through the large gates and wondered if he would ever see them again.

It took a few days for the fallout from the Emperors visit to die down. Plautius and his senior officers were glad to see the back of him truth be told and his Praetorian Guard. They were never well regarded by the men of the legions who saw them as false and aloof second rate soldiers. Most had never actually served in the legions and their officers were all given their posts gratis as they were the sons of Senators. Legionaries were recruited from Rome and served their time there, deployments like the one with Claudius to Britannia were rare.

Gradually the men of Plautius' army got down to the routine work of establishing a stable settlement and work began within days to transform what was once Camulodunum into a Roman fortress like city. The murder of Adminius went by almost unnoticed which surprised Plautius to a certain extent. They thought that the Britons would blame them for allowing the assassination to occur or would even say that they had done it in order to bring in their own or another governor. When the announcement was made some locals actually cheered, the Britons were a strange lot.

With work on the garrison being carried out, there was still a lot of exploring to be done and Plautius decided upon a three pronged advance into the interior of the country. One Legion he decided would go north, another north west and the final Legion, Vespasian's Second Augusta, would travel west virtually parallel with the coast. When Varro heard the news he was pleased that he would remain with the Second Augusta as there had been a possibility he would be confined garrison duty. It was also rumoured that west was the direction that Caratacus had gone when he had left with what was left of his war bands.

Local members of the hierarchy were questioned at length about his departure but little was disclosed except to say that he had left to save Camulodunum and its inhabitants from destruction. There were rumours that he had cousins and other family members with the Silures, a tribe far to the west so it was presumed that their region would have been his ultimate destination. The Silures were a large tribe said to be similar to his own and very warlike so it would make sense for him and his remaining followers to go there. There were differing rumours as to how many had gone with him from four thousand to six thousand, one thing was certain and that was the Trinovantes had joined him swelling their numbers considerably.

Plautius issued orders to all the legions to engage Caratacus or any other hostile force wherever they were discovered and at the earliest possible opportunity. Caratacus had to be destroyed, that was the priority and anyone caught bearing arms with him. The population of Camulodunum had as Caratacus had believed, been spared as they had not resisted especially when confronted by the Emperor. Caratacus could expect no such mercy however, when the legions eventually caught up with him, they intended to bring about his bloody end. He was known to have taken the cream of the warriors from both the Catuvellauni and the Trinovantes with him, estimated to be some many thousands strong, possibly over ten thousand all told.

Caratacus although now a sworn enemy had at least gained some respect as a worthy opponent as the fallen shields of Rome would testify but he was an enemy nonetheless. He would be hunted down whatever the cost and however long it took, time was not a factor but patience was and one of Rome's greatest virtues was her patience in this regard. Caratacus had highlighted himself as a man and a leader that Rome would not allow to flourish and grow. Important lessons had been learned by individuals who led armies against the might of their Emperor, some of whom had threatened to bring its very walls crumbling down. Caratacus would be pursued for a long as it took, it was said that his wife had fled with him and their children and so now they too would share his fate. Only a complete and utter surrender with no terms may guarantee all their lives and even then he would pay for it with his own in all probability. The Romans also knew that this knowledge now made him and his warriors an even more dangerous foe. He and they would fight to the death as that was what they expected but before that happened they would take as many Roman lives with them they could.

Far away to the west, Caratacus led his large army through the forests of the Durotriges. He had been unsure whether they would be treated as friends or enemies and so had sent riders ahead to speak to the local chieftains and elders. After talks they were to be given free passage through the territory. Word had already reached the people of the Durotriges that the tribes to the east had been defeated by the invaders and they were unsure whether to resist and risk losing everything or to make a treaty with the advancing men of the legions.

Food and shelter was given where possible but no alliances were made, some viewed the army of Caratacus with suspicion as they crossed their lands, rivers and passed the hill forts and settlements along the way. He had warned them of their fate if they chose to lay down their arms which the Romans would demand but still they were undecided, better to rule as an ally of Rome than die as an enemy some had said. They behaved like cowards as far as he was concerned and continued west leaving them to the mercy of Vespasian who he knew was leading the Second Augusta behind him.

As the days began to shorten he knew that if he could stay ahead of Vespasian's Legion they would be relatively safe as the enemy campaigned in accordance with the seasons. At some point he knew their march would be halted and they would make camp, not for a night but for the entire winter until the first days of spring and then they would begin to march west again. It was when that happened, that major halt, that he intended to start making counter attacks. The Britons did not stop fighting because the rains came or the snow fell and he intended to show them what could be achieved when that happened.

As the weeks passed and the march west continued he had more than enough time to think about what had gone before, the battles, the loss of life and the tactics he had used, things that had to change. He had to find other ways to fight, facing this trained and well-armed foe face to face had not and would not work. Every battle had turned into a defeat, something he wasn't used to experiencing. He considered every option available to him but also knew that once he got to the lands of the Silures and the mountains, the advantage of the terrain would be his. These were the things he reminded his people of constantly when he looked into their eyes and saw their hurt and frustration. They were not used to being beaten or retreating, they were not used to being displaced and it was a harsh reality and fate for all of them to endure.

With local tribe's undecided as to whether they would fight the men of the eagles as they crossed their territories, he knew they themselves couldn't risk stopping for any length of time. He had considered sending warriors back to flank the marching columns of Vespasian and attack those who found themselves at the rear. He knew full well that the legions marched with their supplies and baggage at the end of their columns and they would literally stretch for miles, where they were not well guarded and were vulnerable. The men who rode the carts in the supply line would give little resistance as they were paid men, mercenaries. Even if they did fight, they wouldn't be competent and would be quickly killed. He also knew that if he could hit their supply lines hard enough it would cripple their advance and no doubt stop it and they would eventually be forced to retreat. If he could make that happen, his warriors wouldn't stop attacking until they pushed them into the sea.

The subject was a matter that consumed his thoughts throughout the days, nights and weeks and of those ahead but he had finally decided that he wouldn't divide his force. After many discussions with his chieftains it was concluded that for any flanking force to be effective it would have to be many thousands strong and they couldn't afford to be without that many people. It was also argued that if their flanking force was discovered by the Romans scouts, Vespasian would simply change direction and wipe them out.

Word was bound to reach the enemy of any counter attacking force and if that happened there was a possibility they would themselves be attacked and destroyed. It was a hard decision but one that had to be made, he believed their strength lay in their numbers and was content for them to stay as one until they could join with the Silures, who he knew, would fight on their side . The only thing that would stop that would be if the chasing enemy made camp for the winter and before they entered the territory of the Silures, in which event he would reconsider his options.

However as the weather got gradually colder and the leaves started to fall and turn brown, the ground hardened and by that time the army of Caratacus was well inside the boundary lines of the Silures lands and safe, for the time being. As it turned out it was said that Vespasian's own army had not walked freely through southern Britannia but had been fought all the way and had captured many settlements. He had also taken many casualties but he had eventually won every battle and there had been many at both settlements and hill forts. Some estimated that forty settlements had fallen to his swords, it seemed that they were unstoppable but were experiencing fierce resistance.

Vespasian's advance had finally got as far as the River Exe where he turned the capital of the Dumnonii into a major fortification which he named Isca Dumnoniorium. On the east side of the river the march was halted and preparations made for the winter break. With casualties to be tended and replacements needed for those who were permanently removed from their numbers, the winter couldn't come soon enough. The Second Augusta, were as far west as any Roman army had ever been and so had to consolidate and re-enforce and make preparations for the next campaigning season.

Chapter Seventeen

The days had turned cold, very cold and frost covered the ground as Caratacus looked out over the land and down across the valley to the River Exe. He and those around him were wrapped in thick heavy skins with hoods over their heads against the inclement weather.

Vespasian had been busy and so had his men, where once stood hundreds of roundhouses, an enormous wooden fortress now broke the landscape in the middle of those that still existed. Large boats were moored in the ice of the water close by, frozen in place until the thaw of spring. His scouts had informed him that they were still bringing in supplies from the sea route to the south, the last part of the journey on the back of wagons.

The enemy were camped for the winter but the structure looked like something more than that, it had a distinct look of permanence to it and was the largest single structure Caratacus had ever seen. Building and construction was still taking place beyond its walls where stone buildings were beginning to take shape, he knew that wouldn't be happening if they intended to abandon it when the spring came.

He could see the helmeted figures of sentries their bodies covered in fur on the walls where they obviously thought they were safe, they looked out surveying the scene below. Traditionally they didn't commit to combat during the winter months it was a weakness that Caratacus hoped to use to his advantage. Encased behind the high walls they may have been relatively safe but they were also a huge stationary target. With his cousin from the Silures at his side, his numbers had swollen in recent months to over fifteen thousand. Ardwen had not hesitated when he had heard of the threat coming from the east. He had sworn to avenge his brothers and Togodumnus.

The Silures were not merely happy to be involved in the campaign, they were eager as they lived for war when the opportunity arose and more importantly, were good at it. A few weeks before a small group of Silures warriors had literally stumbled over an advance force of the enemy who had crossed onto their land. They too were few in number and were found recording measurements and information for maps and had become an easy target for their warriors who had wiped them out to a man. There was no doubt that Vespasian would guess his soldiers fate but he would never know for sure, vanishing in the hills of Silures territory wouldn't do his legions moral any good and that could only be of benefit to the Britons.

As they looked upon the recently constructed fortress, smoke rose from various chimneys although hardly any movement could be seen from within. A few sentries were posted along its walls and in its towers that were positioned at every corner and above the entrances at the front and rear. Row upon row of tents, were lined up inside the fort as well as some ancillary wooden buildings. Towards the rear near the centre were the foundations of the stone buildings which had quickly taken shape. Ardwin and Caratacus decided to take a closer look, they had told the rest of the army to stay hidden and to move behind the rolling hills to the north where they wouldn't be seen.

They believed that they could go unnoticed amongst the Britons of the area and would try to gather information about the movements, if any of the enemy within the fort. Although they were camped for the winter, patrols would still be sent out to reconnoitre the countryside and they would make for easy targets. Small numbers they maybe but the thought of men not returning from patrols would do enormous damage to the men camped inside.

Warm breath billowed from their horse's mouths as they began their descent to lower ground careful not to slip as steam rose from their shining bodies. Hooves hit the crisp frosty grass as powdered frost puffed up into the air as they made their way closer to the settlement at the side of the fort.

"If we don't stop them, everywhere will soon look like this." Ardwin said. Caratacus looked over but couldn't see his face properly as it was hidden inside his hood. From the outskirts the place looked like most others in Britannia except for the tall fort now dominating the roundhouses. It was an alien site to them and one that brought shivers to both warriors' spines, it was an altogether different shiver than that of the cold.

"If we can take one of these fortresses, just one," Caratacus said, "others will see that they are not invincible and can be beaten."

"That's all it would take," Ardwen replied, "one decisive victory and maybe even the cowards who don't fight will realise that we can win this war and remove the blight from the land."

"We're not all warriors cousin, that's the problem." Caratacus said as they continued to move slowly along. "Some don't fight because they're cowards but I know what you mean, I would rather be dust than live amongst them. Some of them have had the fight knocked out of them, some are terrified for their loved ones and a few just want to live in peace, to work the land and tend their crops. Life is a struggle with that alone."

Ardwen didn't reply but grunted in response as they got to a wide track worn by previous travellers. An old man with a mule and cart was slowly rumbling coming the other way over the bumpy ground.

"Good day to you," Caratacus said as they got closer, "how are things?" He asked. The old man squinted up at them with the winter sun now high in the sky behind them, "Who are you?" He said without any pleasantries, clear and direct.

"We are of the Dobunni." Caratacus replied lying. They had already decided to say, they were from the tribal lands to the north of where they were now and hoped it would avoid any suspicion.

"Are you?" The old man said challenging the response, "You don't sound like you are!"

Ardwen pushed his hood back and looked at Caratacus concern on his face, he turned his attention back to the old man, a harsh stern look on his face. "How are things with the Romans old man?" He asked.

The man stopped, pulling gently on the reins of the mule and looked at them more closely, studying their swords. "You will have them taken from you if they see them," he said nodding at their weapons, "they don't like to see Britons carrying arms, the only thing with a blade we can use is for crops or butchery. Anyone with a long sword will be taken in and questioned." He covered his eyes against the sun. "What business do you have here?"

"We have grain to trade and were thinking that the people here may want some in exchange for goods." Caratacus said.

"So why do you have concern for the Romans?" The old man asked.

The two warriors halted their mounts properly and climbed down. "We expect them to move into our own lands when the spring comes, it's only natural that we are curious as to how you find them." Caratacus replied. The old man turned to look at the fort.

"Well?" Ardwen said, "We are fellow Britons old man are we not and I expect an answer when we ask a question of another about the men who have moved into our lands and taken what is rightfully ours."

"Mm well we didn't actually welcome them as you are probably aware." He got down off the cart and walked forward and patted his mule on the rump. "They take our crops to feed their soldiers, grain mostly, they use our women and they try to persuade our young men to join their legions. Our leaders have been told they are to pay annual tributes to them, in exchange they say they will protect the people and show us things, how to build from stone and how to make life better. They say they will bring civilisation to us, whatever that means, things we are not aware of."

"And how are the people taking to them?" Ardwen said.

"They are different from others who have been in charge before, that's certain." He said, "They keep order and control of what goes on, some say that things are better under them, some say they want them gone and some don't care because life is hard enough. No man likes to be told how to live his life but it always happens, the difference here is that these men come from a different land and speak with a different tongue."

"Do they stay behind their walls?" Caratacus asked.

"For the main they do but not always, once in a while they come out in groups of at least eight. Our leaders go inside sometimes to discuss matters but we normal folk don't really get to hear about what they talk about unless it affects us. I suppose it will be different once the spring comes but that's not for a while. I see mounted patrols go out quite often but where they ride to I couldn't say. They're always back by dark and don't stay out overnight."

Caratacus and Ardwen looked at each other and then back at the old man, Caratacus asked, "Where can we find your leader and what do you call him?"

"He is named Wilmarn and you will find him in the large roundhouse near to the forts entrance." He pointed. "He took over after the Romans came as the old leader and his family were put to death after they resisted, you will see their heads on spikes as a warning to others." He looked back to the fort again. "They're along the bank of the river, their children as well."

"Go safely old man," Caratacus said, "we will look for this Wilmarn and see about trading." They led their horses.

"Remember those swords," the old man said pointing at their hilts, "I would cover them or hide them before you go any further, you can always collect them on the way home."

They nodded in response and continued leading their horses. "It sounds like the locals have accepted them already." Ardwen said.

"Accepted? I wouldn't say that cousin, I don't think they had much choice. We know they tried to fight as did my own people. It makes me wonder how my own fair, are some still resisting or have they settled to their enforced way of life. I wonder what the land looks like now, has it changed? There are so many things that run through my mind especially when I try to sleep at night."

"We could always go and see," Ardwen said, "it would probably take a few days ride to get there though and I'm sure there would be check points along the way."

"Maybe in the weeks to come but we have work to do here first. Come on let's see what's happening. We'll put our weapons here under the edge of this bush. I don't want to risk them getting found." Caratacus said as he halted his horse and lifted the leafy branches from which frost fell, Ardwen put his own sword next to his cousins and then climbed aboard his horse, together they continued down the track. It wasn't long before the first of the roundhouses came fully into sight with smoke climbing high out of the thatched roof. They rode past fields with rows of crops, they had obviously been there long before the invaders came. Fish were set up drying on wooden rails waiting to be smoked, some children came out shouting hello at the strangers as they went by.

"Amazing how normal everything looks isn't it?" Caratacus asked.

Ardwen smiled, "They are living day by day as the old man said. I think we should stay clear of this Wilmarn."

"I was thinking the same thing, it's probably better to keep a low profile and just have a look around, maybe talk to a few of the locals and see what there is to see and if there's anything that would prove an effective target." Caratacus said.

They rode their horses around the bend fully and Ardwen said nodding, "How about that?" The fort came into view, its external walls constructed of long straight tall tree trunks cut from the local forest. The builders had filled in the gaps between the logs with some hardened substance that prevented them from seeing inside. A deep trench had been dug near the track below the wall they now followed. Inside it, were branches and sticks that looked to be covering something below but they couldn't see what. Sharpened spiked timbers stuck out at low angles from the wall, they would make climbing difficult, virtually impossible especially if they were under fire. The wood glistened even with the frost as if it had been coated with some dark substance, Caratacus couldn't make out if it was something oily, slippery or both. They saw that they were being watched from above as they walked slowly past and tried to act normally. One of the soldiers looked out at them his breath apparent in the cold air.

"Don't look up and he'll take no notice." Caratacus said, and he was right. Out of the corner of his eye he saw than the legionary had begun to walk in the opposite direction towards one of the large towers at the corner of the structure. The main entrance was approachable over a wooden flat bridge over the ditch, it was around twenty paces wide. They passed more roundhouses on the opposite side of the track and then came to the river. At first there didn't seem to be any activity aboard the vessels anchored to the bank, on the second ship however, a man appeared wearing a brightly coloured red tunic. He paid little interest to them and went about his business on the vessel. These were the ships they had seen from the outside of the settlement on the hillside. They were locked in the frozen water, also waiting for the spring to come.

There was little movement anywhere else as most people were probably inside staying warm near their fires. The clanging of metal could be heard from a forge as they slowly rode along the track, thick black smoke rose from the chimney at the roof and strong fumes permeated the air. They left the walls of the fort behind and saw that the ice was thinner the further south they went. Continuing along the well-worn path other ships were resting at anchor, they moved and bobbed up and down with the flow of the water where the ice hadn't reached them. Stores and supplies were being unloaded onto carts from one ship roped against the river's edge and secured onto two trees, no doubt the unloaded cargo was bound for the fort and the soldiers within. They carried on along the track that now ran parallel with the river, it was much wider here. Eventually the track became just a foot path, they followed it veering away from the water's edge towards dense woodland.

When they were clear of hearing ears and watching eyes, they stopped and dismounted. "We'd better wait a while before we go back or someone will get suspicious, let's head up into those woods." Caratacus said pointing as they left the path completely. The woodland gave them another view of the area from higher ground giving them a different perspective. It was clear that there was only one real way in and one way out of the settlement area except for the abnormal traveller. They checked the woods which would have made an excellent place for a remote post for the Romans but were surprised to find there was none there.

They decided to continue through the woods instead of returning the way they had come so as not to arouse any suspicion. They changed direction and skirted the woods coming back to where they had hidden their swords, satisfied that they had seen enough they galloped off to the north where the rest of the army waited.

Varro didn't enjoy the end of a campaigning season and he liked being stuck inside a fort in the middle of winter even less. Worse than the two, he hated being stuck on guard duty and that was where he found himself, in charge of all the sentries as the duty officer. He hadn't seen Brenna or her brother Tevelgus for months and wondered if he would ever see either of them again. They had stayed with the army working alongside them where they could, assisting with Britons and trying to lessen conflicts where possible at Camulodunum.

He passed a group of legionaries playing dice sat at a table. They were due to rotate with the current guards on his next signal at the second hour after midnight. One of the men asked if he would like to join them but he declined saying that he wasn't very good at the game and was going to make one last check on the men on the wall. He collected his bear skin cloak from a hook on the wall and wrapped it around his shoulders. Leaving the warm building, heated by a large fire he shivered as he went outside into the still night, biting fresh icy air on his face. He climbed the wooden ladder up the wall and made his way to the nearest guard.

"All quiet?" He asked, the sentry looking out into the dark night.

"Yes sir. I haven't seen anyone for hours but an owl has been keeping us company hooting from those trees over there." He nodded out into the darkness to where Varro could just about see the outline of a large tree set amongst others beyond the local roundhouses, their canopies just standing out against the sky. Smoke drifted up into the clear night air from numerous fires kept burning throughout the night inside the Britons dwellings. He looked up and could easily make out various constellations that were familiar to him.

"It's freezing out here, much colder than home during the winter," he said and stamped his feet banging them on the wooden surface, "the fire will soon warm you up inside though." The sentry acknowledged his words with a shivering nod. "Not long, I'm just going to have a word with the artillery crew." The sentry nodded as he walked around the guard straining his eyes to see the men under the cover of the tower.

"Sir." Acknowledging his arrival one of the two ballista crew said.

"How's it going?" He asked.

"Well my balls are now frozen solid and I can no longer feel my hands but apart from that it's as quiet as the grave sir." The other man said from behind the first.

Varro laughed, peering under the low roof he could just see the other man sat down huddled up, "I know the feeling believe me but it won't be long and you'll be back inside and in the warmth where you can get some food and a hot drink, the feeling will soon come back to you, I doubt the damage is permanent."

"I hope not sir or my woman will want to have a word with you I'm sure."

Varro smiled, "Everything quiet then?"

"Apart from that fucking owl hooting away all night, it's kept us awake." He joked looking towards the tree line. "If it keeps going with that racket on our next shift I'll send a bolt flying in his direction, see how he likes that." He crouched and came out from under the roof. "This bastard of a country is freezing in winter, why couldn't we have gone to Greece or somewhere warm, somewhere near the coast, Sicily maybe or even Macedon? The cold gets right into your bones I don't think I'll ever be the same again. Can't you ask the General to have a word and have us replaced with another Legion sir?"

"I think you overestimate my influence soldier and his for what it's worth." He replied.

His companion said, "I wish you'd stop complaining about the fucking cold, it just reminds me how bad it is." He said to his companion. "Obviously it's fucking cold but on the wall we can't do anything about it can we. If we had a fire those hairy bastards would be able to see us from miles away

285

and you'd look a right cock with an arrow sticking out of your face, wouldn't you?"

All three men laughed as they rubbed their hands together and moved from one foot to the other in an attempt to stay warm. Varro looked over the wall at the white frosty ground below.

"One good thing about this weather is that any Briton worth his salt is wrapped around his woman, next to a fire if he's got any sense." Their commander said as he continued to peer over the palisade. Movement suddenly caught his eye, frowning and looking over to the left he saw a fire blaze into life aboard one of the vessels moored along the river bank.

"Sir." One the guards said.

"I see it." He replied quickly, he knew that the sentries aboard the vessels rarely had fires aboard the ships and then only under strictly controlled conditions inside the iron braziers.

"Sound the alarm." Varro ordered without hesitating as one of the men he had been passing the time with just a moment before, began rattling a large metal triangle.

Varro turned to the remaining guard, "Let's get that ballistae cranked up and ready to fire just in case." As he spoke these words, the ship next in line, sparked to life with flames of its own on board. There was no question now that someone must have deliberately set the fires. As he watched both blazes trebled almost instantly in size, pushing flames into the air, something must have been used to accelerate the fire. A horn sounded from inside the fort sounding the alarm, in moments it would be brought to life.

As the area beyond lit up Varro saw dark figures moving about on the decks of the boats, they clearly weren't Roman. He ducked under the low roof of the tower as the sentry struggled to wind the ballista back. "Here let me help you." He said. "Your hands are probably frozen."

"What about our men on-board sir?" The legionary asked.

"I would guess that it's a little late for them now soldier, they're probably lying dead with their throats cut." He looked towards the growing flames and felt pain as his eyes hurt in the glare. The woolly figures on the ships looked as if they were now jumping onto the ice off the far ship of those in the frozen water.

"Ready?" He asked the soldier.

He stopped turning the handle and the man nodded.

"Fire." He ordered standing back. There was a crack as the bolt was launched into the cold night air and went streaking across the track and landed somewhere on the deck of the nearest boat or just beyond, its flight lost in the flames. It was hard to see where it actually embedded itself at that distance especially with the fire.

"Prepare to fire again." He ordered as the sentry collected another missile and loaded another bolt turning the handle again, the ratchets clicked with a metallic clunk as they struck each other. Varro heard activity from below and inside the fort as men raced to their designated positions. Vespasian had them trained and drilled for eventualities such as this and the men knew instinctively where their individual stations were in the event of an attack.

Shadows skittered across the ice beyond the boats as one man fell shouting some obscenity as he skidded and slid over the frozen water. He was dragged upright by another and continued to slip and slide whilst trying to get to the far bank.

"Concentrate your fire on them and the ice." Varro ordered pointing to the escaping Britons. The next bolt flew straight and embedded itself into the ice in between some of the running men, shattered chunks flew up around them as they turned. Another fire started on the ship third along the row farther along the riverside.

"Jupiter's fucking cunt." The soldier behind the bolt thrower shouted straining his eyes towards the fourth ship and sure enough within seconds it was the next to be set on fire. Archers began to take up their positions on the wall, some of whom were still throwing on uniform and bits of armour and helmets as they struggled with their bows. He heard men asking what was going on, why had they been woken, looking out over the wall they soon found out. Stringing their bows they discarded their armour dropping it onto the wooden floor for the time being and concentrated on sending arrows towards the men who were lit up by the fires they had started.

Varro heard a commotion down below and saw a column of men forming up just inside the main gate. They were quickly checking the strapping on each other's segmented armour. A shout from somewhere ordered the doors open as the men in the column turned to face front, shields up, javelins ready.

"At the double." The voice shouted again and Varro saw an Optio leading the men out from the side of their ranks as they began to jog forward. The doors creaked open and multiple hobnail boots hit the wooden bridge over the trench. The junior officer wheeled the men left and towards the ships now totally ablaze. Unable to do anything except launch the occasional arrow, carefully now because of their own men on the ground. Those on the wall had a bird's eye view of the column below as they approached the first ship some distance from the safety of the fort. As they began to slow down another column left the gate with a Centurion jogging at their side and the original was ordered to halt. They did so and some of the troops instinctively crouched, behind their shields as the Optio surveyed the scene before him. It was obvious that nothing was to be gained by trying to fight the fire. The vessels were roaring with flames now as timbers burnt and cracked, the mast aboard the first ship already looked like it was about to fall as it lurched to one side.

Varro was aware that locals were coming out of their homes to the right further along the track away from the chaos, to see what all the commotion was, some pointed excitedly as they realised the ships were ablaze. As he turned back, movement caught his eye somewhere to the rear of the crouching soldiers in the shadows, he realised that it was another armed group of Britons emerging from the trees off to the left and behind them. A soldier tried to shout a warning further along the wall. From this distance and with the roaring fire it was impossible for them to hear and he looked on in horror as spears were launched towards the backs of the formed up column. A moment later the first of the soldiers fell forward into the back of the man in front of him, a spear piercing his armour somewhere in the middle of his back.

The Optio turning saw the danger but he was too late and was quickly engulfed by flailing Britons as they hacked him down around the legs with their swords. The enemy were upon the rest of the men so quickly that they didn't have time to react and form up properly into a defensive square. Within the blink of an eye the legionaries were overwhelmed by the fur covered Britons, those who were still standing began to run towards the other column as it approached at a run forming a testudo.

Varro watched as the two groups collided and then realised more Britons were emerging from the trees to the left. The second column had managed to form it's protective shell just after the survivors from the first were absorbed into their ranks and began to retreat slowly. The screaming Britons hurled themselves onto their shields as bowmen on the walls didn't wait for the order to open fire, they launched arrows at the sides of the defensive rectangle as it struggled to get back to the main gate.

From behind the battle below Varro heard a loud cracking sound followed by hissing and realised that the first boat to be set alight was now sinking, flames being exhausted by the freezing water as steam rose upward and outward. Warriors on the far bank of the river cheered as it sank lower and then stopped at an unnatural angle.

As the retreating column got to within fifty paces of the entrance, the attacking Britons broke off the assault, whether it was the result of an order or a pre-determined plan or even the fact that the archers were homing in on them now, Varro wasn't sure. The running fur clad figures looked like some large strange creatures as they lurched and scurried back towards the woods, their shadows highlighted by the remaining fires. As they began to vanish into the undergrowth of the trees one of them stopped and then another, the others continued running and disappeared completely. Varro watched as the larger of the two cupped his hands to his mouth and shouted.

"Romans," A voice shouted in heavily accented Latin, "I am Caratacus, King of the Catuvellauni." Everyone on the walls stopped what they were doing and turned to look at the two men standing beside the wood. Mutters of the name that had just been shouted at them were repeated along the line of the wall. Some had thought that Caratacus had probably died months before at the battle of the River Medway. He had not been heard of since except for rumours claiming that he had gone west.

He continued, bellowing above the sound of the flames. "You have invaded our lands, slaughtered our women and children but still we are here to defy you." Cheering erupted from the dark trees and from across the other side of the river as hordes of barbarians appeared waving weapons. Another voice shouted above them demanding quiet.

"Romans," the voice paused, slightly higher in pitch than the first as the other man still visible to those on the wall waved his sword above his head, "I am Ardwen of the Silures, we are one with our brothers the Catuvellauni. Know this, we will not rest until we kill you all or push you back into the sea. These are our lands, the lands of our fathers, the home of Albion and we will not give them up and we will not pay your taxes or tributes. Go home, leave our land and we will leave you alone, refuse and face more of this."

He lowered his sword and suddenly fire arrows were launched from the far side of the river roaring and rising like a fiery curtain. They rose high into the night sky and through the smoke of the burning vessels, the soldiers on the walls scrambled for their shields as they began to descend. They started thudding into the wood of the fort and embedding themselves into shields, armour and men. A few landed inside the dugout palisade and instantly set pig fat aflame that had been laid in the event of an enemy attack. The ditch burst into a life of flames as some soldiers jumped from the wall and into the interior of the fort as the roaring fire licked up around its exterior wall enveloping some who weren't quick enough to jump.

Varro dodged back into the cover of the tower but not before he felt the heat of the flames threatening to set him alight, almost instantly he could smell singed fur and wondered briefly if it was his own or the guard he had been talking to just moments before. He fell over the ballista in his panic and stumbled along the other wall out of reach of the fire as it took hold of the forts frontal defences. He had time to check his cloak but didn't see anything on fire.

He struggled to his feet and ran along the wall with the sentry close behind. He heard someone already shouting for water to fight the flames as he got to a ladder and virtually fell down its length to the relative safety of the ground below. It was only when he got to his feet that he felt the pain of a large wooden finger length splinter embedded into his right palm, he swore in frustration ripping it free. Soldiers were already throwing buckets of water against the walls at the forts entrance and along the walls length, trying to cool the wood as he threw the splinter to the ground.

Suddenly without warning an avalanche of night arrows began to land inside, hitting men sporadically at random. Those who weren't struck, took cover under their shields once more, others cried out in agony as the barbed hot arrowheads punctured their bodies. Medics ran from cover to help them, seemingly unconcerned by the deadly barrage from above. Archers fired blindly into the night hoping to hit their attackers in the dark. He didn't know how large a force the Britons had outside but if they managed to burn through the outer wall, the fight could turn into a free for all. With the flames lashing up around the towers now, the ballista were already useless and out of action. He ran to the lines of men that had already formed up from the well as they quickly passed buckets to each other to pass forward, dark black acrid smoke seemed to be everywhere as men coughed and choked.

"Form another line and another here." He ordered pointing and quickly arranged the men so there were three lines handing buckets forward to throw onto the hot wood of the wall. It was impossible to tell what was happening outside now, the Britons could be formed up ready to run into the place as the wood burned through. For now he could do nothing but concentrate on dampening the wood as much as possible, it was already starting to steam and crack.

In the background he was aware of squares of soldiers forming up ready for any eventuality, if the Britons got through they would be met with heavy infantry. The fight to control the fire seemed to be never ending as the pig fat continued to burn, the smell was foul and the smoke blacker than the night sky but eventually it started to die down.

Varro saw that some men had stopped passing buckets and shouted for them to continue. It looked as if the wood on the inside of the fort had held but it now looked like charcoal, black and crisp, shining wet with the water, hissing and steaming in places. The main gate was a ruined husk and far too hot to open as it had before, the great metal hinges glowed red. It was decided to let it cool and settle before any attempt was made to go outside where they didn't know what waited for them. Men sank to the floor exhausted holding ripped material from their tunics over their noses to try and stop the smoke from entering their lungs, faces black with soot looked about relieved that it was over for the time being. The injured were carried and dragged to the infirmary where they could receive better treatment.

As the sun began to rise and the dark sky started to lighten with the first few rays of daylight a few hours later, the forts occupants were still on a high state of alert and were ready for another attack. After the last of the night arrows had fallen the offensive against them seemed to have ended or at least paused but they couldn't be certain from their position inside and so they waited. A few brave souls ventured to the front wall still smouldering from the flames but they couldn't see beyond the palisade and its own smoke, so had quickly backed away.

"We'll wait until daylight and we can see properly," A centurion shouted, "nobody is to approach the wall again until I give the order. If you do I'll shove my vine cane where you don't want it" His previously white tunic was now blackened by smoke where he had been in the midst of the fire fight during the night. Varro saw Vespasian behind the centurion, he looked furious and barely able to contain himself. The Britons had caught them unawares, something that the Legate was not used to happening. He remembered back to Caratacus shouting from the edge of the woodland, the image raw in his mind. Clearly the wily Briton had regrouped and re-enforced his army and now had another tribe fighting under his banner. The enemy obviously had no regard for the conventions of war, attacking outside the campaigning season and when they were bottled up inside their walls. Caratacus was still a worthy and dangerous opponent Varro thought to himself, would this ever end?

"Centurion," A familiar voice shouted, he turned and saw Vespasian wave him over. He ran towards him holding his armour still at the neck under his furs as it had a tendency to bounce when the wearer jogged or ran.

"Sir." He said coming to a halt, he saluted.

"As soon as it's light enough to get out there safely," he said immediately discarding any pleasantries, Varro feeling his pulse quicken, "I want you out there on their trail, I want them found, I want to know where they are so we can destroy every last fucking one of them. Do you understand Centurion?"

"Yes sir." He had never seen Vespasian so angry before.

"I don't want you to be seen, I don't want them to know we're coming. I want you to take your men and find out everything there is to know about these Silures is that clear?"

"Yes sir."

"I want to know who these fucking Silures are as well as this Ardwen. I want to know where their tribal grounds are and how many of them there are, I'm going to hit them so fucking hard their dead ancestors will feel it." He turned to the senior Centurion standing by his side. "I thought we had got rid of that barbarian Caratacus back at the Medway, hasn't he learned his lesson already? Now he turns up with another tribe and sets fire to my fort and kills my men." He turned back to Varro. "Find out who this other cunny is, he's probably fucking Caratacus in celebration as we speak." He turned to survey the damaged wall at the front of the fort. "You will take Quintus' section of men as well and those Britons, Brenna and her brother. They're due to arrive in the morning," this came as a surprise, "you will command. Find them for me Varro." The Legate turned and walked off quickly to survey more of the damage.

Varro didn't reply but saluted and turned to go to the stables to begin to ready his horses and men, he looked up at the sky and shuddered. He wasn't aware that Brenna and her brother were due to arrive that day, they were in for good welcome on the frontier.

***

Already miles away to the north, Caratacus and Ardwen led their men back towards the rolling valleys of the Silures. Snow had begun to fall and people huddled inside their furs trying to stay warm against the days chill. Snow capped the mountains in the distance of Ardwen's land where they knew they would be relatively secure. The attack upon the fort of Vespasian had gone exactly according to plan and at a cost of only five dead but the Roman cost must have vastly outnumbered their own. In addition to their dead and injured the fort was badly damaged and a number of vessels sunk or put beyond repair, it had been a very successful night's work.

Caratacus could have led a full assault on the installation but with it burning and the ditches of the palisade on fire, they would have been sitting ducks for the Roman archers inside. The great Vespasian Legion had suffered a bloody nose during the attack and he would no doubt be seeking revenge but it would come at a cost.

After the battles of the Medway and the Tamesa, Caratacus had learned that he didn't have to face the beast head on every time, he could sneak up behind it and plunge a lance into its side, that was what he had decided to do. He would use every natural advantage he could, cover, hills, trees, rivers, deceit and surprise and he would show no mercy to the enemy that would show him and his people none. He didn't know if it would be enough to drive them from his shores but it would make them falter and the soldiers hesitant. The problem with wounding a dangerous animal however, was that it was even more deadly after it was hurt, so as they had planned, they would now melt into the hillsides and disappear into the winter of the lands of the Silures.

"I really don't see how you were having so many problems with these Romans cousin." Ardwen remarked from his saddle smiling broadly.

Caratacus gave a cautious smile in return knowing that Ardwen wasn't being serious but was trying to make light of the situation, "How so cousin?" He asked regardless.

"You seem to have encountered all kinds of problems with them, letting them land from the sea, cross rivers, set up their armies behind their shields, make camps and forts and even drive you from your own lands." He pushed the hood back over his head so he could see his cousin, "I would say that during the summer months you should relax with your woman and children, go hunting, fishing, travelling maybe, cultivate some crops. When the Romans march we can rest and when they withdraw into their forts for the winter, we can attack. In the summer you could spend your time recruiting more warriors for your army," he paused, "our army. Then as the nights get shorter and the leaves start to fall from the trees, prepare to fight and then when winter comes and the enemy is safely tucked up warm inside their forts, you can destroy them, simple really." He smiled again.

Caratacus laughed, "If only it were that simple my friend. You will see when the spring comes and they creep out of their shells, it's not as easy as you presume, they'll be spreading like disease all over. You would have fought them as I did, had they crossed your lands first."

Now Ardwen laughed, "Ah but cousin your ground is flat like a twelve year old girls breasts, it is suited to them and the way they fight." Caratacus screwed up his face at Ardwen's words but he continued, "They take their time and they set their army out like loaded dice, then they wait for the local barbarians that's us by the way" he remarked, "to come along and courageously but bravely throw ourselves upon their blades."

"And last night was how you would have fought them bearing in mind that it was my idea." Caratacus countered, it was now his turn to smile again.

"Well yes and no really. You see my hills and valleys are like a mature woman's breasts and you can do more with them you see. We can let our friends the Romans enter our valleys where they won't be able to play soldiers like they're used to doing and then once they're in," he slammed a fist into his palm and closed the hand around it, "we annihilate them." He smiled looking up at the last remnants of the night sky and the snow that was still falling, "Thirsty work all this slaughtering isn't it?" He grabbed his water skin from the side of his horse and took and few cold gulps. "Ah beautiful that spring water and nice and chilled thanks to all this snow and ice, not as nice as the mead we'll be celebrating with tonight though eh cousin?"

Caratacus looked at him, "You actually enjoying fighting don't you cousin, bashing heads in and killing men?"

Ardwen looked at Caratacus the smile now gone, "When someone or something threatens my family and my way of life, of course I do and do you know why?"

Caratacus looked at him, "No, why?"

"Because if I am bashing his brains out and killing him, then he isn't doing the same to me or mine. I love it I do Caratacus and I freely admit it and you should learn to love it as well. Forget what happened before, we are where we are my friend and we have to make the most of it, look at it another way, it's got to be better than planting crops eh?" He laughed again and Caratacus laughed with him.

"There's something else I think you should consider." Ardwen added.

"What's that?" He asked.

"You should seriously consider using your own name not the one given to you by your parents when all was well with Rome. The people would respond better to being led by Caradoc of Albion the Celt not Caratacus the Romanised Briton. You know it means the Ram, it would be a fine symbol on your banner." Ardwen said.

"It would be strange to suddenly change my name, it is all I've ever known but I know what you mean, I will consider it although I don't think my wife would be very happy."

Chapter Eighteen

It was just after midday and the sun was high in the sky when Ardwen and Caratacus led the army over the river that naturally separated the lands of the Dobunni and the Silures. Caratacus turned and looked back one final time but there was nothing to see except their own warriors snaking through the cold countryside. He had continually expected to hear shouts from the rear as the Romans sought revenge and attacked their ragged column stretching for as far as the eye could see but it didn't happen.

Despite their success of the night before, the men and women were now looking weary as they tramped along and splashed through the cold water. The hills of Ardwen's land were now in sight in the distance, the snow-capped mountains unseen hidden by grey cloud. It almost felt like coming home to Caratacus he suddenly realised as the walk of his horse rhythmically helped him relax more as much as the symbolic crossing of the river. He began to feel something that he hadn't for what seemed like an age, safe and comfortable.

They followed the path of a small stream that ran down from the valley and into the great river and slowly started their journey upwards on an incline that was almost imperceptible at first. Shale and stone littered the ground over the grass and moss where it had broken off the slate and rock sides of the valley they were about to enter. It looked very different from their journey a few days before when the snow had yet to fall but that didn't matter now, they were nearly 'home.' As they got further up the valley, the hillsides rose higher, the path got steeper and it began to snow.

"Don't worry my friend you'll soon be nice and warm with your wife, sat round a fire and telling tales of a great victory." Ardwen said.

"It cannot come soon enough, my feet have lost all feeling and are like blocks of ice, my hands are useless, if we were attacked now I wouldn't be able to defend myself. I'd have to roll you towards them." Caratacus laughed in response his face hidden by the hood drawn over his head to keep out the chill.

"Mott will soon warm your bones I'm sure." He heard Ardwen say as the wind began to blow. He didn't reply lost in his own thoughts as he realised that his entire legs were as cold as his feet, he tried to feel his thighs but there was virtually no sensation in his fingers tips. He considered getting off his horse and walking but didn't think his legs would carry him properly and imagined crumpling to the ground.

He tried to take his mind off the extreme weather and its effects as he thought about the coming year, it would be crucial and his decisions could determine survival or death not just for him but for many, many thousands. His imagination showed him every possible outcome from slaughter to victory and even to living in peace with the Romans although that was a last resort, it was probably possible. If it ultimately meant the survival of the people who were now under his charge, he would consider it.

He thought of his brother and his brutal death, and wondered was he looking down on them now as they filed along and up the valley. The image of Togodumnus and his wounds entered his mind's eye and once again, it helped to confirm that he was doing the right thing. In reality it was the only thing the forces of Rome had given him and for the time being there was no other choice.

He was dragged from his thoughts by the sound of hooves approaching. Looking up he saw a band of Silures warriors riding down the valley towards them.

"Sadgem." Ardwen shouted as the men got closer.

"Greetings to you Ardwen, Caratacus." The man said as he reined in his horse and pushed the hood off his head. He had brown shoulder length hair and dark brown eyes, his face was chiselled with taught skin over his prominent cheek bones. He looked around and up at the falling snow "Did all go well?" He asked breathing hard.

"Better than expected." Ardwen shouted in reply. "We fired the fort and many boats." He guided his horse to Sadgem and stopped pulling to the side out of the path of the army. "What news of home?" He asked as he waved for the warriors to continue. They had only been away for four days but four days trying to avoid settlements and the local inhabitants was hard work. They shared a border with the Dobunni and some had said they would fight Rome but they couldn't take the chance that someone would betray them for a bag of gold.

"Peaceful and calm," he looked to the grey white snow filling the sky again as his horse snorted and moved closer to Ardwen's, "most are content to stay near a fire and keep out of this damned weather. What of losses, how many dead, injured?" He asked.

"Five died during the fight but two more on the journey, there will be more from the wounded I'm sure but the enemy must have sustained more than three times that number on their vessels alone. They were caught like fish in a pound and couldn't escape, we gave them a better death than they deserved.

We slipped aboard their ships and found their guards sleeping, they didn't even realise their throats were cut until it was too late. Once we torched the forts walls any re-enforcements were stuck inside and couldn't help. We rained night arrows into the fort itself and soon it was ablaze and warming our skin in the cold night air. Something we could do with now, its freezing."

"Everyone will be glad to see you return, the families of those who have lost loved ones will be cared for and a feast of celebration has been arranged for tonight. I'll get fresh horses onto the carts of the wounded and get them back as quickly as possible." Sadgem said. "The rest of us will go south and make sure your trail is clear. I know the Romans don't like to venture out when the snows come but they may on this occasion if they mourn so many dead. I'll take twenty men with me, if we see them coming north we'll not engage them but return as quickly as we can."

Ardwen smiled, "Very well thank you my friend," he said, "I don't have to tell you that we cannot have them following you and your men home if you are sighted."

Sadgem nodded, "I understand, they will not follow us here but if I have too I'll go east and lose them in Dobunni territory. The Romans won't know these lands and so we have the advantage." He turned his horse and kicked it into a gallop and led his men away, snow flying up into the air.

"I don't envy his journey." Caratacus said.

"It's safer than ours was and Sadgems a good man, I trust him completely and wouldn't want anyone else covering our rear. I'm sure the Romans already know where we are roughly anyway, they have enough quislings around them. Come on let's get home and into the warmth."

A long way to the south a group of riders left the fire damaged fort and nudged their mounts into a trot. They were wearing the clothing of the Celts and were undistinguishable from those who lived nearby, who were watching them leave along the track standing outside their homes. A row of legionaries stood in line to stop the Britons from approaching the smouldering fort and the ships that lay in the water at odd angles after their bows had burnt through. All that could be seen of one vessel was the top of its mast, now sticking out of the water at a severe angle where it lay in the middle of the river. The heat of the fire had helped to melt the rivers ice of the night before but it was now reforming around the dead and damaged ships.

Work had already begun to replace the charcoaled embers of the forts wall that still smoked along what was once the strong fortress of Vespasian. Axes were used to fell what remained of the walls and carts were piled high with blackened wood. Soldiers were busily cutting down trees in the nearby forest as heavy infantry and cavalry watched on in case of attack. The soldiers on guard moved their feet trying to keep them warm whilst warm breath came from man and beast alike.

Vespasian walked along the path at the river's edge and surveyed the damaged to the supply vessels. He could barely contain his anger once more. The Britons had been allowed to get aboard the ice bound ships, there had been no alarm raised by those on-board, the sentries who in all likelihood were dead before the first flames caught.

"What supplies did we lose?" He asked the senior centurion by his side.

"Everything sir," he replied, "What didn't go down is either burned or soaked wet through. There will be amphora's we can save I'm sure but we'll have to do something about all the grain we've lost."

Vespasian looked along the side of the river where only the day before a symbol of Rome had lay at anchor. Five ships were now submerged their bows fully below the waterline and two others listed awkwardly. The remaining two had only partially survived the attack as the thick ropes that secured them to the bank were still intact as the Britons had failed to cut or burn them.

"We'll have to report this and ask for supplies as soon as possible. The remaining stores will see us through for a few days and if need be we can go on half rations. Those fools were lucky they died aboard the ships because if they had survived, I'd have had them crucified for negligence."

A naval officer approached and saluted, Vespasian recognised him as the captain of the lead ship and commander of the small fleet. He wore a blue cloak as was traditional for naval men, the colour sacred to Neptune.

"Report." Vespasian ordered.

"We may be able to salvage something of the vessels sir but without a dry dock and with this weather it's going to be very difficult. I've lost twenty one marines, three on each ship when the attack occurred and more later. As things stand I have received no reports as to how they were able to get aboard. Given the sentries on the forts walls and the men on-board, I would say that they approached over the frozen ice and the woods beyond. Without any survivors I can't be certain but I'd bet a thousand gold coins that's what happened."

"Very well keep me informed, give my condolences to the men, I'm sure those on-board died bravely given the circumstances." Vespasian said and dismissed the naval officer and turned to return to the fort. "Perhaps crucifixion would have been a bit hard considering the conditions." He looked back at the charred wrecks. "We need to salvage whatever we can from this mess and we need to start on constructing a proper harbour area that's secure with a dry dock. I think that in future we'll make sure that any supply ships are docked at the sea harbour and the contents brought in by wagons. I'm not going to let this happen again, I let my guard down and we paid for it but it could have been worse." The centurion looked at him. "If those barbarian butchers had got into the fort it would have been a complete blood bath. The palisades did the job they were meant to do thank the gods. I want them dug deeper and wider however, with cal traps hidden under the foliage and I want the guard doubled around the fort for the foreseeable future."

"Yes sir." The centurion acknowledged.

"Right let's get back inside and get cleaned up, we must both reek like smoked fish." Vespasian said turning and heading back to the main entrance where work still went on and would for some time to come.

Some miles to the north, Varro led his small group of ten through the snow filled countryside. They looked like ordinary Britons as they followed the trail left by Caratacus and his army. It wasn't difficult as they had left foot and hoof prints and wheel tracks on the trail and either side, so wide had been their force. They hadn't found any bodies which meant if any others had died, they were carrying them with them.

They had slowed to a walk sometime before not wanting to exhaust their mounts and their disguises would only work if they could avoid contact with the locals, racing north after a war band would only bring suspicion. Brenna and her brother would do any talking that was necessary but they knew their subterfuge wouldn't last forever. The cold was biting into their limbs even though they were covered in thick skins. Hoods guarded their heads but didn't keep out either the cold or snow entirely.

Varro shouted over to Brenna, "We should find somewhere to rest for a while, make a fire and warm up. The trail won't disappear for days with this frost on the ground. We're in no hurry and anyone seeing us would find it suspicious if we were found following their path."

"Very well," she replied, "we'll continue until we find somewhere suitable to shelter and get a fire going and some hot food, we'll feel much better after that."

"Agreed." He said, he estimated that the retreating force were at most, half a day's ride ahead. The mission was to find out where the attackers settlement was and to report back, avoiding all contact with them if possible. There was no point rushing and walking into a trap from which they no doubt would not return.

After a while they came to a small copse in a valley, it was out of the wind that had begun to develop on top of the freezing temperatures and snow, it was the last thing they needed. The snow barely covered the ground under the trees due to the thick cover overhead, as soon as they arrived and tied their animals up they went in search of suitable pieces of wood for a fire.

"Let's get it going as soon as possible and don't worry about the smoke, we're just travellers caught in the storm if anyone finds us, if anyone else is stupid enough to be out in this." Varro said looking around, "Which I doubt."

It took a while for the flames to catch thanks to the damp wood but after a while it dried off. Later with the fire roaring and preparations made to heat salted pork and vegetables they had brought with them, they settled in and waited to see if the weather changed, it didn't. As it was getting late they decided to pitch camp for the night so they huddled next to each other under blankets watching the snow fall from the grey sky as the fire began to cast shadows from the surrounding trees.

Just before the sun fell beyond the horizon, somewhere to the west under a snow filled sky, Caratacus and Ardwen led their army up the final valley path and into the beginnings of the settlement at the top of the mountain. They passed the cultivated areas where crops were grown on the flatter levels inside the huge basin and eventually the first roundhouse came into view. People came out to greet them and scurried about looking for loved ones searching desperately. Those related to the injured ran to the rear while those related to the dead were either struck dumb with shock or began to wail when they were told the news.

It took some time for the entire column to reach the settlement and by the time the final carts were rumbling along slowly past the roundhouse where Ardwen, Caratacus and the elders were, they were already in fresh dry clothes with warm soup in their bellies.

The dead were honoured and a total of eleven families now grieved. More had died in the wagons on the way back with four others seriously injured through sword or arrow wounds. There were more who were walking wounded but in time they would recover to fight again. It was decided that it would be inappropriate to celebrate the raids success for the time being and with everyone exhausted from either travelling or worrying about those out on the road, most settled down in their homes and simply went to sleep.

Caratacus and Ardwen however, together with a few elders stayed awake long into the night quietly discussing their next move, what strategy would they employ next, now that they knew they could defeat the invaders. They knew that Vespasian would want to avenge the humiliation of the attack and drew up plans to counter them and take the fight to the Roman officer and his Legion. They drank mead and finally relaxed as the snow continued to fall covering everything on the mountain home.

Early the next morning a long time before the sun rose, Varro awoke shivering. He was curled up at Brenna's side with Tevelgus her brother curled into a ball under his cloak beyond her. He turned to find Decimus' face partly hooded behind him, snow covered him still snoring oblivious to the conditions. He sat up and saw that the fire was still smouldering just and pushed himself up to his knees and stood up. Brenna groaned but turned and went back to sleep under an arm unknowingly put out by Decimus.

He stood and stretched, shivering, seeing that even more snow had fallen during the night, outside the copse it was a few feet deep now. He could however, see clearly for some way, thanks to the white all around despite the lingering darkness. He collected fallen branches and twigs from the ground under the trees and put them by the fire to dry. He broke and twisted others from low branches, pulling the leaves off, brushing the snow away and set them down beside the fire. The wood cracked as it dried and smelt quite rank. He sat down on a log, one of the few they had found the night before and stared into the falling snow.

"Humph." Someone sighed stirring behind him. He turned to see Decimus had opened his eyes.

"Fuck a pig it's freezing." He said blinking himself awake, he saw Brenna and smiled, "Hello couldn't resist could you?" He said to her sleeping face, she murmured something and opened her eyes, frowned and then suddenly sat up. Her cloak fell away and she quickly raised it round her shoulders, looking round.

"More snow then?" She said sleepily.

Varro threw another stick on the fire, "It's a good job we found this place when we did or we'd be a few feet under it by now. Outside the copse it's at least two feet deep, the trees kept most of it off us. It's still freezing though as Decimus so articulately pointed out."

She looked at him with just his eyes peeping out from his cloak wrapped round his head, "Yes I heard him dreaming last night he was talking and blabbering in his sleep about his love for a huge fat pig called porky or something. He said people wanted to slaughter and eat it but he was saying that he had grown up with it and wanted it to marry him instead." She raised her eyebrows and smiled. "Is it traditional for you Romans to have romantic relationships with your bacon?"

"Ho, ho fucking ho." Decimus replied from under his cloak. "I'll have you know there are some very attractive young swine where I come from." He looked from her to Varro. "Not just pigs either, horses and even cows are known to marry their men folk and when they get too old, you eat them and get another." He struggled up and got to his feet, "I find it makes for a quieter life than a human female. They don't nag nearly as much and when you tire of them, you eat them, simple." He turned and walked away from the growing fire.

"It wouldn't surprise me if you're not joking." Brenna said watching him as he stood away from the group rummaging with his tunic.

"You see what I mean? A man can't even take an early morning piss without being disturbed by a woman." He turned laughing as others in their group began to stir.

Quintus said, "Keep that steaming thing away from my horse will you? I don't want you getting any ideas and ruining her mind. If she catches sight of that mouldy little maggot, I may never get her to breed again. "

Decimus half turned, "Ha-ha don't worry I wouldn't want my fleshy sword going where yours has been anyway, it may never work again afterwards and imagine how upset all the females would be?"

They all laughed as the others got to their feet still wrapped in their cloaks. They prepared a bowl of lentils and chestnuts sweetened with honey and warmed themselves around the fire.

"It's going to be near impossible to track those fuckers in this snow." Quintus said blowing on a hot spoon full of food.

"The only way to do it is to keep clearing the snow and checking the tracks underneath. If we knew this area and where the tracks went, it wouldn't be too bad but as it is we're as good as lost." Tevelgus said adding, "The winters in Britannia don't always provide snow but when they do, it can be here for days, weeks even. Crops are buried and people die if they wander far from their homes, we always stay close when this happens and stay by our fires."

Varro finished his bowl of food, "Well one thing is certain, our friend Caratacus isn't staying by the fire but I agree with what you say. The other thing is that if the snow stops falling and the skies clear we'll be seen for miles in this white blanket if we're caught out in the open. Anyone would see us coming from miles away." He stood up and rinsed his wooden spoon using a leather water skin.

"The question now then is what do we do? If we can't risk going forward, dare we risk trying to find our way back to the fort, things look totally different normally when you try and retrace your steps but when they're covered in snow it's a different thing altogether." Decimus said.

Quintus put in, "How do you think we would be received if we did go back and we had no information about the enemy position. I know the good General Vespasian is a fair man but I don't think he'd take too kindly to us turning up empty handed and with no information."

"I think your right," Varro said, "but I also believe he would understand given the circumstances." He returned to his upturned tree log and sat down. "The other alternative is to wait a while and see if it clears," He added looking up at the sky through the branches of the trees, "we've got food enough to last two more days but after that we'd have to find our own or another settlement."

"And we'd be out of fresh clothes but that I can deal with for a while," Added Quintus, "after that I don't want my balls rotting and swelling like some stinky Briton."

Tevelgus laughed, "Ha-ha, and I wouldn't want the small round rotten berries that you carry about down there anyway." He said pointing to Quintus' groin, they all chuckled.

"Right," Varro said, "we'll wait here another day and see what things look like tomorrow, if it's still snowing we'll think about heading back. In the meantime let's make a better shelter and see if we can find anything nearby worth hunting." He walked to where he'd left his bow, "Quintus, you look after things here, I'll take Brenna, Decimus, Lucius and Marcus and see if we can find anything better for dinner." He looked at Tevelgus, "If you stay here with Quintus and his men in case any Britons turn up and do the talking." He nodded in agreement.

"Good, let's get cleaned up and see if there's anything out there." he said as they prepared to move.

Sometime later and north of their temporary camp, the five hunters dismounted from their horses. They hadn't seen anything so far, nothing moved in the snow it seemed.

"We'll leave them here" he said referring to the horses, "and go on foot for a while, tie them to these trees if we kick the snow away at least they can get something to eat." He said brushing the deep snow aside with his boot where he had tied Staro, they all did the same. Having secured their mounts they moved off following Varro, he and two others carrying bows. They crunched through the snow and entered a wooded area and eventually came to a clearing. They stood still for a moment and listened but all that achieved was tingling feet. Varro was about to give up when the briefest of movement caught his eye.

"There," He whispered crouching, the others following his gaze, "can you see anything?" He asked. Brenna strained her eyes looking in the direction he was now pointing towards, "What was it, I can't see anything moving?"

"A deer, I just caught it's white tail against its back as it moved away to the left." He said now whispering. "Follow me slowly." He lifted his feet carefully and walked forward, the virgin snow was softer here but still made a slight crunching noise in their footfalls. Instinctively they all began crouching as they moved searching the cold white woods. Varro found the deer's hoof prints and waved the others on grinning. A short time later he saw that the prints got longer with more space between the front and rear hooves.

"It looks like it started to run here." He looked around. "Something may have startled it, maybe it picked up our scent."

Brenna examined the prints and whispered, "It's the only thing we've seen since we left." She looked up following the direction of their quarries travel. "If it sensed us, it will be long gone, if it was something else that startled it," she looked around, "we could be in trouble."

Varro looked into her dark eyes and then about at the ground around them, he indicated with his hand for them to crouch lower. Pointing to his eyes he looked at Decimus and directed that he should advance to an outcrop where a tall oak stood with Marcus and to see if they could find anything. As the rest of them crouched lower still into the snow, they watched as the two soldiers moved to the area that Varro had indicated.

The woods were quiet, very quiet and Varro noticed that it had just stopped snowing. He kept his eyes on the men as they carefully made their way over fallen branches and through the grounded snow. Something wasn't right, he didn't know what it was but sensed something, as if he should be able to see what it was that had spooked the deer.

"This isn't right." He whispered to Brenna who was at his side. She didn't look at him but kept scanning the woods to the front.

"There," she said, pointing, "there's something ahead of your men." He looked to the direction indicated and frowned, Decimus and Marcus were still slowly moving away from them.

"I can't see a thing I think this snow has……"

"Shhhhh," she replied. "Look at Decimus and then go right and up, there's something darker in the trees on the bank near that outcrop." He moved his head towards her to try and get a better view.

"It's not natural, not a part of the wood." She said slowly placing an arrow on her bow.

He moved his head forward and strained, "I can't see a……wait, yes I can see it now." He looked at Decimus and Marcus who were oblivious to the danger. They still had their backs to them but had reached the oak and had gone to ground. Whatever was waiting there in the trees must have had a clear view of them as they had approached.

"I can hit it from here." Brenna said sighting the arrow to the small target about eighty paces ahead of them. Varro looked at his men Decimus turned and saw that he was holding a fist up. He angled his wrist to the right and Decimus tapped Marcus on the shoulder and both of them got as low as they could. Decimus had recognised the signal and knew there was danger ahead of them to the right.

"Wait we don't know what it is, there could be more hidden beyond the trees." He said but she didn't lower the bow, he realised he was now talking as if the mysterious object were the enemy. He turned to Lucius, "Go back and come around to the left," he said pointing, "let's see if we can surprise whoever or whatever it is. Take my bow just in case." Lucius nodded and picked up the weapon and quiver and moved off. Varro looked back to the front and saw that Brenna had released the pressure on the bow string but still held the arrow ready. He could hardly see Decimus and Marcus now, they must be lying flat he thought.

"We can't stay here, we'll freeze." She whispered.

"Just give Lucius time to get around them, it won't take long. Once he's gone far enough back so as not to be heard, then he'll quickly flank up to the left." He fidgeted with his feet now frozen again and tried to get some blood into them and waited. It seemed to take forever for Lucius to flank the target. In the meantime they could do nothing but wait and get colder, not daring to move.

Decimus and Marcus had crawled forward to the bank below the large oak tree and were now lying against it, head to foot parallel to the rise. From the position they were in they couldn't see what was above or their comrades behind them due to foliage, low branches and snow. They lay there getting colder and colder straining their ears for any sign of what was going on. They both knew that Varro would not have told them there was danger to the right if he didn't fear for their safety and they also knew he wouldn't be idly waiting for something to happen without doing something positive to rectify the situation.

After what seemed like an age, Varro saw something in the corner of his vision, move to the left. As soon as he saw it his eyes moved to its location, whatever it had been had moved behind a tree.

"Left side forty paces from Decimus and Lucius." He whispered. Brenna looked but couldn't see anything. He saw her screwing her eyes up trying to see what it was concentrating, "Went behind that fat dark tree at the base."

"Was it Lucius?" She asked.

"I can't be sure, I only just caught it as it went to ground behind the tree." He answered. "I'm sure it wasn't a deer, thinking about it, it couldn't have been because it wouldn't get that close to those two hiding by the bank, it would have picked up their scent long before getting that close."

She looked at him, "I can't lie here anymore." She put her hands under her chest onto the ground, "if I don't move I'll never bear children."

"Don't get up." He pleaded but it was too late she was already on her knees peering forward.

"Nobody move." A voice shouted, everyone froze, almost literally. The voice was clearly that of a Briton with an unusual accent. "Come out where we can see you." He ordered, no-one moved. "If you don't come out, the men lying below us will die." He shouted.

Brenna stood up hesitantly, "Who are you," she shouted back, "why are you hunting on our land?" She said bluffing. There was no reply, just silence.

She whispered to Varro, "Stay low, he is Silures, I can tell by the voice. I can see Lucius to the left of the tree he's aiming your bow towards him.

"If you kill my friends or injure them you will not leave these woods alive." She shouted. "I will ensure you will die here and you will be left hanging naked upside down from a tree with your entrails open to the wolves and crow." There was silence.

She shouted again, "I am Brenna of the Dobunni, whoever you are you are not from these lands, come out to where I can see you clearly. I will order my men to stand and return to me, do not hurt them or you will die."

She shouted at Decimus and Marcus but they didn't move. She whispered down to Varro, "They're not moving, I can see them now but they're just lying there."

He looked up, "They do not know your words Brenna, remember." She had got so used to talking to the Romans in their own tongue that she had forgotten that not all them could talk to her in her own language. As her mind raced to try and think of something a man dressed in deerskin appeared from behind the trees above the bank, he was pointing at Lucius who was aiming the bow at him.

"Don't shoot Brenna of the Dobunni." He shouted over the snow. "I am Sadgem of the Silures," He stepped forward to the edge of the slope and looked down at the two prone men.

"You can go." He said and gestured waving with his hand for them to return to their friends. Decimus and Marcus slowly got to their feet, they didn't have to understand his words to know what the gesture meant.

"Why are you in our territory, you have broken the treaty." She shouted attempting to take the emphasis from the two retreating men.

"We come in search of a common enemy." Other men then appeared at his sides from behind trees, there were a lot of them. "We hunt Romans and heard they are here on your land, have you seen any?" He said.

"Romans," She answered, "there are no Romans here, they haven't moved from the Exe in months. They are in the fort by the water and won't come out until the leaves turn green and the frost goes. They don't like to venture out in the cold you should know that."

He smiled. Decimus and Marcus were almost back to them now, still walking slowly backwards, she had lost sight of Lucius who she thought must have slipped back into the undergrowth. She could see at least ten men with the one who called himself Sadgem, there were probably more still hidden from view.

"Our army fired the fort and sank their boats a few days ago, we thought they would come out and follow us to our lands. We meant no offence to you or your people but are merely safeguarding our own." He said.

"There are no Romans here, if there were, they would be hanging from trees. They may have subdued some of my people but not all." She replied, the two men were now with her and moved beyond where she stood, the relief on their faces evident.

"Go in peace Brenna and we will return to the mountains. Your people, those who are free should join us, together we a stronger than standing alone and can defeat this common enemy." He said not waiting for a reply. He moved backwards still facing Brenna then he turned as did the men with him and disappeared from sight.

Varro let out a breath that he didn't realise he had been holding and slowly got to his feet. "That was too close," he said to her, "come on let's get the horses and get out of here."

She walked with him quickly turning to make sure the Silures were gone and weren't following one last time, there was no sign of them. When they got back to their mounts they had eaten all the grass that they had uncovered previously and they found Lucius was waiting for them.

"Well done," Varro said, "if you hadn't come out from cover with that bow anything could have happened."

"No problem sir." He said. He untied his horse and jumped up, "There were at least another ten of them behind that Sadgem hiding below the bank." He said. Varro exchanged a look with Brenna they had been lucky, very lucky.

"It's a good thing you were with us Brenna. They would have known that I wasn't a Briton if they had heard my voice and with that my men we wouldn't have stood a chance." Varro said and got onto Staro.

"It doesn't matter now, what matters is that we are alive and we know the Silures are on Dobunni land." She climbed up onto her own horse, "It was probably just a scouting party, the main force is probably already in the mountains to the west but they aren't afraid to come south and into other territory."

"At least we know where they are now." Varro said.

"You don't understand Varro, the lands of the Silures are mountainous and the area is huge." He looked at her with a surprised expression as they cantered away.

They found the way back to the overnight camp and told the others what had happened. Even with all of them, they would still be outnumbered nearly two to one if the Silures found them again. They knew the next time, they probably wouldn't be so fortunate to hide their true identity. Varro decided that he would run the risk of Vespasian's anger and broke camp. At least they knew the Silures were probing the countryside of the Dobunni and would try to ally any Britons to their side, that information alone was invaluable.

They packed their equipment away quickly and dismantled the low shelters that Quintus and his men had made from branches and logs, small and triangular in shape. Each would have only housed three people lying flat next to each other but that would have created body heat for them and shelter from the falling snow. The wood was thrown onto the fire to burn itself out. After the next snow fall there would be little sign that anyone had ever been there but it didn't really matter now.

They left the smouldering wood piled up on the fire and headed in a south easterly direction. They were unhappy to see that the skies were still grey and full of snow but it held off as they travelled. For the first time in a while they were suddenly aware of the cold again and welcomed the feeling after the day's events and the meeting with the Silures. They were alive, that was what mattered most.

The journey back to the fort was fairly uneventful except for the snow that had already fallen. It made it hard going for the horses and in places the riders had to dismount to get through the deeper drifts. It made movement difficult and in some places the snow was four to five feet deep but where it had drifted was substantially deeper. The terrain looked very much the same everywhere they went which at times made their direction of travel difficult and twice they realised they were heading too far west.

Eventually they found tributaries of the Exe the smaller streams were a welcome break to the solid white they had been used to seeing. A few hours after midday the fort came into view and all amongst them felt a real sense of relief. The front wall had already been replaced entirely and work was continuing on the new watch towers. The palisades looked deeper and wider and were clear of snow where soldiers still worked to carry out the last elements of engineering work. Legionaries now patrolled the tracks around the roundhouses and a check point had been set up. Any future attackers would find it a lot harder to get so close again. Wagons laden with freshly fallen tree trunks, were still being brought from the local woods, no doubt to strengthen the garrisons defences even more. The enemy had been underestimated, it wasn't a mistake that would be repeated.

Chapter Nineteen

As they entered the new gates of the fort, the Centurion of the watch acknowledged them from above and raised a hand in greeting. He was silhouetted against a bright blue winter's day sky and they all had to squint as they looked up. Varro smiled more from the relief of being safe and in familiar surroundings than anything else. He looked forward to being comfortable and under cover and most importantly, to being warm again. He wouldn't have exchanged his role for any other in the military but being exposed to the elements during a harsh winter and in a hostile environment, was not something he enjoyed. Even little things became a major problem and not just the cold; the damp and permanently wet clothes, food, even water when the frosts came, it wasn't natural to be outside and isolated. He was eager to thaw out properly and to submerge himself in a hot bath, to have the wilds of Britannia scrubbed and scraped from his skin.

Unknown to Varro and unseen from the local village, further down the track at the edge of a small group of roundhouses, Sadgem watched from the side of a house where locals went about their daily business. No-one around them noticed the stranger or the man standing next to him, looking at the group of shabbily dressed riders as they entered the fort. Outsiders often came to the area to use the waterways or to trade and since the arrival of the Romans other visitors just came to satisfy their curiosity and to look upon them as they would at a rare or strange animal.

"I knew there was something different about that whore." Sadgem said under his breath as he turned to the man beside him. It had been easy for them to follow the group unseen from the woods as they had trekked through the snow, leaving their foot and hoof prints behind to follow. The rest of his men were well outside the settlement a few miles away dispersed in a forest where they wouldn't arouse suspicion or be seen. It was one thing for a couple of strangers to appear near a Roman encampment but a group of so many heavily armed men was a different matter altogether, unless of course they were their allies.

"It's traitors like that who make places like this, possible." He said waving an arm at the fortress. "We should have killed her when we had the chance." His face was screwed up in hate. "Her day will come when she regrets this and any others who betray our lands to the invader." He turned, "Let's get out of here, the putrid stench of this place is making me want to vomit." The two men untied their horses climbed aboard and kicked their animals into a gallop, no-one turned or noticed them leave.

Inside the fort Varro saw that the damaged buildings from the attack had been levelled and new ones had already been built to replace them or were under construction. Troops were digging and excavating areas for underground heating, it was apparent that Vespasian intended to keep a permanent presence here. The air was full of sawing and banging as other construction continued, it looked as if the attack of a few days before had actually encouraged a growth spurt inside the installation.

Soldiers wore just their white Second Augusta tunics as they worked, laughed and joked, it appeared that the assault by the Britons of a few days before had done little to damage morale. Armour and weapons were lined up nearby against the internal wall, in the event of another attack. He looked up and saw that the guard was still doubled on the high walls, the chance of the enemy striking again with such success was remote. When the better weather came, these soldiers and others would move out and seek those who caused such destruction and death.

The watch centurion climbed down a ladder and approached as Varro dismounted and the two men clasped arms in greeting, "Good to see you all present, how was it out there?" He asked.

"Freezing cold, wet and damp, the snow is a lot deeper further north than it is here and it made for hard going. My balls are like frozen plums and my feet will take days to thaw, as will my hands." He answered stamping his boots and rubbing his hands together, half smiling as he removed his hood.

"I'll escort you to Vespasian's headquarters building, the new praetorian, it's nearly finished already. In a couple of months this place won't be recognisable. There are already plans to expand the fort to accommodate fresh troops, this place will be fucking huge." He continued talking as they passed busy soldiers sawing, digging, mixing concrete, laughing and talking to each other.

"The wrecks in the river were sunk after we recovered any supplies from them and the water is virtually clear, some of the rotten hulls were swept along in the current of the river. I'm sure when its warmer weather in the spring what's left will be dragged out. Until then we're carting in goods from the south." The centurion said happily chattering away, he turned to the others in the group, "You can go and get cleaned up, get warm and get some food inside you." He pointed to a canteen area covered with a leather awning where a few cooks toiled over large bubbling pots preparing food for the hungry legionaries.

"I'd like Brenna to come with me," Varro said, "if that's alright? She can elaborate on specific details especially concerning the Silures we encountered."

The centurion paused, thought for a second and then smiled, "Good yes, anything we know about them and their whereabouts will certainly help. Those goat fucking, sheep poking bastards will be getting seen to in a different way soon enough, with Roman iron." He laughed to himself touching the hilt of his sword as he led them on. They walked along the path that ran along the centre of the fort that was to become the main street to the forum where on the other side, construction was already underway and large foundations were being dug.

"Our men can do most of the work but specialists have been brought in to survey the land and for more permanent structures in brick and stone. You should see the sand that has been brought in, cartloads of the stuff in rows over to the rear." He pointed. "It won't be long until we have decent baths, proper baths not those wooden fucking tubs and all the comforts of home, just you wait and see." The centurion continued as he led him to the building beyond the digging, where Aulus Plautius no doubt waited. He exchanged a glance at Brenna raising an eyebrow the duty officer was obviously getting on his nerves.

The two officers returned salutes to the sentries that stood guard at the entrance to the large wooden structure, it was the focal point of all military and civil activity in the area. The high ceiling corridor was dimly lit by oil burners along the walls compared to outside and it took a few seconds for his eyes to adjust as Varro was led into a substantial room. Plautius was standing talking to a group of men dressed in togas, as they got closer he saw they were studying plans and designs of buildings, they waited.

The room was lavishly decorated in comparison to the Spartan accommodations of the ordinary soldier but that was to be expected. Windows allowed light through, stretched skins and large iron oil burners were scattered about here and there providing more light and warmth. Depictions of Rome were draped from the walls and pots containing burning incense helped freshen the air as two slaves stood waiting to receive orders. Dominating the walls, were the emblems of the Second Augusta, and a large white depiction of Pegasus stood out amongst the others.

"Good, good," Plautius said to the men, "the sooner we have some permanence here the better, you can only live in tents and wood for so long, well done gentlemen. If you need any further assistance don't hesitate to come and see me." Dismissed, the men turned acknowledged the new arrivals with a nod and left the room. Plautius looked at the plans on the table and smiled clearly happy, he looked up.

"Ah Centurion Varro, back so soon?" he said, "Please come forward." They walked closer to a large table that was covered in scrolls of varying sizes some were maps and others written orders, requests, supply, manning lists and the plans the men had been studying. Plautius turned to the duty centurion and asked him to locate Legate Vespasian and request his presence and thanked him, dismissed he saluted the governor and left.

"Well how did you find it out there, did you have any success in locating the Silures and their Catuvellauni friends?" he asked.

Varro looked at Brenna standing next to him and then back to Plautius, "We did sir but our task was gravely hindered by the weather. They have returned to the mountains of the north west, if I may?" He said indicating to the large cattle skin map that hung on the wall behind the desk."

"Of course," Plautius said standing, at that moment Vespasian arrived, he saluted and removed his helmet. "That was quick Legate," he said, "you weren't eaves dropping lurking about out there listening to my plans were you?" He joked laughing.

"I was just returning from checking on the delivery of the grain and food stuff sir. You'll be pleased to know three galleys arrived this morning. We should have fresh food this evening, there's meat and amphorae as well, enough to keep the men happy for a while. Once the ships have unloaded they'll be ready to set sail on tomorrows tide. With regular supplies getting through, it will be one thing we don't need to concern ourselves with."

"Excellent, excellent," he said, "Centurion Varro," he turned and indicated the thawing soldier, "he will be most pleased I'm sure after spending the last few days tracking Caratacus and his Silures friends. I'm sure that you and your party will welcome a good feast later after a hot bath of course."

"I can think of nothing better after we've thawed out properly and had some sleep sir." He replied walking to the map pointing, "We got as far as here, when the weather closed in and made further travel virtually impossible." He indicated a location south east of the river that separated the lands of the Dobunni and Silures. Plautius and Vespasian exchanged a curious look. It wasn't where they had expected the patrol to go and walked closer to inspect the map. Realising that the two senior officers were clearly concerned Brenna broke into the conversation.

"It was here that we encountered a small group of twenty or more heavily armed Silures scouting the territory."

The officers looked to Varro concerned etched across their faces.

"Brenna," Varro said as he turned to the Briton, "here was able to converse with them and they confirmed that the main army of Caratacus had retreated into the mountains of the south of their territory, here." He pointed to the area concerned. "They said they were hunting for Romans but with such a small group they were probably just a rear-guard sent out to see if we were pursuing them in force."

Vespasian approached the map and pointed to the location that concerned them most, the lands of the Silures. "It's an area that will warrant at least half legion strength, maybe more I should imagine to go into if we want to pluck them from their perch. Those mountains, hills and valleys will make for difficult terrain not too dissimilar from Thrace where I campaigned not long after joining up. At least here we won't have the sun burning our flesh to a crisp. However, at the moment it's the opposite, with this blasted cold. It's not a time for pursuing an elusive enemy buried like ticks on a hounds arse." He turned to Varro. "What were conditions like underfoot Centurion?"

"Quite bad sir, at times we had to dismount and walk the horses through snow drifts, we wondered if we'd ever find our way back. Everything looked the same, white and we found it difficult to find our bearings. There were times when it was so white we couldn't see any landmarks and the snow was so thick we couldn't see more than twenty paces in front of our faces." He answered.

"Mm," Plautius murmured looking at the details of the map, "it's as we suspected. They have returned to their mountain hideout and the country is virtually impassable between them and us with this weather. I'm not willing to lose any men through the cold and the winter pursuing an enemy that can wait until we are ready to engage them. Things will be different, a lot different come spring." He turned to those gathered around the map.

"We'll continue to concentrate on things here and wait until the weather improves before seeking them out. In the meantime we can send out light infantry to scout the local area but that's all. No-one and I mean no-one, is to go beyond the two mile marker point." He looked at those listening to him. "If they can see the bloody things that is." He laughed.

"We can develop our relationship with the people of the land here, speak with their elders and show them that we're here to help those allied to us." He smiled, "Very good, thank you Centurion and Brenna," he looked at the Briton, "this help has been invaluable once more. I'm to return to Camulodunum leaving the Legion to manage efforts here in a few days so I will say goodbye for now. Go and get yourselves cleaned up, warm and some decent food inside you."

Varro saluted and he and Brenna left the two men to their plans, entering the darker corridor again he said, "That went better than I thought it would." as they almost immediately walked out into the bright winter sunshine.

She said, "We were lucky to get back after our encounter with that Sadgem, if he had suspected that I was with Romans we would still be out there now, cut open and food for the wolves." She looked at him. "I think that both Plautius and Vespasian knew full well that we could have achieved little more in the conditions. I'm sure they're just glad to know that Caratacus hasn't stayed south. It would have been a disaster if they had chosen to stay in the region, especially after what they will no doubt be regarding as a success against us. They are not stupid though and know they cannot fully rely on the local population to assist them. People are more concerned with surviving the winter than fighting, whoever the enemy may be. The Silures and the Catuvellauni are virtually as foreign in these lands as you remember."

"I hadn't thought of it that way." He replied. "I suppose that my lands were the same once, many years ago divided by tribal boundaries. Even Rome was said to have been segregated by the seven hills that initially made up the city and look at it now."

She smiled, "I hope to one day."

He let his hand touch hers briefly, "That makes me happy, happier than you know, maybe one day we will see it together." He led her away from the praetorian and to where he knew the baths were. There were numerous rooms containing large wooden baths served by slaves from Gaul. He knew it would be quiet at the moment as the men of the Second

Augusta toiled working to build the camp. Later the rooms would be packed with men queuing to clean themselves.

They entered one of the many wooden structures set aside for bathing and removed their outing clothing and hung them on pegs on the walls. She followed him into another area where dozens of large wooden baths sat on sturdy looking iron legs. A slave approached and Varro asked him to bring hot water for two baths.

"Two baths?" Brenna asked looking at him disappointed.

He smirked as he started to remove the rest of his clothes, "The first is to wash the dirt and grime off our clothes, the second is for us to enjoy together." He leaned forward and kissed her lips as the slave returned with another, carrying a large bucket of steaming water. They walked to the edge of the nearest bath and poured the hot contents into it, before they turned to walk away. Two more men appeared carrying another bucket. In minutes the bath was two feet deep, steaming and ready to use. He told the slaves he would call them when they were ready for the second bath to be filled.

Brenna removed her clothing as the slaves left, he took in her beauty and together they dipped their hands in the water testing its temperature, it was just right having cooled a little against the wood.

"Mm that feels good," she gave him a smile and reached out holding onto him as she climbed in, "I want you to make me feel even better though."

They splashed into the water gasping as the heat took their breath away, "I'm sure that can be arranged my lady." He said as he reached out wrapping his arms around her.

Construction of the fort's interior and the surrounding area continued unhindered by Caratacus throughout the winter and as the trees began to grow fresh green leaves and birdsong could be heard, the men of the Second Augusta prepared to face their enemies again. Training had intensified as the New Year was born and the sound of wooden training swords and men's efforts to fight each other, echoed around the newly constructed buildings. The fort now covered a large area but it was small in comparison to the planned forty two acre site that would dominate the landscape for miles around.

Nevertheless, the Roman settlement was now a huge busy rectangle of buildings, shops, forges, sleeping quarters, training and parade grounds and there were even plans for a Temple to be built. Seeds were planted outside the forts walls with the local population in an attempt to close the gap between the two people. Any attack on them was also an attack on the local folk who had worked with their new Roman friends so hard to cultivate and grow them.

Patrols were sent further and further into previously unexplored territory, there were no signs of hostile activity, but where there were, they were put down. Surveyors were sent out to plan routes and roads, the river was cleared of the wreckage from the attack during the winter and supplies once again were brought directly to Isca as it was now known by most, shortening the settlements name.

Although the weather and conditions had improved there was still a cloud on the horizon in the form of Caratacus and he and his warriors were never far from the soldiers thoughts. Nothing had been seen of the Britons warlord since the attack, although rumours were a constant source of chatter amongst the locals. Relations were improving slowly between soldier and civilian however, as the first benefits of their crops came to fruition and local dignitaries were allowed access to the fort once more.

As a sign of their successful co-operation, Vespasian suggested that a feast be organised which Plautius had agreed to. Rows of tables were set out and both military and local dignitaries enjoyed a day and night of entertainment together. Plans were made and possibilities were discussed for Britons to join auxiliary cohorts as free men but not in Britannia, they would serve elsewhere, Hispania, Gaul or maybe even Italia itself. The Britons had proved they were proud and fierce warriors second to none, that the soldiers had faced in battle and so with professional training they would be invaluable serving next to the legions. Those plans would have to wait for the time being and days after the feast, Legate Titus Vespasian led a column of thousands of men northward in search of Caratacus.

Varro and his small party of scouts had left at first light, it had been decided that he would take Decimus and his men as well as Brenna and Tevelgus. They were ordered to ride ahead of the column but not to get more than a day ahead of the slower moving main body. The countryside had been transformed from a white rolling blanket to a lush green landscape. Shepherds herded their sheep with bleating new lambs as they crossed the land and rode through small settlements where the inhabitants stopped their daily chores to stare at the strangely dressed travellers.

Once in a while Brenna and her brother would ride ahead and ask the locals how they had faired through the winter and ask if they had sighted any armed men from the north, none had been seen. They were warned of the advancing army and told not to be afraid and as long as they weren't hostile, they would be left alone to live in peace.

Most inhabitants weren't actually particularly interested in their presence especially when they were told that they would be left alone and wouldn't be hurt or have their livestock taken. They had enough to occupy their daily lives as things were, with crops, hunting and maintaining their homes, just surviving from day to day was a battle in itself.

On some occasions they would offer water which was plentiful as most villages were near rivers or streams and when they did, Varro and his men joined them. The Britons gazed at the men curiously as they were in shining chainmail, red cloaks and helmets. Most of them were invariably taller than their guests, excluding Tevelgus who stood taller than even most from Britannia. Small children looked at them in wide eyed fascination, some afraid, who ran away hiding in their homes and some laughing and pointing at their equipment and clothing.

No Briton showed them any hostility, they were actually hospitable and Varro couldn't help wishing that they had found some of these places when they were frozen to the core during the winter and their foray into the wilds. He always carried a pouch of coins hung from his belt and as a sign of friendship, he gave them out before they left. The Britons especially the children looked upon them with glee as they saw the faces printed on them surrounded by strange marks they didn't understand.

People who lived in isolated areas had probably never seen coins before and would depend on bartering if they wanted goods from others. Cattle, chickens, pigs, hares, crops and even ornaments fashioned from bronze or other metals were used to exchange property in the world where they lived. Varro knew that every time he encountered such people, their lives were about to change but he believed that it would be for the better.

He admired those who lived secluded, far outside settlements because they lived truly independently, sometimes in groups of roundhouses as small as two or three buildings, originally they must have been family settlements. They lived hard lives where their mortally was high with the young. Women especially were at risk during childbirth and many didn't survive, it was a sad fact of life but also something else that would be improved in time.

On a few occasions they came across abandoned roundhouses, where signs of the previous occupants were still present. Crops were overgrown, growing wild nearby and overrunning boundaries, fencing and tracks on the ground. Maybe the occupants had tired of living their solitary lives and had moved to live with others, perhaps they had died during a raid from wounds received from different tribal regions. Inhabitants tended to live as far from borders as they could to avoid being the first victims when cross border clashes occurred, but raiding was still a way of life in some places.

As they travelled through the rich green countryside with birds twittering and singing in the trees all around them, it was hard to believe that a real danger lurked somewhere ahead. The first day was uneventful and before the daylight began to withdraw, the scouts returned to the main column where they found they had already halted. The daily routine was underway with trenches being dug, defences re-enforced with large wooden spikes that each eight man squad carried with their kit and tents were erected. After the marching camp was secure, food would be prepared and the exhausted troops would be allowed to relax, after checking their kit and cleaning their armour, all those except for the men detailed for sentry duty.

As they were in relatively unknown and possibly hostile territory, Vespasian ordered extra guards be posted inside the temporary structure and sentries outside each eight man tent. Guards patrolled the internal perimeter and static posts manned the embankments that had not been there, just the day before. He ordered that wolf mouths were to be half buried in the ground outside the palisade in the trench they had created and that caltrops be sprinkled liberally over the surface. They were sharpened thin twisted strands of iron that would pierce the feet of men or hooves of horses, should they get into the ditch. The men rotated their duties after the hour, allowing them all to get a decent night's sleep so they were refreshed and ready for another days march.

The next morning, the men not on guard awoke to the patter of rain on their tents. The night had been uneventful and the daily routine of preparing for another hard days march was underway. Horses as well as men were fed and any mounts that had slight injuries or had gone lame from the day before were rested. They wouldn't be ridden again until they were healed and would follow at the rear of the column. Replacements were found and the injured animals allowed to walk un-ridden tethered to a cart.

As the final preparations were made to advance, weapons were checked and tents secured on carts or mules as the case maybe for each squad. The last thing to be taken down as the men prepared to march were the sharpened wooden staves that had been embedded into the palisades. The Roman army had learned long ago that taking them out before the men were ready to move had cost lives and sometimes entire legions.

The next two days proved to be the same routine and there were no incidents or sightings of hostile forces. The men were trained to march, build an encampment, guard and sleep and take it down again the next day. On the fourth day however, as they began to prepare their defences for the night, in the distance were the hills and mountains that marked the territory of the Silures.

Vespasian had sent scouts out and knew that by midday the next day he and his men would be entering the lands that had adopted Caratacus as their leader. The atmosphere around some of the campfires that night was tense. It was the first time since they had set out from Isca Dumnoniorum that men looked out of the palisades with real concern on their faces. More men were detailed for sentry and picket duty and each tent party was ordered to have a two man guard outside.

The night passed by without event and in the dawn of a new day the men of the Second Augusta quietly prepared their kit and dismantled the camp. A few men who were in the minority were overly loud and went about their business telling their comrades how many Britons they intended to kill high in the mountains of the Silures. The more experienced amongst them knew it was probably just nerves or foolishness and that by nightfall they may have the answer to which, one thing was certain, from today they would have to have eyes everywhere.

Miles to the north, halfway to the summit of one of the mountains, the Britons watched the Roman camp in the distance. From their vantage point they couldn't make out specific details but the large encampment was clearly visible on the landscape. The large dark rectangular mass had never been there before and once in a while the wind would carry the sound of a trumpet to them, faintly but distinguishable from everything else on the morning breeze.

They waited until they could see the first thin line of men leaving the safety of the temporary encampment, as they began to slowly move towards their position, weaving through the lowland countryside below.

"Let us prepare to receive our guests." Caratacus said as he climbed onto his horse. He took one last glance at the enemy before kicking his horse and going further up the mountain.

By the time the legionaries felt the incline starting to burn their legs, the hills and mountains blocked out most of the sky before them. They had been ordered to wear their helmets and carry their shields for the first time on this expedition and they knew that an attack could occur at any moment.

Varro and his party scouted ahead but at all times were ordered to stay in sight of the leading column, Vespasian didn't want to risk losing any men in a fool hardy manner so close to the enemy. Tracks and trails were evident everywhere and ran in many different directions, it was impossible to identify specific traces that would show any real evidence of the direction of Caratacus and his warriors.

The day wore on as the inclines got steeper and Vespasian was forced to call regular breaks for his men and animals to take on water and rest. He knew there was no point in being engaged in a battle with weary thirsty soldiers; it would be a recipe for disaster even before the first arrow took to the air or the first blow was struck.

Even though they were climbing higher and higher all the time, there were still paths and valleys through the hills and mountains. Varro stopped looking forward to the top of the next rise because there was always another beyond that one that and he wondered if the local people were actually part goat. They had seen no settlements or roundhouses since crossing the river that divided the lands of the Dobunni and the Silures, just the occasional deer that ran as soon as it sensed the advancing column. White dots broke up the green land ahead where sheep grazed in the distance, at least food wouldn't be hard to find here. Higher and higher and further into the valley they marched until by midday Vespasian called another halt. He had chosen a relatively flat and open area that was surrounded by thick forest and called his senior officers together to discuss what he intended to do next.

Varro and his party it was decided, would for the first time since entering the valley and mountains, scout ahead and try and locate somewhere suitable to establish the army for the night. It was better to advance slowly and securely rather than at speed with little haste Vespasian had told them looking around the high peaks now surrounding them in every direction. It was suggested by one centurion that Varro take an entire cohort with him for safety but the Legate chose against it, deciding that a small group was less conspicuous and would be able to move more quickly in the event of an attack. He was to be back with the column well before nightfall, which would give the men time to establish a camp using the trees nearby if necessary.

The sky was grey and cloudy as he led his squad on horseback into unchartered territory. He moved at a slow pace knowing that to go around a corner at speed could mean certain death. It meant progress was time consuming which they could ill afford but he had no choice. The ground was littered with shale and rocks, so even if they wanted to move quickly it would be virtually impossible unless they wanted to risk a horse slipping and breaking a leg. He made sure that those following were strung out in single file on their own with at least ten feet in between each rider.

The track they were following was covered in shadow but the sun was now bright and looked warm on the mountain further up. With the shadow came the cooler air and Varro involuntarily shivered as he felt a slight breeze find its way under his tunic and chainmail, sweat trickled down his spine. He turned and saw eager expressions watching him from behind, eyes darted from him to beyond searching for any signs of movement. The hooves of the horses were quieter than usual due to their slow pace but every once in a while a hoof would strike a rock or a piece of shale and send it skipping over the ground bouncing and making noise that made them all cringe. The sound it caused echoed up around the natural walls that now seemed to envelope the scouts.

He turned forward again and slowed Staro's pace even more as he approached a sweeping corner. There were thick trees on the slopes on either side of the worn path covering the steep banks and making it impossible to see if anything lurked in the darkness beyond. He felt his heart beating stronger, faster, pulsing blood through his veins, it almost felt like his chest was about to explode.

From somewhere further around the corner he suddenly heard signs of movement. Something had moved, a rock or a piece of shale and he heard it bouncing over the broken surface. He swallowed and stopped his horse raising his right arm, indicating for those behind him to do the same. He didn't dare turn around again but sat still in his saddle straining his ears moving his head from side to side listening and half closing his eyes in concentration as he sought out more information. The only thing he could hear now was his mounts tail swishing about behind him and his breathing.

"Shhhh boy." He whispered and very slowly lifted his leg over Staro's rump and climbed down in one swift movement. He risked a look backward now and saw Decimus waving his hand in an upwards motion asking him to get back in the saddle. Varro put his finger to his lips warning them to be quiet as he saw those behind Decimus leaning out to see what was happening up ahead, trying to see why they had stopped. He pulled his shield from the horse and stood still listening.

He slowly walked in front of Staro almost tip toeing trying not to make any sound on the littered surface and stood still raising his hand for him to stay where he was. The horse looked to the side at the long grass at the base of the trees and Varro nodded his head forward and down quickly in frustration frowning at his horse and raised his hand higher. Staro whipped his head up quickly and then back down again showing his disappointment at being told not to move and eat the grass. Varro didn't truly know if that meant he understood what his master wanted from him or not and mentally tried to tell the horse to stay still, pleading in his own mind for him not to move or make a sound.

He turned slowly and faced the corner where the track vanished from view, almost in the same movement he took a step forward, crunch, the shale noisily moved together grating as his hobnail boot compressed it down with his weight. He brought his other foot forward and then listened hovering it above the ground before he gently laid it down, it grated slightly as it landed but it was barely audible. He didn't dare turn to look around to see if his horse was still standing still, although for a second he thought he heard his tail swishing again.

Crunch!

He froze, eyes flashing from left to right bringing his shield higher and then stared at the bend in the path in front of him on the track. He felt for the hilt of his sword and slowly wrapped his fingers around the handle and pulled it slowly up trying to avoid the familiar rasp as it cleared the scabbard. Pulling it clear he took another step forward praying that his boot didn't make too much noise, it didn't this time, the contact was almost imperceptible with the stony surface. He took another and started to lean over to the right trying to see along the path round the bend.

Crunch!

He froze again and could now feel his heart pounding in his chest and a vein somewhere on his right temple pulsing so hard with pressure that he shook his head trying to clear it. Suddenly the single crunch was joined by another and then another. Something was definitely moving towards him building up speed, he crouched pointing his spatha lower, aiming its sharp tip at whatever was moving out of sight, his grip tight on the handle of the weapon. He saw a flicker of white and movement and then it came into full view. It was a lamb, a fat fluffy one. It stared at him and stood stock still as it took him in bleating loudly as if it was as shocked as he was.

He gasped, "You fucking fat furry woolly little bastard." Varro almost shouted in relief smiling. He turned to the others and raised his shoulders laughing quietly and then heard something else, something violent. It was the sound of branches and leaves being struck by something heavy above him and on both sides and then like the sound of heavy rain, the arrows and spears began to fall.

Chapter Twenty

Caratacus and Ardwen had watched and waited whilst the enemy had slowly marched up into the valleys and mountains, snaking their long column past what he hoped would be beyond any safe point of return. Caratacus had said that he wanted to wait until they were so far into the territory, that they would find it impossible for them to get out again. When that time came he intended to close off any route of escape and destroy the soldiers who had marched into this land intent on killing them.

He had surveyed the route himself several times when it became obvious which track through the mountains they would be forced to take as there were so few now and once there, were committed. They would find a change of direction virtually impossible because there were very few and of those that existed, they twisted through the valleys for mile after mile. He believed that even if some were to escape the slaughter he planned, they would easily be hunted down. They could of course, attempt to scale up even higher slopes at either side of the long worn tracks but their horses would soon tire and falter and the result would be the same, destruction.

After so many defeats and the enforced retreating Caratacus had at last found a place where he believed he could fight the enemy on equal terms thanks to the terrain he found himself in. The enemy had the advantage of weapons still but here that advantage would be removed by virtue of the land and twisting narrow mountain paths. This would be the first test of his beliefs where even if they were outnumbered, the valleys, hills and mountains would give him a much better chance for success. He had been pleased to see Vespasian himself riding with his soldiers, the black plume of his helmet distinct amongst the others of white and red. He would have to try and ensure that the Roman Legate was either killed or captured, he hoped the latter as he would make a good bargaining piece with Rome. His warriors were briefed accordingly but if he were to be killed, his head would make a nice trophy impaled on a spear for all to see.

As the Romans had camped so far away from the higher ground the day before, it had given Caratacus and Ardwen time to call more warriors forward from the surrounding settlements and word had even been sent to the northern tribes. Although fairly dispersed through the valleys and mountains, there were more than enough to guarantee that they now outnumbered the advancing soldiers by at least three to one. If the Demeta, Ordives and Deceangli tribes joined them as well, they would be able to stop the invaders from gaining a foothold in this part of the world. He also had the advantage of having Ardwen and his people with him as they knew these mountains better than the goats and sheep that wandered the slopes, the enemy were at a distinct disadvantage in every sense and he hoped to make that tell.

Caratacus had watched from thousands of feet up as the Romans had sent a scouting party into the gorge below. They were already a few hundred feet above sea level and their chance of taking a different route was narrowed with every step they took, until they were down to one. The main party had stopped and were taking a break at a fairly large clearing as the scouts entered the path below. Caratacus watched from his vantage point and began to give orders as warriors scurried down the paths carrying out his orders.

Although he was perched watching the enemy from behind the tops of trees on the slope below him, he felt almost exposed to the dangerous beast he now saw. If only he could reach out with his hand and could grab this army and crush it in his hand and squash it like a mosquito. He stood up and scrambled down the slope through the trees holding the hilt of his sword and pushing it down so its blade faced upward at an angle and didn't scrape along the surface and give away their position. He wanted to wait until the last possible second to spring the trap and kill as many of these intruders as possible.

As arrows and spears began to thud into the ground and flesh alike, causing heavy impacts from their deadly rain, the cries of alarm and pain began from both human and animal alike. As Varro took two giant strides and leapt up onto Staro's back, he saw from the corner of his vision at least two bodies falling from the horses of his own people. As he began to turn, he kicked the horse into a gallop and saw that the fat lamb that had stopped his progress a few seconds before, was now pinned to the floor, a spear impaling it through its back as its legs scrambled to try and gain some purchase on the slippery shale. Rich red blood was already vividly staining the white woollen fur, then an arrow struck it's skull at the side and it stopped moving altogether.

"Follow me." He managed to shout half turning again as his horse built up speed, hooves biting into the stony floor as he ripped his up shield above his head. Arrows and spears continued to land and he heard more shrieks behind in the chaos as they attempted to escape the deadly shower, the noise was almost deafening. Staro chinked this way and that as he moved almost automatically round the tight corners with Varro clinging on for dear life with his legs leaning low.

The first thing that Vespasian knew of the ambush was the instant red hot pain boring into his exposed flesh inside his upper leg, he felt above his right knee and almost collapsed. Crying out in agony immediately and frowning he looked down where he saw a large arrow shaft had embedded itself through his skin and out through the other side. A member of his bodyguard screamed something that he didn't quite hear and ran over to him stopping his fall as he went to go to ground. As the soldier propped him up, other arrows zipped past his head and landed, some hitting the ground but others wounding and killing other men as they desperately looked for cover. In that second he looked up and saw his men taking both arrows and spears which meant the Britons were close, very close.

"Come on sir we've got to move." The legionnaire said half dragging and carrying his Legate up under his shoulder cursing under his breath. Another man ran over to them an optio, and got on the other side of their commander, almost instantly the first soldier was hit. Vespasian turned hearing a thump followed by a cracking sound as an arrow struck and he felt the man go suddenly slack and fall away. He saw it had pierced his face below the right eye and was inches deep into his head. Deep red blood pulsed out and down into his open mouth. The man was dead before he hit the ground his helmet falling clear and landing before he did.

The optio screamed for help as he dragged his Legate towards a cart where the helpless mules were already being hit and injured by a number of arrows. They jerked around helplessly bellowing their anger trying to get free as men fell all around them. He saw that some had huddled together to form better protection under their shields collectively and were virtually crawling, stooped down trying to get out of range of the deadly torrent. Someone unseen was shouting for testudos to be formed. Shrieks of pain filled the air all around him but he knew he had to take control of the madness that now surrounded his world.

Arriving breathless at the wheel of the cart the optio didn't wait for his commander to crawl underneath, he hurled him to the ground, the arrow breaking off in his leg as he did so, Vespasian cried out in agony and fought to get under the wooden surface, fury written over his face briefly at the optio.

"Mars fucking hairy cunt, you fucking barbarian goat fuckers will pay for this." He shouted grabbing at the length of arrow shaft that still remained in his leg. He tried to pull it out but it was already slick with blood. The optio took his neckerchief off and shouted, "Not like that sir, the barbs will rip your fuckin leg apart, turn over."

The Legate frowned but did as he was told mentally scalding himself for losing his composure, he turned his back on the optio who had wrapped the material around the wooden shaft and was wiping blood away. He smothered the deadly barbed head with the cloth and without ceremony or waiting for his commander to ready himself, yanked the arrow free. Legate Titus Vespasian blacked out and was lost to the chaos.

***

Varro rode as fast as he could around the twisting curves of the track, the sound of the animal's hooves loud in his ears. He was faintly aware of the others behind him but didn't dare turn to look and see who was following, who was still with him. Leaning forward low over his mounts back he urged the beast on determined that they wouldn't die in this place. On and on they rode, arrows showering the ground all around them. He knew an archer would be lucky to hit a galloping horse or its rider especially as they jinked and turned around the bends of the track but also knew that an injury out here far behind enemy lines could mean death even if it wasn't severe. Although the odds were low on being hit, he knew that there must be dozens, hundreds of Britons firing and throwing missiles at them because the deadly storm kept coming. A thought quickly entered his head as he knew Parthians were known to smear their arrows in excrement to ensure disease even in the slightest of cuts, maybe the Britons did the same.

In the space of a blink of an eye he imagined all kinds of images, their naked bodies stripped of clothing and armour, barbarians celebrating as they disfigured their torsos, their horses killed and eaten, the men at Isca Dumnoniorum never knowing what had happened to them, lost on the frontier. They could be poisoned by an arrow and left to die a long and painful death. Dark thoughts and images filled his mind as he clung onto Staro as he snorted with effort galloping for his and his masters life, it seemed to go on for an eternity. He was pulled from the nightmare by shouts from somewhere to the rear, a familiar voice.

"Varro slow down, stop, we're clear." It was Tevelgus. He risked turning and saw the big Briton behind him and slowed down and for the first time. He saw that he was followed by only three, Brenna and Decimus were there also, there was quiet from the banks either side.

"Where are the others?" He asked stopping his horse looking up at the sharp mountain slopes either side of them expecting to see more arrows being launched, his chest lurched with the effort of the frantic ride.

"They were hit in the first wave." Brenna said, "There was nothing we could do for them." Automatically they all checked themselves and their mounts to see if they had been injured, they hadn't. Panting Varro jumped off his horse.

"I didn't see them. They must have been hiding in the trees waiting to ambush us, there was no sign, nothing at all." He looked around again certain of more missiles. "We can't just leave them we've got to go back." He said.

Tevelgus got off his own horse and walked towards the centurion, "You saw that hail of arrows, if we went back we would end up just like them, they're dead and if they weren't straight away, they will be by now."

"What if any of them were just injured, how would you feel if you knew your friends had left you to die?" He answered.

The big Briton stared at Varro almost willing him to argue it seemed and then his eyes widened and Varro heard a thump, he fell forward onto the Roman, an arrow sticking into the back of his head. Varro staggered with his weight, took a step back and let him fall face down. Brenna cried out her brother's name.

"Mount up." He shouted grabbing his saddle and swinging his leg back up and onto his horse who, had already started to move forward on his own. Hooves hitting the ground masked the sound of any other flying arrows as they tried to escape again.

From both sides, the Britons scrambled and ran down the steep slopes jeering and screaming towards the men of the Second Augusta who were desperately retreating from the edge of the clearing. Spears were hurled at random from the high ground so thick was the target area below. Legionaries already lay dead or wounded their blood a sharp contrast to the white of their tunics. Despite the deadly avalanche of weapons, the legionaries were already regrouping and forming testudos leaving the dead and injured where they lay as men screamed out for help.

Orders were shouted from centurions and optios inside the formations as they tried to keep order and discipline. One group of such soldiers that were slower than the rest and containing only about thirty men were the first to be attacked.

The Britons swarmed the shield wall and they were stopped in their tracks. Barbarians who had jumped down from other areas not even near them, ran and joined the attack. Spears, axes, clubs, swords and arrows stabbed at their defences, hacking and piercing at the shielded formation.

As other testudos retreated, men who were relatively safe for the time being, watched through gaps in their own shields when movement allowed, as they began to fall one at a time. Shields were ripped from grasping arms as the holders were wounded, spears were hurled over the top of the attacking warriors, axes span through the air landing indiscriminately somewhere in the middle, a hand was hacked off a flailing Roman arm as its shield was ripped from its grasp. It was a blood bath, where no mercy was shown.

As the last two men were simultaneously chopped down, Vespasian opened his eyes. He and the optio were in the centre of the clearing under the cart in front of which the two mules lay dead, hit by umpteen arrows. The Legate saw that the soldier had used his neck scarf as a tourniquet to stop the blood flow.

"Report." He ordered turning and looking out to the scenes of battle around them.

"They've just butchered a testudo sir, at least twenty, maybe thirty men hacked and stabbed to death." He pointed to where he had witnessed the atrocity occur. The Britons were crowding over the slain men picking up helmets, swords and shields.

Vespasian turned in the opposite direction and saw squares of centuries formed up about sixty paces away. "Quickly whilst they're distracted, we've got to get to that testudo over there." He pointed.

The optio gave him a concerned look until he added, "We can either try and get to them and get some cover or wait here until they," he pointed a thumb in the other direction, "come over here and drag us out kicking and screaming and butcher us where we lay. It's up to you but I can't run without your help." The optio turned and quickly crawled out from under the cart on the opposite side from the main body of Britons. He knew in seconds they would be bearing down on other men so he moved as fast as he could. Grimacing in pain

Vespasian shimmied along on his backside. Once clear of the cart, he was pulled up by the soldier who draped his arm over his shoulder and immediately began half running and dragging the Legate towards the waiting formation.

Suddenly they were aware of shouting behind them, as the optio himself shouted at the wall of shields, silently standing in front of them. Neither of them turned not daring to waste any time but hurried forward, now about forty paces from safety. The noise behind them grew as arrows were launched again but this time they were Roman, they flew over their heads and to the side of them landing unseen. Shouts of pain merged with shouts of anger as some at least found their mark.

The optio pushed Vespasian's arm higher to get a better grip and was aware of movement in the Roman line now thirty paces distant. His head was suddenly jarred violently forward, a loud single bang on his helmet signalling that he had been struck with something but he didn't dare look to see what it was. Struggling with the Legate on his shoulder he looked forward and watched as the legionaries launched a wave of javelins into the air towards them. He ducked instinctively as they flew over his head and fell into their intended targets.

He could almost feel the breath of the enemy now and believed that he would die heroically trying to save his Legate. Would his wife hear of his valour? Would they build a shrine in his name? Would anyone survive this catastrophe? Every second he expected to feel a spear puncture his armour and pierce his flesh underneath, snapping his spine. Another volley of pila was launched from the line of shields but it didn't make him feel any more secure. At least he thought his comrades were doing their duty in trying to protect them as they lurched forward. Twenty paces away from some respite, some of the men in the front line of the formation opened their ranks and waited behind their shields peering out. Another wave of Roman arrows sped towards the heathens behind them as he felt the burning hot sensation of an enemy arrow stab into his heel.

"Arrrggggghhh you bastards." He yelled, his face contorted in pain as he fell forward the weight of the Legate on top of him and then everything blacked out.

Caratacus thrust his sword at the armoured demon standing in front of him surrounded by his comrades but it bounced off. The soldier leered at him and stabbed out with his gladius from the side of his shield but his reach was too short. Warriors jostled for position sensing victory over this relatively small and isolated group as men barged passed each other, vying for spoils and death. Spears landed in amongst the Romans, some were deflected off shields or armour but a few found soft flesh to penetrate and pierce.

Screams and squeals of pain, some almost childlike, filled his ears as he cut and thrust with his weapon. An arrow flew past his head so close that he felt the draught of its passing at great speed as it smashed its way into a helmeted forehead just below the rim. The eyes were dead and rolling backward into the head long before the body fell and Caratacus wanted more, much more. They were winning this battle within a battle he realised as more spears were thrown from above and shattered men and bone.

From his peripheral vision he saw Ardwen hacking at a soldiers leg like a maniac chopping at a tree whilst another warrior attacked the upper body. The first slice embedded itself deep into the man's shin before it was wrenched free and another great scything arc removed the leg from below the knee completely. The metallic smell of blood and iron filled his nose. He held his ground briefly trying to assess the situation and saw great rows of soldiers formed up beyond this skirmish, behind their shields. One man was hobbling towards their lines with another draped over his shoulder.

He backed away a few feet from the fighting and gave a hand signal for the archers on the slope to concentrate their fire at the neat rows of silent men waiting to fight. Within seconds the men behind those at the front, hauled up their rectangular shields to form an almost solid roof as arrows struck them. One arrow shaft passed through a small gap and hit one legionary in the face, he dropped from sight instantly. Caratacus signalled Ardwen to break off his attack and follow him, leaving their warriors to wipe out the men before them.

"What is it cousin, why have you pulled me away from our much deserved victory just as we are about to rout them?" Ardwen asked of Caratacus as they ran together.

Caratacus led him to the cover of the trees at the side of the clearing and pointed saying, "Watch what happens cousin, this is one of the things I have learned from fighting these men." They both crouched down behind thick tree trunks and bushes and watched. The warriors made short work of the remaining men that had been unfortunate enough to find themselves isolated and caught out in the open. More spears and arrows penetrated their bodies from above and even their armour occasionally, those who weren't hit from the slopes were struck by swords or axes. It was butchery, man against man, crude, vile and naked aggression and the Britons were winning. The last of the Romans fell with another by his side dispatched just before him but the indiscipline of their men showed as they hurriedly bent down to loot the bodies of weapons and armour.

"See here," Caratacus said, "if those men over there weren't occupied and distracted with those two scurrying back to them, our people would be wiped out where they stood."

Quickly the warriors began to turn their attention to the rows of shields and ran towards them. Caratacus and Ardwen watched a few of them as they tried in vain to spear the two men who were closing the gap to safety. The next second, a flight of javelins were hurled skyward from behind the front row of waiting soldiers. They arced into the grey sky and fell, wiping out lives, in an instant they were joined by arrows that jarred their warriors backward, spinning some as they fell. The Roman spears and arrows took a deadly toll on the previously victorious Britons and their advance began to falter.

Ardwen looked on in horror as their men and women were taken from the world, bodies punctured even before they could reach the Roman lines. They both saw the two men who had been retreating dragged to safety through an area of shields that closed behind them. A trumpet sounded from somewhere in the midst of armour and the entire row of Romans began to move backward as if one giant metallic and wooden beast. Caratacus and Ardwen shouted at their archers to keep firing, they weren't to be given a seconds respite as they retreated.

Caratacus turned and scrambled up the slope behind him quickly followed by Ardwen pulling himself up on trees and branches. He glanced back and saw that the Romans were retreating to the track that they had followed, at the far edge of the bowl like clearing.

"We've got to get the slingers involved when they get to that narrow break in the rock." He shouted back at Ardwen who was already red faced from the effort of hauling himself up. Caratacus slipped on the surface and fell face down and started to slide back down the steep slope towards Ardwen, gravel and loose rock followed his fall.

He swore shouting at himself as he continued to slide trying to grasp branches and roots until he crashed into Ardwen. The two stopped still for a second, looked at each other and then barrelled back down the slope to where they had started.

Varro kept riding until he was certain they were out of sight of the attacking Britons. Eventually he slowed down and turned to see that they had followed the path into another mountainous valley some distance from where the trap was sprung. He guided them down to a small stream where he led his horse to water, Brenna and Decimus followed.

"Gods fucking teeth, this is a fucking disaster." He said crouching down and scooping water onto his face. "Did you hear the battle beyond where we attacked? The main column must have been ambushed as well, if they were cut off in that clearing, every one of them could be dead."

Decimus walked into the water and washed his own face, the water was ice cold, "What now then? We can either ride for help or try and get back to them and find out what happened."

Varro looked over to Brenna who was still on her horse, the animal was drinking from the stream but she was sat staring at the ground.

"Brenna." She didn't reply. "Brenna." He said again, as glazed eyes looked up to acknowledge his words. In the melee he had forgotten about her loss.

"My brother is dead." She didn't move, just sat staring at him. He wiped his face with the red cloth around his neck and walked over to her.

"Come, have some water." He said.

"Will the water bring my brother back?" Tears rolled freely from her eyes down her face and fell onto her dirty skin. He reached up and wiped the tears from her face.

"Come we have to decide what to do, or his death and those of our friends will have been for nothing." She allowed herself to be helped down and Varro put his arms around her and held her closely.

"The Twentieth are supposed to be to the north of here fighting the Ordovices," Decimus said, "maybe we could ride for help." Varro frowned and shook his head slightly telling Decimus that this was not the time. He leaned back and looked at Brenna her head was down facing the ground. Every now and again the sound of battle was carried to them on the wind through the valley, swords clashing, screaming or trumpet sound.

"It sounds like they're still fighting, may the gods protect them." Varro said. "There could be thousands of the bastards in these mountains and we walk in without the support of another legion." Brenna pushed herself away from him.

"It would be as quick to ride back to Isca as to ride north but the Silures are blocking the path so we may never get through, where did your Twentieth legion approach the north from, do you know?" She asked.

Varro walked to the edge of the stream and marked a map in the soil with his sword, "They advanced from the east moving into the northern territories. It's not just the Ordovices they face though as they would have had to march through the lands of the Cornova first who may have resisted as well." He looked up at his two remaining companions. "That's not all," he marked the ground again, "here to the north towards Mona is the land of the Deceangli and there is no guarantee that they haven't joined any fight to the south."

Decimus walked from the stream shaking water from his hands, "At least the Twentieth will be at full strength, they hadn't established any fort and were marching daily or so I heard, they'll be better equipped and manned in comparison to the Second."

"That's true," Varro said knowing the Second had left men behind to guard Isca, he looked at Brenna again, "you would stand a better chance of getting through to them than us through these lands, no-one would have reason to stop you."

She looked back at him, "And why would your Twentieth listen to me? If they're involved in fighting and see another Briton approach them, I may not even get close enough to speak to them."

Varro looked over to Decimus, "Go with her my friend, leave your armour and anything of Rome here, we've got to go for help or those men in the mountains we came with will be destroyed."

Decimus' face showed he clearly wasn't happy with the decision but started to take off his chainmail. "Very well Varro, I will go with Brenna but what will you do? Isn't it better that we all stay together, surely three are better than two are they not?"

"Yes they are but against the odds we are likely to face, I don't think it would make that much difference. We can't just abandon the Legate and the men of the Second, even if it is only to witness their corpses. Besides if anyone sees you two, they will probably think you are man and wife and won't pay any attention." He helped Decimus remove his chainmail as he was struggling to get it over his head.

"Isn't that all the more reason for you to go with Brenna surely?" Decimus said.

Varro looked from one to the other, "You are both dear to me but for different reasons but so are the men fighting for their lives in the mountains back there. I am better suited to staying alone and you are better suited to going, both of you. I wouldn't rest if I were the one to go anyway." He looked over to Staro still drinking at the stream.

"Take my horse, you can ride two and rest one, I can move just as quickly on foot over this terrain." He said pointing up at the almost sheer face of the mountain. "I'll just take my dried meat sack and some water, anything else will just wear me down." He walked to his horse as Staro raised his head, giving him a rub on his ear he whispered something to him and said to the two still watching, "Fill your water skins with fresh water at the stream, you'll need it."

***

The rain of arrows and spears began to falter as the men of the Second retreated back into the pass leaving some dead or seriously injured men behind in the dust. The slingers who Caratacus wanted so desperately to join the battle were caught with the same problem and most of their missiles now just bounced off the re-enforced shields. The Britons in their eagerness to draw blood were too crowded on the slopes and too few of them could get close enough to hurl their spears. Likewise only the bowmen close enough to the pass, could get a clear shot, loosed an arrow. Most of the men lying crippled and injured were quickly finished off by warriors as they swarmed over their broken and shattered bodies. Heads and limbs were hacked off, some still with their helmets on to be used as trophies later. A few men were dragged away kicking and screaming, their fate uncertain but not envious.

With the testudo still formed at the battlefront of the retreating lines, those clear of the pass now broke off and started to gain ground running up hill to the attacking Britons on the orders of their centurions. There were no defences except for the trees and the men of the Legion formed their own testudos in century groups until they reached them. Once there they were ordered to break free and engage the enemy. The fighting was fierce and casualties were taken on both sides but in time the men behind the large shields began to get the better of their opponents and pushed the Britons back over the summit. With the advantage of height, pila were passed forward and hurled at the retreating warriors, which helped speed them on their way.

The respite that the Britons had tried not to give the Romans was now a reality and they now held the higher ground on this particular peak. Those who were in the pass quickly began to make their way up the slope and before the rest were safe, the sound of trees being felled could be heard. Rations and weapons were taken from the carts and hurried upward to the top. Ever organised the soldiers of the Roman army began to build a fortified position which would secure them further, for the time being at least.

Vespasian was carried up to the top where rock provided a natural basin of flat land where they could survey the ground below. Medics and surgeons were brought forward to treat the injured and any supplies that could be carried, were taken from the carts in the valley. With all the animals dead, the remaining wagons were set on fire so they couldn't be used by the enemy. As the daylight began to give way a base camp of sorts was already nearly set up and was preparing for the next attack.

Despite his injury, Vespasian was on his feet as soon as possible against his doctor's advice. With thick padding over the puncture wounds and bandages strapped round his limb, wooden splits supporting his leg either side of the injury, he hobbled around speaking to his men reassuring them that they could hold the Britons off for days if need be. Each man had left Isca Dumnoniorum with enough rations for seven days but they had managed to salvage more from the carts below. He assured them that they were secure enough and would take this opportunity to draw the Britons in and kill as many as possible, all was not lost.

The faces looking back at him told the reality of the matter however, they were cut off and surrounded in enemy territory with limited resources and weapons and had already suffered many dead and injured. He knew he wasn't convincing anyone but to give up now would mean certain death for them all and whilst there was still a chance of survival, he would take it.

He walked to the edge of the rocky outcrop on one part of the peak and looked down, he swallowed heavily. Massing below in the valley were thousands of enemy warriors, swarming like insects in the failing light. They looted what was left on some of the carts his men could not reach and stood shouting up at the Romans, waving spears, bows, swords and axes.

"Mighty Mithras help us." He whispered to himself. Turning he called a centurion over and gave out orders for the defences further down the slope. They would make their mountain fort as impenetrable as they could by angling chopped tree trunks downward but beyond the reach of a standing man, sharpened stakes impossible to climb. Below that would be a ditch dug eight feet deep all around their encampment. Another vertical wall would be built behind the first defence. Pila would be piled at strategic intervals along the line behind the walls, archers behind them would pick off any who got through the walls further up on the land cleared of trees and if all that failed they would defend their land hand to hand until the last man.

As darkness began to fall the chopping of trees and digging continued and once in a while an archer would fire an arrow downward at any Briton that strayed into range, for now the accuracy kept the rest clear as men were speared by the deadly small missiles.

Caratacus and Ardwen watched from the safety of another mountain top close by as the Romans in the distance, the size of peas, toiled at their defences, chopping down trees and digging ditches.

"You have to admire them," Ardwen said, "they took a good beating today and many of them lay dead but still they prepare for more." He bit into a piece of meat as he watched and chewed.

"We too lost men and women but not nearly as many as our friends on the mountain top over there, besides what choice do they have? We should have foreseen this, their retreat, and had enough warriors to stop them gaining purchase over there." Caratacus said in reply.

"If we had that many up there, they would have been seen as they approached and the trap wouldn't have been sprung. Now we can pick away at them at our pleasure, their weapons won't last and nor will their food, it's only a matter of time." Ardwen said looking down at his warriors below them.

"We'll wait until its dark and fire the defences, night arrows should burn the wood quickly enough once we've put oil to them. We'll ask for volunteers to go forward and soak the timber. If they're careful and quiet, they won't even know we've done it until we've launched our burning shafts skyward." Caratacus said, turning to Ardwen he added, "Send some scouts to the local settlements and tell them of our victory today. Tell them we have more Romans trapped and that if they get here quickly enough, they can witness their destruction."

Ardwen turned to do as he was asked, before Caratacus stopped him grabbing his arm saying, "I want warriors here not old men and women. When we destroy these men," he said pointing at the peak opposite, "more will realise that these invaders can be beaten and we can remove them from our shores. Old women looking to slice off dead men's cocks will only get in the way."

Ardwen smiled and summoned a few men who were used as scouts, their short stocky ponies behind them and gave them their orders. He called for more food and retook his place next to Caratacus, "Well we may as well get comfortable, have some food, relax and wait until our guests are settled." Both men looked to the enemy still busy forming their defensive lines.

Brenna and Decimus rode slowly at first their mounts trotting along the mountain paths. They didn't want to draw attention to themselves and the surface was too dangerous to go any faster. The dark night had enveloped the peaks quickly once the daylight began to recede and the paths were difficult to see. They had searched for what seemed like ages looking for a single track that led them lower and eventually they had found one.

"It's going to take forever to get down from here." Decimus said quietly. Brenna ignored his comment at first and concentrated on guiding her mount with Staro trotting behind, tied off.

"We're already a lot lower now and just have to keep going north." She concentrated her eyes, believing she had just seen something ahead, Decimus saw that she was distracted.

"What is it, what do you see?" He asked looking forward in the direction of her gaze.

"I'm not sure. I thought I saw movement up ahead." She replied slowing her horse to a walk. "Did you see anything?"

He stopped and peered into the darkness, "I can't see anything are you sure? It's probably the dark playing tricks on you." She stopped by his side and got off her horse.

"Up there by those bushes." She said pointing along the path they were following. Decimus looked forward straining his eyes and turning his head slightly from side to side, ears listening favouring his left.

"I can't see or hear a fucking thing." He turned to look at her.

"Stay here with the horses," She said, "if I'm not back in a short time, turn around and find another way." She began to walk along the path.

"Wait, wait a moment, let's see if anything moves first, be sure." He said but she held a hand out backwards and continued walking slowly. Decimus got down from his horse and muttered, "Stupid bitch, she'll get us all killed." He said talking to the horses.

Chapter Twenty One

Decimus watched her walk away from him until the darkness swallowed her form, enveloping her completely and waited, and waited, He heard nothing except the breeze and saw nothing except for the darkness all around him. After a while he decided that she had been gone far longer already than the short time she had suggested or he had imagined. He looked around into the dark, cold night and at the landscape around him, he walked along the track ten paces and then back again to where the horses stood. He patted each of them in turn and spoke to them but there was still no sign of Brenna.

"Fucking cunting fuck cakes." He said to no-one in particular under his breath, it was frustration as he realised for the first time he was alone, miles from any friendly faces and surrounded by hostile barbarians for miles around. He looked at the horses who just stared back at him and then at the grass at the side of the track.

"Go on then." He said and let them wander to the side, letting them eat the long green grass. He turned back to where Brenna had disappeared and then turned looking in the direction they had come from, back down the track. They both looked the same, both directions, cold, dark, empty and uninviting.

"Well if you think I'm staying here all on my own you've got another thing coming lady." He said to himself and slowly drew his sword as it quietly whispered out of the sheath. He frowned concentrating and walked slowly along the track in the same direction as Brenna, sword facing forward. For the first time he realised how cold it was despite them now being a lot lower in altitude than they were earlier that day where the danger, real danger was, he thought to himself, danger that he could at least see. He had an ironic grimace on his face as he continued forward grinding his teeth.

"Where in Hades are you Brenna?" He whispered and then he saw movement and stopped dead, standing perfectly still, a shiver went down his spine but not from the cold. Something had crossed his path but it was too far distant for him to see clearly, it looked like a large Briton hunched over clasping his stomach. His senses were stretched to the limit as he tried to pick something up but staring into the darkness he saw nothing. He considered shouting out to Brenna in full voice but knew that if there were Britons nearby, they would be alerted to his position and would descend on him like a pack of wolves. He moved to the side of the track, off the gravel and onto the soft grass verge where he moved more quickly straining his eyes into the dark, every sense heightened.

"Brenna!" He called quietly almost whispering but there was no response, he knew there wouldn't be because she would have had to have been standing right next to him to hear his voice.

"Fucking thunder cunt!" He whispered to himself, now he was scared. The pattern of the track in front of him changed, curving to the left and downwards. At the arc of the curve there were dark trees, many dark trees. He squinted trying to see what lay beneath them but could only make out the nearest low branches with blackness beyond, he turned again and looked back at the horses, they were still happily munching away on the grass oblivious to what was going on around them. He wished he was a horse he decided, they would be looked after by whoever had them unless they were desperately hungry at least. He considered going back to them and riding off but he couldn't leave Brenna alone in the middle of this barren place, could he?

Varro scrambled up a steep slope as he thought about Decimus and Brenna and where they were and if they were safe. The night was cold now and a slight breeze blew down the valley but the sky was clear which at least allowed him to see from his elevated position with the stars shining brightly above. With the help of the gods they would be miles away from this place by now and galloping towards help, somewhere in the lowlands, 'Mithras, make it so' he thought, praying mentally. From somewhere below he suddenly heard noises from the valley over the crest in front of him, blown on the wind. Staying low he reached nearer to the edge and got down on his stomach, the grass was cold but not yet full with nightly dew, something unpleasant to look forward to later no doubt.

He crawled over the ground and could see Britons moving along the track below, tiny from this distance they were so tightly packed, they looked like a human river as they moved through the gorge like valley carrying torches. He followed their direction with his eyes and saw numerous mountains tops and hills in the distance where fires burned. One of them, the tallest peak was especially bright and he could make out the distinct features of a Roman defensive position around its middle.

"Thank Mithras." He said, his voice the first he had heard in hours, it sounded strange, isolated, alone. He removed his helmet placing it down and leaving it behind and edged further forward to get a better view. The last thing he wanted was for his helmet to glint and give his position away. He wouldn't last anytime at all if the Britons saw him and wouldn't be able to get away once they scaled his lofty perch, which wouldn't take long. He looked out over the valley and saw that his Legion or what was left of it, the survivors, had dug palisades and built defences. A swathe of land was bare where they had chopped down trees to build their temporary fortification and he could see a great many men moving about on guard, the size of ants from this distance.

It looked as if they had been forced to use every piece of land available to them right up to the peak where more fires burned. There were no tents erected which could only mean that they were either in enemy hands or had been abandoned, left where they were ambushed. If that was the situation, he wondered how much food and water they had remaining. These were questions he couldn't answer but assumed that if Vespasian were still alive, they would have as many provisions as physically possible as well as weapons. He could make out a line of archers beyond the cleared land and some patrolling the perimeter where he could also see what he presumed was a stock of javelins.

Looking down again at the river of bodies he knew it would be suicide to try and get to the men of the Second from where he was. The other peaks nearby were covered sporadically with their own fires which he assumed were ringed by Britons warming themselves against the night air. Every so often he heard singing carried on the breeze as if in celebration and saw that the Britons on one mountaintop were dancing around a fire, which could only mean that they had already killed many of his comrades.

He lay there feeling helpless, cold, frustrated and hungry and tried to think of something positive he could do to help. He felt his eyes growing heavy as he lay there and tried to shake off the tiredness by blinking his eyes but he knew he was no good to anyone exhausted. He retreated from the edge, wrapped himself in his cloak and curled up in a scoop in the ground out of the wind and allowed himself to fall into a disturbed sleep.

Not too far away on the Roman held mountain, eight legionaries slipped through the defensive perimeter one at a time. A centurion patted each of them on the back and quietly wished them good fortune as they crawled by him on their stomachs. They had removed their armour and blackened their tunics and skin as much as possible using spit and mud dug up from the ditch in the palisade. Vespasian had asked only for men who were willing to volunteer to go on a mission that in all probability would end in all their deaths but he was desperate, as were they all. The eight men were the first to volunteer although there were others. One said he preferred to do something other than sit and wait for a guaranteed death if they did nothing at all.

Vespasian knew that the rations and weapons could only last a certain amount of time, that said, they were now all of them, on half rations which meant they could survive longer. That in itself created problems because as the days went by they would get gradually weaker but it was a chance he had to take, he had to use every ounce of experience now if they were to survive. He actually hoped that the Britons would attack in force and break themselves against his defences and eventually withdraw but knew the odds were against it.

There were three realistic possibilities as he saw things; the first and most probable being the all-out attack with little regard to tactics by the enemy, in which case his men would send as many of them to their gods as possible. As a result of seeing many hundreds of their own warriors die they may withdraw and go home. He knew the Gaul's in particular had such a habit of doing just that when the blood started to flow and they took severe losses but would this enemy be the same? Second and the worst case as he considered it, was that the Britons sat back and waited for their foe to run out of food and water and either become so weak they couldn't defend themselves and were easily overrun or lastly they made one heroic charge down the slopes and onto the waiting spears below.

All scenarios he had considered fully and discussed with his senior officers and the general opinion was that tonight they should defend the mountain and see what it brings. In the meantime, the eight men would try to get down from the mountain undetected and attempt to get help. With no sign of their scouts, who he presumed were dead, the eight men were the only hope.

Once more he looked out at the fires on the peaks surrounding his own and wished that he could reach out and crush them, so tiny they looked from his position. All he could do in reality now was wait, wait and see what Caratacus did, he didn't have long to sit and wonder.

Decimus had lost sight of the horses and the track some time ago and had stopped trying to look backwards except to make sure that no-one or nothing was behind him, which he did repeatedly. He kept having a sense that someone was following him or was about to take his head off with a sword from behind as he turned around. He imagined the hunched over giant he believed he saw earlier, swinging a double headed axe and removing his skull in one swift movement. Who would mourn for him, what would happen to his body, would anyone pray for his soul? He pulled a face, screwing his features up as he dispelled the thoughts and concentrated on the task at hand. Gripping the handle of his sword tighter he continued forward.

"Brenna." He whispered standing still after a while but there was no reply except for the breeze. He took another step and immediately saw something move directly in front of him, it was Brenna he was certain. The shape was fleeting moving fast from left to right and just within his vision in the darkness and he was sure she was running with her sword in hand. He began to jog forward, spatha to the front in his right hand now held tighter than ever. He got to where he saw her and slowed but could see no sign of her passage, he glared at the ground but there was nothing.

Snap!

Something had broken a branch or a twig nearby and he crouched instinctively expecting an arrow. There was light in the distance flickering, a fire maybe but no arrow struck him. He walked towards the flickering flame, lurching from left to right as he went, all the time expecting attack. He was now getting angry at himself for being so scared, he was like a frightened lost child in the woods, the anger helped calm him. Fool he thought to himself, stop being such a prick. Closer and closer he moved, he could now smell wood smoke and hushed talking from around the fire where bodies sat huddled.

Fifty or so paces from them, they still hadn't seen him, one of them looked like Brenna he was sure. He looked at the others and saw they weren't soldiers but were dressed in the same garb as her. Quietly he approached the fire hardly breathing, he could see their faces now in the light of the fire, it was Brenna he was certain. He stood for a while trying to make out what they were saying but could only hear mumbling. As he crept closer, the breeze rustling through the trees and the crackle of the fire made it impossible to distinguish their words.

Suddenly Brenna turned her head and looked directly at him, "Decimus, thank the gods," she said standing and walking towards him, the others all turned to look at the new arrival, "I got lost and came across these people of my tribe." She smiled and approached him. "We were about to set off looking for you. You poor man you must be frozen, come warm yourself by the fire."

He looked at the people sat round the flames, they were wearing swords and axes and he saw a couple of bows lying nearby, two of the men stood staring, hate filled their eyes. He looked back to Brenna and she smiled as she suddenly whipped her hand up plunging a blade deep into his throat and ripped it through his flesh. Blood spurted out splattering her face as he fell, dead before he hit the ground.

The eight soldiers were led by Centurion Varenus Corvus a veteran of the campaigns in Gaul, four optios were also in their number, the rest were made up of legionaries. Although the night was clear and fires lit, some of the landscape around them was hard to distinguish so Corvus stuck to the natural gulley's in the rock and knew they would be hard to spot, or so he hoped. Each man carried only one thing, a sword. They too had been dulled by caking the blades in mud so as not to give away their position as they tried to avoid detection. They moved slowly but swiftly down the slope as they made the descent. They could hear the enemy clearly all around them but would only engage those who attacked them or shouted an alarm.

Corvus had reminded them all not to look at the fires or their vision would be dulled and impaired sight could mean death. They would move and then go to ground sometimes for short periods and sometimes for longer, words would only be whispered and then only into an ear of the man next to them. They were to rely on hand gestures and were to be prepared to lay low for long periods of time even until darkness returned the following night if necessary. The final advice he had given them was the most crucial, if they were discovered and surrounded and there was no chance of escape, they were to fight to the death. By way of reasoning he had explained some of the things he had seen both in Gaul and Britannia of Roman soldiers captured by the enemy.

Crouching low Corvus surveyed the area ahead where he intended to travel. From the height they were at he had an advantage of seeing the lower ground virtually laid out before him as if it were a map, the disadvantage was that someone looking up could just as easily see him and the men unless they were very careful. They were in a slight crevice about eight feet in depth where trees and bushes grew thanks to a trickle of water from the mountain top. He had chosen this route as it ran the furthest down the slope until disappearing over an abrupt ledge somewhere hundreds feet below the palisade. The noise of the trickling water would help mask their movement and the branches would hide them from view but still he took no chances. He turned his head slowly and held out his mud covered arm and gave a signal to the man behind him to lay flat. Head first with his gladius held in his hand, he moved lower on his elbows and toes, moving inches at a time.

After travelling only about fifty normal paces and very slowly, he stopped and indicated to those behind him to rest with his hand by gently lowering it to the ground flat. Their progress would be exceptionally slow, not only because they wanted to avoid discovery but also because after a while, the muscles they were using burned like fire. After the pain had eased significantly and after regaining his breath he moved on again, the line of men moving in tandem behind him, silent and unseen.

Later as the first signs of a new day began to dawn, he had reached the drop that he had seen from a distance hours before when they were selecting which route to take. He looked up without moving his head and saw the first strands of morning in the night sky, soon it would be light and he had to make a decision. He edged forward parallel with the narrow stream and peered over the drop. He saw the trees were thicker and taller below, probably due to the shelter from the wind. He followed the waters flow and saw a camp of Britons in the distance on the flat ground through the branches. They were far enough away for little concern for the present and most of them looked as if they were sleeping. He scanned the area for any obvious guards but saw none, so sure were they of their safety.

Corvus decided on a plan of action and very slowly turned his body to the man next in line behind him and whispered his orders. They were to take cover in the trees below and rest, he considered it too much of a risk to go further with daylight fast approaching. The result of their capture or discovery was far too great for the men still above them, they would wait in the trees, try and sleep and wait until darkness came again.

Caratacus stared up at the Roman emplacement high on the mountain in frustration. They had buried themselves like a lice on a hogs arse and would take some manoeuvring and prodding to displace. Having considered all his options and looking at the defences from every conceivable angle, he had formed the opinion that he had to attack. If it failed badly and many of their people were killed trying to scale the fortifications, he would draw back his warriors from the slopes and starve the Romans out.

He and Ardwen were agreed on their course of action and spent most of the night telling their men and women where to position themselves so as to try and cut off every possible area of escape. If they could contain the enemy fully, they knew the battle was half won, the problem however, was that many of them had stopped on or near the tracks, or by streams where they had arrived at the base of the mountain and there were gaps where the Romans could force an entire Legion through, if they had one.

By the time they had done as much as they could to disperse the warriors fairly evenly, the sun was beginning to show its first glimmers in the sky. Now the problem was co-ordinating an attack with thousands camped in family groups around the base of a large mountain. They had all been told to watch for the first signs of fire around the palisades once it was a light and they would be able to approach under the cover of the smoke and push the attack forward.

Ten men had been sent up the slopes throughout the night with sacks filled with oil, six had returned. That at least meant that there were now six bags full of highly flammable liquid that would burn brightly once they were hit by an arrow bearing flame, or so he hoped. The signal for the bowmen to go forward was to be the first rays of light. Caratacus looked about him and at first saw no movement or indication that his orders were being carried out but then looking to the east, he saw the first group of bowmen scaling the mountain.

He turned to Ardwen and nodded saying, "There will be no better day than this to crush so many of our enemy." He clasped his cousins forearm. "Good luck Ardwen of the Silures, may you take many heads."

"And to you Caratacus of the Catuvellauni, may luck and good fortune bless you today and may our gods crush those of Rome." Ardwen said smiling and then turned and mounted his horse and made off for his position further along the track.

Caratacus watched as the men grew smaller as they climbed the slopes, slippery with shale and morning dew, bows in hand. The first line of defences were about seven hundred feet up and the men would already be tired from their exertions, then would have to light fires before sending their arrows crashing into the palisade. His attention was drawn to a wave of warriors some few hundred feet behind the archers as they took to the slopes, their end not in sight.

Vespasian had instructed his men not to watch the eight as they tried to make their way off the mountain. A group of gawking fools stood standing and staring over the palisade would have given their position away and they would all be doomed. He had also said that if they were found, they would know soon enough, further explanation was not required. The medic had cleaned his wound again with water and applied some herbs that he was told would speed his recovery. He still couldn't put his full weight on the leg unaided so one of his men had fashioned a crutch from a branch which in itself was difficult to use on the uneven surface of their sanctuary, but he was thankful nevertheless. With the crutch and the wooden splits either side of the wound for support, he hobbled from place to place.

He had managed to sleep briefly in between the pain of his leg and the cold disturbing his slumber together with the nightmares he foresaw of his destruction and of those around him. He was standing trying to lean on his injured leg that had stiffened somewhat during the night when the alarm sounded from somewhere below. A lone trumpet at first was quickly joined by others as men raced to put their helmets on and grab their javelins.

Roman archers were the furthest forward, positioned at the top of the defences. As soon as the first alarm was raised arrows were nocked onto draw strings as the men ducked behind the cover of wicker walls made for them to launch their arrows from. The wicker would take some impact and absorb damage but they wouldn't last long against a hail of continued assault. The men crouched behind their small walls hoping that the trench beyond them would be enough to stop the Britons gaining access to where they were.

Legionary Titus Valerius was one such soldier, he looked to the other man, Valerio also sheltering behind the relatively small six foot wicker wall and nodded. To the side of each of them were piles of arrows ready to use against the attackers, neatly stacked and facing the same way to ease loading. The position was mirrored at intervals of fifty paces all the way around the mountain, several hundred feet from the lower ground.

Valerius peered through the small gaps in the wicker and saw movement below, a lot of movement. His fingers felt the reassuring draw string again as he edged to the side of his part of the wicker. The sight before him made him pause and shocked him to the core. There were thousands of enemy warriors struggling up the slopes towards them. A few carried torches and were surrounded by pockets of archers beyond them in the masses were blue painted warriors, men and women carrying long swords, axes and spears. Some he saw wore cloaks against the morning chill their pale skin underneath covered in woad in circular Celtic patterns.

"Fire Arrows!" Valerius bellowed as loud as he was able and drew back his bow, he knew that their own missiles would carry further than those of the Britons due to the height advantage and indeed fly faster through the air. They had to keep them as far away as possible to avoid the wood in their defences catching on fire.

"Loose. Concentrate on the bowmen." He heard the order given from somewhere to his right and estimated the enemy were now approximately two hundred paces away and took aim. The first arrow flew straight and true and landed somewhere in the crowd of bodies eating up the ground below. The second arrow he saw clearly land as it entered the forehead of a baying woman who instantly fell backward and was lost in the crowd.

The Britons lit their arrows and launched the first wave to a sound of cheers and roars as they took to the air. Valerius watched as the bowmen gathered around those with torches lighting their deadly arrow heads coated in oil. He aimed again for the torch bearer almost directly in line with him, his arm wavered slightly as the pressure of the draw took hold. Sighting the big man along the length of the shaft he let loose allowing the barbed missile to fly free. It rose slightly on its downward path as it headed for its target but quickly dropped again arcing toward the flame.

The torch bearer didn't see it approach as he was too busy with his task as archers fought to use his flame. The sharpened iron head penetrated his temple with a violent impact that rocked his huge head sideways as he had turned shouting at another man. It sank deep into his skull and he fell backwards but was propped up by the bodies around him, his torch disappearing from sight as others scrambled to retrieve it. Valerius turned nocked another arrow and drew back again aiming for the same spot where two men he saw were now aflame, their clothing on fire. The torch bearers flames must have ignited their cloaks.

He calmly looked down the shaft of his next arrow and considered shooting at the men screaming as their flesh burnt but instead shot to the side of them, the others could burn. As the first of the enemy arrows began to find length, they landed still on aflame embedding themselves into the wood of the defensive positions. Those that landed in the freshly dug soil of the palisade were extinguished as oxygen smothered them, others set fire to anything they hit that was combustible.

Vespasian had considered having legionaries placed at strategic intervals with the few buckets they had recovered from the spoiled wagons nearby but knew the men would have made all too easy targets. He knew they wouldn't last long silhouetting themselves above the defensive wall but also knew they couldn't afford to use water in such a way. He prayed his gamble would work as the barbarians drew to within a hundred paces of their line.

"Loose pila." A centurion shouted from somewhere behind Valerius but he concentrated on his own task and continued to launch arrows. He was aware of running boots hitting the ground all around him and then a wave of javelins were launched into the air. He looked briefly and saw the soldiers returning to their stock pile for more. Turning back to the front he saw the javelins land as they buried themselves into the men and women who were intent on killing them. Dozens were felled in that first launch and fell backward onto a wave of advancing bodies. They were dragged to the side or pushed out of the way and vanished from sight almost instantly under the feet of those who came after them.

The screams of the Britons were animal like now and a lot louder as they vented their fury at those above. Some were silenced forever in the next avalanche of arrows and spears but still the mass kept advancing, seemingly undaunted. Valerius drew his gladius as the first of them reached the rampart, his face glowing from the flames of arrows burning into the wood of the palisade. He tried to run up the steeper incline of the defensive wall but slipped and fell backwards on loose soil. He took the opportunity of sinking an arrow into the soft ground as his feet scrambled for purchase and tried pulling himself up on its length. Anger bore into the young archer from the enemy as he realised it was useless and nocked another arrow.

"Heavy pila, loose!" Another order rang out from somewhere.

The nearest attacker was now less than fifteen feet below him and jumping to reach the sharpened stakes on the defences. The draw string was allowed to race forward freeing its arrow but in his haste Valerius jerked his arm at the last instant and missed the manic warrior who wanted to kill him. He reached for another arrow blindly, keeping his eyes on the man who was now joined by others, as they sought to gain entry to the mountain fort. Another legionary stepped forward and hurled a heavy javelin towards them, it sank deep into an exposed throat and gurgling, the man fell away.

The sound of battle was almost deafening now at such close quarters as the Britons tried repeatedly to climb the wall. Many died and more were wounded as they were repelled time and time again as they fell in their heroic but foolhardy hordes.

Some climbed up onto the backs of others and grabbed for the burning stakes only to be run through by pila, heavy and light now as the men of the Second butchered away at hands, arms, heads and bodies.

So close were the enemy now that the soldiers could lean out and stab down at the brave, who threw themselves against their spears bending iron as they plunged them into the faces of the screaming few who managed to climb onto the flaming stakes. Burning or stabbed, they fell away, only to be replaced by others. Occasionally one would get over the palisade only to be chopped down by a gladius. It wasn't all one way however, as soldiers were lanced by a thrown spear or hit by the occasional arrow when an archer could free himself from the masses to shoot. The injured men were quickly carried away from the front line and further up the slope to safety and replaced by other troops eager to kill the barbarians.

Caratacus watched from behind a line of heaving bodies pushing to get forward and surveyed the scene above him. The attack had stalled on the defensive line of the mountain encampment and now his people were being slaughtered, bottled up like penned sheep. He watched as a man fully aflame jumped back down from the palisade and landed on top of others who fought to push him away, punching and kicking. The Roman legionaries looked like cloaked devils as they thrust their spears downward lit up against the flaming wood. Helmets glinted and armour shone, reflecting the fires that burned before them as they went about their deadly work. He knew that to continue in this way would mean the death of more brave souls for no gain and knew he couldn't allow that to happen.

"Withdraw," he started to shout, "Withdraw." He ran forward and grabbed at the backs of those crowding forward and spun them around shouting at them to retreat.

"Fucking move." He snarled into faces that turned to see what was happening and who was shouting and what.

"Can't you see this is pointless we're just dying up there?" He spun one woman round and she careened backwards falling down the slope into the legs of others still clambering upward. He grabbed at others and hurled them backward until more and more realised what was happening, who was demanding the retreat. Slowly the tide began to turn and run back down the mountain followed by the occasional javelin or arrow. Those struck slumping forward onto their faces as they were hit, legs flailing into the air. Some lost their footing because of the gradient and tumbled downward screaming as they went limbs breaking. Caratacus turned and joined the retreating army as he fought to maintain his balance, the attack had been a failure and so something else was called for.

The rest of the day was spent helping those that could be helped, down from the slope, those who were dead and there were many, were left where they had fallen. There were injured still below the defensive line crying out for help but when anyone approached to try and recover them, arrows and javelins forced them back. The Romans weren't in any mood to grant leniency even to the injured as they knew their own fate if they were to be taken, a stalemate was reached.

Caratacus withdrew to the lower valley and found Ardwen who had fared no better as he too had lost many brave souls that morning. By the late afternoon the injured that could be moved were taken away on carts heading to their villages wrapped in bandages. Those with life threatening wounds were gathered together to be administered and comforted in their final hours by those who were their kin or friends.

"We'll try again tonight." Ardwen said looking up to where smoke rose to the sky and bodies lay. "Under the cover of darkness, with no moon, we'll be on top of them and inside before they know we're there."

Caratacus looked at him and half smiled at his determination, "Very well but if that fails, we starve them out. We can't lose as many as we did today again. I've seen their iron take too many lives and I tire of the weight on my shoulders, we need the guile of the fox and the strength of the wolf if we're to break these men." He looked upward onto the slope and saw the dead laying strewn everywhere the eye could see, the sight replayed an image of the morning assault in his mind's eye and it was awful.

"Go and find your family cousin, they're camped along the track." Ardwen pointed. "Get some rest and eat and come and find me here later as the sun begins to fall. Tonight we shall climb again and things will be different, you'll see."

Caratacus patted him on the shoulder, "I hope you're right, it would be better to defeat them with swords rather than hunger but defeat them we will." He turned and went to find his wife and family.

Varro had woken up cold and damp when the first sounds of battle had reached his ears. Lifting his head slowly he looked around trying to get his bearings and for a moment was confused. Rolling over he pushed his cloak off his head and looked around. At first he had thought he had been having a nightmare until his surroundings confirmed the reality, he really was alone and on top of a mountain miles from the men of his Legion.

He cursed himself for falling asleep for so long as he realised that dawn was breaking. Looking out over the valley he watched as the Britons had climbed up to the defended held slopes like a tide, only to be halted suddenly in it's tracks. Tiny defenders had cascaded arrows and pila into the swarming masses of the enemy and the advantage of high ground had won them the fight. Fires burned and plumes of smoke rose high into the morning sky from fire arrows and their targets.

After the battle which had raged for a considerable time, he could see many hundreds of bodies littering the slopes left behind as the attack finally subsided and withdrew. He could also see soldiers being carried further up the mountain, obviously wounded. He wanted to be with them but could do nothing except watch as the fate of the men of the Legion was played out before him. Again it brought home his own position as he remembered his isolation but the thought of Decimus and Brenna hurrying north calmed him somewhat. He looked around again and saw hundreds of plumes of smoke from camp fires on the valley floor and suddenly realised he was hungry. He moved backward and rolled onto his back pulling his food bag around and opened it. He chewed at the salted pork slowly and decided that he couldn't stay where he was, he would move lower as a plan began to form in his head.

It took him nearly all day to descend onto the valley floor where the smell of numerous fires was strong to his senses. Moving slowly to avoid detection the day was beginning to draw in and he could hear voices of the Britons as they prepared food. He felt his stomach rumble, the pork had staved off hunger and would continue to do so and keep him going but for now he had more serious concerns than food. He crawled into a copse at the base of the slope and stripped down to just his tunic. The rest he buried roughly only keeping his dagger to hand and then he waited.

Later as darkness covered the land, the light of the fires burned brighter and so did the noise from the Britons as they began to consume their brew before battle. Singing and laughter echoed around the hills and mountains as they celebrated the lives of those who had departed that day. Funeral pyres were lit and a solemn atmosphere enveloped those gathered around them as they paid their respects and then the singing and celebration began again. He watched on waiting for the right moment from his concealed place in the copse. As the celebrating continued, numerous warriors started to walk away towards where he lay to relieve themselves in the bushes.

Just as he was beginning to regret his idea a young man approached, shouting back to his friends and laughing. Varro watched as he pushed branches aside and made his way into the copse where he wouldn't be seen by the others. He stopped about five feet from the covered Roman, hidden under branches and dropped his woollen trousers. Wind escaped his backside as he chuckled to himself and crouched down, starting to groan with effort.

Varro gripped the handle of his dagger and pushed himself up quickly in one fluid movement and lunged forward, the young warrior barely had time to turn his head as cold sharp iron slashed through his throat ending his short life. Varro looked down at the body and quickly dragged the clothing off. He soon realised that his victims shit had landed in the trousers and the smell made him gag. He wiped off what he could using leaves and quickly put the pants and other clothing over his tunic and the cloth cap the man had been wearing onto his head. The rich combination of sweat and shit was foul but he would have to endure the discomfort for the time being. He turned and made his way through the bushes and stooped peering out at the other side. There was another fire some distance away surrounded by more Britons, he pushed his way through the branches and emerged.

    He was seen immediately by two of those sat at the fire and feigned doing up the pants, tugging at the harsh cloth. One of the men raised a hand and shouted a greeting and laughed, Varro waved back and began to walk. He was aware of eyes following him or maybe it was his imagination as he angled away from the light of the fire and made for a dark area ahead. Expecting a shouted challenge at any moment he carried on wanting to run but knowing he couldn't. Reaching darkness his beating heart began to slow, when he was sure he was out of sight he turned and saw no-one was following. The smell from the soiled clothing made him cringe as he found his way onto a track and began to walk faster.

Chapter Twenty Two

As Corvus began to move forward on his stomach, he felt that his limbs were stiff from inactivity and movement was difficult. He and his men had lain unmoving in the ravine for so long, that he had fallen into a restless sleep drifting in and out of consciousness despite the circumstances surrounding them. He paused tensing and flexing the muscles in his legs and arms as he tried to get the blood flowing again and then slowly began to move off. Seven bodies then followed slowly and silently behind him as they made their way to the bottom of the huge gash in the side of the mountain where they had spent the day under cover of the trees. He paused and drank from the stream for the final time and then pushed himself up into a crouch and moved to the edge of the bushes where he surveyed the land.

The Britons had been gathering their weapons and were now moving away from their fires down one of the tracks, presumably he thought to mass before another attack. He looked around and back at his men and signalled for them to wait as he emerged from the trees. He walked slowly to the nearest fire, looked around again and then gestured for his men to follow, the way clear. Slowly they emerged from the damp shelter and searched about around the camp. They found scraps of meat left cooking over the fire and ate greedily having their fill before moving off in the opposite direction to the Britons. When they were sure they were totally out of sight, they began to jog along the edge of the track trying to stay in cover as best they could.
***

Valerius had lost count of the amount of lives his arrows had taken in the dawn attack on their position earlier that day, it was impossible to say, so crowded had the Britons been in their thirst to assault the palisades and outer defences. He had been relieved by his senior Centurion, Marus Fulvious Cortus who was co-ordinating the defences for a few hours, in order to get some food and some sleep but had spent most of the time watching as work details dug out another series of ditches halfway between his own position and the very summit on the mountain, the problem now, was that they would soon run out of space to fight. Cortus knew it meant their commander expected that the Britons would break through the outer perimeter or that it was a distinct likelihood.

In order to try and raise moral, Vespasian had briefed his officers saying that in the event that the first line of palisades were overrun, all legionaries were to fall back to the second line where their defence of the mountain would continue. The men of the Second Augusta, the centurions and soldiers were some of the finest men he had ever had the fortune to serve with and the best in the Empire and they would not fall to a bunch of half-naked savages who tried to mate with goats.

He had also said that he expected re-enforcements in a matter of days but until then they would take as many lives as were thrown against them. He refused to die on this insignificant hillock and wouldn't allow his men to do so either. They would march out of these hills with their heads held high after stopping the assault and would one day return to wipe the scourge of Caratacus from the face of the earth. His men quiet at first had listened in silence but as the speech progressed he had rekindled their spirits, thumping a clenched fist into the air they had cheered and stood applauding the man who would lead them to salvation.

That day, the remaining trees had been felled and embedded into the new ramparts that ran all the way around the upper half of their sanctuary, the ends sharpened with axes. The men went about their business with renewed vigour after the speech by Vespasian and now looked forward to the next attack with renewed optimism. As well as forming a difficult obstacle to overcome, the lengths of timber also helped to re-enforce the ramparts themselves, some of which had been significantly damaged during the first onslaught. Everyman knew that if Caratacus and his warriors broke this second line, they would never leave this mountain alive and it would become their tomb. In order for that not to occur, every effort was to be made to repulse the enemy lower down the slopes, which was where Valerius later found himself once more.

The sky was darker than the previous night due to ominous black clouds overhead and only the light from fires provided any relief but they were not their own. Small fires twinkled in the distance down in the valley, hundreds of them but there were none where they were as Vespasian had ordered a blackout. He realised that he had to ration the remaining timber and didn't want fires illuminating his men once the next attack was underway.

Uncomfortable and cold they maybe, but that discomfort could well be the difference between life and death as they would not silhouette themselves against the night sky. Valerius shivered as he walked out from his wicker barricade once more, a distance of ten paces, looking up he sniffed the air and suspected it was going to rain. Looking down he thought he saw movement and quickly went back to cover, he crouched, nocked an arrow and waited.

Valerio saw him dart back or did he? "It's your imagination," he said to himself but he stayed behind the wicker shield and looked downwards again.

"Men think they see shadows at night, there's nothing there, besides if they try again, they'll get so much iron pumped into them, they'll never come back again." He turned to look at Valerius and smiled, that instant his back arched forward and he gurgled. Horror creasing his face as blood ran from his open mouth and down his chin. Valerius tried to bring up his bow as a hairy limed head grinned out at him from behind his dying friend. Valerio was hurled to one side and over the palisade as a wet glistening sword was removed from his back.

Valerius froze for a moment, finding movement impossible as suddenly all around him the ground came alive below the palisade. A swiping blow chopped through his bow from his side, he saw Britons scrambling up over the defences by climbing onto each other's backs.

"Alarm," he shouted, "Alarm." As loud as he was able and turned to run as another sword swipe crashed into his helmet slicing through the metal like wheat, lurching upward his hands touched the ground as his boots tried to grip the blackened soil. His limbs seemed alien as they betrayed his attempted escape. He was aware of the sound of breaking wood as his wicker shield was ripped from the ground. Arrows began to flash through the air from above as the men of the Second launched their response. He ran scrambling and falling forward, his life flashing before him, expecting to feel a sword or spear blink out his existence at any moment.

Figures above shouted garbled words as his fingers dug deep into the grass now clear of the soil as he pulled himself up. He could hear grunts and shouts behind him and he imagined a sword sinking into his trailing foot, Faster and faster he tried to move, panting with effort, eyes wide, mouth gasping for air. Javelins rained down and thumped, impacting into the surface all around him. He heard an anguished cry close by but didn't dare try to look to see what had caused it.

"Run, keep going, come on you can make it." A voice shouted from above as his helmet fell over his eyes. His legs burned from effort, his calves pumping, ankles hurting like never before as the incline took its toll. One quick push on the rim of his helmet cleared his vision as he saw a legionary shouting from above as he hurled another javelin, it landed close by somewhere behind. Twenty paces from the next ditch above the new rampart, the soldier and another linked hands as one was lowered reaching out. Arrows hammered into the ground, shouts of pain and anger rose closing in on him all around but still he ran, his lungs taking in huge gasps of oxygen.

Six feet away from the outstretched hand he leapt upward, flailing his leading hand to make contact but he fell short, weak and out of breath from his effort to get this far, he slammed into the wall of the rampart, hitting it hard with his face. He gasped again for air turning for the first time since Valerio had been killed and saw blue streaked Britons upper bodies bare, eyes large, mouths screaming, bearing down on him.

"Move your fucking arse soldier." The legionary clinging onto the other man from above shouted, his other hand holding onto a post sticking out from the ground. An archer appeared at his side and fired an arrow as Valerius tried to block out the approaching barbarians in his mind. An arrow flew by his head from the archer, clearly aiming at something close. Taking a deep breath he stumbled to the outstretched arm stretching down to him and jumped up. The strong hand clamped onto his wrist and pulled his body up, feet dangling as he was hurled up and over the trench, he landed hard, gulping for air, leg muscles burning. Grunts of effort filled his ears as men all around him threw javelins at the enemy trying to scale the palisade, their last real defence against oblivion. More men re-enforced their hold on the mountain as pila and arrows were thrown and fired at the attackers who screamed in anger and agony alike as their dead grew. Those who came behind the warriors at the front piled into their backs as a killing field quickly grew and the dead mounted but on they came, fury in their eyes as they sought to take the mountain.

Varro quickened his pace and began to run slowly at first away from the sounds of battle. He knew he had to find help as quickly as possible and to do that he needed a horse. He tried to steady his pace as the incline of the valley helped propel him downward faster than was comfortable, his upper legs straining with effort. Once in a while he would get a whiff of the dead man's shit in his new pants as he ran and decided he would have to find more clothing at the earliest opportunity. He ran on until eventually the ground began to level out, he slowed his pace and stopped catching his breath. Turning he looked back up the track at the way he had come, it snaked curving upward until his disappeared in the dark. He couldn't see anyone following or anything beyond the winding road in the dark.

Controlling his breathing he ran on until the first rays of light started to appear and his knees and ankles felt like the bones were grinding together, sweat peppered his forehead and ran down and into the already dirty stinking clothes. He stopped again and paused leaning forward, hands on his knees that now ached like nothing he had ever experienced before. Wiping at his brow he felt dried salt from sweat just below the hairline, proof if any were needed of his effort. He staggered on trying to loosen his muscles but knew he would have to stop and rest soon or he would collapse exhausted.

He had eaten the last of his pork sometime before and was already starting to feel hungry again when he saw a glimmer of a fire in the distance up ahead at the side of the path. Drawing closer he could just make out silhouetted bodies sat, huddled around the small flames. He carefully moved into the trees that ran along the edge of the path and got closer still using the trunks as cover. As he began to smell wood smoke and the aroma of cooking meat, he heard hushed voices talking, they were Britons.

The dark night had favoured Caratacus as he had pushed forward his attack. Under the cover of darkness he had led two thousand warriors up through the ravines of the mountain as Ardwen had done the same elsewhere hidden by trees and thick foliage. The sudden onslaught had caught the Romans by surprise and had not only overrun their defences but had rewarded them with prisoners as well. So swift and furious had been the enthusiasm to take enemy lives, that over two hundred legionaries had found themselves cut off from their comrades further up the slopes. Some who resisted were hacked to death or hit by their own arrows and javelins from above but as others realised their plight, they surrendered throwing their weapons and shields down.

Ardwen had pushed to butcher them all, stripped naked and in full view of the survivors cowering behind their last ditch above, but Caratacus had refused vehemently. He persuaded him that the men would be taken and given to surrounding villages and tribes as slaves and proof of their own power and the Romans vulnerability. It would pave the way for more to fight against the people who had come to steal their lands and wealth. Ardwen had given in but sought re-assurance that the remainder on the summit would be slaughtered to a man, Caratacus agreed saying that this would be their grave.

The palisade that had proved so troublesome previously now became an effective defence against arrows as they were loosed at the massing Britons baying for more blood. Some of the ramparts were destroyed in places, hacked away by large war axes as effective rough steps were gouged out and dug into the ground ready for the next assault. Warriors now sheltered below the unnatural wall waiting for the order to move again. Ardwen insisted for it to begin immediately but Caratacus was cautious and asked for patience, once again Ardwen impatiently agreed. The Silures leader knew his cousin was better placed to be in overall command and was already demonstrating his more effective leadership.

Before the battle for the summit could begin however, Caratacus sent word of his plan, back down the mountain. A great victory was at hand over the eagle bearers and he wanted their destruction witnessed by as many tribal leaders and chieftains they could find. In the meantime, they would bring their warriors forward to feast and celebrate the victory and consolidate their position making it impossible for even one member of the depleted Legion to escape.

Varro crept forward as close as he dared and crouched down trying to take in the words his ears were almost hearing. They struck him like mighty fists battering his weary body and soul as they shocked him to the core. He leaned with his back to the tree not twenty paces from the fire and listened as Brenna once more told of his friends death.

"The fool died like the rest will soon enough, Vespasian and his lap dogs will never escape these valleys and mountains."

The crackle of the fire was the only other sound he heard now as no-one interrupted her as she repeated the story again as if to convince those sat with her around the warmth of the fire.

"For many months now my brother and I have lived and fought amongst the invader but they never suspected we are of the Catuvellauni. He even died living this lie so we could discover their plans, killed by Silures warriors, allies to Caratacus and sworn enemy of Rome."

Her voice sounded different, almost feral, animal like as she spoke. He slowed his breathing not wanting to give away his position in the foliage behind the tree. Her words were like daggers stabbing at his heart, he had openly given himself to this woman and it had all been a lie.

"I had the opportunity to kill this man and I took it." She said, Varro was frozen with shock as she continued, "Decimus was one of the centurions and trusted scout rider of their leader Vespasian. He and his kind are the eyes and ears of their legions and I even prostituted myself to another, Varro, to gain his trust."

He fought the urge to vomit as the words pounded at him again striking him like cold iron. He fought the urge his rage was directing, as part of him wanted to run into the camp and tear her throat out with his blade. He knew that it would be a futile death and no-one would learn of this woman's treachery and it would result in his own, no doubt by the hands of those she was speaking with. He turned his head carefully as she continued to talk and boast and looked around the edge of the tree, his face against rough bark. To the right of the fire impaled on a wooden stake was the head of his friend Decimus, mouth open, eyes wide in shock.

The final ultimate victory that Caratacus had sought did not occur despite many attempts to achieve it. Time and time again his brave warriors and those of Ardwen climbed above the final rampart of compact mud and were met by a deadly hail of arrows and spears through night and day as they tried to reach the remaining soldiers to take their lives on the summit. Soon there were many dead and wounded on the mountain and he ordered that groups carry them down the slope again and again. After five full days and nights, warriors stopped returning to the summit and simply vanished into the valleys below, exhausted, wounded and mourning the dead.

Ardwen had tried to gather his forces but only a few thousand remained as both leaders finally conceded they would have to starve the Romans out before taking their heads. They were now left with a combined army of less than four thousand strong but it was more than enough to complete the task or so they believed.

Conditions a few hundred feet above the Britons were far more precarious than they knew or could have imagined. Of over four thousand legionaries that marched into the mountains, only four hundred and seventy now survived. They were down to their last days rations and were short on arrows and javelins as they waited for the inevitable final assault. More lay injured, unable to fight on, some dying who would never see Rome or their homeland again. The only surviving medicus had ran out of bandages, poultices, vials and herbs to treat the wounded two days before and now resorted to tearing up the tunics of the dead to staunch the flow of blood from freshly injured men. The crippled and dying had been removed to the very top of the mountain where they were afforded a little shelter by the basin at the top. The same could not be said of those who stood and waited hungry, dirty and despondent behind their barricades for the enemy to return once more.

Soldiers half-starved by days of rationing, stared down the mountain, dirty and covered in blood and grime, exhausted by the unrelenting punishment the Britons had delivered to them. Those injured but still able to wield a blade and hold a shield, guarded the miserable peak with those who had somehow escaped injury and waited, now led by the surviving centurions. Vespasian had developed a fever as a result of his own wound three days into the siege and was barely lucid anymore as he lay with others with stab wounds, lacerations, bruises and broken bones.

Valerius looked out glassy eyed at the view around him and breathed heavily. All day the Britons had been carrying their dead and wounded down the mountain and funeral pyres had burned for days in the valley below, the acrid stench of burning flesh wisped up into the air to fill his nose with its rank stench. He had been told that after the last senior officer had lost his life, the centurions who remained alive were now considering suicide. The rumours had said that they refused to fall into the hands of the barbarians and would prefer to die honourably rather than await a fate worse than death if they weren't fortunate to die in battle.

As he sat watching the enemy lines carrying bundles of bodies file lower, he looked at the blade of his gladius and imagined the cold iron entering his stomach, pushing upward under his ribs and into his heart. He closed his eyes as tears fell and rolled down his cheeks as he realised he would never see his parents again. His father, a former optio with the Thirteenth, had been so proud of him when he had joined the legions following in his footsteps. He remembered the day he had first returned home to stand in front of both his father and mother in uniform, armour polished to perfection and shining brilliantly. He sighed rubbing at his eyes at the memory, wiping his tears away, hoping no-one had seen his weakness but then realised he didn't care if they had. He was nineteen years of age and would never see another birthday or his family again.

As he looked around at the men near him, battered and exhausted, red eyes staring back, he heard a sound carried on the wind and stopped breathing. His head turned in the direction he thought it came from but his eye caught more Britons scurrying down off the mountain. The breeze was strong and he knew it moved sounds playing tricks on the mind, especially at such height. He leaned forward as if a few hand widths would help and listened again.

"If you need a shit, fuck off over there." A legionary said sat next to him, wrapped in his cloak and jerking his head towards the holes dug in the ground for such things. He ignored him and stood up and looked at the Britons again. They weren't just carrying their dead and wounded anymore, they were withdrawing from the mountain by the hundred and as quickly as possible. He looked beyond them into the valley but could see no reason for their obvious panic. He began to move around the edge of the wicker wall that had been his home for what seemed like an eternity.

"You'll get something shoved up you're fucking arse with a barbarian holding the other end of it if you don't get back behind this wicker you daft cunt." He heard the man say.

"Shut your hole for a moment will you?" He replied. "Look!" Pointing down the slope, he stood on his toes trying to try and get a better view. Cautiously the other man came out from behind the wicker and joined him.

"If I get a fucking spear I'll gut you with it myself before I die you little runt." The soldier said joining him frowning. "So what's to be seen then?"

"Shush, shut up for the gods sakes and listen you dirty unshaven smelly whores hole." Valerius said removing his helmet and cupping his hand to his ear leaning out. He frowned concentrating straining his ears.

"I think you need my right boot up your sack young man, there's nothing to hear." The agitated soldier said but Valerius didn't respond. He cocked his head listening. Then he heard it again and his face lit up, the distinctive blare of a Roman trumpet somewhere in the valley below. He turned and ran around the entire line of their defences shouting, almost crying with joy as the blares got gradually louder and others realised they were going to live.

"We're saved, we're saved, Jupiter's cunt we're saved." He shouted tearing off his armour and running round like a lunatic. The survivors of the Second Augusta jumped up and joined in to a man as they too heard the sound of rescue being carried on the breeze as the men of the Twentieth Legion with Corvus and his men marched into the mountains of the Silures.

"Well shave my hairy ball bag and call me Emperor Titus Cock Fuck, I don't bloody well believe it." The previously dour soldier said and joined in the celebration hugging and kissing Valerius.

Caratacus and Ardwen had considered ambushing the advancing legion as it marched, trumpets blaring and echoing around the valleys. They estimated their strength to be around five thousand possibly more, a fully manned legion, fit and well fed and ready to fight and more than twice the amount of men they had under their strength. As Caratacus looked down on the men of the newly arrived enemy, shining as the sun reflected off their armour, he looked to his own people and saw exhaustion and no will to fight on against the odds. They were tired, hungry and weary of death and battle after so many days fighting. He knew they were in no condition to face the new threat.

"We'll go north into the lands of the Ordovices and the Deceangli for the time being. They'll swell our numbers and together we'll crush this plague as it eats away at our land." Ardwen smiled at his cousins words and resilience.

"What of the injured?" He asked climbing onto his horse.

Caratacus looked about him at the wounded lying all around, littering the floor of the valley, "If they can travel, they can come with us but any who have to be carried, they have to be left behind, we can't afford to waste time."

Ardwen considered arguing but knew his cousin was right again, he kicked his horse as it reared up and shouted, "You will not be forgotten." He then raced after Caratacus who was already galloping away into the dust ahead.

The men of the Twentieth Legion could barley recognise the survivors of the Second Augusta as Romans when they reached the first line of palisades. They were gaunt, dirty shadows of their former selves, unshaven and unkempt. The usual inter legion rivalries were forgotten as the injured were treated and soldiers ate properly for the first time in days. Those who had passed away before rescue could arrive, were buried as words were spoken over their unmarked graves. Fit healthy legionaries helped their injured comrades off the rock and down into the valley below. The Britons main force had gone, travelling north, the worst done to defeat those who had defended the mountain.

It took several days until the men of the Second were ready to move and only then, flanked and led by the soldiers of the Twentieth. Cavalry scouts rode ahead ensuring that the way was clear but the Britons didn't return, they were gone as if spirited away. It took several days for the slow moving army to make its way back to Isca where Legatus Vespasian's men could lick their wounds. Of all of them, he was one of the more fortunate, as his fever ensured he was unaware of the entire journey. He finally awoke three days after they returned, in a fresh bed wearing clean dressings and wondering what had happened on the mountain top that had haunted his feverish sleep.

THE END

Author's Note

Thank you for choosing to read Blood of Rome: Caratacus, which is my first novel. I have endeavoured to make the story as accurate as possible based upon historical fact. I chose Caratacus as one of my main characters after studying Roman Britain. I believe to this day that he is an unsung hero who has lived in the shadow of other better and widely known historical figures who have also defended the shores of the country we now know as the United Kingdom.

Studying the events of AD 43, allowed me to discover that everything was not as black and white as it first appeared concerning the Roman invasion of Britannia or Albion as it was known by the indigenous population back then. There had been close ties between Rome and the Celtic tribes of the islands for well over a hundred years prior to the invasion, maybe longer. The landing on the southern shores actually only happened at the last minute and very nearly didn't happen at all due to legionaries refusing to take part, which is covered in the story.

Failure to board the ships of the invasion fleet was because even the great General Julius Caesar, had twice failed to successfully invade and conquer the lands of Albion nearly a hundred years before the events of AD 43. Troops engaged in the invasion truly believed it was not possible to defeat the tribes and had to be bribed to take part, which eventually they did. However, history has shown that they, the soldiers of the Rome were right, as Britannia was never fully conquered. I hope to tell that story through pages and the centuries of the Blood of Rome series.

I sincerely hope that you enjoy the book, it has been a long but enjoyable journey creating it. Any mistakes you may find or grammatical errors are mine and mine alone, for any you discover, I apologise. Aspiring authors always encourage positive feedback for their efforts and I would kindly ask that you write a review of the book on Amazon and or other websites.

Blood of Rome: Caratacus is dedicated to the men and women of the Ermine Street Guard, who professionally recreate Roman Military tactics, dress and deportment and have done so for the last forty years. They can be seen at major historical events and festivals around Britain today. For more information visit erminestreetguard.co.uk.

About the Author

John Salter has always had a major interest in Roman Britain. He was born in Chester on the English/Welsh border in the UK, Chester being the former Roman City of Deva in 1963. He joined the Royal Air Force virtually straight from school at the age of 17 and over the next 25 years travelled and served all over the world, attaining the rank of Flight Sergeant.

During that time his interest in the subject matter grew, as well as studying historical texts, he visited as many sites related to the Roman Empire as he was able. Further inspired by authors such as Simon Scarrow, Ben Kane, Manda Scott, Anthony Riches, Ruth Downie, Douglas Jackson and many others, he decided to try and give something back in the form of his own work, which is what you hold in your hand today or see on your e-reader.

After leaving the forces, he was finally able to settle down and concentrate on writing. Blood of Rome: Caratacus is intended to be the first book in the Blood of Rome series which will eventually cover everything concerning Roman Britain, from Caesars attempted invasions until the day the Romans withdrew from the shores of the island once known as Albion.

I have consciously decided to self-publish this book and those that follow primarily because I want the stories to remain my own and because I still work an 8-5pm job.

Best Regards

John

Printed in Great Britain
by Amazon.co.uk, Ltd.,
Marston Gate.